"I need to know...you remember. Tell me...you remember."

The Cajun's dark eyes were wild with agony, and his face contorted in misery. She hated seeing him suffer.

"Nicole," he repeated, and held a hand out, summoning her to come closer.

At that moment, the morning sun broke over the tops of the trees and shone through the open side door of the helicopter, casting his rugged face in sharp relief. For the first time, she could truly see the man who'd risked his life for her. Her heart clenched, and the prickle of déjà vu returned. He seemed so familiar....

"I...need—" He stopped, clenching his teeth and growling in torment. "Please...I need to know...you remember."

"I remember," she lied, leaning closer to be sure he heard her.

"Then say my name, Nicole."

And in a heartbeat, an echo from her past yanked her back five years to a hotel room in New Orleans. Her heart wrenched, and tears spilled from her eyes.

"Oh, my God!" She curled her fingers into the hair at his nape and buried her face in his neck. "Daniel..."

Other titles by this author available in ebook format.

BETH CORNELISON

started writing stories as a child when she penned a tale about the adventures of her cat, Ajax. A Georgia native, she received her bachelor's degree in public relations from the University of Georgia. After working in public relations for a little more than a year, she moved with her husband to Louisiana, where she decided to pursue her love of writing fiction.

Since that first time, Beth has written many more stories of adventure and romantic suspense and has won numerous honors for her work, including a coveted Golden Heart Award in romantic suspense from Romance Writers of America. She is active on the board of directors for the North Louisiana Storytellers and Authors of Romance (NOLA STARS) and loves reading, traveling, *Peanuts'* Snoopy and spending downtime with her family.

She writes from her home in Louisiana, where she lives with her husband, one son and two cats who think they are people. Beth loves to hear from her readers. You can write to her at P.O. Box 5418, Bossier City, LA 71171 or visit her website, www.bethcornelison.com.

BETH CORNELISON

The Reunion Mission

HARLEQUIN®
entertain, enrich, inspire™

Recycling programs
for this product may
not exist in your area.

ISBN-13: 978-0-373-27787-2

THE REUNION MISSION
Copyright © 2012 by Beth Cornelison

TALL DARK DEFENDER
Copyright © 2009 by Beth Cornelison

www.Harlequin.com

Printed in U.S.A.

CONTENTS

Dear Reader,

As I was writing *Soldier's Pregnancy Protocol* (Harlequin Romantic Suspense, June 2012), I found myself more and more fascinated by Alec's missing partner, Daniel LeCroix. What had happened to him? I asked myself. Just who was this mysterious Cajun? Even though he was not "on screen" most of the book, I felt his presence throughout writing the book. Secondary characters sometimes take over, demanding their own story be told. By the time I finished Alec's book, Daniel's history with Senator White's daughter was already playing out in my head.

I was thrilled to have the chance to write Daniel and Nicole's story…so much so that the opening chapters of *The Reunion Mission* almost wrote themselves. This is a true story of my heart, even though I shook my head at times wondering what I'd done to myself by having characters who needed to speak not just Spanish, but Colombian Spanish, and not just French, but Cajun French. (Yes, there is a big difference!) I hope you enjoy Daniel and Nicole's story as much as I enjoyed telling it.…

Oh, and keep an eye out for book three in the Black Ops Rescues series. I hope to have Jake's story ready soon! As always, more information about all my books is available on my website, www.bethcornelison.com.

Happy reading,

Beth Cornelison

The Reunion Mission

To Keyren Gerlach Burgess, who believed in me and helped bring Alec, Daniel and Jake to life.

Thank you to fellow Harlequin Romantic Suspense author Gail Barrett and her friend, Margarita Unger, for their help with Colombian Spanish translations.

Thank you also to Jennifer Malone and her father, Monte Bonin, for their help with Cajun French, as well as answering questions about Cajun culture.

Thank you to Sara Beth Salyer for sharing her name (as the winning bidder in the Brenda Novak Diabetes Auction for a Cure) and allowing me the honor of paying homage to her beloved kitty, Oreo, as characters in *The Reunion Mission*.

Chapter 1

"Left perimeter clear." Shifting his night vision goggles, Daniel LeCroix peered through the inky blankness of the Colombian jungle, his body humming and ready for action. He focused on the large tent at the far end of the rebel encampment. No sign of the soldiers who slept in the canvas shelter. Lowering the night vision goggles, he cast a glance to his partner, who monitored the camp through an infrared imaging camera. "What do you have?"

Months of preparation had led to this moment. With their objective moments from fruition, he'd be damned if he'd let anything screw up their mission now.

"No movement," Alec Kincaid confirmed. "Looks like the guards watching the ammo are the only ones awake." Alec stowed the infrared imager in his pack and slid his NVGs into place. "Ready to move?"

Adrenaline spiked in Daniel's blood, readying him for battle. "Hell, yeah. Let's go."

Silently, he and Alec dropped from the tree where they'd been perched for hours, watching the faction of rebel soldiers who held several captives in the remote camp. Only one of the prisoners interested Daniel.

Nicole White. A U.S. senator's daughter kidnapped from the medical mission where she was working and held as a political pawn.

Freeing her and returning her safely to the United States was their sole objective tonight.

Leading with his sidearm, Daniel crept down the steep, vegetation-dense hillside to the clearing in the narrow Colombian valley where Nicole had been held for close to thirteen months.

Would she recognize him, remember him?

Daniel shoved down the jangle of anticipation that skittered through him when he thought of seeing Nicole again. Touching her. He had to stay focused on his job if they were to get out of that jungle alive.

When they reached the crude wire fence at the edge of the camp, Alec pulled a pair of wire cutters from his pack and quickly created a hole large enough for them to crawl through on their bellies. Daniel wiggled through first, then Alec. Using hand signals, Daniel directed Alec to the right. Daniel walked backward, following Alec and guarding their six. Keeping to the shadows, they made their way toward the back of the camp where Nicole was being held.

As they rounded the tent where they'd determined supplies were kept, Alec stopped abruptly. He pointed to the guard stationed at the entrance of the supply tent.

I've got this one, Alec signaled, then soundlessly dispatched the man before the guard even knew he had company.

Behind them, a squeak drew Daniel's attention. The door to the ramshackle latrine by the perimeter fence opened, and a soldier stepped out, shining a flashlight toward the camp.

When the beam passed over Alec, Daniel tensed. Just as the man swung the light back and opened his mouth to shout a warning to the camp, Daniel fired a single head shot, and the soldier crumpled. Despite the silencer muffling the gun's noise, Daniel knew someone could have heard the telltale pop. They had to hurry.

By unspoken agreement, Alec set a faster pace toward the fenced area where Nicole was being held. Farther down, they encountered two more guards, playing a game with dice as they monitored the cache of arms stacked in crates under a tarp. Skulking through the night like panthers, Alec and Daniel snuck up on the duo and took them out, as well.

All clear.

With Alec keeping watch, Daniel hurried to the fenced area where the rebels held their captives. The cages holding the prisoners were little more than dog pens, and two teepeed sheets of rotting plywood provided Nicole's only protection from the elements. Rage flashed through Daniel seeing the squalid conditions in which Nicole had been forced to live. Gritting his teeth, he funneled his fury into cutting through the fencing of her cage, then crawled to the tented plywood where she slept.

She wasn't alone. Daniel frowned but dismissed the small form huddled beside her. His mandate was clear. Nicole was his only objective.

Shifting his attention, Daniel held his breath as he caught his first up-close glimpse of Nicole in five years. Her long slender legs and feet were bare. Dirty cargo shorts and a sleeveless T-shirt hugged her womanly curves, and the fetal position in which she slept heightened his sense of her vulnerability. Her arms pillowed her head, and her tangled blond hair spilled over her cheek. Even disheveled and grimy, she was still every bit as beautiful as he remembered.

Daniel's heart performed a tuck and roll, and he allowed

himself the briefest moment just to look at her and thank God she appeared unharmed. But even a few seconds of delay were an indulgence, and he steeled himself for the task ahead. It was go time.

Five years earlier

Daniel stood at attention, watching the parade of national and state dignitaries dressed in their best black-tie finery make their way into the governor's Mardi Gras ball. His buddies at the New Orleans Naval Air Station thought he was crazy for volunteering to work security for the ball. But when he'd heard that Louisiana Senator Alan White would be attending, he'd known he couldn't be anywhere else that night.

Daniel had prepped his Navy dress whites for the event, counting on the other rumor he'd heard to be true—since his wife's death last year, Senator White had brought his daughter, Nicole, as his companion to public events such as this.

Even as he conjured a memory of the last time he'd seen Nicole, a limo flying American flags from the antennae pulled up to the front drive of the antebellum mansion where the ball was underway. Daniel held his breath as Senator White emerged from the backseat, then turned to offer his hand to someone inside the limo. A chill filled the air that February evening, but the weather had nothing to do with the tremor that rolled through Daniel as a graceful young blonde woman stepped out onto the driveway. An ice-blue chiffon gown hugged her curves, and she molded her mouth into a stiff smile as she started toward the stairs on the senator's arm. Jeweled combs winked in the porch lights and held her long hair swept up in a twist, exposing the slim column of her neck.

Daniel tracked her progress with his gaze as she approached, his mouth dry and his gut in knots. With her hand tucked in the crook of her father's arm, Nicole cast a surveying glance to the other partygoers, issuing perfunctory greetings. The politician's daughter, groomed in social graces and good public relations. American nobility, so far out of his league Daniel had to squelch the urge to laugh in bitter irony at the lengths he'd gone to tonight just for a chance to see her again. His studious gaze caught her attention, and Daniel flashed her a lopsided grin. "Hello, Nicole."

Her steps faltered, and a look of confusion dented her brow. "Do I—?"

Daniel blew out a deep breath. He'd been crazy to think she'd remember him after so many years.

But then her face brightened, and she pulled her arm free of her father's to step closer to Daniel. "Boudreaux!"

His heart kicked up a zydeco beat as she seized his hand and squeezed his fingers. "Boudreaux? Is that you?"

He grimaced mentally. As much as he'd wanted her to remember him, her use of the derogatory nickname her friends had given him didn't bode well for *what* she remembered about him. He tugged his mouth into an awkward smile. "Yeah, it's me."

Delight lit her eyes and brightened her grin, and hope stirred in his chest.

"Oh, my God! Look at you!" She canted forward, circling his shoulders with her arms and pressing a social kiss to his cheek.

Stunned by her hug, he was a beat too slow returning the embrace, and his brain snagged when the sweet floral scent of her hair hit him. His body's reaction to her touch, her scent was immediate and carnal.

Still holding the sleeves of his dress whites jacket, she levered back and let her gaze take in the length of him. "I almost didn't recognize you in this impressive attire." She flashed a flirtatious grin and tugged at the breast of his jacket.

"Good Lord, everything they say about a man in uniform is true!"

Daniel rallied his senses, determined not to come off as a flustered sap and to preserve the dignity his uniform required. "You look beautiful, too."

Understatement. She was breathtaking. He'd thought so five years ago on her prom night, when he'd been his cousin's date and met Nicole for the first time.

"Nicole!" Senator White had backtracked to fetch his wayward daughter, not quite managing to hide his irritation. "What's going on?"

Had she been hugging the son of one of his golf buddies rather than a security guard, the senator wouldn't have been nearly so piqued, Daniel wagered.

Nicole extended a hand to her father, waving him closer. "Daddy, I want you to meet someone. This is—" She hesitated, cutting an embarrassed look to Daniel.

"Daniel LeCroix," he finished, offering his hand to the senator before she defaulted to the nickname that mocked his bayou roots.

She twitched her lips in an apologetic grin. "Daniel. Of course! Forgive me. I'm just awful with names!"

Her father arched an eyebrow and heaved a sigh. "To my chagrin. She once called the chairman of armed services by his predecessor's name."

Folding Daniel's free hand between her hands, she faced her father again. "Daniel is the boy who brought me home from prom my junior year." When her father's expression remained blank, she added pointedly, "He's the one who rescued Boudreaux from the storm drain for me!"

Adrenaline kicked Daniel's pulse, and he jerked a startled glance toward her. *Boudreaux?* She'd named the kitten—?

Nicole met his questioning look with a secret smile. "What else would I name him?"

"Ah, yes. Your cat. I remember now. Well, it's nice to meet you, Daniel." The senator offered Nicole his arm, and his raised eyebrows, warning her it was time to go inside. "Nicole, this young man has a job to do, and our hosts are waiting."

Facing Daniel, she squeezed his hand and gave him a lopsided smile of regret. "It was wonderful seeing you again, Daniel."

He returned a polite smile. *Don't leave.* "You, too, Nicole." Then to the senator, "Sir."

The senator met his gaze with a hard look that darted to Daniel's rank insignia on his uniform. "Lieutenant."

The senator's tone carried a warning, a reminder of Daniel's place and the social gap between a boy from the bayou and the senator's well-bred daughter. As if Daniel needed reminding. Though he was proud of his Cajun roots, he was always striving to be better than the next guy—at basic training, in the classroom, in operations—trying to prove his detractors wrong, silencing those who singled him out or who bought into erroneous stereotypes regarding his heritage.

Nicole squeezed his hand before she released it and flashed a rueful smile as her father grasped her elbow and led her inside.

With a cleansing breath, he resumed his watch, shoulders back and hands clasped behind him. Though he stood at rigid attention, his mind writhed with a tangle of emotions.

He'd accomplished what he'd set out to do tonight. He'd seen Nicole again. But, in light of the tumult inside him, coming tonight might have been a mistake.

Nicole needed air. Shoving her way through the crowded dance floor, she hurried to the front porch and gripped the railing as another shudder of disgust rippled through her. All evening she'd put up with the leering glances her father seemed not to notice, but when the president of the Chamber of Commerce squeezed her bottom on the dance floor, she'd had enough. She'd bet her father's fortune that his "friends" never treated her mother with such disrespect.

Thoughts of her mother, stolen from her by cancer just four months ago, brought moisture to Nicole's eyes. She cast a longing gaze toward the parked cars, wishing she didn't have to endure the party any longer, and she spotted the white dress uniform and broad shoulders that had sent her pulse racing earlier that evening.

A smile ghosted across her lips. Daniel LeCroix. She wasn't surprised he'd joined the armed forces. Even in her brief association with him on prom night five years ago, she'd seen his valor, his kindness, his integrity. When her date hadn't deigned to get his hands dirty to retrieve the stranded kitten, when her friends had all abandoned her for "wasting time" on the rescue, only Daniel had stayed behind to help her instead of going to the dance. Daniel had ruined his rented tux moving the sewer grate and climbing into the drainage pipes, then had walked her and her new pet home. And left an indelible mark on her heart.

Nicole couldn't help but wonder how different *tonight* would have been if he'd been her escort instead of her father.

The night's not over. Her breath stilled. Ditching her father in favor of Daniel would be waving a red flag in her father's face. He'd never forgive her for the snub and the damage to his well-crafted public image.

But had her father respected her feelings when she'd complained about his friends' untoward advances? A flash of anger spiraled through her. How long was she supposed to put her life on hold to be her father's PR darling? She was already a year behind her class in nursing school because of his last election campaign and months of filling her mother's shoes as his companion at high-profile events and parties. As much as she loved her father, she just didn't want the high-society lifestyle he thrived on.

Inside, the orchestra began playing the ballad from a popular Andrew Lloyd Webber musical, and Nicole sighed. Fixing her gaze on Daniel, she crossed the porch and approached him. "Dance with me?"

He cut a startled glance her direction. "Nicole." His gaze shifted behind her, obviously noting that she was alone. "Why aren't you inside?"

"I needed a breather. Too much hot air in there." She twitched a grin and hitched her head toward the party. Stepping closer to him, she held out her hand. "So will you dance with me? This is one of my favorite songs."

His gaze locked on hers, his regret obvious. "I can't. I'm on duty."

She moved close enough to slide her hand along the polished buttons of his dress whites. She could feel the strong, steady beat of his heart beneath her fingers, and the life-affirming cadence struck her as powerfully virile and maddeningly sexy. "Just one dance. No one will know or care if you just danced this one song with me." She slid her arms around his neck and twined her fingers in the close-cropped hair at his nape. "Please."

His mental battle played across his face, the tug-of-war between duty and desire. "Nicole…" Closing his eyes, he settled a hand at her waist and halfheartedly tried to push her away.

Suddenly the idea of losing this opportunity to dance with Daniel, because of the rules of his job, or her father's code of conduct, or any other stuffy social convention or arbitrary legal dictate, made her want to scream. She fisted her hand in the back of his dress coat and refused to be budged. Tears of frustration and rebellion puddled in her eyes, and she raised her chin to meet his gaze.

"Screw the rules, Daniel. I want to dance with you."

His dark eyes narrowed on her, and hands that had pushed her away now touched the bare skin exposed by the low cut in the back of her dress. The warmth of his fingers against her night-chilled skin spun a delicious tingle from her head to her toes. A groan rumbled in his throat as he flattened his palm at the small of her back and drew her close.

A tremor of anticipation spun through her when she aligned her body with his. The stiff creases of his uniform and the sensual play of his muscles tantalized her through her sheer dress. Resting her cheek on his shoulder, she melted in his arms, moving with him when he swayed and shifted his feet in a slow dance. The tension that had pounded at her temples slipped away as he held her, and Nicole could almost pretend they were alone, the only two people in this corner of the world.

Daniel skimmed a hand up her spine, sending sparks of shimmery heat through her blood. When he reached her nape, his thumb caressed her sensitized skin with lazy, hypnotic strokes.

"You know," he murmured, his deep voice a low, sexy rumble, "I always kind of regretted that we didn't make it to prom that night. I'd been hoping I'd have the chance to dance with you."

She smiled and curled her fingers in the fabric of his dress coat. "Then this dance was long overdue."

He drew a slow deep breath, then let it out on a hum of pleasure. "And worth the wait."

"Agreed." She snuggled closer, inhaling the crisp scent of soap that clung to him. She closed her eyes and savored the moment. But all too soon the ballad ended and a faster song began. Daniel stopped dancing, but he didn't step back right away. He didn't have to tell her he was thinking about his guard duty, the rules he'd already broken for her.

Nicole mentally scrambled for a way to extend the precious minutes she'd had in his arms. She wasn't ready to say good-night to the thoughtful Daniel she'd gotten to know on her prom night, the honorable soldier concerned tonight for his duty, the sexy man whose touch made her feel thoroughly feminine and on fire.

"I should—"

"Be my date tonight," she interrupted. Lifting her head, she met his dark gaze and gripped his arms to keep him from moving away. Hoping she sounded enticing and impulsive rather than desperate, she flashed a grin. "Come inside with me, and we can spend the rest of the night dancing."

His expression dimmed. "I can't leave my post. Not until my replacement arrives at midnight."

Hope swelled in her chest. "What if someone else covered your post until then? Robert, our chauffeur, is trained in security and often works protection detail for my father." She reached in his front coat pocket, pulled out the cell phone she'd felt there while they danced and dialed.

Daniel opened his mouth to argue, but she turned a shoulder as Robert came on the line. Within minutes, a scowling and skeptical Robert was in place at the front steps, and Daniel had no more excuses not to join her inside.

A giddy sense of victory swirled through her when Daniel finally relented and followed her up the porch stairs. Her triumph was all the sweeter when she thought of the buffer Daniel would provide between her and her father's tedious friends.

Daniel offered her his arm as they crossed the porch. "Is this going to cause a problem with your father?"

Nicole hiked up her chin, remembering the blind eye her father turned to his business associates' behavior toward her. "Maybe. But I don't care. It will teach him a lesson."

Daniel frowned as they stepped into the foyer. "I don't want to get in the middle of some family thing...."

"Don't worry." She tugged his arm, pulling him into the

ballroom, where the volume of music and voices made conversation difficult. "I've got this."

Daniel could feel Senator White's dark glare following him as Nicole led him out onto the dance floor. When she'd explained why Daniel was at her side, the senator had clearly been unhappy with her stunt, and something in Nicole's manner had rankled Daniel, as well. But once he had Nicole in his arms again, the senator faded from his thoughts. With Nicole pressed against his body, his hands on the silky skin of her back, the delicate scent of her surrounding him, he forgot anything beyond that moment, this woman. And the fire that consumed him.

When she threaded her fingers through his short cropped hair or angled her head to flash him a smile with equal parts of sweetness and seduction, his blood ran hot, and his need wound tighter. Months of anticipation and longing coiled inside him.

He'd spent the past five years thinking about Nicole and regretting the chance he'd let slip through his fingers the night he'd walked her home with her new kitten. His sense of honor and propriety, along with a belief that she was out of his reach, had lulled him into inaction when she was sixteen. Since that night, he'd sworn never to miss another opportunity, in any form, when it knocked. For a kid from the bayou, life didn't offer many lucky breaks or second chances.

As they moved together, she chatted amiably, filling him in on her years in nursing school, her mother's illness and recent death, her dream of working overseas in one of the many poor communities where health care was so desperately needed. She quizzed him on his career plans with the Navy, his last tour in the Persian Gulf, his specialty in weapons and explosives.

"Why weapons?" she asked with a frown.

He shrugged. "Because…I'm a guy, and guys like guns and things that go boom."

Her frown turned to a scowling pout, and he was slammed with the urge to kiss her plump raspberry lips. He swallowed hard and determinedly refocused his thoughts. "Because…" he said, schooling his face. "It was where I was needed. It's what I'm good at."

Her smile warmed. "I bet you're good at a lot of things."

He grunted in acknowledgment and brushed his thumb over her bottom lip. "Better at some things than others."

Her pale blue gaze heated, and she canted closer, tracing his ear with her finger. "Do tell."

Lust sent a scalding jolt through him, and as his desire-crazed brain scrambled, weighing discretion against temptation, a firm hand clapped him on the shoulder.

"I'm cutting in," her father said, effectively dousing the flames licking Daniel's veins.

Nicole stiffened. "Actually, I'd rather not." She pulled away from her father's grip and gave Daniel a confident smile. "Daniel was just about to take me home. These shoes are killing me, and my headache from earlier is back."

"Nonsense." The senator took her elbow and guided his daughter off the dance floor. "If you're ready to go home, I can leave now, or have Robert drive you back to the hotel."

"No, Dad, I—" Nicole turned, met Daniel's gaze with a silent plea in her eyes.

Firming his jaw, Daniel wedged through the crowd and cut the senator off at the edge of the dance floor. "The hotel is on my way, sir. It would be my pleasure to take Nicole home."

Nicole beamed, freeing her arm from her father's grasp. "I'll be fine. Good night, Dad."

Daniel seized the chance to pull Nicole toward the front door. He could feel her father's glare burning holes in his back as he escorted Nicole outside and toward the parked cars.

She looped her arm in his and leaned into him as they crossed the grassy lawn. "Thank you. If I'd had to dance with my left-footed father or one of his ass-grabbing friends again tonight, I think I'd—"

Daniel stopped short. "Ass-grabbing?"

She snorted derisively. "Oh, yeah. Right before I came out and found you, the sleazeball from the Chamber of Commerce copped himself a feel."

He tensed and fisted his hands, feeling the thrum of anger pounding at his temples. Performing a stiff about-face, he stalked back toward the mansion. "Show him to me."

Nicole slipped off her high heels and jogged to catch up to him. "Why? So you can defend my honor by punching him in the dentures?" She blocked his path, and when she met his gaze, her eyes sparkled with mirth. "I'm flattered by your chivalry, but save your energy."

He sucked in a deep breath, struggling to calm his raging pulse. "It's just…when I think of some creep with his hands on your—"

She laughed and ran her fingers up the front of his jacket. "You wish you'd thought of it?"

He scoffed and caught her hands in his, tugging her closer. "Believe me, *cher.* I thought about it plenty."

She laced her fingers with his, her expression coy. "Then why didn't you?" She tugged his hands behind her and planted them at the small of her back. "I think I'd like having your hands on me."

The coil of lust inside him yanked tighter. With a groan, he slid his hands down the silky fabric of her dress to palm her bottom. He curled his fingers, testing the supple flesh beneath her dress and tugging her closer.

She sighed her pleasure, and when she tipped her head up, her eyes zeroing in on his mouth, he captured her lips with his. Moving one hand to cradle the base of her head, he held her in place while he explored the taste and texture of her kiss. She clutched at his back, returning his passion and meeting the thrust and parry of his tongue. A sound somewhere between a whimper and a purr rumbled in her throat, and the seductive mewl threw kindling on the fire already blazing in his blood. He wanted her so much he hurt.

"Nicole," he rasped, barely recognizing his own voice, "let me take you home."

"Only if you promise not to leave me at the door." She nibbled her way down his jaw to his ear. "Last time, in high school, you left me…aching for you." Nicole looped her arms around his neck, pressing her breasts against his chest. "I'm still aching for you."

He half moaned, half sighed. "The feeling is mutual."

When he slipped his hands under her dress and filled his hands with her bare bottom, she gasped. "Daniel…"

He shifted his hand, delving a finger into the moist heat between her legs, before the slam of a car door reminded him they were in public. If not for her reputation, he'd take her there in the grassy lawn of the antebellum mansion. But he wouldn't subject her to any scandal or scorn from her social set. Grasping her arms, he kissed her forehead and levered back. "Not here. Which hotel are you staying at?"

She gave him the name of a posh hotel on Canal Street, and as he led her to his truck, he stooped to pick up the shoes she'd kicked off earlier. They seemed ridiculously small to him—size 6—with dangerously spiked heels. "How do you walk in these?"

She grinned. "Very carefully."

He smacked another kiss on her lips before closing her door and circling to the driver's side. The thirty-minute drive to her hotel was torture. He fought the urge to pull to the side of the road and toss her in the backseat, or stop at one of the many lower-rent motels they passed. But Nicole White was not the kind of woman he could take to a second-rate motor inn. He would wait another half hour until they reached her hotel room. Even if his body was strung tighter than a guy wire.

If it killed him, he would wait. For Nicole.

Chapter 2

Present day—Colombia

Nicole woke with a start when a large hand clamped over her mouth and a low male voice growled in her ear, "Don't make any noise."

He gaze flew to the dark figure hovering over her, and panic flooded her brain. In the night shadows, she could tell little about her attacker, except that he was large, and strong, and dark featured. When she squirmed, trying to find Tia, terrified this man could have harmed the little girl, the man's hold on her tightened.

"It's all right, Nicole. I won't hurt you," he whispered, his mouth so close to her that his lips brushed the shell of her ear and his warm breath fanned her neck. In the fog of her fear, it took her a moment to realize he'd used her name. And that he spoke English.

She snapped a startled gaze to his, straining to make out

his face while her heart drummed an anxious beat against her ribs. No use. In the blackness of the jungle night, she couldn't see anything distinguishing about his face.

"I'm an American operative. I'm here to take you home. Do you understand?"

Home. The word held such sweet promise, she couldn't help the whimper of relief that squeaked from her throat.

Her attacker—no, her *rescuer*—loosened his grip on her mouth. "Promise to be quiet?"

She nodded, and tears of joy puddled in her eyes. She was going home. *Finally.* And Tia could get the medical attention she needed. Nicole's heart soared, even though the prospect of escaping the camp filled her with a chilling fear.

As he removed his hand from her mouth, the man dragged his fingers along her chin, brushing her hair back from her face and wiping a tear from her cheek with his thumb. The intimate gesture startled her, and the first uneasy whispers that something was off tickled her nape. He hovered, scant inches above her, and she searched his face, wishing desperately she could see him better in the darkness. Then, with a troubled-sounding sigh, he dipped his head.

And kissed her.

Nicole's breath caught, and her pulse scampered on a fresh wave of panic. Had he lied about his intentions? When her initial, paralyzing shock passed, she gained the frame of mind to resist. But hesitated.

His lips were gentle. The tender caress of his mouth surprised her, intrigued her. Filled her with a sweet warmth. Her body responded to his kiss as if she'd known him her whole life…and yet the edgy prickle at her neck bit harder.

A groan rumbled from his chest, and he broke the kiss to sit back on his heels, muttering a curse under his breath. "Sorry. I shouldn't have done that."

"Damn right, you shouldn't have! Who are you?" she whispered fiercely.

He tensed and angled a hooded glance toward her. "Your ticket outta here. Get up." His tone was gruff now, in contradiction to his soft kiss, and she shivered, despite the clammy heat of the jungle. "I brought shoes and socks for you. Size 6, right?"

"I—yes. How did you know?"

"It's my job to know." He slid a pack off his back and pulled out a pair of boots. "Can you walk? We have a difficult hike ahead of us."

"I can, but Tia's weak." She glanced to the sleeping girl, whose age she estimated at eight years and who'd shared her cage for the past several months. She'd come to love Tia like a daughter, bonding with the terrified child as she protected her from the cruelty of their guards. "She's had a fever and hasn't eaten in days."

Her rescuer followed her glance to Tia and shook his head. "Forget it. She's not coming with us." He shoved the boots at her. "Put these on. Hurry."

Nicole's chest tightened. "What? She has to come. She'll die here if I leave her!" She shifted her gaze down the row of night-darkened cages. "And what about the others? There are twelve of us being held here!"

He clamped a hand over her mouth and growled in her ear. "Keep your voice down." He grabbed the socks up and shoved one onto her foot. "Our objective is to get *you* out. Only you. We can't take anyone else."

She snatched her foot away. "Why? Because they're not American?" Disdain filled her voice, but she didn't care. "Their lives still matter. We can't leave—"

"No. Only you. We only have provisions for you." His tone brooked no resistance, and he tossed a boot into her lap. "Hurry up."

"Then...take Tia instead of me. Please. She's just a child. This is no place for an eight-year-old girl."

He glanced at Tia again and jammed fingers through his short black hair. Hope fluttered in Nicole's chest. Clearly the idea of leaving a little girl behind bothered him.

He released a ragged sigh and cupped a hand at the nape of Nicole's neck. "Don't do this. I have been planning this rescue for months. I'm here to take *you* home. You, Nicole." He kept his voice low, but his tone vibrated with fury and frustration.

An odd sense of familiarity sketched down her spine. Something about his voice...

"I will not do anything that could jeopardize my objective. Got it?"

Nicole's temper spiked. "Did I ask you to save me?"

She felt him tense, his fingers digging into her scalp. "Get your ass moving, or I'll carry you out of here."

A frisson of fear slithered through her. Indecision. Anguish. "I won't leave her. If you don't take her, I'm not going, either." To prove her point, Nicole shoved the boot into his chest and let it drop.

Even with the night shadows, she couldn't miss the lethal scowl he narrowed on her.

"Lafitte!" another male voice whispered just outside her plywood shelter. "What the hell's the hold up? Haul ass!"

Her rescuer bit out another curse, in French this time, and pivoted to where Tia slept. Bending over her, he scooped the girl into his arms.

Relief and gratitude swept through Nicole and left her trembling.

When Tia woke and whimpered in fright, the man clapped a hand over her mouth...which only frightened Tia more.

Quickly Nicole scrambled over and stroked Tia's arm, squeezed her hand. "It's okay, *mija. Es un amigo.*" She tugged the man's hand away from Tia's mouth, then tapped her own finger to Tia's lips. "Shh."

Nicole didn't miss the irony of hushing a girl who hadn't spoken a word since arriving at the camp, traumatized and alone. Tia raised wide brown eyes so full of blind trust that Nicole's heart twisted. She prayed trusting these men, attempting an escape with them, didn't prove a deadly mistake.

When Tia quieted, Nicole jammed the boots on her feet and crawled out of her plywood lean-to in time to see her rescuer pass Tia off to the second man.

"What the hell?" the second man whispered harshly.

"Change of plans," he grumbled under his breath, then stalked back to Nicole. "Ready?" He offered her a hand up, which she took. When he'd pulled her to her feet, he drew her close, and she grabbed one of his muscular arms while she found her balance. "We have to move fast. If you can't run, I'll carry you."

Judging by the size of the arm she held and the width of his chest, she had no doubt he could carry her for miles. The notion started an odd tremble low in her belly. She shook her head. "No. I can run."

"Good. Keep your head down, and do exactly as I say, *when* I say. Got it?" His tone and face were hard and unyielding.

She bristled a bit at his high-handedness but swallowed the sharp retort that came to mind. Under the circumstances, she'd forgive his bossiness. "Got it."

He seized her hand and hauled her with him as he moved to the hole cut in the cage that had imprisoned her. The second man had already carried Tia out and was headed toward the perimeter fence. She scurried through the gap and glanced warily around the dark camp, her heart thundering.

Two shadowy dark figures lay unmoving in the dirt by the weapons cache, and a sick understanding crawled through her.

Her rescuers had killed those men and who knew how many others in order to reach her. Bile rose in her throat, and she fought the urge to vomit.

As he rose to his feet, her rescuer shoved a cumbersome-looking pair of goggles on his head, then pulled a large hand-gun from the waist of his fatigues, reinforcing her recognition of his deadly skill. Her breath hung in her lungs. Apprehension shuddered through her.

Before she could reconcile this lethal soldier with the man who'd kissed her so sweetly and dried her tear moments earlier, he grabbed her arm and ran. She stumbled, trying to keep up with the pace he set, and gritting her teeth, she forced her exercise-deprived legs to move faster. She refused to slow him down, be a hindrance to their escape.

When they reached the hole cut in the perimeter fence, she had precious seconds to rest while the first man shimmied through the hole on his belly. As they coaxed Tia through the gap, Nicole gasped for breath, already winded. The pitch blackness of the jungle loomed beyond the fence that served not only to keep prisoners in, but also to keep wild animals out. Their escape route lay through that dense, wild terrain.

"Nicole." Her rescuer waved her toward the hole in the fence. "Come on, *cher.*"

The endearment reverberated in her head as she dropped to her knees in preparation to crawl through the hole. She recognized the colloquial Cajun French term, pronounced *sha,* which she heard often in her home state. "You're from Louisiana."

He stilled for an instant, and she felt more than saw his gaze boring into hers. "Yes." Before she could respond, he put a hand on her head and shoved her down. "Go!"

She did, with Cajun Man at her heels. Already the second man had disappeared into the thick foliage with Tia. Once through the fence, her rescuer dug in his pack and gave her a pair of goggles like the ones he and his partner wore. "Put these on."

She obeyed, then marveled at the green images that leaped out of the blackness of the night. Night vision goggles. Of course. She studied him with her newly enhanced vision, but he, too, wore a pair of goggles that obscured her view of his face. The goggles only confirmed for her that he was dark-haired and broad-shouldered and had a heavy layer of stubble covering his cheeks and chin. She'd had little chance to familiarize herself with the goggles before he grabbed her hand and pulled her into the jungle.

Behind them, a voice shouted in the camp. A warning. An alert. Someone had discovered the dead guards or her empty cage.

Cajun Man's hand tightened around hers. "Damn! Go, go, go!"

Through the overgrown jungle, she heard the rebel encampment waking, engines starting, angry shouts. He tugged her arm, urging her to go faster, and adrenaline fueled her feet.

Their escape path led them up the steep side of a mountain, and soon her muscles trembled from exertion. Nicole used her free hand to grab limbs and roots, anything she could use to help pull herself up the incline as he hauled her forward by the hand. She couldn't quit, had to find the strength to press on. Letting the rebel soldiers catch her now would mean certain death.

Wide-leafed branches slapped at her legs, her face. Around her, the eyes of nocturnal animals glowed in her goggles, and she fought the fear that threatened to suffocate her. She had to keep moving, keep running. Keep putting one foot in front of the other.

Finally, they reached the top of the incline, and the terrain leveled out. Cajun Man never slowed their pace. The foliage thinned out in places making their progress easier. Many minutes later, when Nicole thought she might drop from exhaustion, he slowed at last and led her behind a wide tree trunk where his partner had stopped with Tia.

She gulped oxygen and collapsed on the ground beside the little girl. Tia crawled close and buried her head in Nicole's chest.

"Where are we?" Cajun Man asked his friend, who'd pulled out a small gadget she couldn't identify in the dark, even with her night vision goggles.

"Chopper's still a couple miles north," his partner answered.

Her heart beat so hard she could barely hear their discussion over the pounding pulse in her ears.

Turning, Cajun Man crouched in front of her and squeezed her shoulder. "How are you holding up?"

She nodded, unable to find the breath to speak.

"And the kid?" He jerked his head toward Tia.

"Scared," Nicole panted. "But…all right."

The night vision goggles helped her make out general forms in an unnatural green glow, but the details of Cajun's and his partner's appearances were still a mystery. She shoved aside her frustration with not knowing what her rescuers looked like. What did it matter as long as they got her and Tia out of that jungle alive? It didn't. Yet she couldn't quash the eerie prickle of familiarity his voice evoked.

He handed her a flask from his pack. "Drink."

She waved his offering away. "I'm okay."

"Drink," he repeated more forcefully, shoving the canteen into her hand. "I can't have you passing out on me later when I need you to run."

Capitulating, she uncapped the flask and tipped it up to her lips. She almost groaned in pleasure as a sweet fruity drink bathed her tongue. An energy drink. How long had it been since she'd had anything but foul water to drink?

Brushing Tia's hair back from her eyes, Nicole gave the canteen to the girl and helped her take a sip. When the little girl tasted the sweet drink, she clutched the canteen tighter and tipped it higher for a bigger gulp.

"Hey!" Cajun snatched the container back. "That's gotta last until we're outta here. Those of us who are hoofing it get priority."

Tia shrank away from him, huddling closer to Nicole with a whimper.

Nicole bit back a retort. She had to remember that this man had risked his life to save her and had brought Tia along against his better judgment and despite the limited provisions he'd made. She raised her chin and worked at keeping her voice nonconfrontational. "Could you please try not to scare her? She's just a kid, and she's already been through a nightmare."

He paused in the act of stashing the canteen in his pack, cast a side-glance to Nicole and heaved an impatient sigh as he shoved to his feet. "Enough rest. Let's move." He faced his partner and gave a nod. "Alec?"

His partner stowed his own canteen and stepped forward to help Nicole to her feet. Cajun Man lifted Tia into his arms and led the way with Nicole following and his partner—Alec, he'd called him—bringing up the rear. Though they were no longer running, they moved at a fast clip, and Nicole had trouble keeping up. The distance between the Cajun and Nicole widened by the minute, until, maybe an hour later, Alec finally cupped his hands around his mouth and made a shrill noise, something between a bird call and monkey. Cajun Man stopped, setting Tia on the ground, and Alec grabbed Nicole's arm to hustle her forward.

"This is taking too long," Cajun Man said as they approached, clearly agitated. "You go on," he said to Alec. "Take the girl and tell Jake to get the chopper ready. I'll stay with her, and we'll be there…whenever." His tone was full of frustration.

"Roger that." Without further discussion, Alec lifted Tia into his arms and disappeared into the jungle foliage. A ripple of apprehension shimmied through Nicole. Not that she didn't trust the Cajun, but having her rescue team halved felt like a dangerous move.

"Are you sure that's a good idea?" She pressed a hand to the stitch in her side.

"Normally, no." He paused, the silence taut with recriminations. "But under the circumstances—"

She grunted defensively. "I'm sorry I'm slowing you down. But all those months in a cage without exercise have left me out of shape."

He faced her and cocked his head as he studied her. The jungle shadows and his night vision goggles made him look like a strange insect from a sci-fi flick. "I know that."

His tone was softer now, almost apologetic, and she slumped at the base of a tree. Yanking off the cumbersome goggles, she rubbed her aching temples with the heels of her hands. His mercurial moods baffled her, set her on edge. "Look, I appreciate the risks you've taken to get me out of that stink hole. I'm doing everything I can to cooperate. But sometimes it seems like you're…" She waved a hand, searching for the right word, then dropped it limply to her lap again. "I don't know…mad at me or something. Have I done something to tick you off?"

Cajun Man was silent, and without her goggles, he was nothing but a looming figure in the blackness. For a moment, she thought he wouldn't answer, but finally he murmured, "Not you. Your father."

Her pulse kicked, and she sat taller. "What does any of this have to do with my father?"

"Everything," he growled, then sighed heavily. "And nothing."

She huffed her annoyance with his cryptic responses. "Which is it?"

"Let's just say it's bitterly ironic that I'm the one who'll be bringing you home to your father."

She blinked, befuddled by his word choice. "Ironic? Why?"

She sensed his hard gaze as a tingle skittered down her spine.

"Because your father tried to kill me."

Chapter 3

A laugh of disbelief erupted from Nicole. "No way! My father is not a murderer." She scoffed and shook her head, amazed she was even debating such an absurd topic. "I may have had my differences with him in the past, but he's an upstanding citizen and an honorable man. He's a United States Senator, for heaven's sake."

The Cajun dropped quickly to a crouch in front of her, and she felt the stir of his breath when he jammed his face inches from hers to growl, "Not anymore. He was censured and later resigned."

Nicole's chest tightened. "Why?"

"Because he's a traitor to the United States."

She huffed indignantly. "That's a lie! He'd never—"

"He did," Cajun snarled. "I can *prove* that he negotiated with a terrorist and gave up classified information vital to national security, trying to get you released." He paused, breathing hard. "And while I respect his goal—clearly I've risked my own life to get you out of this hellhole—I would *never* have betrayed my country to do it."

Nausea swamped her gut, and she shook her head, trying to clear the confusing jumble of information that buzzed through her brain. "I—I don't believe you."

He grunted his disgust and impatience. "You don't have to believe me. I know what I know."

Nicole worked to form enough spit in her dry mouth to swallow. She fumbled to put her night vision goggles back on, to try again to identify her father's accuser. "Who are you, and what is it you think he did? I'm sure there's a logical explanation."

Cajun Man shoved to his feet again and angrily slapped a low-hanging branch out of his way. "A few months ago, he betrayed two American operatives working a top secret mission in enemy territory. He was trying to win your release, but…clearly, it didn't work."

Nicole's stomach swirled, acid biting hard. "Wh-what happened to the operatives?"

He didn't answer for several seconds, and dread screwed tighter in her chest.

"They took it upon themselves to rescue you, despite what your father almost cost them."

Nicole drew a silent gasp as the earth beneath her pitched. "Y-you…?"

Rather than answer her, he flicked his hand, motioning for her to stand up. "Come on. Time to go."

She gaped at him, too numb to move. "So…what? I'm some kind of pawn in your vendetta with my father?"

"Sounds about right. And it evens the score between you and me, too. Don't you think?"

She shook her head, stunned and confused. "Am I supposed to know you?"

He snorted derisively. "Says a lot that you don't."

"Look, stop talking in riddles and tell me what's going on! Who are you?" As hard as she was trying to keep her voice low, frustration and anger sharpened her tone.

"Get—" A loud pop cut the Cajun off and echoed through the dark jungle. Then a series of nerve-rattling cracks. Cajun Man barked a curse and yanked her to her feet. "Snipers! Run!"

Staggering, Nicole ran, fueled by fear. Cajun Man led the way, returning fire with his handgun. Around her bits of bark and dirt flew. The snipers' bullets zinged past her. She charged forward, blindly following the Cajun.

Suddenly, with an agonized scream, he fell.

Nicole skidded to a stop and dropped behind the modest protection of a fallen tree. The Cajun dragged himself forward, clutching his left leg, and an icy chill raced through her. She scrambled to his side. "You're hit?"

He pushed her away. "Forget me and go!" he rasped. "Straight ahead. Alec has the chopper—"

"I can't leave you here!" She moved closer and, with the help of her night vision goggles, she saw the bloody mess that was his knee. "Oh, my God!"

Despite her medical training, her gut pitched. He had to be in excruciating pain. Staying low to avoid the continuing rain of sniper fire, she whipped her shirt over her head. Unmindful of her dishabille, she tore the shirt at the side seam.

"No time!" He batted her away when she tried to staunch his bleeding. "Go!"

Tears filled her eyes. "And leave you here to die? How heartless do you think I am?"

He rolled his head back, teeth gritted and his thick neck arched as he growled in pain. "Nicole!"

Desperation and adrenaline spurred her to action. Wrapping her shirt around his knee, she tied the fabric off, then grabbed the front of his shirt in a fist. "Get up, soldier!" He wasn't the only one who could bark orders. "You *will* go with me. Now!"

She shoved her shoulder under his left armpit and struggled to get him upright and still stay behind the protection of the large tree.

Indecision bit Nicole. The Cajun was twice her size, and they were surrounded by snipers. How was she supposed to get them both to the helicopter safely?

The Cajun clearly read her dilemma, and with his superior strength, pried himself out of her grip. "Leave me, damn it! Run!"

Emotion clogged Nicole's throat, but she choked out, "Promise you'll follow." He jerked a nod that didn't quite convince her, but the hail of bullets seemed to be closing in. She stuck her face in the Cajun's and shouted, "I'll bring Alec back for you."

"No!" he yelled as she turned to run.

Moisture not only blurred her vision, but in the hot jungle, her night vision goggles steamed up. Giving up on the goggles, she yanked them off and tossed them behind her as she plowed forward. The first thin rays of morning sun filtered through the jungle canopy, and with the watery light as a guide, she rushed toward what appeared to be a clearing ahead. The whir of a motor reached her over the pounding of her pulse and the pop of gunfire.

Please God, let that engine be Alec with the helicopter.

"Alec!" Screaming for his help took almost more breath than she had left. Surely he'd heard the gunfire. Where was—?

A hand grabbed her arm and swung her into the thick vegetation. She swallowed her gasp, recognizing the tall, dark-haired man still wearing his night vision goggles. "Alec!"

He shoved her behind him. "Keep your head down!" Leaning against a tree branch with an automatic weapon propped on his shoulder, Alec fired into the trees. "Jake's got the chopper ready. That way!" He freed a hand long enough to push her toward the clearing.

She jerked away. "Where's Tia?"

"On the chopper with Jake."

She nodded in relief, then gasped, "Your partner was shot. We have to go back for him!" She started back the way she'd come, trusting Alec would follow.

"Nicole, wait!" He grabbed at her retreating back, but because she'd shed her shirt, he came up empty-handed. "Nicole!"

"Hurry!" She didn't wait. Desperate to reach the Cajun, she pumped her legs, knocking palm fronds out of her way with her arm, retracing her steps, using tree trunks for cover and the thick foliage to camouflage her progress. The sun was slightly higher now. Shadowy forms separated from the thin gray light that seeped through the jungle ceiling. Terror coiled around her like a python, squeezing her chest, but she forcefully battled the fear down. She had to keep it together. Not just for her own sake, but for Tia. For Alec and for the Cajun who, even though he hated her for some unknown offense, had risked his life, taken a bullet in his leg, saving her.

Alec, moving so silently she didn't hear him until he was upon her, pressed close behind Nicole, his automatic weapon at the ready.

The snipers' fire had slacked off, although she still saw an occasional muzzle flash in the upper branches followed by the chilling thud of a bullet hitting the ground.

"Go back to the chopper. I'll find him," Alec growled.

They'd only gotten half of the way back to where she'd left the Cajun, and something deep inside her wouldn't let her leave the jungle without him. She'd opened her mouth to argue, when one of the dark shadows moved with a lurch and a groan.

Nicole's heart stutter-stepped in admiration and compassion. Despite the obvious pain he was in, the Cajun was struggling toward their extraction point. As he neared, she made out the branch he used as a crutch while he dragged his bloodied leg behind him. He'd taken off his goggles as she had, and no longer had his backpack. Everything in his body language, from his rigidly set jaw, taut mouth, fisted hands and forward canting body as he staggered through the jungle exuded a sheer grit and steely determination. This man was a warrior. A fighter. A survivor.

Your father tried to kill me.

Nicole shook her head to clear the baffling accusation from her thoughts. She'd have time to work through the Cajun's assertions later. Right now, they had to get back to the helicopter.

She hurried toward him with Alec on her heels. Hearing them, Cajun jerked his head up, along with his gun.

She inhaled sharply. "Don't shoot. It's us."

He blew out a harsh breath. "Damn it, Nicole! I told you not to—"

"I know what you said," she countered, as Alec wedged himself under his partner's left arm, and Nicole moved to his right side. "I chose to ignore your orders. I knew and accepted the risk of helping you." She tensed her legs as he shifted some of his weight onto her and limped forward a couple steps. She angled a quick glance at his grimacing face and couldn't resist adding, "I figure it evens the score between you and me."

He stiffened. Whipped a startled look toward her. The thin dappled light still cast his face in shadow, but she felt the intensity of his glare. Without commenting, he hobbled forward. "Faster. I can take it."

"But you're—" The rat-a-tat of an automatic weapon echoed through the jungle behind them, getting closer.

"Don't baby me," he snarled. "Let's move!"

Holding tightly to his arm, his waist, Nicole half jogged, half staggered as she and Alec all but dragged the Cajun. He screamed in pain but demanded they keep up their pace. By the time they reached the clearing where the chopper waited, her legs were jelly, and her arm muscles quivered. As they left the line of trees, Alec shoved his weapon at her and hoisted his partner over his shoulder in a fireman's carry. "Cover us!"

Nicole gaped at the automatic weapon in her hands and shuddered. She'd only seen guns like this one fired. Had never held, much less fired, one.

But a new hail of bullets peppered the clearing as Alec ran for the chopper door with the Cajun across his back. Nicole swung the big gun up and fired toward the muzzle flashes in the jungle. Spinning on her heel, she darted across the open field, praying that everything she'd heard about moving targets was true. She kept her eyes fixed on the open door of the helicopter. Inside, she could see Tia in her pink shorts, huddled with her hands over her ears.

Alec dumped his partner unceremoniously on the floor of the chopper, then ran to the copilot's seat, yelling to the pilot, "Take off, cowboy!"

Panting for breath, Nicole dove into the open side of the chopper. The instant she was aboard, the helicopter lurched off the ground. Her stomach pitched as they ascended and swooped over the treetops. Dropping the weapon in her hands as if it were a rattlesnake, Nicole gasped for air and took a mental survey. She was in one piece, even though nicks and cuts on her arms and legs trickled blood.

And Tia was safe—even if the gunfire and tumult had clearly revived whatever nightmare she'd survived earlier. Nicole scuttled awkwardly across the rocking helicopter floor until she reached the frightened child.

With a whimper, Tia wrapped her arms around Nicole and

buried her face on her shoulder. Tia's warm tears dripped onto Nicole's skin, reminding her that she'd sacrificed her shirt to the Cajun's knee, so she wore only a bra. She closed her eyes and sighed, unable to find the energy to care. Modesty seemed a ludicrous indulgence in light of the situation.

"Nicole…" The strangled-sounding voice was almost lost in the roar of the helicopter turbines.

She raised her head to meet the Cajun's gaze. His dark eyes were wild with agony, and his face contorted in misery when the chopper hit an air pocket, jostling him. She hated seeing him suffer, no matter what vile allegations he'd leveled against her father. Whatever his reasons, his agenda, he *had* saved her—and Tia—from that cesspool prison camp.

"Ni-cole," he repeated and held a hand out, summoning her to come closer.

Giving Tia a reassuring smile, she untangled herself from the child's grip and moved to his side.

Nicole grasped his hand with one of hers and stroked his stubble-covered face with her other hand, wishing she could do something, anything to ease his pain. At that moment, the morning sun broke over the tops of the trees and shone through the open side door of the helicopter, casting his rugged face in sharp relief. For the first time, she could truly see the man who'd risked his life for her. Even with heavy black stubble covering his jaw, mud smudged on his cheeks and his features drawn in a grimace of pain, her Cajun rescuer was a devastatingly handsome man. Her heart clenched, and the prickle of déjà vu returned. He seemed so familiar.…

"I…need—" He stopped, clenching his teeth and growling in torment. "Please…I need—"

Tears puddled in her eyes. "What do you need? Tell me."

She had no idea what medical supplies, painkillers or other provisions the helicopter had, but she'd move heaven and earth to get him the best care when they were back in the States.

He drew a couple shallow breaths, his jaw tightening again. "I need to know…you remember." He swallowed hard, his eyes drilling into hers. "Tell me…you remember."

His request, and the obvious emotional distress behind it, rattled her. Witnessing his physical pain was hard enough. She opened her mouth to ask what he meant, but the tortured plea in his eyes stole her breath and her resolve.

"I remember," she lied, leaning closer to be sure he heard her.

He held her gaze for a moment, sweat beading on his forehead and expectant hope lighting his gaze. Then he scowled darkly and jerked his gaze away. He ground his back teeth together and scrunched his face in agony.

With lightning speed, he seized the back of her head and wound his fingers in her hair so tightly her scalp prickled. She gasped, as he pulled her down so that her face hovered right above his. "Then say my name!"

She stared at him, stunned by his vehemence and trying to reconcile the nagging intuition she'd had since he'd kissed her at the camp that something didn't add up. The niggling familiarity of his voice. Her body's response to his touch.

"Say my name, Nicole," he repeated, raggedly this time. "I want to hear you say it."

And in a heartbeat, an echo from her past yanked her back five years to a hotel room in New Orleans. Her heart wrenched, and tears spilled from her eyes.

"Oh, my God!" She curled her fingers into the hair at his nape and buried her face in his neck. "Daniel…"

Five years earlier

"What do you think?" Nicole asked as she struck a pose wearing Daniel's uniform hat. Only his uniform hat. "Could I be in the Navy?"

From the hotel bed, Daniel stacked his hands behind his

head, a move that emphasized the broad cut of his bare shoulders and the muscle definition in his arms. He sent her a seductive grin. "What I think is that I'll never wear my dress whites again without thinking how much better they look on you."

Nicole dropped her pose and crawled across the bed to him, letting her fingers walk up his chest. "Personally, as hot as you look in your dress whites, I have to say I like you out of them even more."

She flashed him a wicked grin, earning a playful pat on her fanny before he captured her head with his hand and dragged her close for a hot kiss. Despite having made love to him four times already in the past few hours, the heat of his mouth on hers, the stroke of his fingers along her thigh sent a thrill through her blood and made her body quiver in anticipation of another mind-blowing climax. She'd never, in her limited experience, known a man who could so thoroughly and continually elicit such a powerful and carnal response from her. He'd explored every inch of her body and unerringly found and finessed erogenous zones she'd never known she had.

Breathless, she plucked a condom from the bedside stand and ripped it open. "What do you say, Boudreaux? Are you ready for me?"

Holding her gaze, he took the prophylactic from her and covered himself. "Now I am."

In a deft move, he kicked the sheet off his feet and flipped her to her back. She gasped, then laughed as he straddled her, pinning her arms over her head with one hand and running one finger along the side of her midriff. She squirmed, trying to get away from the teasing touch. "Stop," she said, giggling, "I told you I'm ticklish."

He arched a sexy black eyebrow, and his dark brown gaze burrowed into her. "And I told you what would happen if you called me Boudreaux again."

She squealed in mirth as he lightly trailed his fingers over her most sensitive spots. "Stop!"

He traced the curve of her hip and down her leg. "What's my name?"

"Boudreaux!"

He shook his head and tickled his way past her naval, then circled her nipples with one finger. "Say my name. My real name."

She chuckled, flashed a saucy grin. "Afraid I've forgotten it?"

His head cocked to one side. "Have you?"

"No."

"Prove it." He tweaked the tip of her breast and shifted his weight so that his erection nudged between her legs.

Just the promise of what was to come coiled desire in her womb and chased the teasing grin from her lips. The fiery sensations crackling through her were no laughing matter. She wanted him inside her with an urgency that was primal and overwhelming. She angled her hips, straining toward him. "Please…"

Even when she wrapped her legs around him and arched her back, he waited.

"Say my name." His tone held no humor, and his eyes shone with a hunger and passion that stirred a tremor deep in her core. He brushed a kiss across her lips and nuzzled her cheek. "I want to hear my name on your lips when I'm inside you."

The sensual rasp of his voice stroked her, wound her anticipation tighter, while the poignant intimacy of his request seized her heart. She threaded her fingers through his hair and raised her lips to his ear. "Daniel. Daniel LeCroix…"

Nicole whispered his name, rolling the *R* in a sensual purr that vibrated through him and stoked the need that pounded through his veins. His body thrumming, he drew a ragged breath and buried himself inside her. "Ah, Nicole...*cher*..."

A sexy gasp caught in her throat, and she moaned as he filled her. Her body gripped his, and a protectiveness, an overwhelming need to possess her, drove him to hold her closer, thrust deeper, take her higher. When they'd made love the first time, he'd thought he could get his fill of her and satisfy the fascination with her that had begun on her prom night years ago. Instead he found the more they made love, the more he wanted her and the more he lost his heart to her.

With a mewling cry, Nicole bowed her back and shuddered as she peaked. "Daniel!"

The first pulse of her body milking him shattered his restraint, and primal noises rumbled from his throat as he followed her into a mind-numbing climax.

When the maelstrom passed and the sensual haze began to lift, he knew he was in trouble. His caring this much about her gave Nicole power over him. Rather than getting her out of his head, she'd found a way past his defenses and into his heart.

He tried to move away from her, needing distance to clear his head, but she wrapped her arms around his neck and tucked her body against his. "Hold me, Daniel. Please, hold me."

And he did. Until they fell asleep, wrapped in each other's arms. Until the first light of morning peeked through the gap in the curtains and prodded him awake.

Until her cell phone chimed on the dresser, and she rolled out of bed to answer it.

He flopped onto his back and watched her through his eyelashes as she, in all her naked glory, stumbled groggily across the room. The sight of her smooth skin and sultry curves sent a fresh rush of desire thundering through him.

Nicole plucked her cell phone from the dresser and checked

the screen. Her shoulders sagged, and she groaned before she thumbed the answer button. "Hi, Dad."

Daniel tensed.

"Yes, I was still asleep. Why?" She gasped, and her back stiffened. "Oh, no. I completely forgot. I'm so sorry." She sent a quick glance to their bed and winced. "Yeah, I know how important it is to you."

He propped on one elbow, watching her, and she mouthed, *Sorry.* Then turning, she headed into the bathroom. "I'm getting in the shower now. I'll meet you there."

Disappointment plucked at him. He'd hoped they could at least share breakfast before they parted ways.

He heard her turn on the shower and flopped back against the pillow with a sigh. Tossing back the covers, he climbed out of bed and strolled to the door of the bathroom to ask her if she wanted him to order room service. But the door was locked.

Frowning, he raised his hand to knock.

"Yes, I did spend the night with that guy from the bayou," she said, her voice haughty, her tone dripping disdain. "In fact, I had sex with him. Many times."

The taunting tone of her voice sent a chill through him. He lowered his hand and listened with his heart in his throat.

"I'm perfectly clear on your feelings about him," she scoffed, and he heard a thump. "Maybe that's the point."

A sinking sensation knotted in his chest as he saw last night through a new lens. The smug grin she'd given her father when she'd introduced him as her date for the rest of the night. Her repeated use of the Boudreaux moniker. The dark suspicious looks her father had given him.

His sense of being caught in the middle of a family feud had been more on target than he'd realized.

"Because I could, Dad. I can sleep with a Cajun or a frat

boy or the whole naval fleet if I feel like it. I'm not a little girl anymore. You can't dictate my life."

Daniel staggered back a step from the door as if pushed, as if kicked in the gut. Blindsided. Sucker punched. Deceived.

Had last night been nothing but a rebellion against her father? A walk on the wrong side of the tracks so she could flout her father's ideals?

"Who says there'll be a next time?" she said. "Maybe I'm ready to go back to Houston and finish my nursing degree! It's exactly what Mom would have wanted!"

As her argument with her father grew more heated, Daniel raked a hand through his hair and battled down the bitter hurt and anger that roiled inside him.

She'd used him. She'd seen an opportunity to hook a man her father saw as unworthy and dangle her tryst in the senator's face. A sharp ache of betrayal raked through his chest, and he snatched his pants and dress jacket from the closet.

Nicole's voice became a muted drone as he dressed and put on his shoes. By the time he gathered his hat and cell phone from the nightstand, a sour disgust, with himself and with Nicole's betrayal, had risen like bile in his throat.

The shower was the only sound from the bathroom when he gave the room one last glance for anything he'd missed. The rumpled bed served a vivid reminder of what had transpired the night before. He might have been making love to Nicole, but he'd gotten screwed.

Nicole sat on the floor of the shower, silent tears tracking down her cheeks. She had to pull herself together, couldn't let Daniel see how deeply her father's attitude hurt her. Somewhere during the night, making love to Daniel, she'd realized the only way to get her life back under control was to make a clean break from her father. She couldn't be the daughter he wanted her to be, and trying was suffocating her.

Losing her father, so soon after losing her mom, made it all the harder to break free. But if she needed any reminder how differently they viewed the world, it had been obvious when her father had referred to Daniel in such derogatory terms. She'd thrown the words back in his face, hoping her father would hear how elitist he sounded, but Alan White couldn't see what she saw him becoming. And it broke her heart.

Shutting of the water, Nicole dragged herself from the shower and dried off, deciding how much to tell Daniel about the argument he had to have overheard. The truth, of course, but how much of the truth? She was still grappling with the truth herself.

Finally, pulling on the plush robe the hotel provided, she headed back out to the room to face her future. And found no one there.

Chapter 4

Present day—New Orleans

Daniel woke slowly, keeping still, using all of his senses to test his surroundings for possible threats before opening his eyes. He'd been trained to assess every new situation carefully, especially if he was at a strategic disadvantage. Which he was, based on the throbbing ache in his knee and no memory past struggling to the chopper amid gunfire.

The beep of electronics and the murmur of distant voices, too muted for him to distinguish what language they were speaking, met his ears. He lay flat on a soft surface and had covers over him. A bed. His knee hurt like the devil, and he had tubes and needles poking him. His head felt a little muzzy, likely from some kind of painkiller, but he began to build a picture. He could smell antiseptic and…roasted chicken? His stomach growled.

So he was in a hospital room. But where?

And someone held his hand. That fact made his pulse trip. Who—?

He cracked his eyes open, peeking out through his eyelashes, careful not to alert his company to his waking…just in case.

Nicole sat in a wheelchair beside his bed, her head lolling to the side, her eyes closed, her lips slightly parted. Asleep. She wore a blue hospital gown and an IV bag, hanging from a pole attached to her wheelchair, was hooked up to her right hand. As when he'd found her asleep at the prison camp, he was struck by how beautiful she looked, despite the circumstances. And how vulnerable.

On the heels of that thought, he flashed to the jungle. To Nicole pushing herself to keep up despite her obvious exhaustion. To her feisty determination not to leave him behind when he was shot. To her stubborn protectiveness over the little girl.

No. Nicole White might look vulnerable, but a tenacious streak ran through her.

He angled his gaze to their joined hands, determined not to read anything into her presence in his room. Hands he remembered as delicately feminine and soft were now chapped and showed the wear of harsh living conditions. Her once well-manicured fingernails were short and ragged, her skin marred by cuts and bruises. The physical reminders of her ordeal caused a twisting sensation deep in his chest.

Oh, my God! Daniel… He'd blacked out shortly after her eyes had widened in recognition. Finally.

Disappointment pinched him.

But…the jungle had been dark, their situation had been perilous, and their last meeting had been over five years ago. His appearance had changed some over the years.

Still…it stung that she'd not known him immediately. Especially after the intimacies they'd shared their one night together. Daniel sighed. One night five years ago and one night ten years ago. Maybe he was asking too much to think she'd remember him. And even if she did recall everything that had happened that night in New Orleans, where did that leave them?

He had to remember who her father was, the *reason* they'd only had the one night, the way she'd used him....

A spike of bitter resentment seeped through the golden memories and gnawed in his gut. Nothing was settled between them. Clenching his back teeth, Daniel eased his hand out from under hers, careful not to wake her, then shifted in the bed to give her his back.

He sank into his pillow, prepared to nurse his black mood when a soft knock sounded at his door. A sweet and familiar face peeked around the corner.

"Daniel, you awake? Can we come in?" His spirits lifted as his partner's very pregnant wife waddled into the room, Alec behind her, and gave him a bright smile.

Daniel nodded, then hitched his head toward Nicole and signaled for his visitors to be quiet. As Erin Kincaid bent to hug him, he whispered, "Hey, gorgeous. Thanks for loaning me Alec. I brought him back in one piece, like I promised."

She squeezed him and gave his injured leg a side glance. "You promised you'd *all* come back unharmed."

He grunted. "Oops."

She sent him a withering frown and stepped away to allow her husband to greet him. Alec and Daniel clasped hands briefly, tightly. Words weren't needed. Alec was like a brother to Daniel. A brother who'd been through hell and back with him on many occasions. A brother with whom he'd trust his life.

"How's the knee?" Alec asked in a low voice.

"You tell me. I'm a little foggy on what happened after we got airborne. Sit-rep?"

"Pretty simple. We got the hell out of the jungle. Oh, and the snipers? Not from the camp. They were kids."

Daniel frowned. "What?"

Alec nodded. "No lie. Kids, about ten to twelve years old, posted in the trees to guard someone's cash crop. I saw the coca plants once we were in the air."

"Kids. Jeez." Daniel shook his head. "Okay, go on."

"Then we swapped the chopper for the Cessna you'd arranged in Bogotá and flew straight back to the States." Alec, who'd clearly had time to shower, shave and change into street clothes, moved a chair near the bed for his wife. "We were wheels down in New Orleans by early afternoon, some ten hours after extracting the target. Objective complete. Mission accomplished."

His partner crossed his arms over his chest and sent Daniel a satisfied grin.

Erin tipped her head to give her husband a worried frown. "Your last mission. You promised."

He sat on the arm of the chair and kissed Erin's hair. "Yes. I promise."

Daniel watched his partner and his wife with regret. As much as he liked Erin, as happy as he was for Alec, he couldn't help wondering about the future. He'd been Alec's partner on the top secret black ops team most of his career. What was he going to do now that Alec was retiring from active duty?

Daniel touched his thigh, just above his throbbing knee. Would he have a black ops job to go back to, or would his injury sideline him, too?

"I was looking for something more specific. I assume you've talked to the doctors here." He gave Nicole a meaningful glance. "Is she okay? What happened with the kid? Did Nicole tell you anything about her captivity on the flight home?"

Alec arched a dark eyebrow, and the glint in his blue eyes told Daniel he hadn't missed the question Daniel left out. "Nicole's fine. A few dings and some dehydration, but nothing a night in the hospital won't remedy." He folded his arms over his chest before he continued. "Tia is in a room on the pediatric floor getting IV fluids and a psych evaluation. At the moment, the hospital staff and government authorities here believe she is your daughter."

Daniel snapped his gaze up to Alec's. "*My* daughter? Wh—"

"Think about it, Lafitte. Nicole is blond and blue eyed, well-known in the States. No one would believe the girl was hers. And with your tan complexion and dark hair and eyes, you look more Hispanic than Jake or I do."

Daniel dragged a hand over his mouth. "What am I supposed to do with her?"

Alec held up his hands. "Easy. Nicole is working on cutting through the red tape involved in having Tia here without a visa, without knowledge of who her parents are, without consent of the Colombian government...."

Daniel shut his eyes and blew out a frustrated sigh. "I couldn't leave her. Nicole refused to go without the girl, and we didn't have time to argue."

"And when she looked at you with those big sad eyes, your heart melted. Right?" Alec smirked.

Daniel scowled. "Well, yeah. I'd have to be made of stone not to be sympathetic to a scared little girl. Especially in that hellhole. It was no place to leave a kid."

Alec's grin spread. "I was talking about Nicole's sad eyes, but it's good to know you have a soft spot for children, too."

Daniel cut a quick glace at Nicole, who was still asleep, then glowered at Alec. "Wiseass."

Erin and Alec exchanged a knowing grin, then fell silent. Daniel lowered his gaze to the lumpy silhouette of his injured leg under the thin blanket. Questions he hated to ask, dreading the answers, hung with a palpable tension in the quiet room.

"They operated on your knee, patched it up as best they could. You have several pins and screws holding you together at the moment." Alec's voice held a note of apology, commiseration. "The bullet went all the way through, which is good. If it had bounced around in your leg, it could have torn up more arteries, and you'd have bled out. Nicole, being a nurse, got busy once we were out of the jungle and stabilized your leg. She stopped the bleeding, kept tabs on your vitals and found stuff in the trauma kit to keep you knocked out for the ride home."

His gaze drifted to Nicole, almost of its own volition, and his chest tightened when he pictured her laboring over him to save his life. He swallowed hard, despite the cottony feeling in his mouth, and shifted his gaze to Alec. "But..."

To his credit, Alec didn't pretend not to know what Daniel was asking. His partner's brow furrowed in sympathy. "But the surgical repairs aren't a permanent fix. You'll be able to walk with a cane and some therapy, but you're gonna hurt like hell for a while. They recommend a joint replacement in the near future." He hesitated and pinned Daniel with a penetrating gaze. "Your days in the field are over. I'm sorry."

Daniel's gut wrenched, and he battled down the swell of panic with stubborn denial. "Maybe not. Maybe with physical therapy—"

"The team's already issued your deactivation order. I talked to the chief earlier, tried to get him to hold off until after your surgery, but...he was adamant. He can't take a chance in the field with an agent who's suffered a knee injury like yours."

Daniel gritted his teeth, and his hands fisted in the blanket. "He can't take me off the team without even talking to me! How—"

Nicole inhaled a sharp breath and jerked awake, a wild gaze darting nervously around her surroundings. Daniel kicked himself mentally, knowing his angry volume had woken her.

After a few shallow, panted breaths, she seemed to realize she was safe and melted wearily back into the wheelchair. Then noticing the attention she'd drawn, she scooted upright from her slumped position and, rubbing her neck with her hand, sent Daniel, then Alec, curious looks. "I fell asleep."

"Apparently." Daniel gave her a measured scrutiny. He was all too familiar with the time it took to decompress after a trauma, after being held captive and fearing daily for your life. Nicole had a tough road ahead.

Erin introduced herself, and the women exchanged polite greetings before Nicole's eyes locked on Daniel's, all traces of her earlier distress and confusion gone. "How do you feel?"

"Well, let's see…I've got a blown-out knee, a screaming headache and I just learned my injured leg means I no longer have a job." He gave her a churlish smile. "I'm peachy."

Nicole sat back, her expression wounded.

"Daniel…" Erin scolded quietly.

Guilt kicked him, and he tore his gaze from hers to glare at his feet.

"Come on, Lafitte," Alec said. "I know you're ticked about being taken off the team, but don't take it out on her."

"What, are you my mother now?" he growled.

Alec scoffed. "Fine. Clearly you need time alone to process all this." He stood and held his hand out to help Erin to her feet. "When you're ready to talk, you know how to reach me."

Daniel angled a look to his partner and Erin, his guilt and despondency grinding harder into his conscience. "Sorry," he mumbled.

"She's the one you owe an apology to." Alec aimed a thumb toward Nicole, then headed out the door with Erin. "We're heading back to Colorado tomorrow, but we'll stop in and say goodbye in the morning before we head out. Oh, yeah, Jake said to tell you he'd stop by later."

Daniel nodded an acknowledgment to Alec, then shifted a contrite glance to Nicole.

She grabbed the wheels of her chair and turned toward the door. "I should go, too. I didn't mean to be gone so long, and I don't want Tia to wake up alone."

Nicole rolled the wheelchair around the end of his bed, and Daniel saw his opportunity to set the record straight with her slipping away. "Nicole, wait."

She stopped but didn't look at him.

He clenched his teeth, mad at himself for taking out his frustrations on her and uncertain where to begin the conversation they needed to have. "I shouldn't have snapped at you. This—" he waved a hand at his knee "—isn't your fault."

When she raised her gaze, her eyes were bright with tears. The pain in her expression sucker punched his gut.

"I came down here," she started slowly, softly, "to thank you. For rescuing me. For bringing Tia with us." She shook her head and swiped moisture from her cheek. "I don't think I said it before, but I can never thank you enough for—"

"Forget it." He shrugged. "I just did my job."

"No. What you did went above and beyond—"

"Have you seen your father?" he interrupted, uncomfortable with her gratitude.

Her mouth tightened, and a chill filled her eyes. "Not yet. He was in Washington when I called him. He's on his way here now."

"What will you tell him?"

She drew her eyebrows together. "The truth. I have nothing to hide from him." She cocked her head, her expression steely. "Do you?"

He jerked another negligent shrug. "I'd be more worried about what he might hide from you. You deserve honesty."

"Oh? Have you been honest with me?"

"Always."

"Then answer this—why did you leave?"

He frowned and squeezed the sheets in his fist. "What?"

She rolled the wheelchair closer, her eyes shining with blue fire. "Don't pretend you don't know what I mean. On the helicopter, you were eager for me to remember that night. And, yes, I remember it. Vividly. And the morning after."

His gut pitched. What had he said while delirious with pain?

He clenched his teeth. "Then you shouldn't have to ask why I left."

Nicole's eyebrows lifted in surprise. "Excuse me? We barely said good morning. I went to take a shower, and by the time I got out of the bathroom, you'd run away like a roach when the lights turned on!"

Daniel scoffed. "A roach? Really?"

"Sure. It fits. I came out of the bathroom to find nothing but our condom wrappers scattered everywhere like trash after a Mardi Gras parade." She jabbed a finger toward him, and color rose in her cheeks. "You got your wham-bam and left without even a 'thank you, ma'am.' At least hookers get paid!"

Acid roiled in his gut. "Is that what you told your father? 'Cause that would explain a lot."

She blinked and sat back in the wheelchair, clearly startled. "My *father?* What does he have to do—?" She cut herself off abruptly and held up a hand. She inhaled a deep breath and shook her head. "Forget it. This is neither the time nor the place for this conversation."

Daniel shook his head. "Why rehash it at all? It's ancient history."

She shot him a skeptical frown. "You don't believe that, or you wouldn't have needed me to remember you."

Daniel scowled and shifted his gaze from her, hoping she couldn't tell how close to the truth she'd come.

"That's what you said, you know. 'I need to know you remember.' You were agonizing over it."

He shook his head, avoiding her eyes. "I had a shattered knee. It was the pain talking."

She sighed, a resigned, heartbreaking sound in the dim hospital room. "It might have been pain talking, but not pain from your knee."

He jerked his gaze to her, ready with denials, but she turned and wheeled her chair toward the door. "I have to go. Tia needs me."

The door swished closed behind her, leaving Daniel in the dark and silent room alone. He closed his eyes and let the raw ache of memories and regrets roll over him.

When she reached Tia's room on the pediatric floor, Nicole was still shaking all the way to her marrow. She paused outside Tia's door to gather her composure, not wanting any of her own upheaval to upset the girl. When she'd woken from her inadvertent nap in Daniel's room, she'd experienced a few terrifying moments of disorientation. Even now she felt as if a delicate thread wound through her, pulled so taut it cut into her soul. A thread that vibrated like a plucked wire, humming with images, sensations and sounds from her months in captivity. Even though she'd showered three times in the hospital, the rank smell of the prison camp lingered in her nose, and for an instant upon wakening, she'd thought she was back in Colombia.

Nicole drew a deep ragged breath and plowed shaky fingers through her hair, fighting for control, fighting to dampen the humming wire of tension that coiled inside her. It felt like that thread could snap at any moment, and everything she knew and relied on would unravel.

As if mentally breaking free of the Colombian prison weren't enough to contend with, the devastatingly handsome man in the hospital bed downstairs took her life in a freakishly surreal direction.

Daniel was back. She'd thought she'd moved past the hurt and longing associated with that torrid night years ago, moved beyond the handsome and heartbreaking enigma that was Daniel LeCroix. Yet here she was, trembling and fighting back tears, her emotions in turmoil again. Over Daniel.

Who'd braved the Colombian jungle and stormed the enemy camp to free her from her hellish captivity. Who'd accused her father of unspeakable crimes. Who, based on the ache sitting in her chest, still owned more of her heart than she'd realized.

A whimper in Tia's room yanked Nicole from her reflection, and she pushed through the door, quickly rolling her wheelchair to the side of the girl's bed. Nicole shoved all the tangled feelings for Daniel and lingering trauma over her imprisonment down, determined to hold herself together for Tia's sake. She couldn't afford to suffer a breakdown when this precious girl depended on her.

A nurse in pink scrubs was at Tia's side, cooing reassurances and trying to get a temperature reading with a thermometer that fit in the ear. But the frightened child would have none of it.

"Hi." The nurse smiled a greeting to Nicole. "I'm Sophie, and I'll be Tia's nurse tonight."

Nicole forced a friendly smile. "Hi, Sophie. I'm Nicole." She turned to Tia and leaned closed. "*Mija,* it's okay. She won't hurt you."

Tia's dark gaze latched onto Nicole's, and the girl lurched toward her, mewling in fright.

"I tried to explain that it wouldn't hurt," Sophie said.

Nicole nodded. "She doesn't speak any English. At least, not that I can tell. In fact, she hasn't spoken at all since—" Nicole hesitated. *Since she was dumped in a dog pen with me in a rebel army camp in Colombia.* Somehow she wasn't sure sharing the gritty reality of their situation was wise. She didn't need a media circus or the gossip mill interfering with her efforts to locate Tia's real parents through the proper channels. "Since she's been in my care."

"Has she been scheduled for a psych evaluation?" Sophie asked, finding Tia's chart at the foot of her bed and flipping it open to read.

Nicole nodded. "I was told they plan to have her meet with a trauma expert soon."

"What happened to her?" the nurse asked, giving Tia a sympathetic look.

Climbing out of the wheelchair to lie on the bed with Tia, Nicole sighed and smoothed the girl's hair. "I don't know. She was already in shock when I...took over her care."

Sophie glanced at Nicole's IV line and tipped her head to a curious angle. "I heard you all were camping somewhere and got stranded. The guys who brought you in said they found you two and the girl's father last night while they were hunting."

Nicole blinked, needing a moment to catch up, reconciling the cover story in her mind. When they arrived at the hospital, Alex and the pilot, Jake, had claimed Tia was Daniel's daughter. Now, she nodded, and tried to skirt around the lies intended to protect Tia and avoid trouble from outside influences. "I think she's calmer now, if you want to try again to get her temperature. Maybe you could show her how it works on me first?"

Sophie moved close again to take Nicole's temperature. "See? Doesn't hurt," she said and smiled at Tia.

Nicole hugged the little girl and rubbed her arm while the nurse checked Tia's temperature. "It's okay, *mija*. It's okay."

"Ninety-nine point two," Sophie read off the thermometer, then stashed it in her pocket. "Her fever's way down now thanks to the antibiotic and acetaminophen."

Nicole said a silent prayer of thanks that Tia's illness had apparently been nothing more than an ear infection. She'd feared something far worse, such as malaria or dengue fever from a mosquito bite.

Sophie headed for the door. "Well, I'll be on duty all night. Call if you need anything."

Nicole smiled her thanks, and as the door swung closed, she snuggled down on the bed with Tia curled against her in the night-darkened room. They'd spent innumerable hours in just such a position in the rebel camp. Nicole had done all she could to protect and shelter the traumatized child and had grown to love her as if she were her own daughter.

But she's not yours, her conscience prodded. Nicole closed her eyes, resigned to the task that lay ahead—locating Tia's real family and returning the girl to them.

The scuff of feet and crack of light from the hall woke Nicole about an hour later. She squinted groggily at the tall man silhouetted at the door.

"Nicole? Is that you?" The familiar voice broke with emotion.

"Daddy!" She untangled herself from Tia quickly and clambered from the bed.

Her father met her, pulling her into a tight embrace, before she'd made it more than a couple steps. "Nicole, darling... oh, thank God!"

They held each other and cried for several minutes, both too emotional to speak. Finally her father pulled a handkerchief from his pocket and wiped his face while Nicole swiped her cheeks with her fingers.

Her father cleared his throat. "I've been so worried about you, darling. Having you back is the answer to so many prayers." He tucked the handkerchief back in his pocket and cast a searching gaze over her. "You've lost weight, but otherwise you look healthy. Did they hurt you, darling? Are you really okay?"

An image of her captors flashed in her mind's eye, and the thread of panic inside her tugged tighter, a garrote threatening to choke her. Gritting her teeth, she swallowed the sour taste of bile, then inhaled deeply, slowly through her nose. *Hold it together. You can't fall apart.* "It was no picnic, but physically, I'm fine."

Her father narrowed a hard look on her that demanded her honesty. "And mentally?"

Her heartbeat stumbled. What could he see in her eyes? She shoved the tremor of doubt down deeper and refused to shy away from her father's scrutiny.

"Let's just say...some of my memories will take some time to get over. But I'm a White, and we're fighters. Right?" She forced a smile to reassure him.

His graying eyebrows knitted in a frown, and he drew her back into his arms. "Oh, Nicole, I tried everything I knew to get you released."

She squeezed her eyes shut, hearing Daniel's dark accusations in her head. *He betrayed two American operatives....*

"But even with all my connections, I couldn't—" He stiffened and levered back to meet her gaze again. "So what happened? How did you get away?"

Nicole's mouth dried. She'd only just gotten her father back. She wasn't ready to light the powder keg that topic would ignite. "I...was rescued." She turned and motioned to the bed where Tia slept. "*We* were rescued."

Her father leaned to peer around her at the bed, and a frown pocked his brow. "Who is that?"

"I don't know her real name. I call her Tia. She was kidnapped by the men who were holding me and put in my pen a few months ago."

His face darkened, and he stepped closer to the bed for a better look. "She's just a child!"

Her father's volume woke Tia, who sat up on the bed and whimpered in fear before she spotted Nicole and reached for her.

Nicole's heart twisted in pain for Tia's suffering, and she sat on the edge of the bed to stroke the girl's back. "I'm guessing she's about eight, but I haven't been able to get much information from her. She's been so traumatized that she hasn't spoken at all since her kidnapping."

"Not at all?"

Nicole shook her head.

Studying Tia with concern darkening his expression, her father dragged a hand along his jaw and sighed. "Am I right in assuming she's in this country without the proper paperwork?"

Nicole winced. "Well…yeah."

His shoulders slumped. "Nicole, I know you want to help her, but it's not as if she's one of the kittens you like to rescue. You can't bring her home with you like a pet and—"

"Shh!" She held up a hand to quiet him when he raised his voice and Tia cowered closer to her. "I know that."

"There are laws," her father argued in a quieter tone, "both American and international that supercede—"

"I *know!* But I couldn't leave her alone in the jungle with those thugs that kidnapped her!"

Her father scrubbed both hands over his face and jerked a nod of acquiescence. "Do you have any clue *whose* she is?"

Again Nicole frowned and shook her head. She met the

little girl's wide brown eyes and felt a tug at her heart. "My guess would be she's the daughter of someone important or powerful—a chief of police, a drug lord, a military leader or government official, maybe?" She paused and glanced to her father. "I was hoping you would use some of your connections to help me cut through red tape and find out where her family is."

He grunted and lowered himself in a chair at the side of the bed. "I don't know if my connections are worth much anymore. I, um…" He ducked his head and glared at the floor. "I resigned from office a couple months ago."

Nicole's chest tightened. Did she confront her father now or pretend not to have heard Daniel's side of recent events and wait for her father's explanation? Five years ago, she would have played along with whatever charade her father presented. But she'd grown up in Colombia. She'd endured too much and come too far to let herself fall back into her old role as the pliant and obedient daughter. She swallowed hard, forcing down the seesawing nausea that gripped her. "I heard you were forced out of office. That you were censured."

Her father's head snapped up, his expression startled. "Who told you that?"

For a moment, she clung to the belief that his surprise meant she had the story wrong, that he was poised to deny all of the horrid charges against him. She pulled in a cleansing breath and squared her shoulders. "The man who risked his life to save me—Daniel LeCroix."

But her father's face paled, and that hope drained from her, leaving her cold and shaking. Her father's bleak and stunned expression told her every ugly accusation Daniel had made in the jungle had been true.

Chapter 5

"What did LeCroix tell you?" her father asked darkly, his eyebrows dipping low over his eyes.

"Just the highlights. Running through a jungle while under fire was hardly the best time for an in-depth conversation."

Her father blanched even whiter. "Under fire?"

"I did say he risked his life to get me out. They all did—Daniel, Alec and Jake." She paused, her chest squeezing when she thought of the devastating injury to Daniel's knee. "Daniel was shot in the knee. His career is over."

Because he'd rescued her.

Her father stared at her, his shock still evident. "Why… wasn't I informed about this rescue mission before now?"

Nicole laughed without humor. "You're hardly on speaking terms with them. I don't think they rescued me as a favor to you as much as an in-your-face thing." She sobered. "Daniel said you betrayed him. You betrayed the United States by trading top secret national security intel for information about where I was being held."

Her father's back stiffened, and his face grew stony and defiant. "I did what I thought I had to in order to get you back."

"By giving up a team of undercover operatives to the enemy? They could have been killed! And what about the work they were doing? The breach to our operations down there to stop the flow of drugs and root out terrorist cells and—"

"You're my daughter!" her father shouted. "I couldn't leave you down there to die!"

His raised voice frightened Tia, who snuggled closer with a whimper and buried her face in Nicole's chest. Nicole stroked Tia's black hair and crooned soothing words, even though her father's admission churned inside her.

She hated to think she'd been the reason for her father's vile act, his fall from grace. More than that, she hated the idea that Daniel and Alec could have died because of what her father had done. For her.

And then Daniel had turned around and planned a high-risk mission to rescue her.

Nicole sighed and rubbed her temple. Daniel's actions were illogical, confusing…and humbling. She could *almost* believe he'd saved her life because he still cared about her. Except his snarling, icy attitude toward her would indicate otherwise.

So what about his kiss at the prison camp? He'd been tender and sweet. Like the lover he'd been five years ago….

Nicole shook her head to clear it. Deciphering Daniel's confounding behavior was not her priority at the moment.

"So what have your lawyers said? What have you been charged with?"

"Nothing related to…my deal with Ramirez. At this point, I don't think either LeCroix or Kincaid has reported what I did."

Nicole gaped. "Excuse me?"

"Don't ask me why." He sighed heavily. "There was a nasty mess one night this past January that I was involved in. And while General Ramirez, a known rebel leader and drug smuggler, was apprehended, my lawyers are working on a defense as to why I was there. I don't know what LeCroix and Kincaid told the authorities about that night but—"

"Daniel and Alec were there?"

Her father frowned. "He didn't tell you?"

Nicole rolled her gaze to the ceiling. "Apparently there's a *lot* I haven't been told."

She heard her father shift in the chair and exhale heavily. "I'll make a few calls and see what I can find out about the little girl. Are you sure she's Colombian? Not from Ecuador or Peru—"

Nicole lowered her gaze to meet her father's and shook her head. "Daddy, I'm not sure of anything anymore."

His expression softened, and he leaned toward the bed. "I love you, Nicole. You can be sure of that."

Tears prickled in her eyes, and she blinked them away. "I would appreciate any help you can offer. I know the authorities will try to take custody of Tia from me, and I can't let that happen. She's alone and scared, and she needs me. Until we find her family, I have to protect her."

The next morning, Daniel sat on the side of his hospital bed and rubbed his injured leg. Even with major painkillers in his system, he hurt like hell. He'd snatched only erratic moments of sleep last night while his conversation with Nicole replayed in his head.

It might have been pain talking, but not pain from your knee.

Maybe so, but the physical pain had lowered his guard, allowed emotions he'd kept securely locked away for years to resurface. In light of the current throbbing in his knee and the promise of continued pain for several weeks as he healed, he'd better find a way to jam all those dangerous feelings for Nicole somewhere safe and out of reach. Better yet, he should avoid any further contact with Nicole. His mission was complete. He'd saved her from the Colombian prison camp. The end.

"Whenever you're ready," said the nurse who stood beside his bed, waiting. She handed him a pair of crutches, then reached for his arm to help him to his feet.

His doctor had left orders that Daniel put some weight on the bad knee and practice walking on the injured leg so that the joint didn't get stiff and inflexible. Daniel clenched his back teeth and hoisted himself from the bed onto his good leg. The nurse moved in close to steady him, and he waved her away. "I can do it."

"Now put some weight on the other leg, and use the crutches to take a step."

Daniel did as directed and bit back a scorching curse word when a nearly blinding pain shot from his knee up his leg. His bad leg buckled, and he wobbled on the crutches. *Fils de putain!* His leg hadn't hurt this much when he'd been dragging it behind him in the jungle. Of course, he'd had an ample supply of adrenaline coursing through him, blocking his pain at the time.

He squeezed the hand grips on the crutches harder and sent his nurse a warning scowl when she tried again to steady him. A cold sweat popped out on his brow and upper lip, but he took a cleansing breath and planted the crutches another foot in front of him. Braced. Shifted his weight.

He let another string of Cajun French curses fly, but he didn't sway this time. While his nurse gave him trite words of encouragement, he took a couple more steps. A bead of moisture rolled down his temple despite the chill air-conditioning, and he clenched his teeth until his jaw ached. But he was walking.

Big ef-ing deal. He used to run a five-minute mile with a forty-pound pack on his back. Now he had a nurse praising him for each step as if he were a baby learning to walk. He glared his discontent and frustration at the woman. "Look, when I run a marathon again, compliment me all you want. For now, I could do without the false cheer."

The woman's face reflected a moment of hurt and surprise, and regret for his curtness kicked him in the gut. Before he could apologize, a voice from the door stopped him.

"Still in a grumpy mood, I see."

Daniel mustered all his strength not to falter as he jerked his gaze toward Nicole. Thirstily, he drank in the sight of her, taking note of her street clothes and the return of color to her cheeks. She looked damn good, in fact, if still a bit thin. "Been discharged, I take it?"

"Yeah. Something like that."

He pivoted on his good leg and hobbled back to his bed.

Nicole hesitated a few seconds, as if uncertain she should enter the lion's den, then she moved closer. The nurse propped his crutches near the head of his bed and stepped out of the room, giving them privacy to talk.

He scrubbed a hand over his face, hoping she didn't see him surreptitiously wipe the sweat from his brow. "And the girl?"

Her cheek twitched in a grin as if his simple inquiry about the child was gratifying to her. "Tia is supposed to be released later this afternoon, so I have to work fast to get approved as her guardian while the embassies search for her family." She fidgeted with her purse strap and took another step toward his bed. "My father is pulling some strings with a judge or two he knows to make the arrangements."

Daniel grunted and swallowed the snide retort that would

only alienate himself further from her. If this was goodbye, he didn't want her last memory to be him acting like a surly ass. He inhaled deeply, rubbed his aching knee and blew out a cleansing breath. "Well, good luck. I hope things work out for you."

Another awkward smile twitched at the corner of her mouth. "Thanks. When you see Alec and Jake again—"

"Alec and Erin went back to Colorado." As happy as he was for Alec, starting a new life with the woman of his dreams, Daniel couldn't help the kick of envy in his gut. "Her doctor didn't want her so far from home this close to her due date."

"Oh." She shifted her weight, clearly disappointed. "I'm sorry I missed them. I wanted to tell Alec thank you again." Nicole locked an earnest gaze on his. "When you talk to him—and Jake—please tell them how grateful I am for their part in our rescue."

Daniel jerked a nod. "Sure."

She tore her gaze away from his and stared at the floor while she chewed her lip, toyed with her earring. Even without his body language training, he'd have known she wanted to raise a difficult topic, probably delve into their history again. The last place he wanted to go.

She lifted troubled eyes to his and opened her mouth.

"Do you have a cell phone?" he asked before she could speak.

"Uh, yeah." She blinked, clearly caught off guard by his question. "My dad got a new one for me this morning."

Daniel held out his hand. "Let me see it."

Furrowing her brow, Nicole eyed him suspiciously before she dug in her purse and gave him the phone.

He tapped the on-screen menu to open her address book, entered his cell phone number and passed the device back to her. "Your father's not the only one with valuable contacts. If you have trouble with ICE or Homeland Security because of Tia, I'll do my best to help cut through red tape." He nodded to the phone, which she studied with a spark of intrigue lighting her eyes. "That number is the best way to reach me."

She tapped her screen a couple times, and on the tray table beside his bed, Daniel's cell phone buzzed. He arched one eyebrow, and she flashed a nervous grin. "Just checking."

"Thought I'd given you a fake number?"

She straightened. "No, I—" A blush rose in her cheeks as she fumbled. "I was making sure *my* phone worked." She ducked her head and made a production of stashing her phone.

A chuckle rumbled from his chest. "Right. And now I have your number, too."

Her chin shot up, and wide blue eyes latched onto his. "Oh. Yeah." She wet her lips. "Will you use it?"

He tensed, but his gaze never wavered. "I'm not sure that'd be a good idea. Things didn't work out so well for us last time."

She folded her arms over her chest and frowned at him. "And whose fault is that?"

"There's plenty of blame to go around."

Her shoulders slumped. "You're probably right." Heaving a sigh, she slid her purse strap in place on her shoulder. "Pity, too. Before that morning, I thought we had something pretty good between us."

So did I. Daniel bit back the reply. No point dwelling on could-have-beens. "Takes more than hot sex to make a relationship work."

Nicole scowled. "I know that."

She continued to glare at him, but he saw the heat that flared in her eyes. Heat that said she was remembering the sultry tangling of limbs and slap of flesh as their bodies writhed together. Daniel's body hummed as his brain easily conjured an erotic image from that night.

She cocked her head at a haughty angle. "Relationships take time…to learn each other's interests and tastes—"

"They take trust. Respect. Honesty," he snarled. He growled his frustration and waved her off. "Forget it. Like I said, it's history. Leave it alone."

"What makes you think we didn't have trust or…respect or…?"

"Leave. It. Alone," he repeated, his gaze drilling into her.

She threw up her hands and shook her head. "Whatever." Spinning on her heel, she stalked to the door and yanked it open.

Daniel's pulse stumbled, and acid gnawed his stomach. He was about to blow it again. He'd spent his final minutes with Nicole fighting about the past rather than repairing the tensions between them. But if he saw no future between them, why did he care so much where their relationship stood?

He squeezed the bedsheet in his fist. "Damn it, Nicole. Stop."

She waited for him to speak but didn't turn.

His heart thundered as he searched for something to tell her. *You complete me. You make me want to be a better man. We'll always have Paris.* He pinched the bridge of his nose as a parade of clichéd movie lines filled his head. Finally, he sighed and muttered, "It was a good night. But…we were too different to make it work."

She sent him a sad look over her shoulder. "It was a *great* night. But you didn't give us a chance to work."

Nicole disappeared into the hall, her hurt and disappointment still hovering in the air, reverberating around him. Daniel sank back in his pillows as a shard of hope lodged inside him like a splinter. Was it possible he'd read the situation wrong that morning years ago? Had he missed the most important opportunity of his life—the chance to be with Nicole?

He closed his eyes and swore under his breath. Hope was

a painful, double-edged sword. Just when he thought he'd finally cut Nicole out of his life, she cast a new light on his dark memories from their past.

Despite assurances that Tia could be released from the hospital that afternoon, legal red tape and delays kept Tia in the hospital another 24 hours. But Nicole made the most of the extra time, pushing the Department of Children and Family Services to complete an emergency home inspection and interview that allowed her to be appointed Tia's temporary legal guardian. Nicole took Tia to her father's New Orleans garden home, making a mental note to add apartment hunting to her to-do list once matters with Tia were settled.

"Hello?" she called as she and Tia entered the kitchen through the back door. "Anyone home?"

"Miss Nicole!" A thin, prematurely gray-haired woman bustled in from the laundry room and rushed to hug Nicole. "You're home! And safe, praise the Lord!"

Nicole beamed and embraced the woman who'd been her father's housekeeper for as long as she could remember. "Sarah Beth, how good to see you!"

Nicole introduced Tia to Sarah Beth Salyer, who traveled with her father to his many homes depending on where he was in residence at the moment—Washington, D.C., New Orleans, Baton Rouge or his ski cabin in Breckenridge. The two women caught each other up briefly on their respective status quos, then shared another tearful hug.

"I've taken good care of your Boudreaux and Oreo. They're around here somewhere." Sarah Beth searched the floor for Nicole's cats. "Probably on the sun porch."

Nicole's heart swelled. "Then the sun porch is my next stop. I've missed my babies. Want to meet my kitties?" Nicole asked Tia in Spanish.

The girl's face brightened, and Nicole had her answer.

Sarah Beth led them through the house to the sun porch, and Nicole spied Boudreaux on a chaise longue chair, basking in the sun.

"Hey, old man," she cooed, crouching next to the chair and waving Tia over.

"I'll start lunch for you, all right?" Sarah Beth headed back toward the kitchen.

"Thanks, Sarah Beth," Nicole called and scratched Boudreaux behind the ear. The kitten Daniel had rescued for her ten years earlier stretched and purred when she ruffled his fur. He was thinner than she remembered, but his yellow coat still looked glossy and sleek. Tears pricked her eyes when she thought of that prom night years ago when she'd first met Daniel. She'd lost a piece of her heart to him that night, and Boudreaux had been an ever-present reminder of Daniel's kindness and gallantry.

Leave. It. Alone. Why was Daniel so reluctant to discuss their past? Unless she meant less to him than she'd believed. He'd never professed any undying affection or loyalty, so maybe the tender emotions had all been one-sided. But if that was true, why had he risked his life to get her out of Colombia?

Tia's giggle pulled her out of her reverie. Oreo, the black-and-white tomcat she'd found as a kitten, had strolled over to greet them. She'd rescued Oreo at a work site while on a church mission trip to rebuild storm-damaged houses. The tomcat rubbed against Tia and butted her hand with his head. In return, Tia patted Oreo and laughed each time he bumped her hand asking for more attention. Nicole silently blessed Oreo for helping bring Tia out of her shell.

When her cell rang, Nicole dug her phone out of her pocket and checked the caller ID, foolishly wishing the caller was Daniel saying he'd changed his mind about having that long overdue talk about why he'd abandoned her. Instead, the call was from Washington, D.C., and she answered with her heart in her throat, praying for good news about Tia.

Leaving Tia to play with the cats, Nicole stepped into the next room to take the call.

"Miss White, this is Ramon Diaz. I am an attaché with the Colombian embassy. I believe we have a lead on the identity of the girl in your custody."

Relief washed through Nicole so hard and fast, her knees buckled, and she dropped onto the nearest chair. "That's wonderful! What did you find out?"

"She fits the description of Pilar Castillo, the daughter of Mario Castillo, a prominent judge in Bogotá whose family was attacked on the way to mass several months ago. Castillo's wife and other daughter were murdered, and Pilar was taken hostage. The BACRIM— that is, the *bandas criminales* or band of criminals—" Nicole kept silent, not bothering to tell him she was well familiar with the term for the many criminal gangs and rebel groups terrorizing Colombia "—claiming responsibility has used Pilar as leverage in blackmailing Judge Castillo regarding several critical cases he has presided over this year."

Nicole's stomach roiled, imagining the terror Tia—or Pilar—had witnessed, seeing her mother and sibling slaughtered. No wonder the poor child was traumatized. "Are you sure Tia is Pilar? Do you have a picture you can fax to me?"

"I do, and I have a picture of the judge you can show the girl. I'd ask that you send me a picture of the girl for cross confirmation from the father."

A picture of Tia? Nicole thought a moment. "I can take her picture with my phone and text it to you. Will that work?"

"*Sí,* that works," Diaz replied.

Nicole jotted down the cell phone number to text to and headed out to the sunroom again. Nicole had her own test in mind. Tia was still playing with Oreo, dangling a string for the cat to bap and giggling at the cat's antics, and Nicole watched for a moment, savoring the sweet sound of her laughter. Finally, she said calmly, "Pilar?"

The child froze, then jerked a wide-eyed glance up to her.

Nicole's pulse drummed as she stepped closer and squatted next to the girl. "Is that your name? *Es ese tu nombre?*" she asked. "Are you Pilar Castillo?"

Fat tears puddled in the girl's eyes, and she nodded.

Nicole pulled her into an embrace and rubbed the girl's back. "Oh, *mija.* We found your father. You'll be going home soon."

Nicole pulled the page from the fax machine in her father's home office as it fed from the printer. The image of a swarthy middle-aged man in a black robe stared back at her. Pilar's father, Mario Castillo.

"Chicken salad?" Sarah Beth asked from the office door, a plate in hand.

"Sounds heavenly. I'm starved." Nicole's stomach rumbled, and she thought of the many days in the prison camp when she'd eaten foul canned meats and stale crackers, dreaming of Sarah Beth's cooking. "Is Tia still on the sun porch?"

No, not Tia. Pilar. That would take a little getting used to.

"I think so. I set a place for her in the kitchen. Should I get her?" Sarah Beth asked.

"No, I'll get her. Thanks." Nicole folded the picture of Judge Castillo, jammed it in her pocket and headed toward the sun porch. Not wanting to upset the little girl and spoil her appetite, she decided to show Pilar the picture after lunch.

She'd just reached the French doors leading to the sunroom when she saw a hulking shadow cross the far wall.

Pulse jumping, Nicole swung through the door and took in the scene in a glance. Intruders had broken in.

She watched in horror as a dark-skinned stranger descended on Pilar.

Chapter 6

Pilar saw the man and screamed.

Boudreaux and Oreo spooked and scampered away. The man tripped over the bolting cats, landing on one knee. Pilar stumbled out of the man's reach, only to back into the grasp of a second man who appeared from the shadows.

"Pilar!" Acting purely on instinct, Nicole burst through the door, grabbing a decorative statuette from an end table. As she darted toward the first man, she hefted the figurine and smashed it on his head as he fumbled back to his feet. He toppled with a groan, clutching his head.

The second man had reeled Pilar in and held her against his chest, her legs dangling, as he fought to subdue her flailing arms.

"No! Let her go!" Nicole rushed forward with no thought for her own safety. Everything inside her had focused on freeing Pilar from the man's grip. She reached for the little girl, battling the man's arm when he tried to push Nicole away.

An all-out fight for Pilar ensued. He pulled Nicole's hair. Wrenched her wrists. Bit her arm.

In return, Nicole gouged at the man's eyes. Clawed his face. Scratched his arm. She realized they were in a tug of war with Pilar as the rope. The poor girl was being pulled like a Thanksgiving wishbone. To spare hurting Pilar, she needed to let go, but—

"Augh!" the man cried out and crumpled, grabbing his crotch.

Nicole hauled Pilar into her arms and spun away. On some level, she knew Pilar's flailing feet must have kicked the man in his family jewels, but she funneled her energy on one thing. Running. As she dodged a chaise chair, heading inside with Pilar clinging to her, the first man rolled on his back, snarling. He raised something small and black. A flash. A loud crack. *Gunfire!*

Nicole kept moving. Adrenaline fueled her legs. Panic buzzed in her ears.

"Nicole!" Sarah Beth stood by the door of her father's office, waving her in. "Hurry!"

Behind her, Nicole heard a shout. Another crack of gunfire. A crash and pounding footsteps.

A third gun-wielding man materialized from the kitchen. Aimed. Something hot stung her neck, but she ignored it as she charged across the living room and into her father's office. Nicole headed to the protection of her father's oversize desk and set Pilar on the carpet beneath it. Sarah Beth slammed the massive mahogany door closed and threw a bolt lock.

Loud thumps reverberated through the room as bullets pocked the office door.

"Get away from the door!" Nicole shouted to Sarah Beth.

"The second door—" the housekeeper said, pulling a thick metal door from a side pocket in the wall.

And Nicole remembered the construction project her father

had ordered in the months after Katrina. The central room of the house, his office, had been reinforced for hurricanes with iron beams, metal sheeting and a heavy secondary steel door. A safe room.

She ran to help Sarah Beth roll the heavy door over and lock it in place.

"We need to c-call 911," the housekeeper said, her voice shaking.

Nicole nodded and, with trembling hands, she reached in her pocket for her phone. The first tears of fear prickled her eyes, blurring her vision as she tried to steady her hands enough to hit the right spots on her touch screen. Meanwhile, Sarah Beth snatched up the desk phone and dialed.

Nicole stumbled behind the desk and slumped on the floor. Pilar huddled close, hands over her ears as she whimpered.

Her own panic, vivid with images from her imprisonment, crowded her brain, drawing the thread of tension inside her tighter. It would be so easy to give in to that pull toward chaos, but Nicole battled it away, one breath at a time. *Keep it together. For Pilar.*

Struggling to clear her mind, she thought of the Kevlar vest her mother had bought her father years ago after he'd sponsored his first controversial bill and received a series of death threats. The bulletproof vest was upstairs in her father's closet. No help.

Blinking away the moisture in her eyes, Nicole stared at her cell phone screen. Right now, she only wanted one man.

Daniel. Who'd saved her in Colombia. Who'd taken out her captors. Who'd made her feel safe.

The shouts and deafening thumps on the office door told her their assailants hadn't given up. And they were chipping slowly through the first barrier.

Nicole swallowed the bitter taste of fear that rose in her throat and struggled to steady her hands. Her thumb skipped to the button to bring up her contacts. With a stroke of the screen, she scrolled to the number Daniel had programmed in her phone just yesterday. And hit *Call*.

"Going home soon?" Jake asked as he strolled into Daniel's hospital room, wearing his trademark cowboy hat, and took stock of Daniel's latest attempt to put weight on his injured leg.

"Not soon enough. I feel useless sitting around here all day." His leg hurt less today and could bear more of his weight, but Daniel didn't harbor any illusions of a miraculous healing. His immediate future included walking with a cane at best and knee-replacement surgery as soon as it could be scheduled, followed by weeks of physical therapy.

His black op teammate—correction, *former* teammate, since Daniel had been canned—helped himself to the only chair in the room and stacked his hands behind his head. Jake narrowed his navy blue eyes on Daniel. "Looks like you're making progress. Your doctor give you an idea when you might bust this joint?"

Daniel shrugged off the question. He had nothing waiting for him when he left the hospital, so he hadn't given his release much thought.

Setting his well-worn cowboy hat on the table beside him, Jake rubbed a hand over his short-cropped sandy-brown hair and hedged. "Have you…talked to the chief about a job at headquarters?"

Daniel's cell phone chirped, and he hobbled toward the tray table where he'd left it. "I don't want any damn, soul-sucking desk job."

Jake turned up a hand. "You have one of the best minds in the business. You could coordinate missions, develop strategies—"

"Screw that." Holding Jake's gaze, he snatched up the

phone and dropped heavily on the side of the bed. "I'd rather leave the agency than push paper the rest of my life." He jabbed the answer button and barked, "What?"

"Daniel!" He knew the voice instantly, recognized the tremble of fear, heard the steady crashing in the background.

He jerked to attention, stiffening his back and squeezing the phone tighter. "Nicole, what's wrong?"

Jake sat forward, meeting Daniel's gaze.

"Men broke in…at my father's. They…tried to grab Pilar." Her voice was breathless and full of tears.

Daniel signaled Jake with his free hand. *Shoes. Pants. We're moving.*

"Are you hurt?" His own fear for Nicole sharpened his tone.

"We're in the safe room, b-but…they're shooting at the door, at the locks."

Jake whipped out a large pocketknife and sliced off the left leg of Daniel's jeans above the knee. With one hand, Daniel worked the jeans over the brace around his injured knee, while Jake shoved Daniel's shoes in front of him, ready to step into.

"Daniel, I…I need you," Nicole said, her voice breaking.

A fist closed around his heart, and a shudder rolled through him. *I'm coming, cher.*

Jamming the foot of his good leg in a shoe, Daniel lifted his arm for Jake to pull out his IV line. "Call 911," he grated, his own voice made rough with emotion. He thumbed disconnect and slid the phone in his jeans pocket.

Jake tossed him a shirt, and Daniel jerked it over his head and grabbed his crutches. "Let's roll."

"Daniel?" Nicole shouted, numb with disbelief. "Daniel!"

No answer. *Call 911,* he'd growled. And hung up on her. *Hung. Freaking. Up.*

Fury, hurt and disappointment coalesced inside her, a bitter brew. Her life was in peril, and he'd fobbed her off to 911. Never mind that the cops were in a better position than a hospitalized and injured Daniel to come to her rescue. Common sense did little to dull the sting of his rejection. His curt refusal to get involved.

She swiped at a tickle on her neck, and her fingers came away bloody. The sting she'd felt on her neck. Had a bullet grazed her? The bright red on her hand made the vibrating tension wire inside her tug tighter. She swallowed hard and sucked in a calming breath.

Don't lose it. Keep it together.

Sarah Beth was still on the line with the emergency operator, giving them the address, detailing their unfolding horror. From the sound of it, the men at the office door were making progress getting through the first door and could blast the lock on the inner steel door any time.

Nicole crawled under the desk with Pilar and wrapped her arms around the whimpering child. The men would have to come through Nicole to get to Pilar, and with her own fear jammed deep down inside her, Nicole was ready to put up a fight.

"I have a 9 mm in the glove box," Jake said as they roared down the highway in his pickup truck toward the address displayed on his GPS. "Take it."

Daniel opened the compartment in front of him and took out the weapon. After checking the chamber to make sure it was loaded, he shoved the gun in the waistband of his jeans. The GPS showed them nearing the address a Google search listed for Alan White's residence. Daniel checked his watch. Nicole had called eight minutes ago.

From under the brim of his cowboy hat, Jake shot him a dark glance, but Daniel saw the keen look of preparation in his eyes. "All right, man, this is your show. What's the plan?"

"Park one street over. We'll approach from behind. Obviously, you're more mobile than I am, so you take lead. I'll cover you. Nicole said they were in a safe room, which means center of the house, no windows. If our targets are still there, they'll be working on getting inside that room." Daniel didn't bother elaborating on what it meant if the gunmen weren't still at the senator's house. He shoved down the frisson of panic that swirled in his gut at the notion of anything happening to Nicole. He had to stay in battle mode. Had to focus.

Tossing his cowboy hat on the back seat, Jake pulled to a fast stop on a residential street lined with multilevel garden homes. Shouldering open the truck door, Daniel grabbed his crutches, cursing his limited mobility when he needed speed and agility more than ever.

"Go." He waved Jake away, and they started across the neighbor's lawn. By keeping his weight off his bad leg, Daniel could plant the crutches and swing his good leg forward in a large hop that moved him at a decent clip. As he approached the senator's house, he scanned the scene, picking out spots he could dive for cover if a gun battle erupted, choosing the best point of entry, searching for the best vantage point to survey the scene. As they neared the back garden gate, a steady thumping reached his ears. He hobbled up beside Jake, who'd pressed himself against the back garden wall to peer through a crack in the gate.

"What d'ya got, cowboy?" Daniel asked, finding the padlock that secured the gate had already been cut off.

"Garden's clear. Back door's ajar." Jake moved to get a different angle view. "Brick grill pit twenty paces to the left. No window to the right of the open door."

Daniel jerked a nod confirming their destinations. A sheen of sweat beaded on his brow as he pushed open the gate. Senses alert to his surroundings, heart pumping, Daniel hurried to the protection of the grill pit. Then while he covered

Jake, his teammate skulked to his position by the door. Flattened to the wall of the house, Jake reconnoitered the situation inside. Using hand signals, Jake waved Daniel closer. In four silent hops, Daniel took his position next to Jake. Propping his crutches beside him, he pulled out his gun. Balancing on his good leg, he leaned against the house for support.

More hand signals.... *Three tangos. All armed. Two by safe room door, third watching front yard by window.*

Daniel nodded and craned his neck for a look. The men at the door of the safe room were chopping their way through the wood frame around a steel barricade with an ax.

The goal of any operation was minimal casualties. Dead men couldn't give up valuable intel, lead them to those higher up the food chain.

The contingency plan, if they met resistance, was simple. Lethal force.

I'll go high. You take a knee, Daniel signaled. *Take the lookout. Head shot.* Which left the men by the safe room for Daniel.

Jake jerked a nod, sank to his knee and raised his sniper rifle.

In the distance, Daniel heard the wail of approaching sirens. Inside he heard a woman's scream as the men with the ax broke through the door frame. No time to wait.

Adrenaline charged through Daniel's blood. He funneled the surge of energy into focus, concentration, training.

"Freeze!" he shouted. "Drop your weapons and lie on the floor! Now!"

The three men turned. Both the lookout and Daniel's target raised their guns.

In a heartbeat, Daniel and Jake reacted.

The concussion of twin gun blasts pounded his chest. The man by the front window dropped. One down. Jake shifted his rifle and re-aimed.

Daniel's target staggered back a step, then clutched his neck. The third man dropped the ax and scrambled for his weapon.

Daniel re-sighted and squeezed the trigger again. Plaster splintered from the wall behind the ax man. A miss. *"Merde!"*

The man Daniel had shot in the throat slid down the wall but raised a handgun. Daniel finished the wounded man with a second shot that hit its mark.

Ax Man jumped behind a massive entertainment center and returned fire. As Ax Man shot at Daniel, Jake darted inside, running in a crouch until he reached the sofa.

"Drop your gun and get on the floor!" Daniel repeated.

Axe Man fired again, keeping Jake pinned behind the couch. Daniel needed a better position, preferably inside the house if he was going to help Jake. Gritting his teeth, he did a quick mental inventory of his surroundings, strategizing. Keeping his injured leg straight in front of him, Daniel slid to the ground, then crawled on his belly and elbows into the house. When Axe Man spotted him and opened fire, Daniel log-rolled until he was behind the couch with Jake.

Staying on his stomach, Daniel peered around the couch and zinged a few bullets near Ax Man's head. While Daniel distracted the gunman, Jake snuck from the other end of the couch to the opposite end of the entertainment center. He gave Daniel a hand signal, and Daniel took his cue, firing at a vase near the front window. The gunman jerked his attention across the room where the vase shattered. And Jake pounced. Before Ax Man could react, Jake took him down and held him pinned to the floor with a knee between the gunman's shoulders.

With adrenaline numbing his pain and his crutches still outside, Daniel hobbled over on his injured leg and disarmed Ax Man. He gave Jake a nod of thanks. "Get whatever information you can from him before the cops arrive."

"Roger that."

A whimper filtered out from the safe room, and Daniel's chest constricted. "Nicole!" He pounded a fist on the steel door. "Are you all right? Open the door. It's Daniel." He paused, listening, but blood whooshed in his ears, drowning out all but his own thundering pulse. "Nicole!"

Chapter 7

Nicole snapped her head up. In the silence following the barrage of gunfire, a familiar voice called to her from outside her father's office. "Daniel?"

Heart in her throat, Nicole eased Pilar into Sarah Beth's lap, then scurried to the battered reinforcement door. She threw the massive bolt that locked the steel door in place and struggled to push the door back in the wall pocket. Once the barricade had slid a couple inches, a large male hand grabbed the edge and shoved it aside in one powerful thrust.

Nicole's breath caught seeing Daniel's brawn filling the portal, a gun in his hand and a concerned scowl furrowing his chiseled face. *Daniel.* Fierce, handsome and...*here.* A familiar thrill tripped down her back and settled low in her belly.

"You came," she rasped in disbelief and joy.

His frown deepened. "Of course I did. You were under assault. You said you needed me."

"I know, but...you were in the hospital."

He lifted one eyebrow. "I checked myself out."

Nicole blinked, her ears still ringing from the gunfire and her post-adrenaline crash muddying her brain. "But you... hung up on me."

Daniel jerked a shrug. "I mobilize faster if I'm not on the phone."

"Your knee—"

"I'm getting the impression you're not glad to see me." He narrowed a dark penetrating stare on her and stepped closer. "Did you really think I'd ignore your call for help?" The intimate whisper and deep pitch of his voice sent a ripple of pleasure to her marrow.

"No." Maybe that's why her first instinct had been to call Daniel instead of the police.

He reached for her chin and swiped his thumb across her damp cheek. "Who are they? What did they want?"

Nicole took a few seconds to answer, needing time, unlike Daniel, to mentally shift from the deeply personal moment they'd been sharing back to the frightening business at hand. "I don't know who they are. I've never seen them before in my life. They were trying to take Pilar."

His eyebrows drew together. "Pilar?"

She nodded. "That's Tia's real name—Pilar Castillo. Her father is a prominent judge in Bogotá. I was in the process of confirming her identity through the Colombian embassy when the men attacked us."

A muscle in his jaw twitched, the only outward sign of what was going on behind those dark eyes. "You're bleeding." He touched the stinging spot on her neck.

"It's just a nick. Slap a Band-Aid on it, and I'm fine." She forced a smile, hoping he couldn't tell how shaken she was knowing that a bullet had only missed her carotid artery by a few inches. *Keep it together.*

He scowled his discontent. "You can't stay here," he said

at last. "You're not safe until we figure out how Pilar's location got leaked."

A chill shimmied through Nicole. Not safe in her own home? Two days ago, when she'd walked on U.S. soil again for the first time in months, she'd believed the nightmare was behind her. She'd been wrong.

Nicole glanced at the dead man lying in the hall behind Daniel, and her stomach roiled. "So what do I do? Go to a hotel?"

The front doorbell rang, interrupting any reply from Daniel. "This is the police. Open the door. We have reports of shots fired."

"I need to deal with the cops now." He gave her shoulder a squeeze. "But I'll be moving you and the girl to a safe house as soon as possible. Be ready."

A safe house? She opened her mouth to ask for elaboration, but Daniel spun away and limped on his bad leg toward the front door where the police knocked loudly. Nicole turned and staggered back into her father's office where Sarah Beth and Pilar still huddled together behind the large desk.

"Is it over? Is it safe to come out?" Sarah Beth asked, her face still pale with fright.

Nicole held her arms out to Pilar, who tumbled into her embrace, and nodded stiffly to Sarah Beth. "The police are here, and Daniel…"

She shuddered and tried to erase the image of the blank stare of the dead man in the hall. Daniel and his teammate had arrived just in time. She didn't want to think about the lethal means they'd employed to save her, Pilar and Sarah Beth.

Over the next couple hours, the police interviewed everyone at the scene, including the surviving man from the trio that had attacked the women. Nicole's father arrived minutes after the police and surveyed the ransacked house in horror. Nicole rushed to her father and hugged him tightly, reassuring him over and over that she was unharmed, only shaken by the attack.

Jake and Daniel showed the police their military credentials, and the preliminary ballistics assessment supported their claims of self-defense in the deaths of the two intruders. Pending an investigation, no charges were filed against them, but everyone, including Pilar, was required to accompany the cops to the police station so their hands and clothes could be tested for gunshot residue, along with other evidence collection.

The first long shadows of evening stretched across the parking lot of the New Orleans P.D. by the time Nicole and Pilar were released to go home. Jake and Daniel, leaning on his crutches, met them on the sidewalk as they exited the police headquarters. Nicole assessed Daniel's clenched teeth, the lines of pain and fatigue around his mouth and eyes, and concern burrowed past her own weariness. "You should go back to the hospital. You need rest and painkillers, and—"

"No." He shook his head, his eyes grim, uncompromising.

"Daniel…"

"No. We're going back to your father's place, but only long enough for you to pack a few necessities. Jake's agreed to drive us to the safe house I mentioned." He hitched his head toward the street. "His truck's down here. Let's go."

"Daniel, wait. Don't I get a say in this?" Nicole squeezed Pilar's hand and squared her shoulders.

Daniel's stern expression hardened further. "There's nothing to discuss. These men— whoever they are, whoever sent them—aren't going to give up just because this attempt to take Pilar failed. This is bigger than just an attempted kidnapping, and you're in their way. They won't hesitate to kill you to get the girl."

Nicole released a shaky breath, nodding. "I get that. But my father can hire men to—"

Daniel's chin jerked up when she mentioned her father, and Nicole hesitated. "Hold on. You can't think my father had anything to do with this!"

Pilar inched closer, casting Nicole a wary look when she raised her voice.

Daniel arched one eyebrow. "I can't?"

"Damn it, Daniel! Do *not* try to pin this on my father!"

Raising a hand to quell her argument, he leaned toward her, pitching his voice lower. "He may not be behind the attack, but we can't rule him out as the source of the leak. You told him about Pilar, didn't you?"

"I—" Nicole snapped her mouth shut. She had. Her father had promised to make phone calls to locate Pilar's parents and smooth over any red tape regarding her presence in the U.S.

Daniel clearly took her lack of response as capitulation. "Until we know where this threat against you and the girl is coming from, I'm not going to trust your safety to anyone else." Pivoting with his crutches, Daniel moved aside to let her precede him to Jake's truck. Sighing her resignation, Nicole led Pilar to the street and climbed inside Jake's dual-cab Ford F-150.

When they reached her father's house, Jake ran interference with the senator while Nicole packed. Pilar clung to her as she gathered what few belongings she'd amassed since getting back to the States, including some clothes and toys for Pilar. Oreo, clearly recovered from the ruckus earlier in the day, hopped up on the bed and tried to curl up in the suitcase. Pilar's face brightened when she saw Oreo, and she left Nicole's side in order to pat the cat.

Daniel, who'd accompanied Nicole to her bedroom, sat on the opposite side of the bed with his bad knee stretched in front of him. He knitted his brow as he watched Pilar with the feline. "That's not the cat I rescued for you, is it? The one I got from the storm drain was orange."

Nicole paused in folding a nightshirt and shook her head. "No, that's Oreo. He's a more recent addition to the family. Boudreaux is around here somewhere. Boo is an old man now." She cast a glance to Pilar and Oreo, remembering the events of that afternoon. "You know, Oreo and Boudreaux may have saved us today. They ran when the trouble started, but managed to trip up one of the gunmen, buying me a few seconds to grab Pilar and get to the safe room." She grinned at Daniel. "They're heroes."

He tugged a corner of his mouth up and scratched Oreo behind the ear. "Sure, they get all the credit."

Nicole placed her hand on his arm and held his gaze. "Not all. I'm fully aware that you risked everything to help me. Again." She bit her bottom lip. "I'm not sure I can ever repay you for—"

He gave a disgusted grunt. "I don't want repayment."

"I only mean—"

"Is this everything you need?" He made an impatient gesture toward the suitcase. "We have to get moving."

Fine. So he didn't want her gratitude. Nicole raked her fingers through her hair and turned on her toes to check her room for anything else she wanted to pack. Boudreaux sat in the door to the hall blinking at her sleepily. Shooting a glance back to Pilar, Nicole said, "We're taking the cats."

Daniel jerked his chin up. "What?"

"Look at her with Oreo." Nicole waved a hand toward the little girl, who stroked the black-and-white cat and snuggled close to Oreo's furry warmth. "The cats calm her. Comfort her. And…I've missed them. Why can't they go?"

Daniel rolled his eyes in resignation. "Whatever. But they stay inside. There are alligators where we're going."

"Alligators?" Nicole whipped a look of concern toward Daniel.

He raised a hand, forestalling her arguments. "It's perfectly safe."

"Why won't you tell me where this safe house is?"

"Because if you don't know, you can't tell your father." When she scowled, he added, "Or anyone else."

Nicole let her shoulders droop in surrender as she moved to the back of her walk-in closet to retrieve the cats' travel cages. Boudreaux saw the carrier and headed under the bed.

Nicole pointed to the absconding feline. "Grab him."

Leaning from the bed, Daniel scooped the old orange tomcat up and eyed him. "So we meet again."

"It's okay, Boo. We're not going to the vet this time." Nicole held out the cage, and Daniel guided the wiggling cat inside. Pilar gave them a curious look when they caged Oreo, as well, and zipped up Nicole's large suitcase.

"We're taking the kitties with us, okay?" she told Pilar, and fumbled for a few words of Spanish. *"Llevémonos los gatos con nosotros."*

Pilar gave her a weak smile and nodded as she scooted close to Nicole's side again.

"I'll get your bag." Daniel pushed off the bed and positioned his crutches under his arms. "You and Pilar go on down to the truck. Jake can get the cats."

Nicole hoisted her suitcase from the bed and extended the handle for rolling. "Don't be silly. You're on crutches."

He tried to nudge her aside. "I responded to your 911 on crutches, didn't I?"

She nudged back with her hip, noticing how hard and lean his body felt as she brushed against him. "True. And I'm sure you could wrangle my suitcase down the stairs and out to the truck, if you had the chance, but…" She started toward the door, wheeling the luggage with one hand and holding Pilar's hand with her other. "So can I."

Nicole bumped her suitcase down the steps from the second floor, feeling the weight of Daniel's disgruntled scowl following her.

At the bottom of the stairs, she met her father's frown and sighed. Somehow her father's disapproval bothered her less than Daniel's, a switch from years past that didn't escape her notice.

"I still think this is a mistake." The senator stormed toward her, blocking her path. "Let me hire protection for you. Your safety is my concern, not these guys'."

"I trust Daniel and Jake, Daddy. They're who I want."

"At least take my Kevlar vest with you, in case there's more shooting," her father pleaded.

"I'll be fine, Dad. Really." When Jake took the suitcase from her, she motioned toward the second floor. "The cats are upstairs in travel cages if you'd get them, too, please."

Jake arched an eyebrow and glanced to Daniel. "We're taking pets?"

Daniel swung to the door on his crutches, then paused and rubbed his temple. "Apparently."

Jake lifted a hand in concession, then tugged on the brim of his cowboy hat. "This is your gig."

Daniel faced her father and narrowed a steely stare on him. "If you want your daughter to be safe, don't breathe a word of any of this to anyone. The fewer people outside this room who know, the better."

Her father puffed out his chest and squared off with Daniel. Quickly, Nicole wedged herself between the men and patted her father on the shoulder. Pilar scuttled with her, holding tightly to the hem of her sweater. "I'll call when I can, Daddy."

"No, you won't," Daniel grated.

Senator White aimed a finger at Daniel. "Listen here, pal. Don't you try to—"

"Dad, stop!" Nicole knocked his hand down and divided a frown between the men. "We're all on the same side here.

Can't you two stop warring with each other for even a little while?" She smacked a kiss on her father's cheek and flashed him a taut grin. "Love you. Try not to worry. And you be careful, too."

Jake finished loading the truck, squeezing the cats' cages on the backseat next to Nicole and Pilar, and they got on the road just as the night blanketed the city. Pilar curled against her and fell asleep not long after they reached the dark highway bridge that crossed the marshes surrounding the city. After the first few miles, Oreo and Boudreaux ceased their plaintive mewls, and the truck grew quiet.

In the tight space of the backseat, surrounded by darkness, Pilar huddled against her, Nicole experienced a déjà vu that sent a shudder to her bones. Gritting her teeth, she battled down the panic that tried to climb her throat. *You're not in that cage anymore. You're safe. Keep it together.*

Sucking in a deep breath, she sought out Daniel's profile, reassuring herself with his presence. The lights from the dashboard cast harsh shadows over the rugged lines of his face, and she couldn't help but flash back to the night her hands had traced his chiseled cheeks and square jaw while her body had been tangled with his. That night he'd been smiling, his dark eyes alight with warmth and humor. Her heart pattered with longing. She missed his smile. She had yet to see it since he'd swooped in to save her from her Colombian prison.

"Now that we're on the road, can you tell me where you're taking me?" she called over the road noise. Roused by her voice, Oreo meowed, as if to say, "Yeah, where are you taking us?"

Daniel turned in the front seat and met her gaze. "My turf."

"Excuse me?"

"With my bum knee, I need every advantage I can get against these cretins. We're going someplace I know inside out." He cast a narrowed gaze out the side window and muttered something to Jake she couldn't hear.

A tickle of suspicion crawled up her back. "Meaning?"

"We're going to the bayou."

Daniel peered through the darkness to the weathered house on the bank of a southern Louisiana bayou. He'd spent many nights in the old wooden home. Set on a pier foundation with a wide front porch and a tin roof, his *grandmère's* one-hundred-year-old house looked exactly as it had the day he'd come to live there as a newly orphaned boy.

From the bayou waters, the eyes of creatures large and small reflected the headlights with a preternatural glow. Daniel had learned to respect the wildlife as he grew up, but Nicole and Pilar would have to be taught basic precautions. As beautiful as the moss-draped bayou was, the murky swampland teemed with hidden dangers.

"The circuit box is just inside the back door," he told Jake as he handed him a key. "Turn the power on while we unload, will ya?"

Jake nodded, jammed his cowboy hat on his head and climbed out of his truck, leaving his headlights burning, the only illumination on the house, other than the gibbous moon.

Daniel slid out of the truck and pulled his crutches from the backseat, along with one of the cat carriers. Nicole whispered to Pilar, who sat up, rubbing her eyes and glancing around warily.

"Whose house is this?" Nicole asked, rolling the kinks from her shoulders and craning her neck to gaze through the windshield.

"Mine now." Daniel massaged his sore knee, stiff after sitting so long. "It was my grandmother's and her parents' before that. *Mémère* left it to me when she died three years ago."

Behind him the security light blinked on with a hum that

said the power had been restored. One by one lights came on in the windows, indicating Jake was making his way through the rooms, checking things out.

Nicole popped open the truck door and climbed out, then helped Pilar jump to the ground. After circling the front bumper, she took a cat carrier in each hand and looked up at him. "Lead the way."

Slinging his duffel over one shoulder, Daniel planted his crutches on the soft earth and headed inside. The warped front steps creaked as he climbed them, and he batted a large cobweb out of his way as he hobbled to the front door. He gave the grimy window a quick knock, and Jake opened the door and stood back.

The musty smell of mildew and age assailed him, and as he limped into the familiar living room, he imagined he could still smell *Mémère's* crawfish gumbo and spicy boudin cooking on the gas stove. When his grandmother didn't round the corner from the kitchen and spread her arms for a hug, a pang settled over him. The house seemed lonely, lifeless without *Mémère*.

"I'll grab the suitcases," Jake said, moving to the door. "Which room do you want them in?"

Roused from his memories, Daniel waved a hand toward the back of the house. "Put Nicole in the master bedroom and the girl next door. I'll sleep on the couch."

Nicole stiffened. "No. Pilar stays with me." She stroked the child's head and shrugged. "I doubt she'd stay in a room by herself, anyway. You can have the master bedroom."

Daniel lifted a shoulder and pulled a dusty, protective cover from a stuffed chair. "Whatever."

In their travel carriers, the cats meowed and pawed at the cages' doors. Nicole squatted to peer in one carrier, cooing to the feline inside. "Can I let them out?"

"Go ahead." Daniel moved to the next piece of furniture

and yanked on the sheet cover. A plume of dust rose in the air, and Pilar sneezed.

Yeah, with the accumulated dust and mildew, the house would be full of allergens, but it was secluded, safe. He'd take a stuffy nose over Colombian mercs any day.

Nicole opened the first cage, and the old orange cat crept out, giving the air a cautious sniff. "What do you think, Boudreaux?"

When Nicole pointed to the other cage and nodded to Pilar, the little girl crouched to open the second carrier. The black-and-white cat trotted out and gave an unhappy meow before taking off to explore his new digs.

"How long has this place been shut up?" Nicole asked, joining him in uncovering the furniture and using a corner of one of the sheets to wipe dust from a lamp table.

Daniel wadded up the dirty sheet in his hands and tossed it in a corner on the floor. "Last time I was here was two, two and a half years ago, I think, right before I left for Colombia on an undercover mission with Alec."

"Is there any food here or other supplies?"

Daniel dragged a hand over his mouth and grunted. "Maybe a thing or two. I'll ask Jake to bring in some supplies for us first thing in the morning."

"What did I do?" Jake asked with a grin as he backed through the front door hauling in Nicole's rolling suitcase and his duffel bag.

"He's volunteered you to go shopping—" A loud crash and the predatory howl of a cat cut Nicole off. More rustling and thumping drew everyone's attention to the back of the house.

Jake and Daniel exchanged a telling look, and both drew weapons from under their shirts. Adrenaline kicking and his muscles taut, Daniel moved down the hall on his crutches as silently as he could while keeping a grip on his handgun.

Pressing his back to the wall, he slid a hand into the first bedroom and turned on the light.

Empty.

Drawing a deep, quiet breath, Daniel sidled farther down the hall and repeated the process at the next door. When the lights flashed on, he swept his gaze over the twin beds, scarred dresser and rag-rug-covered floor.

In the center of the room where he'd slept as a teenager, Nicole's black-and-white cat stood with an arched back and ears plastered to his head, hissing at a fat, disoriented-looking raccoon. While his chest loosened a degree with relief not to find anything more threatening skulking in the shadows, he kept a wary eye on the raccoon. A frightened animal of any size could prove dangerous, and raccoons could carry rabies.

"Casse-toi!" he shouted, waving a hand at the critter. As if animals at his *grandmére's* spoke Cajun French by default. "Scat!" he added, in case this raccoon preferred Southernisms.

Jake eyed him and chuckled. "Scat?"

He shrugged. "Always worked for my grandmother."

The raccoon turned and waddled to a bookshelf, where he climbed up until he reached a hole in the drywall and scampered through.

"Looks like someone's been living here, after all." Jake shoved his gun back in the waistband of his jeans.

Daniel groaned. "And chewed a hole from the attic." He stashed his own gun away and looked around the room for some way to block the varmint's hole for the night. "I'll have to evict the rascal tomorrow and make some repairs."

"Sounds like fun," Jake said, his tone dripping sarcasm. He knocked his cowboy hat back enough to scratch his forehead. "I can stay a day or two and help out if you want."

Daniel shook his head. "Naw. I have another assignment for you, if you're willing."

"I've got some personal time coming. I'm game."

Daniel nodded his appreciation, then frowned as a thought occurred to him. He pulled out his cell phone and checked his reception. "Hmm. Signal's weak, but it might do in a pinch. You have a satellite phone in the truck by chance?"

"No, but I can get you one."

Daniel nodded. "Thanks, cowboy." The satellite phone might be overkill, but with Nicole's life at stake, he'd rather not risk being incommunicado should trouble arise.

And lately, trouble seemed to be following Nicole.

The next morning, Nicole dug her phone from her purse and walked over to a window, searching for the best possible reception, which proved to be rather dismal. When her call was answered, she smiled at the voice at the other end of the line. Stiffly formal, yet familiar and oddly comforting. Some things never changed. "Hi, Daddy. It's me."

"Nicole!" Instantly, warmth tinged with worry suffused the businesslike tone. "Where…you? Where…take you? Are you…right?"

She leaned her head against the window and closed her eyes. "I'm safe, and… Daniel's asked me not to tell you where we are."

"Damn it, Nic—! I'm…father. I…right to know. Does LeCroix really think…going to let anyone or an…hurt you? That's ludicrous."

"Not you, necessarily, but…it's just a precaution."

Through the crackle of static, she heard her father sigh. "If he thinks…shut me out of this situation, I—"

"No one is shutting you out. I promise I'll check in with you from time to time so you know I'm safe. Okay?" Static answered her. "Daddy?"

"You had a call…from Ramon Diaz at the…embassy."

Nicole perked up and crossed the room to a different window, still searching for a clearer connection. "What did he say?"

"The judge has disappeared. Mario…heard about the attempted kidnapping…went into hiding."

"Wait, are you saying *Pilar's father* is missing now?"

"In hiding. He doesn't trust…because of the attack here involving you and Pilar. Diaz isn't happy about you disappearing…Pilar, either. She's a Colombian citizen and you're—"

A loud burst of static cut him off.

"Dad?" Nicole checked her phone. Her screen read, *dropped call.* She tried to call her father back, but couldn't get a strong enough signal now to place the call. "Fudge."

So…Pilar's father was in hiding, as well? Great. How was she supposed to reunite him with Pilar now? Stewing over this turn of events, she carried her phone into the kitchen with her, in case her father called back.

Pilar was sitting at the kitchen table with Jake and Daniel, watching with wide, wary eyes as the men conferred.

"Good morning." She sent Pilar a smile, and the men acknowledged her with mumbled greetings. Her stomach rumbled, and she turned to the cabinets to search for food.

"We're making a list of supplies Jake will get when he goes out in a few minutes. If you have any preferences, speak now."

"Coffee," she said emphatically, then checked the counter for a coffeepot. She sighed her relief when she spotted one. "Fresh fruit and vegetables. Milk. All the stuff a little girl needs for a healthy diet. Cat food and litter for Oreo and Boudreaux." She chose to ignore Jake's eyeroll as he scribbled these items on the list.

Nicole fixed the only breakfast she could find in the empty cupboards. Instant oatmeal that Daniel warned her was likely several years old. When the kettle water boiled, she stirred up two bowls of instant oatmeal and grimaced. "Add eggs and whole grain bread to the list for breakfasts."

Jake winked at her and scribbled on his list.

She put the two bowls on the table and watched as Pilar bowed her head over her breakfast, then crossed herself before eating. Though not Catholic herself, Nicole had attended a Catholic high school and had numerous Catholic friends growing up, and it touched her to see the young girl practicing her faith even after all she'd been through.

"I need ammunition for both my Sig .45 and my .22 hunting rifle," she heard Daniel say, even though he spoke in a hush. She shivered, hating the idea of loaded weapons around Pilar, even if she understood the need.

Daniel must have sensed her gaze, because he glanced up at her and narrowed an all-business look on her. "Can you shoot?"

Alec hadn't bothered to ask when he'd shoved the automatic weapon in her hands as they fled the jungle. "I can pull a trigger, but I make no promises about what I'll hit."

Jake and Daniel exchanged a look before Daniel returned his attention to her. "I'll teach you to handle a gun. I want you ready next time those cretins show up."

"Next time?" Her grip tightened around her spoon. "I thought the point of hiding out here was so there was no next time."

Daniel shrugged and ducked his head to study his notes. "We have to be prepared for anything. No hideout is foolproof."

Learning to shoot. Hiding from assassins. Dodging bullets. When had her life become so…*hazardous?*

Daniel hitched his head toward her phone, which she'd left on the end of the table. "And another thing…no cell phone. A signal can be traced. If you have to use a phone, my cell is encrypted."

"Oh." Guilt nibbled at her. "So…I guess I should tell you that I called my father this morning."

Daniel sent her a tell-me-you-didn't look, then scrubbed a hand over his face. "Okay. We'll deal with it."

"There's more."

Jake and Daniel both raised worried gazes to her.

Nicole glance quickly to Pilar, who stared bleakly at her oatmeal. "Her father heard about the kidnapping attempt somehow. He's gone into hiding. Ramon Diaz, my contact at the Colombian embassy, called my father's house to tell me that, and my father let Diaz know we'd moved Pilar to a safe house. Diaz is upset, presumably because he wasn't informed."

"No one can know we're here," Daniel interjected, anticipating her next argument.

She studied Daniel's unshaven jaw and dark, serious eyes, and a ripple of uneasiness shimmied through her. Her guardian could well be the most dangerous element in this equation. Dangerous to her sanity, her heart, if she didn't figure out how to rein in her wild obsession with him.

Knowing he was sleeping in the next room, Nicole had spent hours staring at the ceiling last night, wishing she could curl up next to his muscular body. Imagining a young Daniel growing up within these walls and becoming the mysterious man he was today had teased her brain in the late hours. The idea of living under the same roof with Daniel for who knows how many days made her skin feel too tight and her blood hot.

She shifted her gaze to Jake, a rugged, incredible-looking man in his own right, yet the powerfully built, sandy-haired pilot didn't stir Nicole's deepest passion the way Daniel did—and always had.

Pilar poked at her oatmeal and sent Nicole a sad look.

"You don't have to eat it if you don't like it, *mija*." The gray-beige goop reminded her, too, of the gruel they'd eaten in the jungle. Nicole shoved her bowl away and pushed her chair from the table.

The sights and sounds of the attack at her father's house flickered in her memory, and Nicole shuddered. If she hadn't gone to check on Pilar when she had yesterday, would the men have succeeded in kidnapping her? And why had she left the girl alone in the first place?

She'd assumed her father's house was safe. Why wouldn't it be? How could she have known such terrible men were already on their trail?

The questions pounded at her temples. What she and Pilar needed was an activity to keep them busy, something to distract them from thoughts of the men who'd attacked them. Cleaning the safe house topped that list.

Nicole raked her hair back from her face and remembered the picture of Mario Castillo she'd received just before the attack yesterday. The photo was still folded in the pocket of her pants. "Wait here," she told Pilar. *"Espérate aquí."*

She hurried to the bedroom to retrieve the crumpled picture, then smoothing the paper against her chest as she returned, she sat next to Pilar and laid the photo on the table. "Do you know this man?" she asked. *"Conoces a este hombre?"*

Pilar leaned forward to examine the photo, and her eyes widened, lighting with happiness. *"Papi!"*

Daniel and Jake glanced over from their huddle.

A thrill raced through Nicole, not only hearing Pilar speak at last, but seeing the pure joy and longing on the girl's face. She smiled and nodded, pulling Pilar into a hug. "Good. That's so wonderful."

"May I see that?" Daniel asked, holding a hand out.

Nicole passed him the crumpled sheet. "That's the judge who's in hiding. Mario Castillo. That picture had just been faxed to my father's home office yesterday when the men attacked. So we have our confirmation of who she is. *Whose* she is."

Daniel studied the photo a moment, then passed it to Jake. "Will you see if—"

"I'm on it." Jake shot Daniel a smug grin as he interrupted. "Do you want me to bring him here when I find him or meet you somewhere?"

Nicole cleared her throat. "Um, gentlemen. May I remind you that I already have the Colombian and U.S. embassies working on this? They're the ones who faxed me the photo and got in touch with Castillo yesterday."

Daniel leaned back in his chair and angled his stubbled chin as he regarded her. He lifted one eyebrow. "And may I remind you that your contacts are likely the ones responsible for leaking Pilar's location to the men who tried to kill you? Until we know what and who we are dealing with, Jake will be doing our legwork in Colombia, looking for Castillo."

His gaze hardened to a scowl as he glanced at his injured knee, and Nicole didn't need to ask how he felt about relying on his teammate to do his fieldwork while he babysat them and nursed his bum leg. Sympathy she was sure he wanted no part of tugged at her. He'd already sacrificed so much for her and Pilar, but losing his mobility—and therefore his position on his black ops team—had to be the hardest for him to accept.

The men finished their discussion, and Jake headed out to buy supplies. Daniel patched the raccoon hole in Pilar's bedroom, leaving the attic repair for when Jake could help him, then moved to the living room where he began cleaning his guns.

Nicole cleared away their untouched breakfast and turned to the girl who now clutched the faxed photo of her father close to her chest. "Well, we might as well start our cleaning in the kitchen." She found a rag and turned on the faucet at the sink. The water that sputtered out was a rusty shade of brown and smelled like eggs. Nicole wrinkled her nose and glanced at Pilar. "Yuck."

Pilar scrunched her nose, too.

After running the water for a few minutes, the accumulated dirt and smell in the pipes cleared enough that Nicole felt comfortable using the water with some liquid soap she found in a cabinet to wash the dishes and wipe the counters, table and chairs. As they worked, Nicole continued the quasi game she'd played with Pilar in their cage in Colombia. Moving through the kitchen, she pointed to objects and told Pilar the English name for each item. Though Pilar never repeated the words, her bright eyes reflected intelligence, and Nicole felt sure the child was soaking the information in.

They'd nearly finished wiping down the kitchen and all the pans when Oreo sauntered in, tail twitching and something furry in his mouth. Nicole jumped back with a screech.

Startled, Oreo dropped his prize. The white fuzzy thing didn't move.

Daniel scrambled from the living room into the kitchen, his gun at the ready. "What happened?"

"Oreo had something in his mouth…." Nicole nudged the wooly thing with her toe, realizing it was a toy. "At first, I thought it was alive. Sorry. I didn't mean to alarm you."

Pilar picked up the toy, a small stuffed lamb that looked like it came from a child's fast food meal, and held it out for Oreo to sniff.

"Hey, where'd he get that?" Daniel asked. "Lamby was mine when I was a kid."

"Lamby?" Nicole's cheek twitched with a grin.

"Cut me some slack. I was five." Daniel stepped closer to reach for the lamb, but Oreo swatted at the small stuffed animal and snagged it with his claw. "Hey, *minou,* gimme—"

Pilar giggled as Oreo batted Lamby across the floor, and she chased down the hall after the cat.

Nicole covered a laugh. "If Lamby is an heirloom you want protected, I'll get it back from Oreo…."

"Pfft." Daniel waved a hand and sighed. "It's a cat toy now."

Nicole cocked her head and tried to read Daniel's expression. "But if it's important to you…"

Daniel hitched his head toward the hall where Pilar played with Oreo, giggling. "Listen to her. That's more important than some old dusty toy."

Nicole's heart swelled, and smiling warmly, she caught Daniel's gaze with her own, held it. "That's the Daniel I remember."

Something in his hard gaze shifted, softened, but before Daniel could reply, Jake burst through the back door, his arms loaded with bags. "Ho, ho, ho. Santa came early this year." Jake set the bags on the kitchen table, then aimed a thumb at the door. "There's more in the truck. A little help?"

"Pilar?" Nicole headed out the back door, crooking a hand to tell the girl to follow. When Nicole saw the pile of groceries and supplies mounded in the bed of Jake's truck, she stopped to stare. "Geez Louise, Jake!"

Jake shrugged as he marched past her. "Tell me about it."

Daniel swung next to her on his crutches and paused. "There a problem?"

She motioned to the huge pile of supplies. "Just how long do you think we're staying?"

His returned gaze was hard and flat. "As long as it takes to make sure you're safe."

Chapter 8

Jake left for Colombia to search for Judge Castillo as soon as they'd unloaded the supplies from his truck. Jake was one of the best agents the black ops team had, and Daniel felt confident the native Texan could track down Pilar's father within a week or two.

Over the next two days, Daniel watched Nicole buzz around his grandmother's house, cleaning up a storm. Guilt nibbled at him every time she picked up a rag or broom, as if her housekeeping was an indictment against him and the safe house he'd provided. Or an unspoken commentary on the home of his youth.

At first, he tried to ignore her, but that exercise was futile. If Nicole was around, she had his full attention. When he tried to help, she shooed him away.

"Cleaning keeps me busy, and if I'm busy I'm less likely to dwell on things that are out of my control." She rinsed her rag in the kitchen sink and headed back outside to wash the porch windows. "Besides, I had enough idle time while I was held captive to last me a lifetime." She aimed a finger at the sofa. "You should sit. Rest your knee. You've earned it."

Daniel raised his hands in surrender and settled on the couch, frustrated with his own idleness.

Pilar found a children's book in a storage box of his childhood things and brought it out to the living room. She sat next to him and opened the cover. A fuzzy warmth filled Daniel's chest. He wasn't sure what to do with the tenderness he felt toward the little girl. He hadn't spent a lot of time around kids, except when he was supposed to be in soldier mode and not focusing on things like how sweet a little girl's smile could be or how a child's laugh could lighten even the tensest mood. Living with Pilar over the past two days, watching her interact with Nicole, cast his protective duties in a whole new light. Pilar had an innocence and vulnerability that stuck under his ribs and crowded his heart.

The first day, as she'd clung to Nicole, Pilar had looked at him with a heartbreaking mix of wariness and hero worship. He was the brute with the guns and the loud voice and the gruff appearance who'd rescued her from even scarier men. He hated the idea that he frightened the girl, so by the second day, he shaved the black stubble that made him look like a thug. When she glanced his way, he made an effort to smile, and with no immediate threat warranting barked commands, he consciously lowered his volume and softened his tone.

Not only did his efforts seem to calm the little girl, but Nicole noticed the changes and sent him appreciative smiles that shot straight to his soul. Though he wanted more from Nicole than her gratitude, Daniel welcomed the points he scored with her because he'd built a good rapport with Pilar.

He didn't know where things with Nicole might go. They had a lot of crap in their way—like her father. But his body ached for her, and his heart bled a little more every time he thought of the happiness he'd known with her for one magical night. If they could get past their differences, could they recapture that bliss, that passion? Or would he always be *that guy from the bayou* to her…a convenient chump from the wrong side of the tracks to use and discard when he'd served his purpose?

A niggle of irritation poked him for the umpteenth time. Nicole's pride had been hurt when he'd walked out on her five years ago. She was determined to rehash the events of that morning, root out his reasons for leaving and exact her pound of flesh for his slight. But how could he relive the pain and humiliation of that morning? His pride and dignity had already suffered one nearly crippling blow thanks to her. He was no glutton for punishment.

The crinkle of yellowed pages drew his attention to Pilar and the book in her lap. The text was in Cajun-English dialect, and the girl stared at the pages, frowning.

He'd heard Nicole chanting English words to Pilar many times in the kitchen or bedroom when they were alone, and he wondered if the English lessons were helping the girl's comprehension at all. Scooting closer to Pilar and readjusting his injured leg, he pointed to the book in her hands, *Cajun Night Before Christmas.* "May I?"

When Pilar handed him the book, looking chastened, he reassured her with a wink and a warm smile. The shadows in the girl's eyes dissipated, and she flashed him a shy grin. Flipping to the first page, Daniel studied the pictures, nostalgia stirring an ache in his chest.

"My *grandmére* used to read this to me when I was little," he told her quietly, knowing she wouldn't understand. "Even when it wasn't Christmas." He pointed to the bearded man in his sleigh. "There's Santa Claus…'cept around here, we call him *Père Noël,* Father Christmas." He glanced down, looking for any signs of recognition in her face. "Oh, yeah. Y'all celebrate with *El Niño Jesús,* right?"

Now Pilar's face lit with a smile.

Daniel had an idea and pushed off the sofa to hobble to a cabinet across the room. He dug in a pile of dusty books until he found the photo album his grandmother had kept of him and his parents. Planting himself next to Pilar again, he turned the pages of aged photos until he found one of himself at about age three. "See, that's me." He pointed to the picture, then to himself. "Daniel."

Pilar examined the picture with a small furrow in her brow, then glanced up at him, a wide smile brightening her face. He turned the page and found another picture of himself with *Mémère.* "That's my *grandmére.*" He motioned around them. "This was her house."

As Pilar looked around then back at the photo, Daniel sent a glance to the front window where Nicole was scrubbing madly. As if feeling his gaze, she paused in her work and met his stare. When she spotted Pilar beside him, the book spread between them, she smiled. Warmth expanded in his chest until he could barely breathe. Damn, Nicole was beautiful.

Pilar tugged on his sleeve and pointed to another picture of him as a young boy, wearing wet cut-off jeans and a sappy grin while he showed off the catfish he'd caught. "*Oui,* that's me, too."

On the next page, he tapped a picture of himself at about five years old, pouting. "Look-a dat *bahbin!*" he said with a thick Cajun accent, remembering what *Mémère* used to say about that photo. *"Quoi faire tu braille?"*

Pilar laughed and imitated his exaggerated pout.

"Oh, just what we need in this house," Nicole said as she walked back into the living room from the porch, her tone wry, "a *third* language." She sent him a teasing grin and headed back into the kitchen to rinse her rag again.

"De rien," he called after her.

As she returned from the kitchen with the rinsed rag, Nicole spotted the picture album he held, and her teasing grin faltered. "What's that?"

"Nothing." He gave her a dismissive shrug. "Just some old pictures of my grandmother's."

"Can I see?" Nicole joined him on the sofa, her thigh brushing his as she settled close enough to see the photos, the lemon scent of dish soap clinging to her.

"Go ahead," he said, trying to sound casual, even though his heart thrashed as hard as that catfish in the picture had flailed when he'd pulled it from the water. He loosened his grip on the album so Nicole could angle it toward her.

Daniel's gut tightened, suddenly all too conscious of how Nicole might react to the Cajun lifestyle depicted in the photos—isolated, poor, living off the bayou. His grandmother had never received a formal education, never embraced modern conveniences and technology. Daniel had been the one to update the house with modern amenities in recent years.

But as out of date as this house had been, the Gatreau family's tiny shack on stilts, deep in the bayou, where his grandmother had been raised, was even more primitive. He'd pointed Alec and Erin to that bayou shack when they'd needed a hideout last winter.

Pilar carried *Cajun Night Before Christmas* to a chair across the room and settled in to study the pictures, while Nicole perused the photos.

A sunny smile lit Nicole's face, and she pointed to the proud boy with his catch. "Is this you?"

"Yeah." His voice sounded tight. Willing his muscles to relax, he forced the air from his lungs. "Yours truly."

Nicole's blue eyes brightened, and she laughed—a happy sound of discovery, not derision.

Daniel slid a covert side glance to her, studying her reaction as her gaze moved from one picture to another.

"Oh, my gosh," she chuckled, "I bet you hate that picture. Look at your pout!" She met his eyes, her lips twitching with humor. "Were you a grumpy little boy, Mr. LeCroix?"

The urge to kiss her teasing grin slammed him so hard he had to catch his breath before he could reply. "No more than most. I'm smiling in all the other pictures."

Her attention returned to the photo album for a moment. When she raised her head again, warmth filled her face.

"So you are." She smoothed a finger over one of the photos, and his skin reacted as if she'd stroked him instead. "That's the smile that stole my heart the night we met."

Stole her heart? The phrase sent a shock wave through him, though with effort, he masked his surprise, suppressed it. His smile hadn't been enough to build a relationship on after she'd used him in her rebellion against her father years ago.

His fingers tightened on the photo album as a familiar knot of bitter disappointment swelled in his chest. He couldn't allow himself to forget the pain and sense of betrayal he'd known that morning and in the months that followed. He'd buried himself in special operations training, praying he could forget Nicole and the hope she'd crushed in that overheard phone call to her father. But he'd never completely erased her from his heart or his mind. And now, here he was sharing the house he'd grown up in with her, protecting her from an unknown threat…and in danger of falling for her all over again, if he didn't find a way to fight the old feelings stirring to life again and keep her at arm's length.

"Oh, there's the requisite I-lost-a-tooth shot." Nicole angled another grin at him, and he ignored the acceleration in his pulse. "Do you remember what the tooth fairy brought you?"

"I didn't have a tooth fairy."

"What?" Nicole sounded truly offended on his behalf. "Why not?"

"Doesn't matter. I had a good childhood," he said, hearing the note of defensiveness in his tone. "I had plenty of reason to be happy, to smile, even though I lost my parents when I was twelve. We didn't have much materially, but I never knew it. What we lacked in things, my parents and *Mémère* made up for in the love they gave me."

"Oh, Daniel…" Nicole stared at him with a certain sadness in her eyes. A bittersweet smile that felt too much like pity to Daniel tugged her lips.

He closed the photo album with a grunt and shoved to his feet, wincing when a sharp ache shot through his knee. The pain only fueled his frustration with the elusive dissatisfaction that nagged him. "I'm not looking for sympathy! I have no regrets from my childhood. I'm proud of my family, my heritage."

Pilar raised a startled looked, and Nicole blinked her surprise at his outburst. "As you should be. I never said otherwise."

Daniel sucked in a deep breath, his nose flaring and his hands fisting at his sides. *Get a grip, man.* She *hadn't* said anything derogatory about his Cajun roots. Not today, anyway, and not since he'd brought her home from Colombia. But being with her in this house had him on edge.

"Forget it," he grumbled, picking up his crutches and heading outside. "I'll be on the porch."

The weight of Nicole's stare followed him as he left, and his gut tightened. Like a storm rolling in from the Gulf, a showdown between them was coming, and he dreaded the fallout.

Nicole carried her glass of iced tea toward the front porch but stopped behind the screened door when she spotted Pilar sitting with Daniel. He sat in one of the rocking chairs with his injured leg propped on a large bucket he'd turned upside down, and Pilar stared at the ugly red surgical scar visible through Daniel's knee brace.

"Pilar," he said softly, and the little girl glanced up. He crooked his finger, motioning her closer. She walked to his side, and Daniel put an arm around her shoulders, turning her and pointing toward the bayou. "Look."

Nicole looked the direction he indicated and spotted a beautiful blue heron strutting through the water, searching the shallows for fish.

Pilar angled her head to grin at Daniel, and Nicole's heart tripped. The little girl had a beautiful smile, and Nicole's spirits lifted seeing the child happy at last. Was it the new hope Pilar had of being reunited with her father that made her feel safer, more cheerful, willing to smile?

No sooner had that thought filtered through her mind than Daniel flashed a warm grin back at the little girl. Now Nicole's heart thundered. When he smiled, Daniel could melt the hardest heart. This was the man she'd fallen so hard for five years ago at the Mardi Gras ball, the man with whom she'd spent a sensual night and with whom she'd envisioned her future. Perhaps part of Pilar's happiness had to do with Daniel. She couldn't blame Pilar for developing a crush on the handsome man who'd rescued her twice.

With a flap of its massive wings, the heron took flight, and Pilar tracked the bird with her gaze, until it disappeared behind the cypress trees that lined the bayou. Pulling her chair closer to Daniel's, Pilar settled in, staring again at the injured knee.

"Te duele?" Pilar asked in a tiny voice, her finger lightly touching Daniel's scar.

Nicole was so startled to hear Pilar speak, she gasped.

Pilar and Daniel both swiveled their heads toward the door

where Nicole stood. Caught spying on the duo, Nicole pushed through the screen door and took the rocking chair next to Daniel's. "She asked if your knee hurts."

He shot Nicole a strange look, then arched one black eyebrow and said dryly, "Thanks."

"Wh—"

Before she could finish, he turned back to Pilar and, with a devastating smile, replied, *"No mucho. Espero que la cicatriz tan horrible que tengo no ahuyente a las chicas bonitas."*

Pilar giggled and shook her head. *"No creo."*

Nicole kicked herself mentally. Hello? The guy had worked undercover in Colombia for who-knows-how-long. Of course he spoke Spanish.

He met her stunned, somewhat embarrassed look with a smug grin. "I told her I hoped my ugly scar didn't scare away all the pretty girls. She said it wouldn't."

"I'm sorry. I forgot you would know Spanish because of your work in South America."

"Instead, you assumed I couldn't understand her. Why?"

She blinked, taken aback by the bitterness behind his question. "Well...most people wouldn't have."

"Most *Cajuns* wouldn't? Is that what you mean?"

She bristled. "What is that supposed to mean? I'm not a bigot!"

He waved her off. "Forget it."

Nicole tensed and leaned toward him. "No, explain. Why do you think I would make any judgments about you based on your heritage?"

"You have before."

She sputtered a laugh. "What? When?"

He rolled his eyes and shook his head, frowning. "Are you kidding me?"

Nicole spread her hands. "No. Please enlighten me."

A muscle jumped in his jaw. "The night we spent together, five years ago."

Her pulse sped up, remembering the sensual glide of his body against hers, the heat of his kisses and the breathy moans of satisfaction they'd both made. But she couldn't recall anything he could have misconstrued as bigotry. She shook her head. "Still clueless. What did I do?"

He glanced at Pilar, and Nicole noticed the girl's worried frown for the first time. Even if she couldn't understand the words, Pilar could obviously tell from the tone of their voices and their expressions that the conversation had turned angry and personal.

"Dang it," Nicole fussed under her breath then flashed the girl a forced smile. *"Todo está bien.* Everything's all right, *mija."*

Pilar looked skeptical and shifted her gaze to Daniel.

With a lopsided grin, he turned up a palm and shrugged. *"Alguien debe haber puesto un insecto en su desayuno."*

Again Pilar giggled.

"What did you tell her? Something about breakfast."

Daniel gave Nicole a nonchalant glance. "That someone must have put an insect in yours."

Rolling her eyes heavenward, she leaned closer to Daniel. "We're not through with this conversation." She kept her volume low and shot Daniel a pointed look. "We have to talk about it eventually... Soon, preferably."

"Let it go," he returned flatly.

Gritting her teeth, Nicole huffed her exasperation, then met Pilar's gaze and pointed at Daniel. *"Él está loco."*

"Sí, loco." Daniel wiggled his fingers on either side of his head and crossed his eyes.

Pilar laughed and snuggled closer to Daniel's side. *"Sí."*

Nicole grinned, touched by Daniel's attempts to bring Pilar out of her shell. "Well, it seems we're all in agreement."

Daniel grunted and returned his gaze to the still waters of the bayou. "Pilar, my dear, have you ever been fishing?" He met the girl's eyes and repeated the question in Spanish.

When she shook her head, Daniel seized his crutches and hoisted himself out of his chair. "Then I'm going to teach you."

He limped to the other end of the porch and grabbed two cane poles that leaned against the house. Leaving one of the crutches behind, Daniel started down the porch steps and hitched his head, signaling Pilar to follow. "Come on, tadpole. Let's catch dinner."

Pilar's glance asked approval from Nicole.

"Go on." She waved her away with her fingers. *"Te puedes ir."*

Her expression curious, Pilar rose from her seat and joined Daniel on the lawn, taking the fishing pole he handed her.

"Be careful," Nicole called, not sure if she was more worried about Pilar, experiencing the wildlife of the bayou for the first time, or Daniel, dealing with his injured leg on uneven, sometimes murky terrain.

Daniel tapped the walkie-talkie clipped to his hip. Jake had purchased the short-distance radios for just this type of circumstance. At the moment, Nicole's was still sitting in the charging cradle plugged in the kitchen outlet.

He leveled a penetrating gaze on Nicole. "Keep your radio close. If anything seems off, if you so much as think a mosquito has gotten in the house, call me."

Nicole straightened. "I thought we were here because it is so remote, so safe. Do you really think—?"

"No. I think you'll be fine. And I'm only going a few yards down the bank to my old pirogue dock." His eyebrows lowered, deepening his scowl. "But I'd rather not take any chances. There's a gun in the first kitchen drawer. If you need it, don't hesitate to use it."

* * *

After Daniel and Pilar left, Nicole carried Daniel's encrypted cell phone out to the porch, hoping to get more than one bar of reception so she could check in again with her father. The connection was marginally better outside, so she settled in the rocking chair Daniel had vacated and held the phone to her ear.

After assuring her father that she was fine and refusing once more to tell him where they were, Nicole asked if Ramon Diaz had been in touch.

"He's called every day, Nic. He's getting pressure from his government to bring Pilar home before this turns into a political issue. You are holding the child of an important Colombian official, you know."

"I know, Dad, but Daniel thinks we—"

"LeCroix? He shouldn't even be involved in this! He's trouble, Nic. He's up to something. I know he is."

"He protecting us the best way he knows how."

"He has an ulterior motive. Just a few months ago, he swore to my face that he'd destroy me. How can you trust him?"

"Daddy, stop. Please?" Nicole rubbed her eyes and groaned. "Can't you two put your differences behind you and realize that we're all on the same side? This bickering and hostility between you two…" She opened her eyes in time to see a turtle scuttle from a log into the brown bayou. "Well, it hurts me. I care about you both. Deeply. And—" She stopped abruptly when she realized what she'd said.

She had deep feelings for Daniel. But what feelings? Gratitude, certainly. He had saved her life several times. Admiration, yes. Daniel had risen far in a short time and made a difference in the fight against terrorism. Lust? Definitely. In spades.

"Nicole." Her father's wary tone intruded on her reflection. "Are you telling me you're in love with this man?"

A tremor shot to her core. "I…don't know. He's changed since I knew him before."

He scoffed. "Did you ever *really* know him?"

Nicole scowled. "What do you mean?"

"Well, you had a reckless one-night fling with him a few years ago, but then he left town and… I thought that had been the end of it."

Out of habit, Nicole bristled a bit at the word *reckless*. When she did something impromptu—like leaving her nursing job to help at a medical mission camp in a poverty stricken area of Colombia—she was reckless. When her father made snap decisions, he was bold and daring.

Then the rest of his comment resonated inside her. "What do you know about his leaving town?"

Her father hesitated. "Only what you've told me."

"I never said he left town. Even when I left for Colombia, I still had no clue what happened to him. The Navy wouldn't tell me anything, and he never called. I…" A chill of suspicion slithered through her. "Daddy…what…" She took a slow breath for courage. "What did you do?"

"Do? I don't know what you mean, what did *I* do?" Her father might be good at bluffing with reporters and his colleagues, but she heard the slight wobble in his tone.

Acid pooled in her stomach. What part had her father played in keeping her and Daniel apart? Was her father behind the bitterness that Daniel felt toward her? "How did you know he left town?"

"Like I said, I thought you told me that. But it's been years, honey." He laughed stiffly. "I've slept since then."

"Fine. I'll ask Daniel." Nicole rolled her eyes. Liked he'd tell her! Keeping mum about the past was one thing Daniel had in common with her father.

"Nicole, I just don't want to see you get hurt again. I remember how you felt when he walked out on you last time. Who's to say he won't abandon you like that again?"

His question cut her to the quick, because he'd hit on the very fear she'd been skirting around for days. *Don't fall for him again. Don't let yourself form those old attachments to him,* she'd warned herself. Not only had he made no promises for the future, he sometimes acted like he couldn't wait to be rid of her. So why was he here with her at all? She'd give anything to be able to read that enigmatic mind of Daniel's, see past his shuttered expression. Years ago, he'd worn his heart on his sleeve. He'd been open about his passion for her, his hope for the future, his zest for life.

His black ops work, she realized with a sinking heart. They'd trained him to hide his thoughts, show no emotion.

"Nicole?"

When her father spoke, she yanked herself from the silence into which she'd lapsed. "I don't know what will come of my relationship with Daniel, Daddy. But for my sake, if you two could put your differences to rest and at least be civil…" She sighed, wondering if such a truce was even possible.

"So…you are looking for a future with him? You have feelings for him? Real feelings? Because any adoration you have for his heroics in rescuing you is not enough to build a relationship on."

Nicole pinched the bridge of her nose. "I'm aware of that."

She heard her father blow out a breath. "All right. I'll do my best to accept him. For your sake."

She opened her mouth to tell him his concession might be premature, that there was nothing between her and Daniel to accept. But the murmur of voices called her attention to the bank of the bayou where Daniel and Pilar were making their way back up to the house.

Just the sight of Daniel, his skin a deeper bronze after only an hour in the sun, made her pulse stutter and her breath snag in her lungs. The bright daylight accentuated his ebony eyes and the masculine cut of his cheeks and square jaw. He flashed Pilar a white smile as they crossed the yard, and a bayou breeze ruffled his black hair. Her fingers twitched around the cell phone, remembering the silky feeling of his hair threading through her fingers as they'd made love. His dark Cajun features easily topped her list of reasons to love his heritage.

"I just want what's best for you," her father said, interrupting her ogling and sensual memories of Daniel.

Nicole cleared her throat. "Thank you, Dad. I've got to go now." She started to disconnect then added, "I love you."

"Same here, sweetheart. Be careful. And call again soon so I know you're okay."

"I'll try." She tapped the disconnect button and set Daniel's phone aside just as he and Pilar reached the foot of the porch steps.

He sent her a dubious look. "Who was that?"

She shook her head, dismissing the call as trivial, and focused her attention on the fish dangling from the line Pilar held. "You caught some!"

The girl's face lit with excitement, and she held up their catch—two good-size catfish and one very small fish Nicole couldn't identify. Keeping her tone cheerful and bright, she asked Daniel, "Isn't that third one too small to keep?"

He smiled back, keeping up the pretense. "Yeah. But there was no way I was going to make her throw back the first fish she'd ever reeled in. That'd just be mean."

"Cena!" Pilar said, beaming. *Dinner.*

Nicole braced a hand on her hip. "I hope you don't think I'm cleaning those!"

"Squeamish, are we?" Daniel asked, using the porch railing and one crutch to help him hop up the steps on his good leg.

"Just sayin'."

When he reached the porch, he stepped toward her, so that she had to angle her chin up to meet his eyes. So that he was near enough for her to feel his body heat, near enough to smell traces of the soap he'd used in the shower that morning. His proximity caused a quiver deep in her core. The intensity of his gaze as he hovered over her shot longing through her like liquid fire.

For the first time in days, she saw a vibrance and...*life* in his expression that had been missing since he'd woken up in the hospital. Here at his grandmother's home by the bayou, he was in his element. More than that, teaching Pilar to fish, seeing the girl's joy, clearly fed his soul. Though he'd never admit it to her, she could imagine how his injury and the loss of his job with the black ops team had bruised his ego and his sense of purpose. For an alpha male control freak like Daniel, those blows had to have been crushing.

Still holding her gaze, his wide chest so close that he brushed against her when she took a deep breath for composure, he asked, "You know how to make hush puppies and slaw?"

Sarah Beth made the best hush puppies Nicole had ever put in her mouth. Maybe she could call her father's housekeeper for help. "I can try."

Daniel arched a skeptical eyebrow, then shrugged. "Then I'll take care of the fish. Cleaning. Seasoning. Frying. Deal?"

She twitched a grin. "You're on."

With a satisfied nod, he moved away, and Nicole felt the loss to her marrow. Like losing her bedcovers on a winter night, she felt a cool emptiness course through her.

"You okay with her helping me clean the fish?" he asked, taking the string of fish from Pilar.

Nicole frowned. "I'll leave it up to her if she wants to watch, but I don't like the idea of her using a knife."

Daniel glanced toward the bayou before facing Nicole

again. "I was her age when *mon père* learned me how to cut up *la barbue*."

Nicole folded her arms over her chest and gave Daniel a measuring scrutiny. Had his thick Cajun accent, mixed Louisiana French and English, and blatant use of a common, though grammatically incorrect, Southernism been for her benefit? With a prickle of uneasiness, she recalled his earlier accusation that she held a negative bias against Cajuns. On the contrary, she admired the resilience, traditions and sense of community in the Cajun population. She envied Daniel the unconditional love and support he'd had from his family, while she'd struggled to win her father's approval or five undistracted minutes of his time.

She raised her chin and kept her tone neutral. "I'm sure your father taught you well, but you asked if I was okay with Pilar cleaning fish. And I'm not. You do the cutting, okay?"

Pilar watched them with wide, inquisitive eyes, and Daniel gave her an oh-well glance and a shrug, before starting toward the side yard. "How do you say 'worrywart' in Spanish?"

Dividing a look between Daniel and Nicole, Pilar bit her lip, clearly undecided about who to stay with, then scurried after Daniel like a puppy. Nicole couldn't blame her. Given the chance, she'd spend every minute she could with Daniel, too. Especially the kind, smiling version of himself that he showed Pilar.

Nicole turned to go inside, wondering how long they'd be in hiding here with Daniel. And more important, what would happen once Daniel felt they were safe? Would he disappear from her life again without a word? Would he give their relationship a second chance?

Back in the kitchen, she began searching the groceries Jake had brought in, pulling out the ingredients to make hush puppies, but her mind dwelled on the one question that seemed at the root of everything with Daniel. What had happened five years ago that changed his feelings for her and made him leave without a goodbye?

For her sanity's sake, she had to find out, had to get the truth. Tonight.

Chapter 9

Nicole quietly closed the door to the room she shared with Pilar and tiptoed back to the living room. "Well, I don't think we'll be hearing anything from her until morning. She was asleep before her head hit the pillow."

Daniel paced across the room, using only one crutch for support, then turned and walked back the direction he came. "Wore herself out running around the yard today."

Nicole watched him retrace his steps with a knit in her brow. "I'll say. After being cooped up in that cage in Colombia, I can't blame her for wanting to run herself ragged." She stopped behind the couch and propped her hip on the back of the sofa. "Speaking of which, what are you doing? Shouldn't you be resting your knee?"

"Not if I want to walk without a crutch again. Physical therapist in the hospital told me to use my knee, not let it get stiff. Put more weight on it every day."

Nicole sent him a worried frown. "Does it hurt?"

"Not as much as it used to."

She watched him stalk back and forth, clearly making progress in his recovery, but a far cry from the agile special ops agent who'd stolen through the jungle to rescue her. Did he hold his injury against her? Was that why he seemed so angry with her most of the time?

She wiped a sweaty palm on the seat of her blue jeans and looked for an opening to hash out his grievances. Knowing he wouldn't appreciate her dancing around the issue, she squared her shoulders and dove in head first. "Tell me what happened that morning at the hotel. Why did you leave? What did I do?"

Daniel stopped midstride and whipped his head toward her.

"And don't say I already know," she said, aiming a finger at him. "Because I don't. I've never understood why you left, why you never called or answered my messages."

He sighed heavily and scowled. Cursed under his breath. "Do we have to talk about this?"

She tamped down her rising frustration. "Yes, we do. Because I deserve answers." She tapped her chest with her finger, fighting the hurt that swelled in her chest, still as sharp and ruthless as that morning years ago. "I deserve to know why you broke my heart, why you abandoned me. Why you stayed away for so long."

Daniel closed his eyes and gritted his teeth, making the muscle in his square jaw jump. With a harsh exhale, he met her gaze evenly. "I heard everything you told your father."

The mention of her father hiked her frustration level up a notch. She didn't want to beat that drum again.

"Daniel, I—" But she hesitated, catching her protest before it escaped her lips.

His expression didn't have that shuttered quality it had had in the past when she broached this topic. The wall that said he was shutting her out. She thought back to that morning, replaying the details.

She'd awakened in Daniel's arms, exchanged sleepy good-morning smiles and a languorous kiss…and rolled out of bed to answer her cell phone. Her father had been looking for her, wondering why she was late for a political brunch.

Nicole's gut clenched as she struggled to recall exactly what had been said in that conversation. She'd still been angry with her father for his blind disregard for her feelings, his manipulation and dictatorial attitude toward her life. Because of the deeply personal issues between her and her father and so that Daniel could sleep if he wanted, she'd taken the phone in the bathroom and prepared to shower. And not seen Daniel again until he appeared from the dark of night in the Colombian prison camp.

She spread her hands and shook her head, at a loss. "I remember taking his call, but…I can't remember what I said that—"

He scoffed. "Of course you don't. Because it meant nothing to you. It was no big deal."

She bristled at his bitter tone. "I argued with my father. I remember that. And that argument was not nothing to me. It changed everything. You changed everything for me."

He snorted his disbelief.

She drew a steadying breath, not wanting to let the discussion evolve into another fruitless shouting match. "I'm sorry, but I just don't recall any specific thing I said that you would interpret as offensive."

His obsidian eyes drilled into hers. "You flaunted the fact that you'd slept with 'that guy from the bayou.' You told him you knew his feelings about me and that was the point." Anger and hurt washed over his face, disproportionate to the comments he quoted.

"But what—?"

"There was more. But that's the gist." His entire body was tense, vibrating with pent-up emotions.

"And that upset you?" She shook her head, confused. "I don't get it."

He bit out another sour curse. "It was the way you said it, Nicole. I heard the meaning behind what you said." A husky rasp thickened his tone, and he jerked his gaze away, visibly steeling himself, grappling for control over his pain and fury.

Nicole held her breath, waiting as he shifted his weight uneasily.

When he raised his gaze to hers again, shadows flickered over his face and a storm brewed in his eyes. "You *used* me, Nicole. You used me, because I represented the worst-case scenario to your father. It wasn't bad enough that you had a night of indiscretion, but I was bayou scum."

Nicole gasped, stunned silent by his accusation. The depth of his pain and anger toward her stole her breath, gnawed her soul. How could he have believed such things about her after the intimacy they'd shared the night before?

Color rose in Daniel's cheeks as he growled, "You couldn't wait to rub your walk on the wild side in Daddy's face. You practically chortled with glee as you told him how we'd done the nasty, repeating for him that I was a *Cajun,* so that he wouldn't miss just how low you'd sunk in your scandalous rebellion. You didn't give him a name, because who I was didn't matter. Only *what* I was."

"That's not true," she whispered, her voice choked with dismay.

He curled his lip in a snarl. "I was the butt of the joke you pulled on Senator Daddy."

She shook her head, reeling, stung by his accusations. "No. You're wrong."

"Am I? You didn't sleep with me to prove a point to your father?"

Her stomach lurched. She had been making a statement to

her father. Just not the one Daniel believed. "You misunderstood. I didn't think of you that way. I'm not a bigot."

His glare was skeptical.

She sighed. "Yes, I was mad at my father, and I flaunted our night together to make a statement, but I cared about you. I wanted to see you again, if—"

"The facts say otherwise." His tone was cold. The bitter anger that rolled off him left her trembling and sick inside.

"What facts? You didn't give me a chance to explain! You left the hotel without telling me where you were going, where I could reach you, how I could—"

"You knew where I was. And you made sure I didn't stay there long enough to cause trouble. You and Daddy certainly arranged for me to be transferred out of state fast enough."

Nicole blinked her confusion. "I don't know what you're talking about."

He scoffed and sent her an impatient frown. "You sure about that? Why else would I get singled out for an exclusive black ops program less than twenty-four hours after sleeping with you? Your father's fingerprints were all over that transfer."

Nicole recalled her father's earlier comment about Daniel leaving town after the night they'd spent together. A prickle raced down her back. "Maybe my father's, but not mine. I was heartbroken that you'd left." Her voice cracked, and she paused to clear her throat, swallow the knot of frustration and disappointment choking her. "I called the Naval base looking for you and kept running into dead ends. I left messages...."

Daniel's gaze narrowed. "You didn't know about the transfer?"

She battled the tears that burned her sinuses. "I swear I didn't. Not until now."

He turned, shaking his head in denial and lifting a disgusted look to the ceiling.

"I never knew where you went," she persisted, "or what happened to you until you rescued me from Colombia." As soon as the words left her mouth, a whole new flood of questions washed through her alreadyspinning thoughts. Her knees buckled, and she braced an arm on the back of the couch to keep from crumpling to the floor. "All this time... you've hated me."

Daniel jerked his chin down and swung a stunned gaze toward her.

Her mouth dried. "You've believed such terrible things...." Her thoughts shifted again, scrambling to keep up as she saw the past five years from a fresh, startling perspective. "But...if you hate me so much, why..." A tremble started in her core, spreading until her entire body shook. "Why did you risk your life to save me? Wh—why are you here now? What's your game?"

An unfathomable expression of shock darkened his face. The tension coiled in him was a palpable vibration that charged the air. "You think I *hate* you? Are you insane?"

"You said—"

Daniel threw his crutch aside with a clatter and closed the distance between them in two stiff strides. Trapping her between the back of the couch and his large body, he captured her head between his hands, his fingers digging into her scalp. Nicole's heart lurched at the flash of heat that blazed in his eyes as his mouth crashed down on hers so hard and fast their teeth clicked and she bit her tongue.

She, in turn, curled her fingers in his hair and returned his frantic kiss with her own desperate need. A thrum of desire surged through her veins, hot and fast. A rumble of satisfaction rose from her throat, and Daniel slid a hand to the base of her back to pull her closer. She tasted blood from her cut tongue but didn't care. She'd waited too long for this, dreamed of having Daniel back in her arms. The kiss was rough, untamed, but his mouth felt right against hers. Preordained.

When Daniel finally tore his mouth from hers, his breathing was ragged, as if he'd just run a long distance. He still held her nape with a firm grip, and his eyes blazed with a dark, dangerous fire.

"I got you out of Colombia," he said in a low growl, "because the thought of you being in the hands of those rebel bastards made me crazy. Knowing they could be starving you, hurting you, *touching* you haunted me. Made me sick."

Nicole raised her hands to stroke his taut jaw. "Oh, Daniel…"

"I have tried every day for the last sixty-three months to get you out of my head. Wanting you is a physical ache I live with every minute of every hour."

Nicole's heart tripped, and her eyes filled with tears. As romantic as Daniel's words were, his expression and his tone reflected misery and frustration rather than rapturous love. The incongruity twisted in her chest.

"I can't erase the memory of how you felt beneath me, how sweet your hair smelled, how warm your kiss tasted, how erotic your moans were when I pushed inside you."

She caught her breath, recalling that earth-shaking moment. Feeling the proof of his current arousal pressed against her belly, her body pulsed with the same anticipation and heat as the night they'd made love.

He sucked in a shallow breath, his eyes fierce. "I wish to God I could hate you, Nicole. Maybe then I could break this hold you have on me. Maybe then I could stop wanting you and missing you so much I hurt." His voice dipped to a whisper. "Maybe then I could move past the betrayal I felt that morning, hearing you tell your father I'd only been the lowly means to your rebellious end."

When he tried to step back, she grabbed his shirt in her

fists and met his gaze with a determined stare of her own. "I never said that. Whatever you thought you heard, you were wrong. I've never thought of you as anything but heroic and thoughtful and maddeningly sexy."

He frowned and turned his head, but she grabbed his chin and dragged his face, his gaze back to hers.

"Listen to me, Daniel. You stole my heart that night in New Orleans." Her voice cracked, but she forged on. "And you broke it the next morning when you left me."

His mouth tightened, and his brow furrowed, as if hearing this truth pained him. She plowed her hands into his hair, pulling him closer. "I felt betrayed that morning, too. But it didn't change my feelings for you. You're not the only one who couldn't forget. Except I'm *glad* you were in my head all those months."

He squeezed his eyes closed, clearly trying to shut her out. Giving him a firm shake, she waited until his gaze met hers again before she continued. Tears dripped onto her cheeks and strangled her voice, but she needed him to hear her out. "My memories of you kept me sane while I was caged like an animal in that godforsaken prison camp. I clung to the hope that I'd survive and see you again. Hold you again. Make love to you again."

He stiffened, his expression tormented. He seized hold of her, framing her face with his hands. "Damn it, Nicole...."

Her gaze drilled his. She was determined to make him understand how she truly felt. "I wasn't entirely surprised to see you when you rescued me, because deep inside, I knew you'd come. I'd prayed you'd come for me. And I—"

"Stop!" he rasped, his eyes suspiciously bright. Beneath her hand, his heart thundered, hard and fast.

Drawing a ragged breath, she licked her tears from the corner of her mouth. Daniel's eyes tracked the path of her tongue, and with a groan, he captured her lips again. His kiss was gentler this time, but no less needy, no less toe-curlingly seductive.

Nicole wrapped her arms around his neck, and he angled his head to deepen the kiss. When he drew harder on her mouth, she responded with equal fervor. When he backed off and soothed her lips with tender kisses, she sighed at the sweetness of his caress. When he searched with his tongue, she met him, stroke for stroke. Tangling, teasing, savoring…

Nicole tugged his T-shirt out of her way, eager to feel the heat of his skin, feel taut muscle and sinew. Soon he'd slipped a hand under her shirt, and his fingers closed over her breast. His palm abraded her beaded nipple through the thin satin of her bra, and the rush of sensation that washed through her stirred a moan from her throat. Without thinking, she hooked one leg around his hip, straining to feel him closer, hating the clothing barrier between them.

"Mon Dieu!" he rasped, and remembering his hurt knee, she panicked briefly that she'd hurt him somehow. But those thoughts fled as he cupped her bottom, lifted her and tumbled with her over the back of the sofa and onto the cushions.

He stretched across her, his weight pressing her into the soft couch, their bodies aligned so that there was no mistaking his desire for her. She wrapped her legs around his, canting her hips forward to rub against his steely length. His breath hissed through his teeth, and with shaking hands, he shoved her shirt and bra up and off of her. With hot, obsidian eyes, he drank in the sight of her, then laved the peak of each breast with his tongue, molded them with his fingers.

Nicole gasped and writhed beneath him, burning and trembling as her need built. She helped him push her jeans down her legs, kicking them to the floor. When he insinuated a hand between her legs, the intimate stroke of his hand shot liquid fire to her core.

"Daniel!" She teetered on the brink of climax, felt herself

careening toward that sweet oblivion, free falling. "Not…yet. I want you…inside me."

He pressed a warm kiss to her lips, then nuzzled her ear. "It's all right. There'll be more. Let go, *cher.*"

The whispered endearment was her undoing. The rich rumble of his voice rolled through her, and the tenderness in his tone melted her bones and pierced her heart. He sank two fingers inside her, and she shattered with a soft cry. She clung to him as she floated back to earth, wanting to weep with joy and love. After so long, she was finally back in Daniel's arms.

His day's growth of beard scraped lightly as he trailed nibbling kisses along the curve of her throat. "We should move," he murmured against her skin. "We're too exposed here."

She tipped her head to meet his gaze. "You think Pilar—?"

"Anyone." He jerked his head toward the front window and door to the porch. "I want to see my target before he sees me."

The reminder that dangerous men were looking for them sent a shiver down Nicole's spine.

"Don't worry, *cher.*" He dragged a crooked finger along her jaw. "I always get my man."

A cocky smile tugged the corner of his mouth, and Nicole grinned. "I can imagine."

Daniel sat up, pulling Nicole with him, and his gaze grew smoky once more. "I've waited a long time for this."

She brushed a kiss on his cheek. "Too long."

With amazing agility and strength, he swept her into his arms and rose from the couch, despite his injury. Nicole struggled, wanting down. "Daniel, no! Your knee!"

"Is fine." His level gaze echoed his assertion. "Let me do this."

She opened her mouth to argue, but having seen the pain and frustration in his eyes when he dealt with his injury over the past several days, she knew she couldn't deny him this chance to reclaim his sense of his manhood. She laid her head on his shoulder and looped her arms around his neck, and as he carried her back to the master bedroom, her heart swelled with affection for her stubborn hero. She caught his occasional grimace but knew he'd rather die than let the ache in his knee interfere with his gallant gesture. Once they were in the room where he'd slept the past nights, he kicked the door closed and followed her down on the mattress.

She fumbled with the button at his fly, murmuring, "You, sir, are overdressed."

"Roger that." He caught her mouth for a quick kiss before rolling on his back to toe off his shoes. Once he'd worked his jeans past his knee brace, she skimmed her hands down his chest to his briefs, pushing them down his legs to join the jeans on the floor.

"That's better." She flashed him a sultry smile, then swung her leg over him to straddle him. He moaned his satisfaction when she settled on top of him, and the teasing light fled his face. His dark eyes held hers, the intensity and hunger in his expression sending ripples of anticipation through her blood.

Once he'd stripped off his shirt, Daniel picked up where they'd left off on the couch. His hands covered her breasts, tweaking and arousing. His kisses ravaged her mouth and explored her bare skin. He moved unerringly from one erogenous zone to another, as if...

"You remember what I like," she said on a breathy sigh as he kneaded and nibbled a sensitive spot at her nape.

He pulled back to meet her gaze, his hands still stroking her. "I memorized everything about you. I remember it all. Every." He kissed her. "Last." Kiss. "Inch."

Her hand smoothed over his chest, and she sighed. "I thought I'd memorized you, but—" She traced a jagged scar on his shoulder. "You've changed." Her fingers drifted to another scar, pale against his tanned skin, and a dull ache jabbed her heart. "I don't think I want to know how you got all these." She let her finger trail to another pucker in his skin. Clearly a healed bullet wound. She shuddered. "You lead such a dangerous life. I hate the idea of you facing death as a regular part of your—"

"Led." His fingers closed around hers, and he pressed his lips to her palm. "Past tense. I've been benched from field-work, remember?"

She laced her fingers with his and resumed her position on top of him. "I know you're disappointed, but…I can't say that I'm sorry. I want you safe."

He tucked her hair behind her ear, his expression serious. "As I want you."

Nicole bent down to kiss him, lingering over his lips, sa-voring the heat and passion. Then, wrapping her fingers around his arousal, she covered him, first with the condom he had waiting and then with her body, taking him deep in-side her. Lacing her fingers with his, she moved with him, the pumping sway of their bodies causing a sweet tension to coil at her core. Closing her eyes, she recalled their first night together and the promise their future held. The magic in their lovemaking. *Say my name.*

Daniel moaned as she rode him, and in her mind, she was back on the rumbling helicopter in Colombia, holding his hand as his eyes, wild with pain, searched hers. *Say my name.*

Her chest contracted remembering the heartache in his eyes when she woke in his hospital room. *Say my name.*

She opened her eyes and met the ebony gaze that had been full of fear when he'd burst into her father's bullet-riddled of-fice to save her from the hired gunmen. *Say my name.*

"Daniel," she whispered in his ear, "I'm here, Daniel. I'm yours."

His grip on her hand tightened. "Nicole…*cher,* I…"

Whatever he'd planned to say was lost as he inhaled a sharp breath and shuddered with his climax. She followed him into the fray, her body inundated with blissful sensation. "Oh, Daniel…"

When she was spent, she collapsed against him, her heart hammering, her lungs panting for air. Silently he held her, his fingers strumming her spine, threading through her hair.

After a moment to catch her breath, Nicole tipped her head back to see his face, and she scraped a fingernail along his stubbled chin. "That was…pretty great, huh?"

He tonelessly hummed his agreement, flashed her a lopsided smile. "No argument here." Silently, he stared at the ceiling for a while before adding, "Damn shame, though."

Nicole propped on an elbow to get a better view of his expression. "What is?"

"The blistering heat between us."

She drew her eyebrows together. His now-serious expression nipped her neck with apprehension. "How is good sexual chemistry a bad thing?"

He spared her a glance before studying the ceiling again. "It muddies the water. Complicates the real issues."

Nicole's felt her stomach swoop in dread. "Meaning?"

"My job, my reason for being here, is to keep you and Pilar alive. Anything else is a distraction."

"Including how we feel about each other," she concluded with a sinking heart.

"Yeah."

And there it was, the protective wall slamming into place around his heart, keeping her distant. She shoved down her hurt, determined not to let her disillusionment show. "So this was just sex. Nothing more?"

"Has to be. I can't afford anything else. Not until this mess is over, anyway."

She released a breath slowly, careful not to let him hear the tremor that seized her. "And after this is over?"

He was silent for so long she wasn't sure he planned to

answer. But, finally, his low voice rumbled through the dark room like distant thunder. "I don't know."

Squeezing her eyes closed, she battled down the sting of disappointment as she curled against his body and rested her head on his chest. Her body was sated, but her heart craved more. She wanted what she feared she might never have from Daniel...his love.

Chapter 10

The next morning, Daniel's side of the bed was empty when Nicole woke. A chill filled her, burrowing to the bone, when she thought of the empty hotel room she'd found after her shower the last time they'd made love. Within minutes of making love last night, Daniel had been withdrawing again, erecting the barriers that kept his heart off-limits to her.

She curled her fingers into the sheets on his side of the bed. The covers were cool. He'd been gone for a while. A knot twisted in her chest, and her pulse kicked. Had he left the house, abandoned her and Pilar?

She drew a slow, calming breath. He wouldn't leave them here. Not with kidnappers after Pilar, men willing to kill anyone who got in their way. Daniel was first and always a protector, a defender. No wonder he was so good at guarding his heart.

Sliding out of bed, she padded over to Daniel's duffel bag and found a T-shirt to wear until she could get her own clothes from the room where Pilar was sleeping. His shirt hung almost to her knees and held a trace of his scent, a sexy combination of man and fresh air and soap. Just that hint of Daniel turned her insides to mush and stirred a flutter in her veins. Surviving his disappearance from her life had been hard enough last time. She wasn't sure she had the strength to handle losing him again. But how did she get past his defenses? Why did he still feel he had to hold her at arm's length?

Maybe she'd be better off guarding her own heart, giving up her delusions of a future with Daniel. She wanted roots, children, cats, a house with a garden and a husband who was there for her every night, physically and emotionally. But Daniel craved danger, adventure. Except for his partner and friend, Alec, he'd been a loner most of his professional life. Could she really expect Daniel to settle down and be content with home and hearth?

The tinkle of a child's laugh drifted to her from down the hall, and she headed to the kitchen to check on Pilar. As soon as she opened the bedroom door, the smell of bacon and fresh coffee greeted her, and Nicole's stomach rumbled. In the kitchen, Pilar sat at the table, a plate of toast and eggs in front of her and a grin on her face. Daniel stood over a pan of sizzling bacon, a pair of tongs in his hand and a chef's apron that read *Laissez les Bon Temps Rouller!* draped over his bare chest—presumably to protect him from popping grease.

Nicole was busy ogling Daniel's wide shoulders and gauging his mood in the wake of their night together, when a chipper voice said, "Good morning, Señorita Nicole!"

Jerking a stunned glance to Pilar, Nicole blinked...grinned. "Good morning, Pilar." Turning back to Daniel, she widened her eyes in query.

He lifted a muscled shoulder, his mouth twitching with amusement. "Don't look at me. I didn't teach it to her. I was as surprised as you when she greeted me that way."

"I taught it to her while we were in Colombia. That and a few other words and phrases. I just never knew if she was retaining any of it since she wouldn't speak."

Daniel turned back to the bacon, flipping the slices in the pan. "Apparently she did."

"Apparently. I'm just…relieved that she feels safe enough now that she's talking again."

He shot a glance over his shoulder at the little girl, then raked an encompassing look at Nicole. She felt his slow, heated perusal like a physical caress.

He arched a black eyebrow, but his expression remained neutral. "That shirt's never looked better."

She flashed him a crooked smile, hoping to elicit one from him. "Hope you don't mind my borrowing it. My clothes got left in the living room last night."

"Pas du tout."

She deflated a bit. Though he seemed in a pleasant mood, an improvement from his grim scowling earlier in the week, he also seemed reserved, except where Pilar was concerned. She watched with a prick of envy as he offered the little girl one of his smiles. "Is it good? *Está bueno?*"

Pilar bobbed her head. *"Sí."* The little girl paused and grinned. "Yes! Good."

Daniel winked at the little girl then shifted his gaze to Nicole. He hitched his head to the coffeepot. "There's coffee."

"Thanks. Smells wonderful." She padded over to pour herself a cup, watching Daniel from the corner of her eye. As she sipped from the ceramic mug, Boudreaux rubbed against her legs, greeting her with a meow. "Hey, Boo. How are you, old man?"

She squatted to pat him and scratch his cheek, which earned her a purr of appreciation. Oreo sat in the chair next to Pilar, eyeing the eggs on her plate and sniffing the air. Casting a quick, guilty look to Daniel, whose back was turned, Pilar plucked a bite of egg from her plate and fed it to Oreo. When she discovered Nicole watching her, the little girl's eyes widened.

Nicole sent her a wink and a grin, then gave Boudreaux a final pat before rising to her feet again.

"Thought I'd take Pilar out in the pirogue today. My family still has a shack in the bayou where my grandmother grew up." Daniel shot her a hooded glance that seemed to be daring her to judge him for his family's simple, live-off-the-land history. "The fishing there is the best in the swamp."

Nicole smiled pleasantly. "I'm sure she'd love it."

He stepped closer to her, holding her gaze. "Want to come with us? I promise not to let the alligators get you."

Daniel stood near enough that she could smell the soap from his shower. Mingled with the mellow aroma of fresh coffee and frying bacon, the scents were a feast for her senses. She laid a hand on his chest, and his heart thumped strong and steady beneath her palm. "I'd love that."

"After breakfast, then." He slid a hand into her hair and nudged her forward for a quick kiss.

Relief flowed through her at this indication that he didn't regret their lovemaking, even if he viewed their liaison as merely an outlet for their sexual chemistry.

A giggle reached them from the table, and they turned as one to find Pilar grinning at them. Daniel cocked an eyebrow. "Should I not have done that in front of her?"

"Didn't your parents kiss in front of you?"

"All the time. But we're not her parents."

Nicole squeezed his shoulder and brushed another kiss across his lips. "Is that bacon ready yet? I'm starved."

"Help yourself." The heat in his eyes as he massaged the nape of her neck with his fingers said he was also hungry… for her. A tingle raced through her from his touch, and just the intensity of his dark gaze made her bones feel as if they were melting.

As he pulled away, he whispered, "Beautiful," so quietly she almost missed it.

While Daniel tended to the bacon, Nicole collapsed in a chair at the table, her legs trembling with the rush of adrenaline and passion Daniel had stirred in her.

Pilar practiced her English throughout breakfast, correctly naming each food they were eating and repeating the list of birds and animals she'd seen the day before while fishing. The scene felt so natural, so blissfully domestic, that Nicole couldn't help but imagine what it might be like to sit around a table with Daniel and two or three children who had their father's dark Cajun good looks.

I can't afford anything else. When Daniel's words replayed in her head, Nicole forced the fantasy of family dinners with him, along with the stab of heartache, to a back corner of her mind. She and Daniel still had a lot of work to do before that dream stood even a remote chance.

With the long, sturdy pole that he dug out of his grandmother's storage garage, Daniel guided his old pirogue through the muddy bayou water, the way to his family's old shack as familiar to him as his own reflection. Nicole and Pilar sat together at the opposite end of the long flat-bottomed boat, pointing out wildlife to each other. A family of turtles on a log, an egret wading in the shallows among the ancient cypress trees, a nutria lumbering along the shore. Smiling to himself, he kept quiet whenever they passed a snake coiled on a branch above them or when he spotted a pair of alligator eyes watching them from the murky depths. He monitored those potential threats, ready to take action if needed but not willing to frighten the females unnecessarily.

As the skiff glided through the water, Daniel's attention drifted to Nicole over and again. Images and sounds from last night flashed in his memory, making his entire body hum and his nerves jangle. Sleeping with Nicole hadn't tamped the fire inside him. The first touch of his lips to hers had been gasoline on the smoldering embers. He hadn't imagined he could burn any hotter for her, but he was discovering new things about himself every day since returning from Colombia with her.

For instance, he found himself enjoying quiet time with Pilar and caught himself wondering what it might be like to take his own daughter fishing or teach his son to bait a crawfish trap. Before this week, he'd never considered himself a father figure. After all, what father spends ninety-nine percent of his time infiltrating dangerous cartels and street gangs in the world's seamiest neighborhoods, then goes mucking through muddy jungles or lurking in remote caves for days waiting for his human prey to make a wrong move?

Except those days were over for him, thanks to his bum knee. So where did that leave him? How did a guy who'd spent so much time in the field make the transition to a life of bedtime stories and lazy afternoons with a fishing pole?

And where did Nicole fit in the picture? He gritted his teeth as a sharp pang of longing gouged his heart. Since that fateful morning five years ago, he hadn't allowed himself to envision a future with her. The parts of that dream his pride hadn't squelched, his life on the black ops team had made impossible.

But last night, having her in his arms, burying himself deep in her welcoming warmth, had revived a glimmer of his youthful optimism. That seed of hope burrowed deep inside him, taunting him and raking his heart with painful illusions of what could never be. His life and Nicole's were still as different and incompatible as ever. They both had a mountain of issues to deal with, careers that took them all over the planet, and ambitions for the future that had no room for family. And she had loyalties to her father that Daniel would never ask her to deny. Because family mattered. *Mémère* had taught him that, and he believed it, even when it meant accepting that Senator White was a permanent fixture in Nicole's life.

Last night had been soul-shaking, and he refused to regret any part of it. But he couldn't let Nicole believe it was more than what it was—hot, even-better-than-he-remembered, burned-into-his-DNA sex.

He watched Nicole tuck her hair behind her ear and laugh at something Pilar said in broken English, and a fist squeezed his lungs. He'd survived without her before, and somehow he'd find a way to move on this time, as well. Once Pilar was back with her father, he'd launch a new career and put Nicole behind him, just like he had five years ago.

When the old shack came into view, a bittersweet nostalgia settled over him. As a boy he'd loved coming out here with his father to fish, and when he'd grown older, he'd taken on the job of caring for the tiny house on stilts for his grandmother, who'd loved to tell him happy stories about her childhood in the swamp.

As they approached, he tried to see the weather-beaten shack through Nicole's eyes. The warped and rotting wood, the rusty tin roof, the moss-covered walls and dingy windows. Yet the shack wasn't a total disaster, since he'd made some repairs and cleaned the inside a few months back, before directing Alec here to use the house as a hideout from the men tailing him.

The pirogue bumped the rickety dock, and Daniel lashed a rope from the boat to a post.

"Can we go inside? I'd love to see where your grandmother grew up," Nicole said as she climbed out onto the floating wooden platform at the base of the stilts.

"Sure. Let's unload the boat, then I'll give you the fifty-cent tour." Daniel handed her the cooler with the lunch they'd packed and gave Pilar the set of cane poles and tackle box.

"Want help?" Nicole asked, offering her hand to help him negotiate the awkward gap between the dock and the pirogue.

He waved her away with a scowl. "I can do it." When he stood, the boat rocked, and unable to put his full weight on his bad leg, he fumbled for balance.

"Daniel." Nicole shoved her hand at him, her blue gaze steady and determined. "Don't be so stubborn. Give me your hand."

He hesitated, hating to appear weak in any way in front of her, but finally grasped her arm at the elbow while she grasped his arm and pulled him onto the dock beside her.

"Thanks," he grunted, then set to work moving their cane poles to the other end of the platform where they'd be fishing.

As promised, he took Nicole and Pilar for a quick tour of the two-room shack, but getting inside required climbing a ladder made of two-by-fours nailed to one of the stilts. Daniel ascended the rungs by pulling himself up until his good leg had a foothold, then performing another pull-up to repeat the process. He didn't give the tactic a second thought until he saw the gleam of appreciation in Nicole's eyes as she squeezed his biceps and wiggled her eyebrows. "Impressive. I like."

In deference to the little girl watching them, he limited his response to grin and a smoldering gaze. But later...

Nicole turned and took in the decor. "Hey, not bad."

Despite its outer appearance, the shack had several new items of furniture, including a new mattress on the bed. He'd paid extra to the delivery man for his help to bring it out on a boat and carry it up the two-by-four ladder. The living space had a small table, a couple of chairs and a kitchen area where he could cook over a camping stove. The tiny back room was a bathroom with a shower, sans hot water, and a toilet hooked up to an underwater septic tank.

"See? All the comforts of home," he said, pulling a wry grin.

Nicole gave him a dubious grin, and Pilar, standing at a window, stared out at the water. "Fishing?"

Daniel chuckled. "Yes, fishing. Let's go."

For the next hour, they tossed their lines off the small dock, swatting mosquitoes and working with Pilar on her English. Despite their chatter, which Daniel knew was scaring away most of the fish, they managed to hook a couple medium-size crappie. When Nicole's line pulled taut, Daniel wrapped his arms around her to help pull in a struggling catfish. The excitement in her eyes when they dragged the catch onto the dock spun a mellow warmth inside him.

"Aye-ee!" Nicole whooped in her best Cajun accent.

"Aye-ee!" Pilar echoed, and Daniel laughed.

"You're pretty pleased with yourself," he teased.

She flipped her hair behind her. "Of course I am. I've never caught a catfish before. This is a red-letter day!"

He raised his eyebrows. "You grew up in Louisiana and never…?" Daniel shook his head. "Well, this *is* an occasion, isn't it?" He pulled her closer and dropped a kiss on her lips. "Congratulations, *cher*."

They took a picture with his cell phone, then released the fish at Nicole's request.

"My work here is done." She laid her pole aside and headed toward the two-by-four ladder. "I'll be right back. Bathroom break."

"Check the seat for spiders before you sit down," he called to her, earning himself a frown of dismay. He grinned and cast his line into the water. "I'm just sayin'."

"Check the seat for spiders?" Nicole grumbled as she marched back to the tiny bathroom. "Not funny." Though, if she was honest, she should be glad the shack had such facilities at all. She could be holding it until they got back to Daniel's house.

Nicole squeezed into the small bathroom and forced the rusty slide bolt into place. Turning, she eyed the toilet warily before lifting the lid and leaning forward to search for creepy crawlies. No spiders but…

The reek of sewage wafted up in a redolent wave that caught her off guard. Gagging, she staggered back a step and gasped for a fresh breath.

But the stench filled the tiny room, filled her nose, filled her memory. In an instant, she was back in her pen in Colombia where the stink of the outhouse and prisoners' waste, of fetid mud and decay hung in the air, an inescapable reminder of the squalor she'd lived in.

The thread of panic and terror she'd held forcibly at bay

since coming home jerked tight around her throat like a garrote. Her vision blurred, and she panted for air as a clawing, frantic horror engulfed her.

Sweat popped out on her face. Her heart thundered. The walls shrank around her.

Spinning toward the door, desperate to get out of the tiny room, she scrabbled with the slide bolt. Her legs shook, and her hands trembled. But the lock wouldn't budge.

Chapter 11

Trapped! She was trapped!

Mewls of fright punctuated her choppy gasps. She had to get out! Had to—

Giving up on the bolt, she slammed her hands on the door. Out! She had to get out!

She heard the guards' cruel laughs. Saw the chain-link fencing. Felt the desperate despondency. The fear. No!

Tears dripped onto her cheeks. "No! No, no, no! Let me out! Please God!"

She barely recognized her own voice, strangled by anxiety and panic, unable to pull herself back from the edge. Screaming, terrified, she battered the door with her fists. "Noooo!"

Over her own moans of fear, the thump of uneven footsteps reached her ears. "Nicole? Nicole! What's wrong?"

"Help me!" she sobbed. "Please!"

The door rattled. "Unlock the bolt."

"I—I can't. I—help me!" Her head spun as she panted shallowly for air. "T-trapped…"

"Okay. Stand back."

Numbly, Nicole stumbled a step away from the door, until her back hit the opposite wall. She squeezed her eyes shut, quivering to her marrow. A cage. Leering guards. Mud. Bugs. Heat. Despair. No, no, no! Not again!

A loud thump sounded at the door, then another. The door buckled, shook. Finally, the slide bolt tore away from the wall, and the door crashed open.

She jerked a startled gaze up, gulping the fresh air.

Through the opening, Daniel frowned at her, rubbing his shoulder. "Nicole? *Cher*, what—?"

"I…I smelled…the camp," she muttered between gasps. He knees gave out, and she slid to the floor. "Prison camp… I couldn't…get out. Trapped… Oh, God—" She buried her face in her hands and sobbed, "So…sc-scared."

Warm arms wrapped around her, and a smooth, deep voice crooned, "It's okay, *cher*. You're safe now. You're free."

Nausea rolled through her, and she shoved Daniel aside to retch in the toilet. Only to catch another waft of putrid stench in the process. "Oh, God," she moaned as the horror crashed down on her again.

"Hey, take deep breaths, Nic. You're hyperventilating." Daniel put a hand under each of her arms and pulled her to her feet. "C'mere, *cher*. You're safe. Breathe for me, Nic."

She stepped to the tiny sink to rinse her mouth out, then cast a sodden gaze toward him, too battered by her roiling emotions and dark memories to do anything but crumple against him. "Hold me. Please."

"Ah, *cher*. Always." He scooped her into his arms and carried her into the main room, where he sat on the bed with her in his lap. "Let it out, Nicole. You've held it in too long. You've earned the right to fall apart a little."

Fall apart.

More like disintegrate. She clung to Daniel's broad shoulders and let his presence, his strength wash through her. If she had to come unraveled, she could think of nowhere she'd rather be than in Daniel's arms. Hiding her face in the curve of his throat, she curled her fingers into his shirt and held on tight, shuddered.

"Let it out," he murmured, and caressed her back.

She'd tried so hard to be strong. To keep it together for… "Pilar," she whispered.

"Is fine." He stroked her hair, kissed her forehead. "I told her to wait outside. I'll check on her in a minute."

Nodding, she closed her eyes, fought to get her ragged breathing under control. "I'm sorry. I just—"

"Don't," he growled, his arms tightening around her. "Don't you dare apologize. You're human. And you've been through hell." He wiped the moisture from her cheeks. "To be honest, I've been waiting for this. I knew it was coming."

She raised a forlorn look to him. "Because I'm weak."

He huffed an exasperated sigh. "No. Because I've seen enough hardened soldiers suffer breakdowns after a trauma to know PTSD can affect anyone. And you have a tender heart. You care. You let things in, including the horrible, evil things men are capable of." He threaded his fingers through her hair and massaged her scalp in a slow, relaxing caress. "It will get to anyone after a while."

"I was fine until…I smelled the septic gasses…" She shivered and nestled closer, savoring the heat of his body. "And then…it was like I was back there…in Colombia…in that pen."

"Smell is one of the most closely linked senses to memory." He slipped a pack of breath mints from his pocket. "This might help get the stink out of your nose."

Nicole accepted a mint gratefully and sucked hard on the

candy. After drawing and exhaling a lungful of musty, though septic-stink free, air, Nicole hummed her agreement. "I've heard that about smell and memory. I know the sm-smell of cut grass…reminds me of my mother."

"Cut grass?"

"Not because she mowed our lawn." She forced a staccato laugh. "But because I used to work in our flower garden with her, pruning roses, weeding daylilies, planting tulip bulbs. You'd think the smell of flowers or soil would make me think of her, but it's grass. Our yard man was almost always out at the same time, mowing, so…" She sucked in another tremulous breath, feeling a fresh rush of tears. "I miss her so much."

Daniel pressed a kiss to her head, squeezing her again in his embrace. "Shrimp boil reminds me of my *grandmére*. For the obvious reasons."

They were quiet for several minutes, except for her soft sniffles as she cried, releasing months of tension and fear and heartache. The silence was comfortable, soothing, and Daniel's gentle ministrations lulled her frantic pulse back to a normal rhythm.

"Nicole?"

She tipped her chin up to meet his gaze and was startled by the pain that flashed in his dark eyes.

"Did they…" He paused, clenching his teeth, as if his question was to vile to speak. "Were you…raped?"

Placing a hand on his cheek, she shook her head. "They knew I was an American, that my father was a senator. I think they left me alone because they feared an American retaliation if any harm came to me. They were in a better position to negotiate with my dad for my release if I was unhurt."

Relief flooded his face, and he sighed. "Thank God."

"I like to think that, in that way, my dad was protecting me, even from thousands of miles away."

Daniel twitched a quick lopsided grin. "Yeah."

Her returned smile faltered as another memory crowded her brain. "But…" A shudder rolled through her.

He cupped her chin and stroked her cheek with his thumb, his expression morphing to reflect her own gravity. "What?"

"There was another woman there for a few weeks. I don't know who she was or where she came from, why they were holding her, but…" Her stomach churned with bitterness. "The guards raped her…almost every day. They made sure I saw." She bit her bottom lip as fresh tears welled in her eyes. "I wanted to help, but I…couldn't. I felt so helpless. Hearing her scream was…a whole new kind of hell."

"Merde," he muttered under his breath, his jaw rigid and anger clouding his eyes.

"When Pilar arrived, I made it my mission to protect her." The maternal determination that had motivated her to guard the little girl surged through her now. "Taking care of her… saved my sanity. Comforting her, shielding her, teaching her, keeping her spirits up gave me something to take my mind off my own plight."

Daniel traced her jawline with the back of his fingers, his attention fully focused on what she was telling him.

"I felt like, in some small way, I had control again. I could protect Pilar, if I did nothing else."

"And soon she'll be going home, thanks to you."

Nicole sighed. "Seeing her leave will be hard. She means a lot to me."

"I can tell." His eyes held a soft glow of compassion and concern that burrowed deep inside her, chasing away the chill her memories of the prison camp evoked.

But here she was safe. Here she was protected. Here she was…loved?

Nicole searched Daniel's expression, and although he'd never professed any feelings for her other than lust, she could've sworn she saw affection and commitment in the way he looked at her. Or was that wishful thinking?

Her heart kicked, and suddenly she needed his kiss more than she needed her next breath. Plowing her fingers into his hair, she dragged his head down and caught his lips with hers. A quiet rumble of satisfaction hummed from Daniel's chest, and he cradled her nape as he angled his mouth for a deeper kiss. Unlike the frantic urgency that had ignited their passion last night, the tenderness of Daniel's lips echoed the comforting gentleness he'd shown her since breaking down the bathroom door to reach her. The warmth of his lips flowed through her like a balm, soothing the last jagged edges of her frayed nerves and filling her with a sense of security and belonging she hadn't experienced since…the night they'd shared in New Orleans five years ago.

After breaking free of her father, she'd buried herself in her nursing career, traveled with the medical mission to Colombia, dedicated herself to guarding Pilar, but only Daniel had given her the deep-seated joy and fulfillment that satisfied her searching heart.

Nicole tangled her fingers in his thick hair, savoring the sweet sensation of holding him, tasting him, feeling the answering tremors that shook him, just as her own body trembled with desire and an overwhelming joy. When he traced her lips with the tip of his tongue, she welcomed him with a soft sigh of pleasure. After a moment, Daniel gentled the kiss again and pulled away to look into her eyes.

"Are you okay? No more flashbacks?" His concern was etched in tiny lines beside his eyes and the softening in his penetrating gaze.

She stroked his cheek and nodded. "Thanks to you." She closed her eyes as he placed a small kiss on her nose, her eyelids, her forehead.

"You're strong, *cher.* Don't forget that. And you are safe now."

When she felt his lips on hers again, she wrapped her arms around his shoulders, wanting to hold him close forever. Wanting that moment to last. Wanting—

A frightened squeal rang through the shack. Tensing with alarm, Nicole and Daniel broke apart, and she scrambled, two steps ahead of him, toward the ladder.

"Daniel!" Pilar screamed. "Daniel!"

"Pilar?" Heart thumping, Nicole scurried down the first few rungs of the two-by-four ladder, only to run into the little girl clambering her way up. "*Mija,* what's wrong? *Qué te pasa?*"

Pilar tugged at Nicole's leg, then pointed toward the water. *"Una serpiente! Una serpiente!"*

Inching down next to the little girl, she looked out at the bayou and saw a snake swimming away, his body wiggling as he glided through the murky water. Nicole shivered.

"He's gone. It's okay, *mija.*" Nicole guided Pilar down the last steps to the dock, allowing Daniel room to descend.

"What did it look like?" he asked. "What shape was its head?"

Nicole shot him a withering glance. "Snake-shaped. All snakes look the same to me." She shuddered and hugged Pilar to her. "Creepy."

With one eyebrow cocked, he divided a considering look between Nicole and Pilar. "I'm assuming our visitor has spoiled your enthusiasm for fishing?"

Nicole nodded. "Kinda."

Heaving a patient sigh, Daniel shuffled toward Pilar's abandoned fishing pole and began to pack up.

Daniel sat at the kitchen table under the pretense of eating a plate of the cookies Nicole and Pilar had baked that afternoon for dessert, but his focus never left the woman snuggled on the couch. She read a book to the drowsy girl in her lap while Boudreaux napped at her feet.

If keeping his mind, his attention off Nicole had been difficult before, now it was impossible. Daniel dragged a hand over his face and exhaled a harsh breath. Over the past few days, she'd systematically chipped away at his defenses until he could no longer deny how important she was to him. How much he wanted her back in his life. How much the thought of losing her again frightened him.

And because nothing had been settled between them, despite their recent cease-fire, losing her was still a real possibility. *Merde!*

The terror that had filled her eyes when he'd busted through the bathroom door at the shack had sucker punched him. Knowing the horrors she'd seen and survived wrenched inside him and fueled the burning anger toward her captors. Realizing how much worse it could have been for her chilled him to the marrow.

Her heartbreaking sobs and tremors had been hard to witness. Wanting to take away her suffering, but being helpless to do more than mutter useless platitudes and provide a shoulder for her tears, left him raw and restless.

Daniel shoved another peanut butter cookie in his mouth and chewed, tasting nothing, his mind preoccupied. Having spent so much of the past five years trying to forget Nicole, Daniel didn't know what to do with the feelings she was awakening in him. His knee-jerk response to her was still to keep his guard up, waiting for the left hook he hadn't seen coming.

But maybe the real knockout punch was her claim that he'd gotten it all wrong five years ago. That she hadn't been using him in her rebellion against her father, that her feelings had been real, that she held no prejudice toward his family history and Cajun heritage. If that were true, if that night had meant as much to her as it had to him, then he'd thrown away a precious gift. He'd walked out on the best thing to ever happen to him. He'd been a damn fool.

"Couillon," he scolded himself under his breath and shoved the plate of cookies away. Folding his arms over his chest, Daniel rocked back in the kitchen chair and listened to Nicole pronouncing words for Pilar to repeat.

"Shirt."

"Shirt," Pilar echoed.

"Shoes."

"Shoes."

"Socks."

The soft brush of fur and a quiet meow roused him from his observation. Glancing down, he found Oreo rubbing on his leg. Lamby lay on the floor near where Oreo paced. Daniel picked up the toy and tossed it across the floor. Oreo scampered after it.

Hearing the skitter of cat feet, Pilar sat forward and grinned at Oreo. "Silly cat!"

When the little girl tried to scurry after Oreo, Nicole caught the back of Pilar's pajamas, bringing her up short. "Nope, it's bedtime."

Bedtime was a word Pilar knew, and she poked out her bottom lip in disappointment.

Nicole cast a disgruntled look at Daniel. "And thanks for getting her riled up again after I spent thirty minutes calming her down for bed."

He spread his hands and gave her a what-did-I-do? look.

She quirked a lopsided grin, taking the edge out of her chastisement.

To redeem himself, Daniel shoved to his feet and clapped his hands together the way his father used to before he'd lay down the law. "C'mon, tadpole. Time to *fais do-do.*"

Pilar continued pouting, and Daniel, using the antique

cane he'd found in his *grandmére's* closet, crossed the room to her. With a fake growl, he wiggled his eyebrows playfully and scooped her under his arm like a football. After a high-pitched squeal that shattered his eardrum, peals of girlish laughter tumbled from Pilar as he toted her back to her bed.

Nicole groaned as she followed them. "She'll never fall asleep now."

Daniel dumped Pilar in the pile of pillows and blankets, and her giggles turned his insides to mush. Nicole wasn't the only one who'd miss Pilar when she went home.

"Now." He arched one eyebrow in a mock scowl and pointed to the bed. "*Fais do-do.* Go to sleep." Then, for good measure, he added the Spanish, *"Duérmete."*

He turned to limp out of the room, and hearing scrambling and rustling sheets behind him, he stopped at the door next to Nicole and faced the bed again. Pilar had crawled out of the bed and knelt bedside it, hands folded and head bowed.

He sent a side glance to Nicole, and whispered, "What do you think little girls pray for?"

She smiled at him. "Same thing big girls do. Safety, their family, their dreams. Oh, and to marry Justin Bieber."

He snorted. "Who?"

Nicole rolled her eyes.

After making the sign of the cross, Pilar crawled back into the covers and pulled the sheet up to her chin. Nicole moved to the side of the bed and kissed the girl's head. "Good night, *mija.* Sleep well."

Daniel switched off the light and closed the door behind Nicole. Remembering how they'd passed the evening after Pilar's bedtime last night, he gave Nicole a hungry glance and murmured, "How fast do you think she'll fall asleep?"

She stepped close to him, her hand sliding up his chest and a coy smile tugging her lips. "Not fast enough."

* * *

Thirty minutes later, Nicole had finished straightening the kitchen, and she dropped wearily onto the sofa next to Daniel.

When he opened his arms and patted his chest, she happily accepted the invitation to snuggle against him and rest her head on his shoulder.

"So...I've noticed you've been using a lot of Cajun French and colloquial phrases this week." She tipped her head back to gauge his reaction.

He tensed a bit. "That bother you?"

"Not at all. Except that it might confuse Pilar while she's trying to learn English." She paused. "And...I don't recall you using so much French in the past. "

"I didn't. When I was around anyone except my grandmother, I made a point of not using French and keeping the Cajun accent out of my voice."

"Why?"

He snorted. "You have to ask?"

"Apparently so."

He drew a large breath, as if explaining himself were a burden. "You know the stereotypes about Cajuns in Louisiana. We're uneducated...which in some ways is true. A lot of folks around here, especially the older generations, didn't bother finishing high school, since they made their living off the land, harvesting oysters, crawfish and shrimp. Hunting alligators for their meat and hides. Raising catfish for market." He drilled a hard look on her. "But that doesn't mean we're stupid."

"I know that."

"And yet we're the butt of Boudreaux jokes around the state."

She sighed. "As long as there is ignorance and cruelty in the general population, there will be bigoted jokes. And not just about Cajuns."

"Yeah, well…we're also seen as backward, since some of the older generation have been slow to embrace modern technology."

"Or it could be said that they're trying to preserve traditions passed down for generations. I love the idea that someone values their culture's history enough to do that."

"I—" he started, then snapped his mouth shut, apparently unable to find a counter-argument. "Regardless, most people have preconceived, stereotyped ideas about Cajuns. For instance…when I met my cousin's and your friends on your prom night, your date started calling me Boudreaux as soon as he heard my accent and learned where I was from."

"Grant Holbrook was a jerk. A fact I learned well enough when he abandoned me and went to prom with your cousin when I wouldn't leave the kitten to die in the sewage drain."

Daniel grunted. "Doesn't say much about my cousin, either. Although, in her defense, she saw the error of her ways and has straightened up in recent years."

Nicole smoothed a hand over Daniel's chest. "Last I heard, Grant's still a jerk."

"Yeah, well…he did me a favor. He showed me that I needed to be proactive in the way people perceived me. I had to erase the swamp from my voice and be better than the next guy in everything I undertook. I had to try harder, run faster, be smarter, reach higher and never make excuses. I was determined to prove critics wrong and never let an undeserved stigma keep me from achieving my goals."

Nicole sat up, swinging her feet to the floor, and gave Daniel a narrow-eyed scrutiny. "You know what I think?"

He raised his eyebrows and cocked his head slightly, inviting her to continue.

"I think you're the one who has a problem with your heritage."

Daniel scoffed loudly. "Bull."

"You're certainly sensitive about it. You assumed the worst five years ago when you heard half of a conversation I had with my father. Your prove-the-critics-wrong philosophy reeks of a personal prejudice at the least and an insecurity about your roots at worst."

Daniel's dark eyebrows snapped together. "Wanting to do my best, be the best, doesn't mean I'm prejudiced," he growled. "I love my *grandmére* and everything she taught me about life on the bayou."

"I'm not saying you don't love your family. But—"

"*But* even my parents recognized that they had to move to another part of the state if they wanted to achieve the goals they had for themselves and for me. Cajun people have always isolated themselves. On purpose—with their language, their location, their traditions, their lifestyle…"

"So do dozens of other cultural groups around the country. The Gullah in South Carolina. The Amish in Pennsylvania and Ohio. Hasidic Jews in New York—"

"All right!" He held up a hand to hush her. "Point taken. But that doesn't change the fact that being a member of one of those cultures means living with the stereotypes associated with that culture. I chose to stay a step ahead of the stereotypes. I prefer to eliminate any obstacle before it becomes a problem."

Nicole shook her head and studied him with a heavy heart. "And I find it sad that you saw your heritage as an obstacle rather than a strength."

"I don't—" Daniel's phone chirped, interrupting him, and he checked the screen before answering. "It's Jake."

Nicole's sat forward, anxious to hear what Jake had learned.

"LeCroix."

She watched Daniel's expression closely for clues to what Jake had to say.

"Tell me you found the judge." He jammed his finger in his other ear as if he was having trouble hearing, then glanced up and met her expectant gaze. Answering her unspoken question, he gave a quick nod. "Excellent." When his forehead creased with consternation, Nicole's pulse kicked up. Was something wrong?

"No, no. I can't say that I blame him. Hang on." Daniel met her gaze. "Get Pilar. The judge wants to talk to her. He needs proof that she is with us and isn't in danger."

Of course, the judge would be dubious, need proof of life and his daughter's well-being before he'd cooperate. Nicole nodded and started down the hall. "I'll wake her up."

She walked quietly to the bed where Pilar snoozed peacefully and brushed the hair back from her face. "Pilar, *mija*. Wake up." Nicole had to jostle the girl and say her name a few more times to rouse her from her slumber. When she had the girl's attention, she motioned for her to follow. Taking Pilar's hand, she led the groggy girl into the living room.

Pilar squinted against the light and blinked curiously at Daniel, her expression reflecting apprehension.

Daniel held out the cell phone and smiled his reassurance to Pilar. "Your father wants to talk to you," he said in flawless Spanish.

"Papi?" Pilar's eyes widened, and she snatched the phone from Daniel. *"Papi? Papi!"*

Nicole watched the hopefulness in the child's eyes morph to joy, then Nicole's eyes filled with tears as Pilar's puddled with moisture and the child's small shoulders shook.

She pieced together parts of the conversation as Pilar half laughed, half sobbed to her father. Yes, she was fine, she was safe, she told him. Miss Nicole has taken care of her. She was trying to be brave, she said, her chin trembling, and a tender ache stole Nicole's breath. Pilar missed him, missed her mother and sister. She sobbed harder now, and Nicole recalled what they'd learned about her mother and sister being murdered in front of her.

Her heart breaking, she wrapped Pilar in a hug that she knew could never take away the horrible memories or replace the family she'd lost.

Pilar sniffed loudly and told her father, *"Te quiero."* I love you.

She handed the phone back to Daniel, who stroked her head and flashed her another encouraging grin as he raised the phone to his ear. "Jake?"

Pilar buried her face on Nicole's shoulder. She held Pilar and rubbed the girl's back while she followed Daniel's end of the conversation.

"Good enough? Will he trust you?"

The hard lines in his face relaxed a degree, which Nicole took as a good sign.

"Where are you? Do you have a tail?" Daniel shifted his gaze away, clearly concentrating on what Jake was telling him. "How long will it take you to get him out of the country?" He paced a few steps, then turned and limped back toward her. "I just think we need someplace out of the way, neutral ground to make the transfer. Somewhere we know we aren't being watched."

Nicole tried to get Daniel's attention, using hand signals and mouthing, *Why not here?*

He dismissed her idea with a shake of his head, then told Jake, "Good idea. I'll look into getting a boat."

A boat? Nicole furrowed her brow.

"When will you be there? It'll take us a couple hours to reach international waters."

She blinked. They were boating out into the Gulf of Mexico?

"Right. I'll handle that from my end. Text me the GPS coordinates of the rendezvous point. Yeah. Okay. See you then." He thumbed the disconnect and looked up at Nicole with a sigh.

"We're taking Pilar to meet her father out on the Gulf?"

He jerked a nod. "That's the plan." He paused and twisted his mouth in thought. "I have to rent a boat by tomorrow night. We're meeting Jake and Castillo in roughly thirty-six hours."

"We can use my father's cabin cruiser. He keeps it docked at a private marina on Grand Isle." Still hugging Pilar close, she held her hand out for the cell phone. "I'll call him now and make the arrangements."

Daniel shook his head and tucked the phone in his shirt pocket. "I've told you I don't want him involved in this. We have to keep a low profile."

"He's not—" Nicole stopped herself, feeling her blood pressure rise. Before she hashed this out with Daniel, she needed to put Pilar back to bed.

She nudged the girl back by the shoulders and smiled warmly. "You'll see your father—*Papi*—soon. I promise. *Pronto.*"

Pilar nodded, a bright hope in her eyes, though Nicole couldn't be sure how much Pilar understood. Had her father explained anything in their brief conversation?

She led Pilar back to the bedroom and tucked her into bed. As she waited for the girl's eyes to droop and her breathing to deepen with sleep, Nicole mentally rehearsed her argument in favor of including her father in the loop, allowing him to help. With one call, she could arrange for her father's forty-foot cabin cruiser to be fueled, stocked and ready for them within hours.

After pressing a light kiss to Pilar's forehead, Nicole walked back out to the living room and, crossing her arms over her chest, she faced Daniel. "I trust my father."

"Good for you," he said without looking up from the map he was studying. "I don't."

"Because he's just like you."

Now Daniel glanced up, his eyebrow arched skeptically. "Excuse me?"

"The reasons you hate my father—his interference in our relationship five years ago and his giving up your cover to General Ramirez's men—he did both because he wanted to protect me. As extreme and ill-advised as they seem to us in hindsight, he just wanted to save my life. You've done some pretty extreme things for the same reason. Because you both care about me."

Daniel tensed his jaw, making the muscle jump. "I care about you, yes. I'm nothing like your father."

She ignored his denial, taking a seat beside him and spreading her hands in entreaty. "What's more, I care about both of you. I *love* both of you."

Though he clearly tried to mask his reaction, she saw the telltale twitch in his muscles, as if he'd received an electric jolt. She caught the flicker of heartbreaking emotion and surprise that passed over his face in an instant, before he slammed the protective walls back in place.

He dropped his gaze back to the map, but his hands weren't quite as steady now. "The fewer people involved, the better our chances of getting Pilar back to her father safely." He tossed her a side glance. "That is what you want, isn't it?"

"Of course, but my father already knows about Pilar. Seems to me, keeping the boat arrangements within the circle of people already privy to our situation is the wisest move." She thrust her hand out for the phone. "Let me call him. We don't have time to find another boat and still make our meeting with Jake and Castillo on time. I'll ask him to arrange for us to get the key from the marina manager."

Daniel stared at her, his dark eyes bright with penetrating

intensity. Finally he growled under his breath and slapped his cell phone in her hand. "Warn him not to breathe a word of this to anyone. He's not to tell the marina manager anything except to have the cruiser ready to sail by sunrise."

Nicole nodded and gave him a grateful smile, careful not to appear gloating. His capitulation was a small victory for her, but she didn't presume to believe he was ready to cede the war with her father. Still, it was a step in the right direction. Maybe there was hope for them yet.

Chapter 12

The plan was simple. Drive to Grand Isle, take Senator White's cabin cruiser out into the Gulf of Mexico, rendezvous with Jake and Judge Castillo at the set GPS coordinates. After he handed Pilar over to Jake and her father, Jake would deliver the judge and his daughter back to the judge's safe house in Colombia via the same means he'd gotten Castillo out of the country. With Pilar no longer in her custody, the threat to Nicole should be eliminated, and his protection would no longer be needed. They'd be free to go their separate ways. Easy peasy. Clean and simple.

He should feel relieved. This mess was almost over. Mission accomplished.

So why was his chest contracting so tightly he could barely breathe? Why were his nerves jumping and his pulse racing like he'd just run a marathon?

Nicole rode silently in the passenger's seat of the rental car they'd picked up in Baton Rouge. He'd chosen a rental company that would send a driver to his grandmother's house to get them and take them back home tonight. He cast a side glance at Nicole.

I love both of you.

He'd waited half his life to hear her tell him she loved him. And, *damn it,* when she had, her father's presence had overshadowed what should have been his. He'd even had to friggin' share Nicole's declaration of love with the infernal man. Daniel gritted his teeth. He couldn't ask Nicole to exclude her father from her life for his sake, so any future he tried to build with her would always include the man who'd offered him to the enemy like a Thanksgiving turkey. Her loyalties would always be divided.

Irritation plucked at him, and he shifted in the driver's seat, restless and ready to get out to sea.

"We're almost there," Nicole said, reading his mood correctly. "The road to the marina is just past this turn a few miles."

He nodded and used the rearview mirror to check on Pilar. The little girl met his gaze in the mirror, and her doelike brown eyes turned his heart inside out. Nicole wasn't the only one who'd miss Pilar. And wasn't that a kick in the pants? A hardened undercover counter-terrorist agent letting a little girl's giggle and innocent eyes burrow under his tough hide. "*Pronto,* tadpole. *Pronto.*"

Pilar nodded, and her grin reflected her eager anticipation of seeing her father.

When they reached the turnoff to the marina, Nicole directed him to the crushed-shell parking lot and aimed her finger to a large boat moored at the end of the wooden pier. "That's it. The *Serendipity.*"

Daniel cut the engine and studied the cabin cruiser. "The marina manager has the key?"

"He's supposed to. I'll get it and meet you two down there."

Daniel climbed out of the car and retrieved the cane he'd been using the past two days. The loose shells made walking more difficult, and he had his head down, watching his step, when Nicole gasped.

He looked up to see what had startled her, then followed the path of her stunned gaze to the manager's office.

Senator White stalked down the sidewalk toward them. On his heels were two well-dressed Hispanic men.

Daniel stiffened, alarms clanging in his head and white-hot fury roiling inside him.

He'd given her a clear mandate, specific directions. No one else could know about their meeting with Jake. Her father was not to be involved or informed of their plans beyond their need to use the boat for the day.

Had she defied his directives and betrayed his trust? *Again?*

Acid bit his gut hard as he saw his future in clear focus— Nicole deferring to her father, Nicole not trusting him, Nicole second-guessing him and undermining their relationship because of her shaky faith in him. Which, in truth, meant he had no future with Nicole.

Swallowing hard, Daniel choked down the bitter taste of his hurt and anger, and cut a narrow-eyed gaze to Nicole. "I told you your father couldn't be trusted. Apparently, neither can you."

A wounded look crossed her face, and she opened her mouth to defend herself. But Daniel knew all he needed.

"Take Pilar and go wait at the boat. I'll handle this." He hobbled forward, hating the disadvantage he was at because of his damn knee. With his free hand, he unzipped his jacket for faster access to the sidearm in his shoulder holster. The patter of footsteps behind him told him Nicole and Pilar were following him rather than doing as he'd ordered.

When he sent Nicole a glare, she raised her chin and scowled back. "He's my father. *I'll* talk to him."

"Nicole, honey, how are you?" The senator's booming voice reverberated across the marina. He drew Nicole close for a hug, and she gave her father a tight smile and a peck on the check.

"Dad, what are you doing here? I told you we didn't need help with the *Serendipity*."

The senator cocked his head. "Just the same, it is my boat, and I prefer to be the one who pilots it. Besides, I thought it would be nice to have the opportunity to get to know your Mr. LeCroix better."

Her Mr. LeCroix? What did he mean by that? Daniel wondered but shoved the thought aside in the interest of more pressing matters. Like the two men standing with Nicole's father.

"Who are you?" Daniel asked the men, his tone less than polite.

"Ramon Diaz," the taller of the two men said, stepping forward to shake Daniel's hand. "I'm the attaché to the Colombian embassy who has been working with the senator and Miss White in returning Pilar Castillo to our country. And this—" he indicated the shorter yet well-muscled man with him "—is Jorge Menendez, my associate."

Daniel sized Menendez up. The bulge at the waist of his coat was, no doubt, a gun, and the eagle eye with which he regarded the group told Daniel the term *bodyguard* might be more accurate than *associate*.

Diaz turned to the little girl, who scuttled closer to Nicole's legs, giving the stranger a wary scrutiny. "And this, I presume, is Pilar."

Nicole shook Diaz's hand, as well, her expression guarded. "What brings you here today, Mr. Diaz?"

The attaché chuckled. "I'd think that was obvious. Pilar

Castillo is a Colombian citizen, and I'm here to take custody of her."

Daniel tensed and, from the corner of his eye, saw Nicole square her shoulders.

"We've been in New Orleans for days," Diaz continued, "trying to make just such arrangements. But you disappeared with her."

If he was simply here to take custody of Pilar, why did Diaz feel he needed a bodyguard for the meeting? Was the muscle for his protection or for Pilar's? Did he expect trouble from the goons who'd tried once to kidnap the girl?

"How did you know we would be here?" Nicole asked, echoing Daniel's next thought.

"The senator told me," Diaz returned blandly.

Nicole sent her father a stunned look, which the senator met with a guilty frown and shake of his head.

"I called him to see if he'd had any news from you, Miss White," Diaz explained, "and he filled me in on your little jaunt today."

"Only after you threatened to go to the media with accusations that I was an accomplice to kidnapping and harboring an illegal immigrant," Senator White growled, then shot Nicole an apologetic look. "I'm sorry, honey. I was in a bad position, and God knows the last thing I need is any more scandal or bad press."

Nicole scowled her disappointment in her father and faced Diaz. She gave the attaché a tight, businesslike grin. "Well, as much as I appreciate your help in finding Pilar's father and keeping this whole situation amicable, the truth is your assistance is not needed. We've found Judge Castillo and are meeting him today to return Pilar to his custody."

Daniel's gut dropped, and he gritted his teeth. *Merde!* Why had she told Diaz their plans? Too much was still at risk. Too much could still go wrong. Embassy official or not, Diaz was a wild card, an unknown, and Daniel didn't trust him.

Diaz and Menendez exchanged a startled look.

"Castillo is coming here?" Menendez asked.

"No," Nicole said. "We're going to him. Meeting him at a neutral location."

"Where?" Diaz asked.

"Doesn't matter," Daniel cut in before Nicole could show all their cards. "We have the matter under control. Your embassy doesn't need to get involved."

"LeCroix, is it?" Diaz asked shifting his attention to Daniel. "We are already involved... As is proper protocol." His eyes narrowed as he shoved his hands in the pockets of his dress pants and twisted his mouth in a thoughtful moue. "But I'm not an unreasonable man. If you have a custody transfer set up, there is no point in changing those plans."

Daniel's neck prickled with suspicion, but Nicole released a relieved sigh and flashed a bright smile. "Thank you."

"On one condition," Diaz added.

Nicole's smile dimmed, her eyebrows pulling together in a dubious frown. "What condition?"

"We accompany you to the rendezvous point to verify the exchange for the Colombian government."

Daniel squeezed the grip of his cane. "No way in hell."

Blinking her surprise, Nicole shot him a dark look. "Daniel, why—?"

"No. We go alone, as planned." His returned look asked her to trust him. Their plans had been leaked, but he could still salvage the mission. All that mattered was seeing Pilar safely delivered to her father. He only asked for Nicole to have faith in him, give her cooperation.

Diaz heaved an impatient sigh. "It seems to me you have but two choices. One, you allow us to go with you and verify that the girl is, in fact, given back to her father, or two, I call the local sheriff and Coast Guard and have you arrested for kidnapping, child endangerment, child trafficking and anything else I can make stick. This will become an international incident, because I will see to it your government is called to task."

"Now see here," Senator White started, aiming a finger at Diaz.

"Dad." Nicole gripped her father's arm and sent him a pleading look for calm. Turning back to Diaz, she employed another ingratiating smile. "Mr. Diaz, what if we verified the transfer for you. We could send you proof, say pictures of Pilar with her father, or—"

"Pictures can be altered," Menendez countered.

Daniel cursed under his breath. "We're wasting time here."

Pilar's wide brown eyes darted from one man to the next, clearly alert to the tension in their voices. Daniel gave her a brief considering glance. His goal was to get Pilar back to her father. Diaz had thrown a monkey wrench in that plan, but not an insurmountable obstacle.

As much as he hated changing their plans, getting locked in a diplomatic stalemate benefitted no one. He nailed a grim stare on Diaz. "Fine. You can go with us and verify." He hitched his head to Menendez. "But your *associate* stays here. Take it or leave it."

Menendez glowered at Daniel before exchanging a silent but pregnant look with Diaz. The attaché sniffed and scratched his nose, then nodded. "*Si,* he will stay here."

Menendez's expression clearly displayed his hatred of this plan. "Diaz—"

The attaché raised his hand to quiet his associate. "Shall we go, then?"

Senator White rallied, as if afraid the situation could backfire if he didn't hurry. He put a hand on Nicole's and Pilar's shoulders and directed them down the pier.

Daniel opened his mouth to stop the senator but reconsidered. If things went sideways, the senator was safer on the *Serendipity* with them than alone here with Menendez. Sighing his resignation and taut with apprehension, Daniel followed the rest of the group to the senator's cabin cruiser.

While the others boarded, Daniel slipped out his cell phone, hoping to send Jake a quick text, warning him that the attaché and senator were accompanying them.

No signal. *Enfer!*

The two-way radios they'd brought for communication with Jake would only work when they were within five miles of him.

Before Diaz could enter the living space, Daniel pulled him aside and searched him for weapons. He found the man's 9 mm Beretta in an ankle holster and confiscated it, much to the attaché's displeasure.

"This is a simple custody transfer. Why would you need a weapon?" Daniel asked coolly.

"Because the same people who took Pilar in Bogotá, who tried to kidnap her in New Orleans, are still out there. Anything could happen."

"I've thought of that, and contingencies are covered." With a nod of dismissal, Daniel strode inside the main cabin.

While Nicole's father headed to the cockpit and piloted them out of the marina, Nicole opened an overhead bin and removed a child-size life jacket for Pilar. After helping the girl into hers, he showed the men where the other life preservers were stored in case of emergency, then followed the girl out to the bow to watch the waves. Diaz followed the women outside and planted himself in a deck chair.

Joining the senator upstairs in the cockpit, Daniel stepped close to Nicole's father, so his low tone could be heard over the rumble of the engine and whipping slipstream. "Do you keep any weapons onboard?"

The senator cut a startled look to him, then nodded to a compartment beside them. "I have a loaded gun—a Colt .45 single-action revolver that was my grandfather's—locked in there. I thought it was prudent to have some means to defend myself and my passengers in light of recent news about pirates and the violence crossing the border out of Mexico."

Daniel arched an eyebrow. "If you're looking to defend yourself against pirates and drug runners, you better consider an automatic rather than a single action." He sighed. "But keep the Colt handy. Just in case."

The senator gave Daniel a long, hard look. "Listen... LeCroix, I know we have a lot of history. You have every right to hate me and what I did."

Daniel gave him only a brief glance of acknowledgment before setting his jaw and turning his attention to the Gulf.

"I'm not proud of some of the things I've done. But I'd do them all again, if it meant saving my daughter's life. She is everything to me."

Daniel kept silent, searching the horizon for signs of trouble.

"Nicole has deep feelings for you, LeCroix."

Though he tried not to show any reaction to that statement, Daniel felt his muscles give a telltale twitch.

"And because of that, I'd like to bury the hatchet."

When the senator paused, Daniel glanced at him. "Bury it where? In my back?"

Nicole's father shook his head. "I'm trying to offer a truce. A cease-fire for my daughter's sake."

Flexing and balling his hand in agitation, Daniel faced the senator. "I have deep feelings for Nicole, too. I'd like to think we have a future together, but recent events have proven that's nothing but a pipe dream."

The senator drew his gray eyebrows together. "Recent events?"

"Like our extra passenger, Diaz. You put your political well-being ahead of your daughter's safety."

The man's eyes widened. "I didn't—"

"I don't trust you, and I'm learning I can't trust Nicole when it comes to you, either."

Senator White raised his chin, and his expression hardened. "Do not ever question my motives regarding my daughter. Her safety and happiness are my top priority. Always."

"Then act like it." Before heading back down to the lower level, Daniel slapped a scrap of paper with the GPS coordinates of the rendezvous spot on the dash and aimed a finger at the locked compartment. "Have your weapon ready in case it's needed."

On the ladder to the main deck, Daniel cast a glance to the senator to be sure he'd complied. Nicole's father slid the Colt revolver in the waist of his pants at the small of his back and met Daniel's gaze with a nod.

Nicole stood with Pilar at the bow of the *Serendipity,* trying to soothe the knots in her stomach and cool the burn in her heart. If the tension over the Colombian attaché's surprise appearance and her impending goodbye to Pilar weren't enough, Daniel's earlier caustic comment ate at her, leaving her stinging and raw.

I told you your father couldn't be trusted. Apparently, neither can you.

Daniel had avoided her for the past hour and a half as they cruised out into the Gulf of Mexico, and she had tried to stay busy, keep her mind off the newest rift between them, by entertaining Pilar.

The little girl had shaken off the tension from the confrontation on pier, clearly focused on seeing her father, the seagulls clamoring near the boat, and the spray of water splashing her face as she hung over the railing at the bow.

Suddenly Pilar's face brightened, and she pointed toward the horizon. *"Papi!"*

Shielding her eyes from the glare of sun, Nicole squinted at the spot Pilar indicated.

"Mira, Nicole! *Papi!"* Pilar squealed and waved an arm excitedly.

Sure enough, a small boat with two men aboard rocked in the waters ahead of them. One of the men, his hair as black as Pilar's, stood and waved an arm back at Pilar. The second man wore a telltale cowboy hat.

The girl's shouts and excitement brought Diaz and Daniel to the railing, as well. Daniel lifted a pair of binoculars and confirmed that the other boat was Jake and Pilar's father. "Anchor here!" he shouted to the cockpit. "Let them come to us."

Her father gave a nod of understanding, and the drone of the *Serendipity's* engine quieted.

Daniel raised a hand radio to his mouth. *"Serendipity* to Connelly. You there, cowboy? Over."

"Roger that. Over," Jake's voice crackled over the radio.

"We have extra company. Over."

"So I see. What's the plan? Over."

Daniel cast a glance at Diaz and scowled. "Same plan. We're anchoring here. Copy?"

"Roger that."

Daniel's jaw tightened, and he stared across the Gulf at the small fishing boat that was even now turning toward them. Raising the radio to his lips again, he added, "Greek protocol."

Nicole furrowed her brow, shooting him a question in her glance. He returned a hard stare but said nothing.

Having dropped anchor, her father came down from the cockpit and joined her at the bow railing. He put his arm around her shoulders. "You've done well, Nicole, caring for Pilar the way you have. You can be proud."

A bittersweet pang sliced through Nicole's chest and squeezed her lungs. She stroked Pilar's head and winked at the girl when Pilar angled her a grin. "It's hard to let her go. I'll miss her so much."

Her father patted her arm. "I know you will. But you can stay in touch."

When she moved to hug her father, her hand brushed something hard at his back. A gun. She gave him a puzzled look.

"LeCroix's idea," he said quietly.

Pilar bounced on her toes, clapping her hands, as Jake steered the fishing boat within a few yards of the *Serendipity*. "Papi!"

From the fishing boat, Mario Castillo beamed at his daughter and blew kisses. "Pilar! *Mija!*"

Diaz crowded in next to Nicole and her father at the railing, and Castillo's attention shifted to the new face. And his smile faltered.

Nicole barely had time to register the judge's reaction before chaos erupted.

Castillo pointed an accusing finger at Diaz.

Diaz snatched the gun from her father's back. Aimed at the fishing boat. Cocked the hammer and fired. Jake jerked and stumbled backward, and Castillo shrank to a crouch.

Pilar screamed, and adrenaline surged through Nicole. Fear and stunned confusion sent her pulse skyrocketing.

Producing a gun from under his jacket, Daniel swung his weapon toward Diaz. "Drop it!"

Jake lunged at Judge Castillo and tumbled with Pilar's father into the water on the far side of the fishing boat.

His primary target hidden behind the fishing boat, Diaz turned his weapon toward Daniel. Cocked the hammer.

As Nicole turned to grab Pilar, ready to take evasive and protective measures, her father tightened his grip on her shoulders and shoved her behind him.

"No! Pilar!" Panic swelling in her chest, Nicole fought to get past her father, but he held her arm tightly and shielded her with his body.

"Nicole, stay back!" her father growled.

Daniel and Diaz glared each other down in a deadly game of chicken. Nicole stared in horror at the weapon aimed at Daniel, and a numbing terror swept through her, strangling her breath.

"Drop the weapon," Daniel snarled, his dark eyes flinty and unyielding.

"Not until Castillo is dead." Diaz reached Pilar in one giant step and, snaking an arm around her, he hauled her back against him in a death grip. "He is responsible for my brother's murder!"

The girl's eyes rounded, wild with fear, and she cried, "Nicole!"

Only someone who knew Daniel the way Nicole did would have noticed the small tic in his jaw muscle, the slight catch in his breath. Diaz's move had rattled Daniel. Because Daniel loved Pilar.

Diaz cut a quick glance to the water, holding Pilar between him and Daniel. A human shield. "Come out, Castillo, or your daughter will die!"

"No! Don't hurt her! Please!" Nicole cried. Fear pooled like ice water in her veins, and Pilar's pleas shredded her heart.

"Let the girl go," Daniel grated through clenched teeth.

Diaz shook his head. "No, *señor*. She is my bait to draw out *her traitorous father!*" He shouted the words toward the water.

"You are the traitor, you BACRIM coward!" Splashing sounds preceded Castillo's appearance in front of the boat as he swam toward the *Serendipity*. "All of you who murder innocents in our streets and poison our children should be hanged!"

Diaz saw his opportunity and fired at the judge.

"Castillo!" Jake shouted, swimming with one arm from the protection of the fishing boat. Blood trailed Jake in the water, and his other arm hung loosely at his side. Nicole's gut tightened with concern. Jake needed a doctor, but they were miles from shore.

Despite his injury, Jake seized the back of Mario Castillo's shirt and dragged him back toward safety, even as Diaz cocked the gun again and squeezed off another shot. Re-cocked.

From her peripheral vision, Nicole saw Daniel shift, edging toward Diaz. But the movement, slow as it was, drew Diaz's attention back to Daniel, as well. Without hesitating, the attaché fired.

"Daniel!" she screamed, terror sluicing through her.

The bullet flew wide to the right. With a two-handed grip, Daniel aimed at Diaz but clearly had no shot, not with Pilar in the way.

Wearing a gloating grin, Diaz thumbed the hammer back with a click and tightened his finger around the trigger.

Nicole felt her father's muscles tense. His hands released her, and instantly, without a second thought, she lunged for Pilar, jerking her free from a distracted Diaz.

But even as she pulled Pilar close, she watched, as if in slow motion, as her father sprang toward Daniel, as a bullet hit his back, as he knocked Daniel from his feet and lay motionless on the deck. "Daddy!"

Then Diaz spun toward Nicole, his lip curled in disdain, and he pointed the gun at her.

Chapter 13

Daniel shoved the senator off him in time to see Diaz whirl toward Nicole and Pilar and take aim. An icy fear unlike anything he'd ever experienced stole his breath. Nicole!

Acting purely on training, muscle memory, instinct, Daniel jerked his gun up and fired. Fired again. Didn't stop until Diaz crumpled on the deck, his eyes fixed and lifeless.

As the concussion dissipated over the Gulf, Daniel lay still, the aftershock of adrenaline sending a shiver through him. He cut his gaze toward the woman he'd thought, just seconds earlier, he could lose forever. Another shudder rolled through him. "Nicole!"

She jerked her head up from her protective huddle over Pilar. Terror filled her eyes as she looked first to Diaz's body, then at him.

"W-we're all right." Tears spilled from her eyelashes, and she lowered her gaze to her father. "Daddy?"

Daniel holstered his weapon and rolled to a seated position beside the man who'd taken a bullet meant for him. Nicole's father had saved his life. That truth sat in Daniel's gut like a rock, and he shoved the thought aside to deal with later.

The senator lay on his back, and though his eyes were open, he didn't move. No blood showed on the front of his shirt, which was a bad sign. No exit wound meant the bullet had likely ricocheted around inside the man, wreaking havoc with his internal organs.

When Daniel pressed his fingers to the man's neck, searching for a pulse, a thready wheeze issued from the senator's mouth. "Nic—"

Nicole scurried across the deck to her father's side. "Daddy? Oh, thank God!"

The senator's eyes turned toward his daughter. He gasped for a breath. Raised an arm.

"No, lie still, Daddy. Let us help you." She stroked his head with a trembling hand and sniffed as she cried. "How badly are you hurt? Can you breathe?"

Daniel fumbled with the shirt buttons at the senator's throat, loosening the collar to help him draw air.

"Back," he wheezed.

"Pilar!" Castillo's voice rang from the water.

Daniel glanced over his shoulder as, sobbing, Pilar jumped to her feet and reached over the railing toward her father. *"Papi!"*

"Daniel?" Jake this time. "A little help here?"

"Give me a minute! We've got a man down!" he shouted back.

Nicole met his gaze. "Jake's injured, too. The shoulder, I think."

The senator made a strangled noise and tried to sit up. Grimaced and groaned. Wheezed.

Daniel finally freed the buttons at the senator's neck, and as he worked the lower buttons, he discovered a stiff, unyielding garment beneath the senator's undershirt. Startled, Daniel flattened his hand against the garment, feeling the material and weight, confirming his suspicion. His gaze connected with the senator's, and the man read his expression, gave a small nod.

"Kevlar," Daniel mumbled, then gave a chuckle of relief. He caught Nicole's hand to capture her attention, and when her panicked eyes darted up to his, he flashed her a crooked smile. "He's wearing Kevlar. A bulletproof vest."

Nicole's mouth opened, recognition brightening her eyes. She turned to her father and laughed through her tears. "The vest Mama bought you when..."

"Thought...it was...prudent." This time when her father tried to sit up, Nicole helped him, and Daniel worked the senator's dress shirt up to reveal the point of the bullet's impact.

Senator White moaned, then rasped, "Knocked the...wind outta me. Hurts to...draw breath."

"I bet." Daniel sat back, rubbing his own aching knee, which had taken a blow when the senator knocked him down. "You don't have a bullet in you, but you could easily have a broken rib or bruised lung." Guilt kicked Daniel, along with an uneasy gratitude.

He'd sworn he'd hate White forever for his part in keeping him away from Nicole. For betraying his and Alec's cover and putting their lives in peril while they were on a mission in enemy territory. For dividing Nicole's loyalties.

Daniel swallowed the bitterness those memories still stirred in him and met the senator's gaze. "Thank you."

Still panting for air, White nodded. "Because...my daughter...loves you."

Nicole gasped, and fresh tears puddled in her eyes. She divided a look between her father and Daniel, and bit her lip. "Oh, Daddy..." Carefully, she leaned in to hug her father's neck. "I love you, too."

"No, *mija!*" Castillo's shout drew Daniel's attention back to the scene that had been playing out as background noise behind him.

Pilar had climbed under the railing, and before he or Nicole could scramble to stop her, the little girl jumped into the Gulf.

"Pilar!" Nicole cried, dashing to the bow. Daniel groped for his cane and met Nicole at the rail. Below them, Pilar swam into her father's arms and was greeted with tears and kisses and admonishments for her impetuous leap into the water.

Spying them at the rail, Jake called, "Hey, I'm feeling a bit like shark bait down here, bleeding like this. Could you drop a ladder so we can come aboard?"

"Roger that, cowboy," Daniel returned, then faced Nicole. "Help them out of the water. I'm going to raise anchor and find a first aid kit. Then we need to radio the Coast Guard and have them alert the police on Grand Isle to pick up Menendez before we reach shore."

Jake grunted as Nicole shoved a wad of sterile gauze into the hole in his shoulder, and Daniel cringed in sympathy. Even though the bullet had passed through and done minimal damage, Jake had to be hurting like the devil. "At least it's not your gun arm."

Jake nodded. "There is that— Ow!" He sent Daniel a gloomy look. "My own fault. You warned me, and I didn't take enough precautions."

"You warned him? Is that what that Greek protocol business was about?" Nicole asked.

Jake nodded. "As in, the Greeks should have been more wary of their Trojan gift. Proceed with caution." Shifting his attention to the father and daughter reunion across the room, Jake hitched his head toward Castillo. "You oughta debrief the judge so we can vamoose before the Coast Guard arrives."

Daniel glanced at Nicole. "You got this?"

She nodded. "Of course, it would help if the patient would *sit still*."

Twitching a grin at Jake, Daniel stepped over to the cluster of overstuffed chairs where Castillo and Pilar were huddled together, wrapped in blankets and alternately chuckling and crying.

"You speak English," Daniel stated, confirming what he'd gleaned from the day's earlier events.

Castillo nodded. "Enough to get by."

"You recognized Diaz," Daniel said, getting right to the business at hand. "How did you know him?"

Castillo clutched Pilar to his chest and met Daniel's gaze levelly. "I grew up in the same neighborhood with Ramon and his brothers."

"What did he mean when he said you were responsible for his brother's murder?"

The judge snorted. "Carlo was not murdered. He was executed for his crimes." His eyes darkened. "Carlo and their youngest brother, Hector, joined a BACRIM— how do you say—? A street gang…."

"Go on," Daniel answered with a nod, well-familiar with the criminal gangs that were the scourge of daily life in Colombia, dangerous hordes of competing drug runners, rebel factions and lowlifes exploiting the civil unrest in the country as an excuse for lawlessness and personal gain.

"When he came before my court, I gave him what he deserved. Death sentence. His brothers said I was traitor to him. That he was fighting other gangs to keep the neighborhood safe." He scowled darkly and shook his head. "But no one is safe while he runs his drug traffic through our streets and poisons our children with his *cocaína*." He paused and stroked a hand down Pilar's head, his expression sad now. "It was after this that they attacked my family. They murdered my wife and daughter and took Pilar. Only if I, ah…" He fumbled as if looking for the right word. "Obey their demands, turn my eyes away from their crimes, will I get Pilar back."

"Did you do as they asked?"

The judge sneered at Daniel's question. "Never! I will not surrender my country to these criminals!" He looked down at his daughter, his face crumpling in anguish, and he made the sign of the cross. "God forgive me, I couldn't give in to them, even if it cost my daughter's life." He drilled a hard gaze on Daniel. "We are at war with these BACRIM. The drug cartels and traffickers. They have—what's word? Infil—"

"Infiltrated?"

Castillo nodded. "Infiltrated too many *policía* and government posts already."

Daniel sighed heavily. "Like Diaz did in the embassy here in the U.S."

Pilar whispered something in Spanish to her father, and he kissed her head. *"Sí."*

"Is she all right?" Daniel asked.

Judge Castillo smiled. "Eager to get home."

Daniel frowned. "In light of everything, her kidnapping, the threats against you and the turmoil in your country, you still want to go back to Bogotá?"

"I must. It is our home, and we cannot let the evil win. We will go home to fight for what is right." Castillo must have read Daniel's concern for Pilar in his expression, because he grunted and added, "I will be hiring a bodyguard for Pilar. More protection at our house." He arched an eyebrow. "Would you or Jake be interested in the job?"

Daniel tugged a wry grin. "A few months ago, I might have jumped at the offer but…" He rubbed his injured knee. "I'm not the man for the job anymore."

Castillo cut a telling look toward Nicole. "For many reasons. Pilar tells me you and Señorita White are in love."

Daniel's gut rolled, and he battled down the bitter taste of betrayal he'd shoved aside earlier when they'd encountered the senator, Diaz and Menendez at the pier. "I'm not sure what we are. But…I don't see a future for us. It's…too complicated."

Judge Castillo leaned back in his chair, a disappointed glare fixed on Daniel. "Too complicated? For the man who rescued my daughter and her lady-guardian from a rebel camp?" He shook his head and narrowed his eyes. "No. Nothing is too hard if it is also what is right. If you love her, you will not say it is too complicated and walk away."

Daniel opened his mouth, unsure what to say, but Jake saved him the trouble of a response when he strolled up behind them.

"All done here." Jake gingerly tested his freshly wrapped shoulder with his fingers. "I think it's time we hit the road… or the water, in this case. Judge Castillo, are you ready to go?"

Castillo nodded and nudged Pilar, whispering to her. The girl's eyes widened, and she searched the room until her gaze landed on Nicole, who was still packing up the first aid kit. Scooting off her father's lap, Pilar ran across the room to her surrogate parent. "Nicole…"

Daniel couldn't hear what Pilar told Nicole, but reading Nicole's expression was simple enough. Melancholy, the bittersweet ache of goodbye.

Nicole dropped to her knees and wrapped Pilar in a firm embrace. With her eyes squeezed shut, she clung to the little girl. "I'll miss you, *mija*. You are so brave and strong. I know you'll do great things with your life," she told her in stilted Spanish.

Pilar said something softly that made Nicole's face crumple with grief, and she squeaked, "I love you, too, *mija*."

Seeing Nicole's pain, knowing how much he, too, would miss Pilar, Daniel was blindsided by a wrenching ache in his chest. His airway tightened, and he had to clear his throat to loosen the knot of emotion. When Nicole and Pilar joined the men, Judge Castillo shook hands with Daniel and Jake and gave Nicole a kiss on each cheek. "I can never thank you enough for the love you have shown my daughter, the care you've given her and the risks you've taken to bring her back to me."

"There is one thing you can do," Nicole said, wiping her cheeks. "Stay in touch?"

Castillo nodded. "Of course." Taking Pilar's hand, he looked to Jake. "We are ready."

But when her father turned to leave, Pilar tugged her hand free and threw herself against Daniel's legs. "Goodbye, Daniel."

Shifting his weight to his good leg, he bent and lifted Pilar in his arms for a bear hug. He kissed her head, and through the fresh onslaught of emotion choking him, he rasped, "*Adios,* tadpole."

When he set her back on the ground, Pilar took her father's hand, and they followed Jake out to the deck. Daniel paused at the door and looked back at Nicole, who sat on a sofa with her face buried in her hands. "You coming to see them off?"

"No." Lifting her head, she swiped at her red eyes and shoved to her feet. "I'd better go check on Dad."

Without another word, she headed back to the small bedroom where her father was resting. Daniel watched her go, and wondered to himself— if saying goodbye to Pilar hurt this much, how much more would it hurt when he and Nicole went their separate ways?

Because he still had a bad feeling in his gut about where they were headed.

The Coast Guard met the *Serendipity* a couple miles from shore. In addition to examining her father's injury and reaching the same conclusion as Nicole had—significant bruising but no broken ribs, a diagnosis that they would still confirm with X-rays at the closest emergency room once they reached shore—the Coast Guard officers took an initial incident report on the shootings. As they had all agreed to ahead of time, Nicole, her father and Daniel gave truthful accounts of how the senator and Diaz acquired their wounds.

Diaz had joined them for a day trip to discuss business. The senator kept the gun on the boat in case of trouble from pirates or drug runners. He had the gun tucked in the waist of his pants, and Diaz snatched it and threatened them all with it. When Daniel produced his own weapon to defend them, Diaz fired, the senator knocked Daniel out of the way and took a bullet in his Kevlar-protected back. Diaz turned toward his weapon on Nicole and Daniel fired to save her. Initial forensic analysis supported everything they reported, as would later tests. Nicole was confident the case would be closed as justifiable homicide. No mention was made of Pilar, her father or Jake.

When the Grand Isle police were alerted to Menendez's possible connection to the attack the week before at the senator's home, they located him in a small diner near the pier and held him as a material witness. Before they left the Grand Isle police station, Nicole and her father were told that Menendez had clammed up, sitting like a rock, stoically staring straight ahead when questioned. Nicole could only surmise the man's silence was largely due to his links to Diaz and the criminal gang in Bogotá responsible for killing Pilar's family. They also learned that the Colombian embassy denied any association with the thug, but produced an extradition request for his for crimes in Colombia. By nightfall, Menendez was on a plane back to South America, and she and her father were released from police custody to return home. As she walked out to the police department parking lot, Nicole breathed a giant sigh of relief to have that chapter of her life behind her at last.

She couldn't regret her time with Pilar, though, or that the tumultuous past weeks had brought Daniel back into her life. Pain pinched her heart when she remembered Daniel's biting assertion that morning that he couldn't trust her and the cool distance he'd kept from her throughout the day. She'd been as surprised as anyone to see her father and Diaz on the pier but hadn't had an opportunity to defend herself.

By the end of the physically exhausting and emotionally wrenching day, when she found Daniel waiting for her in the police department parking lot, her hurt had grown a callus, and she bristled at the idea of having to defend herself. She was tired of proving herself and reiterating her loyalty to him. After all they'd been through, all the past hurts and misunderstandings, she needed Daniel to love and trust her unconditionally.

She helped her father get settled with a pillow in the passenger seat of his Caddy, then met Daniel, who leaned on the hood of the rental car they'd picked up just that morning. Had it only been that morning? Geez, it had been a long day!

"You okay to drive him back to New Orleans?" Daniel asked as she approached.

She nodded. "I'll stop for coffee somewhere, but I'm fine. What about you? Are you headed back to your grandmother's tonight?"

He gazed into the darkness avoiding her eyes. "Probably. For a day or so. I need to see about my leg. Talk to a surgeon about a knee replacement. After that..." He lifted a shoulder in a dismissive shrug.

She studied his rugged profile in the harsh bluish parking lot lights, and her stomach swooped. His jaw was rigid, and the jumping muscle in his cheek spoke of his lingering anger with her. She sighed, too weary to verbally spar with him tonight.

Why, oh why, out of all the men in the world, had she fallen so hard, so completely in love with this hardheaded, temperamental, obstinate man?

Dreading his answer, but needing to know where he saw their relationship, she asked, "Will you call?"

He didn't respond for a moment, and with each second that passed, Nicole felt her heart slowly cracking, as if a thin wedge were being driven in one tap at a time. Finally, he lowered his eyebrows in a scowl and shot her a dark look. "I don't see the point." *Tap.* "You and I…have never really fit." *Tap.* "I think it's time we both let go of the fantasy we created that night in New Orleans and admit that we could never work."

Tap.

Tears of frustration burned her eyes. "Daniel, you haven't given us a chance to wor—"

"Good night, Nicole." He pushed away from the hood and popped open the driver's door. "I'll get your cats back to you by the end of the week."

She gaped at him. Stunned. Stinging. Furious. "Daniel?"

He paused only long enough to give her one last look, his eyes full of regret. "Take care of yourself. You deserve it."

Without another word, he lowered himself into the rental car and cranked the engine.

Crash. Nicole struggled for a breath as the shards of her shattered heart sliced her chest and left her bleeding inside. She stood motionless, aching to her marrow as she watched him drive away. Only after his taillights had faded into the night did she muster the strength to stumble back to her father's Cadillac.

He sent her a worried look as she turned the ignition key and backed out of their parking space. "Everything all right, honey?"

And because she'd never lied to her father before, she cut a quick glance to him and answered simply, "No."

* * *

Two days later, while sitting out on the porch of his grand-mére's house, Daniel received a text message from Jake saying Pilar and her father had been successfully returned to the safe house in Colombia, and Jake was on his was back to his home in Texas for some recuperative time for his shoulder injury. After reading the message, Daniel set his phone aside and gazed at the bayou, bored out of his skull and missing Pilar and Nicole like crazy. He knew he might never see Pilar again, yet the girl had shown him the joys of fatherhood and given him hope that someday he'd have children of his own.

Children with Nicole's stunning blue eyes and breathtaking smile…

He smacked a fist on the arm of the chair and bit out a curse.

Stop it! You made the only decision you could. Look at the contrail of pain and hurt you two have already left behind you. How could he put his heart at risk again? Just two days ago, she'd broken her promise not to tell her father about their plans. How could he trust her allegiance in the face of that betrayal? No, he'd already suffered enough anguish over Nicole, her self-serving father and her lack of faith in him.

Because…my daughter…loves you.

Daniel shifted restlessly in the rocking chair as the senator's words replayed in his mind. Nicole's father had saved his life…for Nicole. That sacrificial gesture didn't jibe with the ugly picture of the senator he'd locked in his brain for the past five years. Readjusting his perception wasn't comfortable. Neither was admitting he could have been wrong about what had really happened that morning in the hotel room in New Orleans….

I think you're the one who has a problem with your heritage.

I love you both. Love you….

With a growl of consternation, Daniel ground the heels of his hands in his eyes and leaned his head back on the rocking chair. Why did things between him Nicole have to be so confusing, so complicated?

If you love her, you will not say it is too complicated and walk away.

If he loved her? *Enfer!*

He'd loved her since the day he met her. That was what had made her betrayal hurt so much. Except...if he were to believe Nicole, she hadn't betrayed him. She'd been rebelling against her father's ideals, but she'd been invested, she'd wanted to be with him, given him her heart.

The buzz of his phone cut into his frustrating rationalizations.

Snatching up the phone, Daniel checked the caller ID, secretly hoping it was Nicole, but saw his partner's number instead. "So Alec," he said by way of greeting, "Erin kick you to the street yet?"

"Hello to you, too," Alec returned, sounding happier than ever. "And, no, for some reason, Erin loves me and seems quite happy to put up with me."

Daniel twitched a small grin, relieved to have the distraction. "She's a keeper."

"That she is. Especially after seeing her endure twelve hours of labor. The woman is my hero."

Daniel sat up straight. "Labor? She had the baby?"

"This morning. A boy. He's a little small, since he's a couple weeks early, but he's got strong lungs and a head full of his mother's blond hair." Pride filled Alec's voice, and Daniel couldn't help but smile.

"That's wonderful. Congratulations to you both."

"Thanks." Alec heaved a contented sigh. "I tell you, Lafitte. I never thought life could be this good. Marriage, family...you should try it."

"Yeah, maybe someday." He let his gaze drift out to the dock where he and Pilar had fished, and his heart twisted.

"Someday? Dadgum, Lafitte, haven't you kept Nicole waiting long enough? When are you going to wise up and tell her how you feel?"

Daniel pinched the bridge of his nose and sighed. "That ain't happening. Just a couple days ago, I told her we were through."

"Through? Wha—" Alec huffed. "What's that word you called me? *Coullion?*"

Daniel cocked his head, surprised to hear Alec tossing the Cajun term back at him, the term he'd used to shake Alec out of his stupor when he was prepared to let Erin slip away. "Yeah, *coullion.*"

"Because I'd say it applies to you, too. You're a stubborn fool if you give up on Nicole. I was only with her a few hours, but I could see how much she loved you. Do *not* let her get away, Daniel. I will come down there and kick your ass if I have to."

Daniel grinned. "I wouldn't presume to pull you away from your wife and baby like that."

"So you'll call her? Apologize? Beg her for a second chance if you have to?"

Daniel groaned and shook his head. "I— It's not that simple."

"Yeah, well, *hard* isn't in your vocabulary," Alec countered. "I've seen you take on three armed guys with your bare hands and come out alive. I've seen you get past security at a drug lord's fortress and get back out without even waking the guard dogs. 'Not that simple' merely means you have to dirty your hands a bit." Alec paused, and Daniel heard the cry of a baby in the background. "Look, the nurse just brought Ethan in. I need to go."

"Okay. Well, give Erin my best."

"Daniel, do you love her? Because that is what it boils down to, man. If you look at it that way, it is real simple."

Daniel squeezed the cell phone, and his chest tightened. "Yeah. I do."

"Then do right by her, okay?"

Nothing is too hard if it is also what is right. The judge's stilted English bounced through his memory.

"Thanks, Alec. Congrats again." Daniel disconnected and set the phone aside. *Do right by her.*

An energizing warmth flooded his body when he whittled away all the debris that had been cluttering his view of his relationship with Nicole. Alec was right. If he loved Nicole, wasn't that all that really mattered? Couldn't they sort out all the rest if they clung to their love for each other? After all, their feelings for each other had already survived the tempest of the past five years.

He glanced down at his knee brace and began calculating his next moves. Before he could ask Nicole to build a future with him, he had to settle a few matters. He wanted to schedule his knee replacement surgery and get on the road to recovering full use of his leg.

And he had unfinished business with her father.

Three days later, Daniel knocked on the door to Senator White's garden district mansion in New Orleans. The woman who'd been with Nicole on the day of Pilar's attempted kidnapping answered his summons and smiled when she saw him. "Daniel LeCroix, my hero! How nice to see you again."

He offered a polite smile to the housekeeper. "And you, Sarah Beth. Are the Whites home?"

The clack of shoes on hardwood preceded Nicole's appearance behind her father's housekeeper. "Daniel!" Her expression was both heartbreakingly hopeful and cautious. "Come in. What…what brings you here?"

Sara Beth took her leave, and Daniel focused on the woman who'd filled his dreams for the past ten years. Though surprise and concern filled Nicole's face, he couldn't help but notice how the past several days of rest and nourishment had put more color in her cheeks and flesh on her bones. She looked beautiful, and his heart responded with a pure, sweet pang of affection.

"I can't stay long. I'm on my way to the surgery center for my knee replacement now, but…I have some business to discuss with your father first. Is he home?"

Her brows furrowed with suspicion. "Yeah, but…what business?"

"Where can I find him?" he asked, purposely avoiding her question.

She stood back, worry etched in tiny lines around her eyes. "He's in the den. I'll take you."

Heart drumming, he followed her to the spacious room at the back of the house, already repaired after the gun battle with the kidnappers from a few weeks earlier.

"Dad, you have company," she said rousing her father from the television.

Senator White stood slowly and faced Daniel, his curious, somewhat wary expression matching Nicole's. "LeCroix." He offered his hand and Daniel shook it, meeting the man's eyes squarely.

"Senator. Are you feeling better?"

He tipped his head a bit. "Still a little sore and moving slowly, but I'm doing all right. What can I do for you?"

"I have something important to ask you."

Nicole moved next to her father, biting her lip. "Daniel, what's going on?"

He met her eyes briefly before giving her father his full attention. "Senator, I've been in love with your daughter since her prom night ten years ago. I believe I've demonstrated my willingness to do whatever it takes to protect her, even if it costs me my own life."

White glanced at Nicole, then gave Daniel a brief appreciative smile and tight nod. "Indeed you have."

"Sir, I promise you that nothing will change in that regard. I will always love, protect and defend her, no matter your answer."

He quirked a bushy gray eyebrow. "My answer? I haven't heard a question yet."

"Dad!" Nicole scolded.

Daniel wiped his hands on his pants and cleared his throat. "You're right. Senator White, will you grant me the honor of your daughter's hand in marriage?"

Nicole gasped, and her hand flew to her mouth.

White grinned and regarded his daughter with love in his eyes. "Daniel, my boy, I've learned not to make decisions where my daughter's life is concerned. She's a headstrong and capable woman with a mind of her own. If you want to marry her, she's the one you need to ask." He turned back to Daniel, adding, "For my part, however, I give my blessing and wish you many years of happiness."

Daniel twitched a grin, relief pricking the bubble of tension filling his lungs. Shifting his cane, he faced Nicole, his heart thundering. "Nicole, I—"

"Yes!" she cried and flung herself at him so hard and fast he dropped his cane in order to catch her. As a result, his balance faltered, and they nearly toppled.

Senator White laughed. "Honey, once again, I didn't hear a question."

Tears of joy leaked onto her cheeks, and she pulled back from his embrace just far enough to send him a grin. "Sorry. You were saying?"

He flashed a lopsided grin. "I was wondering if you'd drive

me to the hospital, so I don't have to put my car in long-term parking."

She mock-scowled and poked him. "Of course, I'll drive you. Anything else?"

He captured her face between his hands and sobered. "Only this…I love you. I've loved you for years, and I promise to love you the rest of my days on this earth. I can't imagine my future without you in it." He pulled a small pouch from his pocket and took out his grandmother's ring. "*Mémère* wanted me to give this to my bride." He slid the antique ruby and diamond ring on her finger. "Will you be my wife?"

Fat tears dripped from her spiky eyelashes, but a smile of sheer bliss and love lit her face.

"I love you, too, Daniel LeCroix." She wrapped her arms around his neck and kissed the breath from him. "I've waited a long time for this moment. And through the years, my answer has never changed. Yes, I'll be your wife. Absolutely yes."

* * * * *

Tall Dark Defender

To my wonderful editor, Allison Lyons.
Thanks for all you do!

Chapter 1

The lights weren't supposed to be off.

Irritation, tinged with a tickle of uneasiness, skittered through Annie Compton. She fumbled in the predawn darkness to jab her key into the lock at Pop's Diner. Her boss, Peter Hardin, was supposed to have left the outside light on to deter burglars and to illuminate the front door for the employee who opened the diner in the morning. Today, Annie was said employee with the unenviable responsibility of showing up at 5:00 a.m.

She grumbled under her breath as she groped on the shadowed door to locate the lock's slot. The door moved unexpectedly. Just a fraction of an inch, but enough to catch Annie's attention. A bolted door shouldn't have wiggled that much.

Annie pulled the handle, and the heavy glass door swung open. Her pulse spiked. Turning on the front light wasn't all her boss had neglected when he closed the restaurant last night.

Gritting her teeth, she entered the diner and flipped on the overhead lights. The cold bluish-white glow of the fluorescent bulbs flooded the dining room.

"Hello? Mr. Hardin?" She scanned the empty restaurant cautiously. Listened. Waited. "Is anyone here?"

When she heard nothing, saw no one, she released the breath she held and crossed the floor. Annie stashed her purse behind the lunch counter, wishing she could call grouchy Mr. Hardin on the carpet for his gaffes. Considering her boss had only criticism for her waitressing skills, she figured turnabout was fair play.

She huffed a humorless laugh as she plucked out a coffee filter and dropped it into the brewing basket. The man had left the diner unlocked, for crying out loud! Compared to exposing the restaurant to theft, her forgetting to refill the saltshakers was nothing.

Problem was, neglecting the saltshakers wasn't her worst mistake. Her gut clenching, she poured a carafe of water into the coffeemaker. She'd made her biggest blunder ever just a few nights before—a royal screwup that Hardin claimed had cost him two hundred thousand dollars. The amount seemed preposterous to her, but her boss insisted that was how much she'd lost him.

Annie's hands shook as she measured out the coffee grinds. She could never make up for losing Mr. Hardin so much money. She guessed she was lucky she still had her job, lucky he hadn't beaten her senseless the way Walt would have.

Thoughts of her violent ex-husband sent another shiver down her back. She rubbed the goose bumps on her arms and squared her shoulders. *Never again.*

If she had to work this dead-end waitress job the rest of her life, barely making ends meet for herself and her two young children, the price was worth her freedom from her abusive marriage. No man would ever hurt her or her children again.

Annie jabbed the power switch, and with a hiss and a waft of rich aroma, the morning java began dripping into the pot.

A glance around the diner showed numerous cleaning jobs that had been ignored at closing last night. She pressed her lips in a taut line of frustration. Perhaps this was part of her boss's plan to punish her for her colossal and costly mistake three nights earlier. Perhaps she deserved as much.

Two hundred thousand dollars. Acid bit her gut. How could she ever make up for that mistake?

Sighing her resignation, she took a clean rag from the cabinet and headed to the kitchen for a bucket of soapy water to start cleaning tables.

She noticed the foul odor as soon as she stepped through the swinging door from the dining room. Wrinkling her nose, she flipped the lights on and checked for some food item that might have been left out to spoil. But not even rotten milk smelled this bad.

Coupled with the unlocked front door, the putrid scent gave her pause. Too many things seemed off-kilter at the diner this morning.

A ripple of apprehension shimmied through her. Annie hesitated by the main grill, which still sported last night's grease.

"Mr. Hardin, are you there?" She heard the quiver of fear in her tone and pressed a hand to her swirling stomach. "Hello?"

She took a few baby steps forward, scanning the dirty kitchen. Rounding the industrial-size freezer, she crept into the back hall.

On the floor, a pair of feet jutted through the open door to the manager's office.

Annie gasped. Dear heavens! Had he fallen? Had a heart attack?

"Mr. Hardin!" she cried, rushing forward.

When she reached the office door, Annie drew up short.

Her breath froze in her lungs. Bile surged to her throat. Black spots danced at the edge of her vision.

Peter Hardin lay in a puddle of blood, his eyes fixed in a blank, sightless stare. Two bullet holes pocked his chest, and a third marred his forehead.

Annie stumbled backward, horror clogging her throat.

Numb, shaking, light-headed, she edged away from her grisly discovery.

Shock and denial finally yielded to terror. A scream wrenched from her throat and echoed in the empty kitchen.

Her boss was dead. Murdered.

And though she hadn't pulled the trigger, Annie was certain Hardin's murder was her fault.

Three days earlier

He'd stalked his prey long enough. Time to move in for the kill.

Over the rim of his coffee cup, Jonah Devereaux eyed the rotund, balding man across the Formica table from him.

Martin Farrout.

Everything Jonah had learned to date in his investigation told him Farrout was the muscle of the gambling operation, the gatekeeper. Getting past Farrout, rooting out the players up the chain of command was what the past six months had been about.

"Mark my words. Kansas will go all the way," Ted Pulliam, one of Farrout's lackeys, said, jabbing the diner's table with his finger for emphasis.

Jonah grunted and lowered his coffee. "North Carolina. They're a powerhouse with a winning legacy to uphold."

Pulliam scoffed. "All right, Devereaux, put your money where your mouth is." The wiry man with faded tattoos slapped a Jackson on the table. "Twenty bucks. And I'll give you five points."

Jonah schooled his face and divided a bland look between Pulliam and Farrout, sizing them up. Weighing his decision to push his investigation to the next level.

He drained the cold dregs of his coffee and shoved the mug to the end of the table. In seconds, their waitress had snagged the coffeepot and stepped over to refill his cup.

Lifting a hand, Jonah waved her off. "Naw, I'm done, Annie. Thanks anyway."

"Gentlemen, we close in ten minutes. Can I get you anything else?" the attractive brunette asked as she cleared away the dirty mug.

Sure. I'll take an order of inside information about the local gambling ring with a side of details on the money-laundering operation I suspect your boss is running. Hold the onions.

If only it were that easy.

Instead, he'd spent months investigating the illegal activities he'd traced to Pop's Diner, and he still didn't have the evidence he needed to resolve the case and turn his information over to the local police.

The evidence he needed to give Michael justice.

Pushing aside thoughts of his mentor, Jonah flashed Annie a quick smile. "Just my bill."

While posing as a paper-mill worker who'd recently moved to the area, Jonah had eaten enough greasy meals at the small diner to send his cholesterol count into the stratosphere—a lesser-known hazard of undercover work that'd take countless hours in the gym to rectify. At least the coffee was good. God knew he'd guzzled enough of the brew at Pop's to last a lifetime.

But over the weeks, his regular meals at Pop's had gained him the level of familiarity with the locals he needed to loosen a few tongues and open a door or two. Things were finally beginning to fall into place.

He shifted his gaze to Farrout and pitched his voice low. "I want the real action. Five grand on UNC to win it all."

Pulliam fell silent and sat back in the booth.

Farrout lifted a thick black eyebrow. One taut second ticked after another, the tension screwing Jonah's gut into a tight knot. Unflinching, he held the portly man's stare.

Finally, Farrout narrowed his eyes to slits. "Ten."

Jonah sighed, pretending to consider the higher stakes. He couldn't seem too eager or too free with his cash. The working-class stiff he was supposed to be wouldn't have ten thousand dollars to lose on a careless bet. Not that *he* had that kind of money to lose, either.

He rubbed his thumb idly on the handle of his spoon and glanced out the plate-glass window to the night-darkened street. "That's pretty steep."

Farrout shrugged lazily. "I gotta know if you're for real or if you're just wasting my time. First bet is always ten grand, minimum."

Pulliam twisted his lips into a taunting grin. "How sure are you of UNC now?"

Keeping a stoic face, Jonah drummed his fingers on the table in an intentional display of nerves. "I can go eight now, two more next payday."

Farrout's fleshy lips twitched. "Deal."

Annie returned with separate checks for the three men.

When she reached for Farrout's plate, he grabbed her wrist with his meaty hand and squeezed. "Did I say I was through?"

Wincing, Annie gave Farrout a wide-eyed glance. "I'm sorry. I just thought—"

Fury burned inside Jonah, and he stiffened. "Let go of her."

The barrel-chested man returned a cold stare. "Butt out, Devereaux."

Jonah gritted his teeth. "Let. Go."

Annie's cheeks had drained of color, and her dark eyes rounded with apprehension.

A muscle jumped in Farrout's jaw, but he released Annie with an angry thrust. "Watch yourself, Devereaux. I don't like people sticking their nose where it don't belong."

Hell. He didn't need to blow his investigation by pissing Farrout off. But he damn well wouldn't sit by and let him rough up a woman, either. He'd done that too often as a kid when his dad was in one of his moods, and the guilt still ate at him.

Annie rubbed her offended wrist and cast a quick, curious glance at Jonah before hurrying back to the lunch counter.

Over the months he'd been working the case, he'd gotten to know all of the waitresses by name. Annie was the most reticent of the waitstaff, but she was also the most intriguing. Though attentive and polite to a fault, she was far less inclined to engage in good-natured banter and flirting the way the other servers did. An air of mystery surrounded her, partly because of her shyness, partly because she wore her silky dark tresses in a style reminiscent of the sultry movie stars of the 1940s—parted on the side with a curtain of hair covering one cheek.

Jonah had caught a glimpse of that hidden cheek once and seen the scars she was concealing. Those scars added to the enigma that was Annie but, in his opinion, didn't detract from her pretty face. Clearly she thought otherwise, or she wouldn't work so hard to hide the jagged pink lines.

As Jonah dug his wallet out of his back pocket, Farrout and Pulliam slid out of the booth and sauntered to the counter with their checks.

"Put it on my tab, doll face," Farrout said, tossing his ticket on the counter and turning to leave.

Pulliam added his bill and clicked his tongue. "Ditto."

Annie's brow furrowed, and she shook her head. "But… we don't—"

The men ignored her as they walked out, chortling to themselves.

From the booth, Jonah seethed over the men's rudeness. He studied Annie's crestfallen expression, her drooping shoulders and moue of disgust. She slapped the counter with the rag in her hand and huffed loudly.

When she raised her gaze to him, he quickly shifted his attention to his bill and pulled a twenty out of his wallet. He rose from the bench seat and approached the counter where she wiped up the day's mess with more vigor than necessary.

Extending the ticket and cash to her, he smiled ruefully. "Keep the change."

She glanced at the money and frowned. "But all you had was coffee."

He lifted a shoulder as he returned his wallet to his pocket. "Maybe I want to help your day end on a positive note."

Annie gaped at him as if she didn't know what to make of his kindness. As if she'd never encountered generosity before. "But—"

"Annie!" Peter Hardin, the manager of the diner and Jonah's key suspect in the money-laundering scheme, burst through the swinging kitchen door.

Jonah saw Annie tense as her linebacker-size boss stalked over to her.

"I need you to do an errand for me." Hardin slapped a bulky tan envelope on the counter.

Annie's face fell, and she glanced at her watch. "Now? It's almost midnight."

Jonah took his time putting on his jacket, unabashedly eavesdropping on the exchange. Annie's distress around her boss piqued his curiosity.

"Yes, now. This has to be delivered to Fourth Street in the next half hour. It's extremely important, so don't be late with it. Guard this envelope with your life."

Jonah clenched his teeth. Fourth Street was a notoriously bad section of town. This time of night, the area was downright dangerous. What was Hardin thinking, sending a woman on an errand alone in that part of town?

"But—" Annie hesitated, chewing her lip as if debating the wisdom of arguing with her boss. "If it's so important, why aren't you delivering it?"

Hardin glared at her. "I have my reasons. You want a job tomorrow, you deliver that package on time. Got it?"

Annie opened and closed her mouth in dismay, then nodded.

Her boss handed her a scrap of paper and hitched his head toward the front door. "That's the address and the name of the guy you give the package to. *Only* to him. No one else. Got it? Now, go on. I'll close up."

After fishing her purse out from under the counter, Annie tucked the package against her chest with a sigh.

Jonah watched her leave the diner and walk past the parking lot without stopping. He frowned. She didn't have a car? Walking Fourth Street alone at night could be suicide.

Without giving it a second thought, Jonah fell into step

behind Annie. Peter Hardin might not care about his waitress's safety, but Jonah wasn't about to let Annie make that delivery unprotected.

Annie's footsteps reverberated in the dark shadows looming around her. Alone on the downtown street, she clutched the manila envelope to her chest like a shield.

She shouldn't be here. This part of town was dangerous, especially at this late hour. But how could she refuse her boss's order? She couldn't afford to lose her job. She only had a few more minutes left to make Hardin's delivery, and he had been emphatic about the deadline—and the dire consequences if anything happened to the mysterious contents.

Just make the drop and get out of there. Get home. Get safe.

The sound of her shallow breathing rasped a harsh cadence in the quiet March night, and her heartbeat drummed in her ears like a death knell. She slowed her frantic pace, closing her eyes long enough to gather her composure.

Keep your wits and don't blow this.

The drop-off address had to be close. She searched for numbers on the buildings, but the dilapidated storefronts and graffiti-decorated buildings bore no identification.

She gritted her teeth. Damn Peter Hardin for forcing her to do this dangerous errand! If she didn't need her job so much, she'd have told him where to stick his order to do his dirty work. She sighed in disgust, wishing she'd stood up to Hardin.

But she'd always been a pushover. Her ex-husband had known it and taken advantage of that truth.

Squaring her shoulders, Annie kept walking, realizing how this decrepit neighborhood was a reflection of her life. Lonely, scarred and struggling to survive.

She'd had the typical fairy-tale dreams for herself as a

girl—love and marriage, happily ever after. Instead, she'd found a nightmare—fear and abuse, divorce from a man now serving time for a laundry list of crimes. After six years of unhappiness, at least she was free of Walt. Her job as a waitress at Pop's Diner barely covered her bills, but her children were safe now. She was safe. That was all that truly mattered.

Yet as she searched for some evidence of where to take the package, she felt anything but safe. A prick of alarm nipped her neck. Though she heard nothing, saw no one, the uneasy sense that someone was following her crawled over her like a cockroach on her skin. She shuddered.

Annie drew a deep breath for courage, her nose filling with the stench of sewage, mildew and despair.

A scuffing noise filtered through the night from an alley just ahead of her. Her steps faltered. Her pulse jumped.

"H-hello?" she called, her voice cracking.

A hulking figure emerged from the black void. The man descended on her before a scream could form in her throat. He wrapped arms of steel around her, and a fleshy palm covered her nose and mouth. Lifting her as if she weighed nothing, her attacker pulled her into the dark alley and slammed her against a brick wall.

The collision knocked the air from her lungs. Shock and fear froze her limbs.

No! her brain screamed. *Not again!* Slow-motion images of her past flickered before her mind's eye.

"You call this slop dinner?" Walt's hand cracked against her chin in an upward arc.

Her assailant seized the manila envelope she'd sworn on her life she'd deliver only to Joseph Nance.

Panic surged inside her. Her fingers curled into the package, clinging to it for all she was worth. "No!"

"Give me the money, bitch!" he growled. His fist crashed into her mouth, and a metallic taste slid over her tongue.

Red smears stained the floor. Blood. Her blood.

Walt kicked her in the ribs, and crimson drops leaked from her nose and splashed onto the linoleum.

The man's beefy fingers bit her flesh. He shook her. "Give it to me, or I'll kill you!"

Past and present twined around each other. Numbed her. She did what experience had taught her was her best defense. She shut down. Drew into herself. Closed her eyes.

Just endure it. Survive.

Her grip slackened, and the package was ripped from her arms.

Chapter 2

With a frightened cry, Annie slid to the ground, raised her arms to protect her head. Through the haze of her terror, she heard the shuffle of feet. A grunt. A curse.

Opening her eyes a slit, she found a second man in the alley, brawling hand-to-hand with her attacker.

Touching her swollen lip, she scooted farther away from the men who battled in the shadowed alley. She cringed as the newly arrived man landed a solid blow to her attacker's gut. Her assailant responded with a resounding punch to the other man's jaw.

Annie curled into a ball, trembling as fists flew. She squeezed her eyes shut and plugged her ears. She'd seen and heard enough violence in recent months to last her a lifetime. Her ex-husband's abuse was an all-too-present memory that haunted her every day.

Hot tears leaked onto her cheeks, and she conjured a image

of her children, Haley and Ben. She prayed she'd survive to see them again. *Please, God.*

Her kids were all that mattered. The reason she worked the exhausting waitress job at the diner. Her reason to persevere. Her reason for leaving Walt sixteen months ago, despite the horrifying weeks that followed as her abusive ex hunted her, terrorized her, nearly killed her.

A loud, pained shout jolted her out of her protective shell, and she peeked out at the scene unfolding before her. Her assailant was on the ground, the second man rubbing his knuckles. As he stepped back from his opponent, the second man moved through a shaft of light from a streetlamp.

And Annie glimpsed a face she knew from the diner. A regular.

Her gasp drew the man's attention.

She searched her memory for his name. John? Jacob? No— *Jonah.*

"Annie, are you all right?"

In those few seconds of Jonah's distraction, her assailant snatched up the envelope and ran from the alley.

"The package!" Panic wrenched Annie's chest.

Jonah pursued the thief to the end of the alley but apparently decided against a footrace. Instead, he walked back toward Annie, wiping blood from his nose with the sleeve of his shirt. "Are you hurt?"

"He took the envelope," she said, her voice quivering. A sinking disappointment crushed her chest. Though grateful to be alive and to have had Jonah's help, she dreaded what Hardin would do when he discovered she'd lost his package. Peter Hardin was no gentleman, and she doubted he'd be forgiving about her screwup. She buried her face in her hands as fresh tears puddled in her eyes. "He's going to fire me. I know he is. Oh, God…"

Jonah crouched in front of her, and she jolted when he stroked a hand down her arm.

Raising a wary gaze, she scrunched a few inches farther away from him. He may have scared the mugger off, but she'd seen his skill with his fists. Experience had taught her to give violent men a wide berth.

"Hey, come on now." The low, soothing rumble of his voice lulled her. "You won't lose your job. It's not your fault you were mugged." His dark eyebrows drew into a frown, and his tone hardened. "If anyone is to blame it's that bastard Hardin for sending a woman into this neighborhood alone in the middle of the night."

Jonah flexed and balled his hand. Annie's mouth dried, the stolen envelope temporarily forgotten as she focused on the more immediate threat—the man fisting his hand before her.

Taking a deep breath, she eyed Jonah's clenched fist. "Wh-why are you here?"

He cocked his head slightly and lifted a corner of his mouth. "I'd have thought that was obvious. I followed you when you left the diner."

So her sense had been right. Her pulse sped up. "Why? What do you want?"

He raised his hands, palms out. "I only wanted to keep an eye on you. I figured something like this might happen and…" He sighed. "I'm only sorry it took me so long to catch up once the jerk grabbed you. I should have stayed closer, but I didn't want to spook you if you saw me following you."

Annie furrowed her brow skeptically. "So you were following me to…*protect* me?"

He grunted. "I heard Hardin tell you to make the delivery, knew the neighborhood…" He glanced away for a moment and swiped at the blood beading under his nose again. "I oughta wring the jerk's neck for putting you at risk this way."

"No!"

Her vehement protest snapped his gaze back to hers. "Oh, I won't. I'm not interested in being arrested for assault." He held his hand out to her. "Can I help you up?"

Annie hesitated, staring at his large hand. His knuckles were swollen and raw, his palm toughened by calluses. That hand had packed a powerful punch to her assailant.

"Annie?"

Her gaze darted up to his. In the harsh shaft of light from the streetlamp, she studied his face. His bloody nose had a bump at the bridge, as if it had been broken before. A thin, silvery scar bisected his dark eyebrow, and a red blotch on his jaw hinted at a future bruise, courtesy of her attacker.

Yet despite all these visible signs of past and recent fights, his lopsided grin and warm green eyes spoke of a softer side to this man.

"Keep the change."

"Let go of her."

Did she dare trust him? He *had* come to help her. Or so he said.

"If you wanted to protect me…" She paused, second-guessing the wisdom of challenging him on his story. Challenging Walt had earned her more than one beating.

"Go on."

She took a fortifying breath. "Well, why not just walk *with* me? Why follow me?"

He rubbed a hand over his battered jaw. "Fair question." He tugged up the corner of his mouth. "If I had offered to walk with you or drive you to the drop-off address, would you have accepted?"

"I—" She lifted her chin. "Well…probably not. All I know about you is that you like lots of milk in your coffee—skim, not whole—and that you usually sit at the counter. First seat, facing the door."

His grin was a tad smug. "That's what I thought." He offered his hand again.

This time, after a brief hesitation, Annie placed her hand in his and let him pull her to her feet. The warmth and strength of his fingers, curled around hers, sent an odd shiver through her. How could a touch be both comforting and unnerving at the same time? The size of his hand, swallowing her smaller one, sent a tingling awareness through her. His height dwarfed her five feet four inches, and he had more strength in one arm than she had in her whole body. Like Walt had.

Jonah had the power and skill to crush her if he chose.

Her stomach did a forward roll. Snatching her hand back, she rubbed her arms, hoping to warm the chill that burrowed to her bones.

"Did he hurt you, Annie? I can take you to the emergency room if—"

"No! I— I'm fine. Really." *I've taken far worse.*

Uncomfortable under his scrutiny, she averted her gaze, tried to collect her thoughts. "I...I guess I should call the police. File a report."

Jonah's eyes narrowed, and he rubbed his jaw. "Uh, generally yes. But...I'd rather you didn't."

Her gaze snapped up to his. "Why not? He took Mr. Hardin's package. He said the package was important and—"

"The guy is long gone."

"But the cops need to know! I was attacked, and...maybe they can find the package before—"

Before Peter Hardin finds out the envelope was stolen. Fear seized her lungs, and she struggled for a breath. "Oh, God," she wheezed.

"Annie?" Concern knit Jonah's brow as she leaned against the bricks and gasped for air.

"H-Hardin...will kill me. H-he's...going to hate me. H-he..."

Jonah stroked a hand over her back. "Calm down, Annie. It'll be all right. Hardin can't blame you for this."

She angled her head to glance up at him and scoffed. "You don't know him very well." She bit her bottom lip to keep it from trembling. "I don't have a cell phone. I'll have to wait until I get home to report this... Unless you—"

Jonah was shaking his head. "Annie, I know you have no reason to trust me, but...I need you not to call the cops about this."

Annie frowned. "Wha— Why?"

"I have my reasons. I know that's not much to go on, but it's all I can say now." He scowled and ducked his head. "Please, Annie. I need you to trust me on this."

Trust him? She barely knew him. And trust was one thing she had little of when it came to men. Walt had destroyed what little trust she had. But to get away from him, to get out of this deserted alley and get home to her kids, she'd promise anything.

"All right. No cops." *Yet.* She reserved the right to change her mind once she was safe at home.

With his mouth in a grim line, he gave a tight nod. Jonah swept his gaze over her, then stepped back. "I can at least walk you back to the diner parking lot."

"I don't have a car. Can't afford one." Annie lifted her chin, determined not to feel any embarrassment for her financial woes. She had no reason to be ashamed.

"Mmm. That's kinda what I figured when you didn't drive here. How did you plan on getting home?"

She scooped her purse off the ground. "Same way I got

here. Walking. Usually I take the bus home. But on nights when I work late, the bus is no longer running."

Jonah heaved a sigh. "Well, my truck is back near the diner if you'd like a ride."

Annie adjusted the purse strap on her shoulder, steeling herself for the long walk home. "No. Thank you."

He scowled. "You know I'm going to follow you, regardless."

Her heart gave a kick, and her muscles tightened. Walt had disregarded her wishes, too. Done as he damned well pleased, whenever, whatever. She'd felt powerless.

The last thing she needed was another controlling man dictating her life. Especially one who clearly was no stranger to violence. But how did she refuse without incurring his wrath? How did she impose her will on a man whose mind was obviously set?

With the flutter of ill-ease in her veins, Annie backed toward the street. She cleared her throat to steady her voice before replying, faking the confidence she hoped she projected. "I…appreciate your help earlier, but I can get home by myself."

He rubbed his hands on the seat of his jeans, shaking his head. "It's late, Annie. The streets in this part of town are dangerous—as you've discovered."

She shivered, remembering the instant terror when she'd been grabbed. Her arm still throbbed from her attacker's vise-like grip. Defeat settled in her belly like a rock, followed closely by a surge of desperation. How would she explain the lost package to Hardin? Was she destined to be a victim of men's violence for the rest of her life?

Not a victim, Annie. You're a survivor. *Stay positive. Attitude is everything.* The mantras and platitudes Ginny, her counselor from the women's center, preached echoed in her brain. But on days like today, keeping a rosy outlook took more energy than she had. She'd dealt with grumpy customers, poor tippers and a demanding boss. She'd been on her feet since noon, spilled coffee on a customer who then threatened to sue and had had her life endangered thanks to a boss who would likely fire her for losing his package.

Annie shoved aside the sense of impending disaster and squared her shoulders as she faced Jonah. "I can't stop you from following me, but I prefer to get home by my own means."

Jonah ducked his head, his mouth twisted in a frown of disagreement. "Fine. I won't argue with you." He shook his head and huffed his frustration. "But if you change your mind, give a shout. I'll be just a block or so behind you."

The cocky lift of his eyebrow dared her to try to stop him from tailing her. He stepped back to let her pass, and she marched toward the street, squeezing her purse to her chest and giving the dark downtown avenue a wary scrutiny.

A queasy jitter roiled in her gut, knowing she'd disappointed him, upset him. Her innate need to please, an instinct Walt had exploited and pushed to an unhealthy extreme, caused her a moment's hesitation. She almost balked, almost relented.

When she'd risked her life to free herself from Walt, she'd vowed to never depend on a man for anything ever again. Rebuilding her life, her confidence, her inner strength was a daily struggle. Old habits and emotions, ingrained in her during six turbulent years of marriage, died hard. But she'd sworn to shed the debilitating attitudes and knee-jerk reactions from her marriage in favor of strength and self-empowerment.

One day at a time.

She could take care of herself and her children, no matter what. She hated that she needed the job Hardin gave her so desperately, but without a college degree, her employment options were limited.

She glanced behind her a time or two as she made her way home, and each time, Jonah gave a nod as if to say, "Yep. I'm still here."

She sensed Jonah's stare like a weight on her back as she crossed the parking lot and climbed the outside iron stairs to her second-floor apartment. On the grillwork landing, she lifted her gaze and found him in the lawn below. She flicked her hand, shooing him away.

Crossing his arms over his broad chest, he nodded to her door.

Sighing, she unlocked the door and pushed it open an inch. Again she flicked her fingers, sending him away. His lopsided grin flashed white under the bluish light of the security lamp, and he waved. Only when she turned to go inside did he finally amble off in the direction they'd come.

She parted the sheers on the kitchen window to make sure he really left, didn't loiter in the parking lot or try to come up the stairs to her door. His loose-limbed stride mirrored the relaxed confidence she'd come to know when she waited on him at the diner. He poked his hands into the pockets of his jeans, and for an instant, she admired the way his clothes fit his taut, muscular body.

"Miss Annie?"

The young voice jarred her from the intimate perusal of Jonah's physique, a side trip she had no business making. Clapping a hand over her scampering heartbeat, she faced her babysitter. "Rani, I... Sorry I'm late. My boss had me run an errand after I got off."

"It's okay. I was just watching TV. I—" Rani paused, wrinkling her brow. "Gosh, what happened to your lip?"

Annie touched her swollen mouth. She'd almost forgotten about the blow the mugger had landed, splitting her lip. "Nothing really. I'll be fine. Just a little accident," she lied out of habit.

She'd gotten good at making up explanations for the injuries Walt had inflicted.

She was a klutz. The baby had bumped her nose with his head. She'd tripped over a toy in the dark. Her babysitter frowned but said nothing else about Annie's injury.

"Come on." Annie hitched her head toward the back of the apartment. "Let's get you your check." She paused at the door to the kids' bedroom and peeked in.

Ben slept soundly in his crib with his diapered butt poking in the air, and curled in her bed, Haley clutched her stuffed cat, Tom, under one arm.

A tightness squeezed Annie's chest as love filled her heart to bursting. Quietly, she stepped into the room and adjusted Ben's blanket to cover his arms, then crouched to stroke Haley's long, dark hair. Her daughter stirred, and Annie held her breath, hoping she hadn't woken Haley with her motherly doting. She tiptoed back out the door and turned toward her bedroom where she kept her checkbook.

After scribbling out Rani's weekly payment, she walked the teenager to the door.

"You still need me at eleven-thirty tomorrow morning?"

Rani Ogitani had graduated from high school the previous May and started babysitting for Annie the following summer. Now, ten months later, Rani claimed to be looking for a job, thinking about college, weighing her options, but seemed content watching Annie's children and living with her mother for the time being.

"Yeah. Eleven-thirty. The kids give you any trouble today? I know Ben can be a handful."

Rani yawned. "They were okay. Mom says Ben's cranki-
ness is just his age. Typical terrible twos."

Annie grinned. "This, too, shall pass."

"Hmm?"

"Something my grandmother used to say. Never mind."
She held the door open for Rani and stood on the landing to
watch as the teenager crossed the parking lot to her mother's
first-floor apartment.

The March evening still held a nip of the winter just past,
and goose bumps rose on Annie's arms. Before stepping back
inside, she scanned the yard, the parking area, the street.
Jonah was gone. Or at least she couldn't see him anywhere,
if he was hiding, watching.

She shook her head. That was paranoia talking. Walt's
legacy.

Or was it? Jonah had followed her when she left to make
her delivery for Mr. Hardin. Was he really just being thoughtful and protective? Why had he asked her not to call the cops?
Was he her guardian angel—or was Jonah hiding a dangerous secret?

Chapter 3

The next day, Jonah took his place at the lunch counter at Pop's Diner as he had nearly every day for the past several months. With luck, he'd only have to subject himself to the diner's menu another couple of weeks. As he followed through with the bet he'd placed with Farrout the night before, he hoped he now had an inside track to learn more about how the illegal gambling operation worked—how gamblers paid their debts, where the money went, who was involved at higher levels.

Follow the money.

He thought about the package Annie had been given to deliver last night, and tension spiraled through him. He'd bet anything Hardin's package had to do with the gambling money he was laundering through the diner. Whoever had been on the other end of that delivery was a key player in this operation.

Jonah gritted his teeth. He'd been so close to filling in

another piece of the puzzle in this investigation before that bastard had jumped Annie and made off with the package.

It almost seemed as if the guy had been lying in wait for her. As if he'd known that package was to be delivered....

Jonah puffed his cheeks and blew a slow, thoughtful breath out through puckered lips. Who could have tipped the thief off? Where was the leak in the operation? Was someone gunning for Hardin?

Nothing about last night's turn of events sat well with Jonah, especially when he figured Annie into the picture. Hardin had drawn her into the dynamic. She could have unwittingly become ensnared in the sticky web of deceit Hardin and Farrout had spun.

Jonah mulled his next move, then glanced up from his ham on rye when Annie breezed through the front door at ten minutes until noon. She cast him a quick nervous glance as she poked her purse under the counter and rushed back into the kitchen.

Jonah swabbed another greasy fry through his puddle of ketchup, keeping an eye on the kitchen door. Waiting.

Moments later he heard Hardin's raised voice roll from the back of the restaurant like thunder announcing a storm. "You *lost* it? You idiot! I told you how important that package was! How could you *lose* it?"

Jonah craned his neck, trying to find Annie through the service window.

He heard the soft murmur of Annie's response, recognized the frightened tremble in her tone, and his gut pitched.

"Sorry's not good enough!" Hardin screamed.

A loud crash. Annie's frightened yelp.

In an instant, Jonah had jumped from his stool and barreled through the swinging door into the kitchen. He sized up the situation in a glance. Hardin's red face, balled fists and threatening pose as he leaned close to Annie. The young waitress had scrunched back against the wall, her face pale and arms raised defensively to protect her head.

"Is there a problem here?"

Hardin's glare snapped over to Jonah. "What are you doin'? Can't you read? Employees only!"

"Annie? You all right?" he asked, ignoring Hardin.

Frightened brown eyes lifted at his inquiry.

Hardin jabbed a finger toward the door. "This ain't none of your business!"

"I'm making it my business. I don't take kindly to any man threatening a woman."

Annie's brow furrowed warily.

"The bitch lost two hundred grand of my money!" Hardin growled.

Annie gasped, and her eyes widened. "Two hundred grand!"

Hardin narrowed a glare on her. "That's right. Two hundred grand. And it's comin' out of your paycheck!"

Her face blanched a shade whiter. "Mr. Hardin, I can't—"

"Shut up!" He slammed a hand on the wall beside her head, and she yelped, trembled.

Jonah's blood boiled, and he strode closer to Hardin. Grabbing the man's shirt, he yanked him around, then shoved him back against the opposite wall. "Back off! If I see you so much as breathe on her again, I'll tear you apart."

Hardin puffed his chest out and shoved back. "Don't threaten me! She's my employee and—"

"That doesn't give you the right to hurt or intimidate her," Jonah growled through clenched teeth. "Don't touch her. Ever."

"Jonah…" Annie said quietly. "Don't."

"If anyone is to blame for that money being stolen from

her, it's *you*." Jonah poked the man in the chest with his finger. "You had no business sending a woman into that neighborhood alone, especially at that hour. What were you thinking? She could have been killed." He took a deep breath to calm the rage seething inside him. The urge to smash the guy's face was too strong. He needed to step back, cool off. He released Hardin's shirt and moved away, his hands still bunched at his sides.

Hardin's eyes narrowed, and his face flamed red. "Get out of my kitchen! Out of my diner!" He turned to Annie, aiming a finger at her. "And you! You're fired!"

Annie bit her bottom lip and squeezed her eyes shut.

Jonah moved between Annie and her hostile boss. "Not so fast, pal. Unless you'd like to explain to the cops what that two-hundred-grand delivery was about, where the money came from."

Now he had Hardin's attention. The man's eyes widened, and his face leeched of color.

"She can file a wrongful termination lawsuit whether she has grounds or not, and the delivery you asked her to make is sure to be called into question. You got an explanation ready for the judge about that two hundred grand?"

Tensing, Hardin glared darkly at Jonah, then cast his glower toward Annie.

Jonah held his breath, second-guessing his rash challenge. Tossing down the gauntlet with Hardin might not have been his wisest move if he wanted to keep a low profile as he worked his investigation.

But Hardin, in his rage, had spilled the tidbit about the huge sum that had been in the package. Hardin knew Jonah had been at the diner last night when Annie left to deliver the envelope. And Jonah couldn't help but wonder if his intervention now hadn't provoked Hardin to fire Annie.

Guilt pinched Jonah. He couldn't let her lose her job because of his temper.

"Fine," Hardin snarled, spittle spraying Annie's direction. "Consider yourself on notice. You screw up again, and you're gone."

With another scalding glance to Jonah, Hardin stomped into his office and slammed the door.

Annie pressed a hand to her chest and slid to the floor, shaking.

Pulling in a deep breath for composure before he approached her, Jonah studied Annie's trembling body and wan expression. He'd seen reactions like hers too many times in both his personal and professional life not to know what he was dealing with. If her fearful reaction to Hardin wasn't enough, her scars and her distrust of him last night bolstered his assessment.

She'd likely been abused. Husband, father, sibling—didn't matter who. The devastating legacy of violence and mental cruelty didn't differentiate.

Acid roiled in his gut, and he took another couple of seconds to cool off before squatting in front of her.

"Annie—"

"You shouldn't have gotten involved," she murmured. Raising her eyes to meet his, she shook her head. "He's my problem, and I have to learn to deal with him."

He frowned. "Annie, he had no right—"

"That doesn't matter! Right and wrong isn't the point." Annie hiked her chin up a notch and firmed her jaw in a display of moxie that sparked hope in him.

He held his tongue, giving her the chance to speak her mind. Her body language as she gathered herself and recovered from Hardin's intimidation spoke volumes to him. She was strong. A fighter. She had the mettle to overcome her past. Warmth swirled through his blood as he held her rich-coffee gaze.

Annie swallowed hard and squared her shoulders. "This was my problem, not yours. I have to learn how to handle these situations for myself, if I'm going to—" She tore her eyes away and shook her head again. "Never mind."

When she pushed up from the floor, Jonah put a hand under her arm to help her to her feet. She shrugged out of his grip. "I'm all right. I don't need—"

"Okay." He held his hands up and backed away one step.

Stroking her hands down her uniform apron, she angled a dubious look toward him. "Why have you decided to be my protector? You barely know me."

He shrugged. "How well do you have to know someone to want to help them?"

She ducked her head and didn't answer.

Jamming his hands into his pockets, he cocked his head and studied her bruised cheek and swollen lip, evidence of last night's attack. Even with the injuries marring her ivory skin, her beauty shone through. Annie was a curious blend of childlike fragility and womanly allure. She had a dusting of freckles across her nose that lent to her young, waifish appearance, while her bowed lips and thick-lashed brown eyes contributed to the seductive movie-star quality her hairstyle evoked.

He cracked his knuckles, working off the remnants of adrenaline following his confrontation with Hardin. "Look, are you all right?"

A pointed, dark brown gaze snapped up to his, half hidden by the curtain of hair she kept over her left cheek. "I'm fine. I appreciate your help, but—"

"But nothing. Forget it." He waved a hand in dismissal and pivoted on his heel. He'd made it as far as the swinging door

before he reconsidered. "No, don't forget it." He marched
back to Annie and drilled her with a hard gaze. "You want
to learn to take care of yourself? To handle men like Hardin
and that guy in the alley last night?"

Annie blinked her surprise. "What are you talking about?"

"You said you had to learn how to handle situations like
this, guys like Hardin." He flicked a thumb toward the spot
where Hardin had stood earlier. "Did you mean it?"

A deer-in-the-headlights look froze her face.

"I can teach you to handle yourself when a man attacks
you. I can show you how to defend yourself, protect yourself."

She eyed him skeptically for several silent moments.
"What about my children?"

"Kids?" Jonah fumbled, caught off guard by her question.
"I…I guess I could teach them, too."

"No, they're too young. I mean, can you teach me to protect them from men like…" She paused, bit her lip, then lowered her voice. "Men like Hardin?"

Jonah held her gaze, moved by the depth of fear, the passion and motherly concern he saw reflected in her dark eyes.
A degree of desperation shadowed her expression and tugged
at dusty memories deep inside him.

"I can…if you're willing to trust me."

His answer seemed to douse her interest with a cold slap
of reality. She frowned and jerked her gaze away with a sigh.
Trust was clearly in short supply for Annie. Not surprising.

Jonah twisted his mouth to the side as he thought. "May I
have your order pad and pen?"

With a puzzled look, she took the items from the front
pocket of her apron and extended them to him.

"What time do you get off work tonight?" He scribbled an
address on the pad and clicked the pen closed.

Again she hesitated before answering, her gaze narrowed

on him as if she could detect his motives, any ill intent or hidden agenda if she studied him close enough. "Eight. Why?"

"That's my gym." He tapped the front of the pad. "I'll meet you there at eight-thirty and give you a few pointers on self-defense, if you want. There are plenty of things a woman can do to protect herself, even from a man twice her size. I'll show you a couple of the most effective ones tonight."

He handed her back the pen and pad, and she perused the note he'd made. She worried her bottom lip with her teeth again and wound a strand of hair around her finger. "I don't know. I...I'd have to call my babysitter and make sure she could stay late. And I hate to miss the kids' bedtime. I see so little of them as it is." Her shoulders slumped a bit, and he heard working-mother guilt rife in her tone.

Seizing the opportunity to learn more about her and make her feel more at ease with him, Jonah grinned. "How old are they?"

Her head snapped up. "What?"

"Your kids. How old are they?"

Her expression softened, and warmth flooded her eyes. "Haley is five and a half, and my baby, Ben, is almost two."

Her obvious affection for her children needled a vulnerable place in Jonah, an emptiness he hadn't allowed himself to dwell on. The idea of having his own family stirred a complicated mix of emotions in him. He longed for the domestic ideal of home and hearth, but his memories of family left him in a cold sweat. Norman Rockwell dreams of a picket fence and two-point-five kids were a fantasy for him. Out of reach. Too risky.

His broken family, his only experience with home life, was a recipe for disaster.

Clearing his throat and shoving aside his own bitter memories, he flashed her another smile. "A boy and a girl. That's great. You have a matched set."

A corner of her mouth quirked up. "Hardly matched. They're as opposite as can be."

Jonah chuckled. "Funny how that happens, huh?"

Her mouth curved a bit more, forming the first hint of a grin he'd seen on her lips in weeks. "Yeah. Funny."

"I'd love to meet them someday."

Her smile vanished in a heartbeat, replaced by the damnable wariness again. "Why?"

He shrugged. "I like you. And I like kids. Stands to reason I'd like your kids."

Her brow lowered. "Mr. Devereaux, I'm not interested in—"

"No, you're right." He raised a hand to cut her off. "Too fast. I didn't mean to be pushy." He nodded toward the order pad still in her hand. "But please consider coming tonight. For your safety's sake." As he backed toward the door, he threw in a parting shot he knew was pure manipulation. But he didn't care. "Do it for your kids if not yourself."

Annie needed to learn to protect herself, to stand up to bullies like Hardin, to revive the spark her abuser had extinguished. Jonah wasn't above a little manipulation if it motivated her to make changes in her life.

The truth was, Annie had been the delivery person when a two-hundred-thousand-dollar transfer of funds was stolen. Had the thief intended to kill her to keep her quiet, stop her from identifying him? Would the party who'd expected the cash seek retribution? Could Hardin become more desperate and, therefore, more dangerous?

No matter how he looked at this turn of events, Jonah didn't like the crosshairs Annie had found herself in after last night. She needed more than just a few self-defense techniques if someone tried to keep her from talking. But his lessons would be a start.

Meanwhile, he'd be extra vigilant. Annie needed someone with his experience and training to watch her back.

Annie surveyed the last few diners who'd come in for a late meal, then faced Lydia, who was working the last shift. "Can you handle things if I go now?"

"Sure thing, honey. I got it covered." The older waitress smiled and jerked her head toward the door. "Get on home to those babies and give 'em a kiss for me, too."

"Thanks, Lydia." Annie untied her apron and stashed it under the counter. Grabbing her purse, she headed back to the kitchen, walking with careful penguinlike steps to avoid slipping on the greasy film that had accumulated on the floor through the day. As she neared Mr. Hardin's office, she heard his raised voice, and her heart beat a little harder.

"That's not enough time! I said I'd get it to you!" he ranted.

As Annie tiptoed past his half-open door to clock out, she caught her reflection on the stainless-steel side of the industrial freezer. The image rubbed a raw nerve.

How many times had she cowered around Walt, tiptoeing through their house in order not to wake him, or quietly keeping a discreet distance to avoid triggering one of his tantrums?

She'd thought her days of treading lightly around hostile men were past, yet here she was skulking past Hardin's office like a guilty child. Frustration and self-censure stabbed Annie.

She'd come too far and paid too high of a price to be free of Walt to fall back into old habits now. Habits born from fear.

Damn it, she didn't want to live in fear anymore! Annie jammed her time card in the clock so hard it crumpled in the middle. Spinning on her heel to leave, she marched back by Hardin's office, her chin up and her back straight.

"Annie!"

She froze, dread slowing her pulse and snagging her breath. *Please, Lord, not another errand like last night.*

Heart thumping, she turned toward Hardin's office and stepped to the door. "Yes?"

"Where do you think you're goin'?" he asked around a cigarette dangling from the corner of his mouth. His eyes mirrored the same dark resentment she heard in his tone.

"My shift is over. I was going home."

"Not if I say you don't."

A rock lodged in Annie's stomach. She dragged in a smoke-laced lungful of air, trying to steel her nerves and battle down the building panic.

And anger—the most dangerous of emotions.

Dealing with the repercussions of Walt's rage had been enough to teach her just how dangerous. But her own temper had led her to say foolish things at times that had only inflamed Walt's wrath. Fury over Walt's unfairness and controlling nature had seethed in her gut like a corrosive waste until she would throw up, so she'd long ago learned to suppress her temper, swallow the bile and deny the heat of anger that flashed through her blood.

Yet despite her best efforts to erase her ill will and moments of irritation, she still carried a boatload of frustration and ire for the desperate circumstances of her life. She blamed Walt's abuse and her submission to his violence for the dark cloud his threats still cast over her. Now Hardin was doing his best to intimidate and control her, and she struggled to keep the poisonous emotion at bay.

"My shift is over, Mr. Hardin. I need to get home to my children." Her voice quivered with anxiety and barely suppressed indignation. She curled her fingers into her palms, and the pulse of rising adrenaline throbbed in her temples.

Her boss narrowed his eyes and stabbed out his cigarette in the overflowing ashtray on his desk. "Seems to me there's a matter of two hundred thousand dollars you either have to pay back or work off."

The flutter of fear taunted her, beating hard against her breastbone.

"Mr. H-Hardin, I could never work enough hours to repay—"

"Well, if you ain't going to work the extra hours, then maybe you could settle your debt with me…another way." Surging to his feet, he raked a lascivious gaze over her and smirked.

Annie fell back a step. Disgust slithered over her, and she shivered. Taking a slow breath, she searched for enough confidence to reply without her voice quaking. "No."

He crossed his arms over his chest, and his gaze continued to roam over her.

"I'll find a way to repay the money," she said, though the words were sour knots in her throat that she had to force out. "It will take me a while—" *Like forever.* She cringed at the thought of tightening her budget even further and scraping together small payments for Hardin. "But I'll find a way."

A muscle twitched in Hardin's jaw, and his flinty eyes drilled into her. "I want the money by next week."

The ice in his tone, his stare sent a deep chill slicing through her. Trembling to her marrow, Annie whirled away and hurried toward the dining room. Her feet slipped and skidded on the greasy kitchen tile, but she didn't slow down. She had to get away from Hardin. Get out of the diner. Get home to her children—the only place she felt even remotely safe anymore.

"I can show you how to defend yourself, protect yourself."

As she rushed out of the diner, Jonah's promise filtered through her head. Her steps slowed, and she reached into her pocket for the scrap of paper he'd given her with his gym's address.

If only—

Forget *if only*. Dreams and wishes were for other people. She had to deal in reality. In truths and concrete facts.

Her truth was she had to pay her hostile boss a hell of a lot of money.

Picking up her pace again, she jogged to the bus stop, still quaking from Hardin's chilling threat. No way could she find two hundred thousand dollars to repay him, even if she had a year to pay him. Much less a week.

Her bus rumbled up to the stop just as she reached the street corner. While she waited for an older man with a walker to board, she fished in her pocket for her bus pass.

Once more her fingers brushed the crumpled paper Jonah had given her.

"Do it for your kids if not yourself."

Guilt and fear squeezed her chest, tangling with irritation over Jonah's obvious manipulation of her love for her kids. She stared down at the address. What could it hurt just to go and see what Jonah wanted to teach her? He'd already proven he wanted to help, not harm her. And a gym was a public place. She'd be safe there. Right?

"You coming or not?" the bus driver called, jarring her from her deliberations.

"I—" Annie exhaled a deep breath of resignation. She had to at least *try* to protect herself from Hardin and men like the thief who jumped her last night. She was tired of living with this fear. She'd come too far to lose everything because she let a bully like Hardin intimidate her.

Annie raised her chin and met the bus driver's gaze. "Not." With a puff of exhaust, the bus chugged away from the curb, and Annie headed toward Jonah's gym.

Chapter 4

The scents of body odor and rubber floor mats greeted Annie as she entered Jonah's gym minutes later. Wrinkling her nose as the unpleasant smells assailed her, she cast a wary glance around the cavernous warehouse.

When Jonah had invited her to his gym, she'd pictured an upscale facility where beautiful bodies jogged on treadmills, followed a perky blond instructor in aerobic dance or toned their muscles on expensive weight machines. This gym was a far cry from her vision.

Dingy and dark with nary a perky blonde in sight, the large room housed four boxing rings and numerous punching bags suspended from the bare rafters by steel chains. A litany of grunts and curses reverberated from the concrete block walls, while burly men in scruffy shorts and sleeveless shirts pounded the weighted bags—or each other.

Apprehension slithered through Annie as she crept deeper into the room. Like a brewing storm, the raw power and the brute violence on display filled the room with an ominous and suffocating energy. Struggling to pull air into her lungs, Annie scanned the men's faces for Jonah.

With every passing minute, she grew more uncomfortable and self-conscious. One by one, sweat-drenched men paused from their training to eye her with curious, even lewd, glances. Her discomfort spiked as a man in the nearest boxing ring caught a bone-jarring blow to the chin that sent him to the mat with a groan.

"That'll teach you to talk back to me!"

She pressed her throbbing cheek to the cool floor, not daring to get up before Walt stalked from the room. Getting up only gave him the opportunity to knock her down again.

The images before her blurred as tears pricked her eyes.

She staggered backward, edging toward the door. She shouldn't have come. Shouldn't have risked—

As she passed a different boxing ring where two men sparred while a third coached from the ropes, recognition slammed through her. She squinted at the face barely visible behind the protective headgear, and her heart tapped double time.

Jonah.

Stunned, she stared while Jonah exchanged jabs with the other man, shuffling his feet to dodge blows. Sweat glistened on his arms and glued his tank-style T-shirt to the flat plane of his abdomen. Well-defined muscles in his shoulders and chest spoke for the hours of training and conditioning Jonah had put in.

Annie gawked at his brawny build, and heat prickled her skin. An unfamiliar flutter stirred in her chest, and realization that his size and strength had piqued her feminine interest startled her. Had she learned nothing in her marriage to Walt? She'd been physically attracted to Walt when they married. He'd been especially handsome in his military dress uniform the day they wed. But all the sexual chemistry in the world didn't outweigh the suffering he'd put her through in later years.

Yet she couldn't help but stare at Jonah's toned and powerful physique, his smooth style as he moved around the ring. With practiced skill, he ducked a swing and landed a solid hook to his opponent's pad-protected jaw.

Shocked out of her gawk-fest by his potent punch, Annie gasped.

Jonah's gaze darted to her.

In that split second of his distraction, his opponent struck back with a blow to Jonah's ribs.

Annie felt the blow as surely as if she'd taken the hit herself. The air whooshed from her lungs, and tension screwed her muscles tight. Clapping a hand over her mouth, she fell back another step.

"Devereaux, what the hell are you doing?" the silver-haired man by the ropes shouted. "You gotta keep your eyes in the ring!"

Grinning through a grimace, Jonah raised his boxing gloves. "Time. I've got company."

She sidled toward Jonah as he climbed through the ropes and jumped down to meet her.

"You came." Equal measures of pleasure and surprise colored his tone.

She nodded tightly and gave the activity in the room a meaningful glance. "If I'd known what kind of gym you meant, I don't know that I would have."

His dark eyebrows drew together. "Why?"

Eyeing the muscle-bound giant battering a small punching bag beside her, she inched closer to Jonah. "I'm...rather out of place, wouldn't you say?"

A warm grin lifted a corner of his mouth. "Hey, I know these guys look pretty rough, but I assure you, you're perfectly safe here."

He rubbed his ribs and winced.

"Are you all right?" She knew more than she cared to about the sting of fist-imposed injuries.

He glanced down at his chest. "It's nothing. Just a reminder that when you're in the ring, you gotta stay focused on your opponent, not be distracted by what's happening outside the ring."

The older man who'd been coaching winked at her. "Even if the distraction is mighty pretty."

Jonah tossed a towel at the other man. "Down, boy."

Annie frowned. "I'm sorry if I—"

"No, no." He waved off her apology. "My fault. I'm just glad you came." To the silver-haired coach, he said, "Frank, I think I'm done for the day. Same time tomorrow?"

Frank nodded. "Sure." To the kid in the ring he called, "Okay, Billy. Hit the showers."

Jonah bit the lace on one glove and pulled it with his teeth, then moved on to the second.

Annie fidgeted with her purse strap. "I can't stay long. My kids—"

"Pull?" He lifted his hands toward her.

Annie blinked her surprise.

"Please," he added with a lopsided grin.

Unaccustomed to refusing any man's request, she awkwardly grasped one bulky glove and tugged. It didn't budge.

"Harder. You gotta really muscle 'em off."

Annie hesitated, jitters dancing in her gut. She slid her purse from her shoulder and set it on the concrete floor. Grabbing Jonah's boxing glove with both hands, she pulled. Hard.

As he freed each hand, Jonah shook his arms and flexed his fingers.

"Thanks." He took the gloves from her and tossed them next to a duffel bag on the floor at the edge of the ring. Hitching his head toward the locker room, he said, "Give me five minutes to grab a shower, and we'll get started."

Annie sent another uncomfortable glance around the gym and bit her lip. "I should probably just get home. Maybe this was a mistake."

Furrowing his brow, he took her hand in his. His touch sent another flash of tingling heat over her skin.

He ducked his head to meet her gaze and squeezed her fingers gently. "Don't go. Just five minutes. I need to talk to you, but right now I smell like a goat."

His farm-animal comparison earned a half grin from her. And her concession. She nodded. "Five minutes."

With another handsome smile, he snatched up the gym bag and headed toward the locker room.

"Jonah?"

He turned.

"Do you have a cell phone I can borrow? I need to call my babysitter and tell her I'll be late."

"Sure." He fished in his duffel and extracted a small flip phone. "Catch." He tossed the phone toward her, and, caught off guard, she barely snagged the cell before it hit the concrete.

While she waited for Jonah, Annie found a corner where she was out of the way and called her apartment. She filled Rani in on her delay, then talked to Haley, who bubbled with excitement over a new lost tooth.

"I saved it to show you, Mommy. And Rani says if I put it under my pillow, the tooth fairy will give me money!"

Annie smiled, loving the joy in her daughter's voice and

trying to recall if she had any change in her wallet to hide under Haley's pillow.

"Hey, Mommy, maybe you could put *your* teeth under your pillow and get some money from the tooth fairy, too!"

Annie sputtered a laugh. "My teeth?"

"Yeah, then maybe you wouldn't have to go to work at the diner all the time and could stay home and play with me and Ben."

Remorse stabbed Annie, cutting her to the quick. "I don't know, sugar. I think the tooth fairy only wants kids' teeth."

"Oh."

The disappointment in her daughter's tone wrenched Annie's heart. "I'm supposed to have this Saturday off, though, and I promise we'll do something fun. Just you, me and Ben. Maybe go to the park? Okay?"

"Okay."

But Haley sounded skeptical. Too skeptical for a five-year-old. Knowing how many times she'd had to cancel plans with Haley when she had to work extra hours at the diner flooded Annie with fresh guilt.

Jonah emerged from the locker room, wearing a clean T-shirt and jeans, his wet hair combed back from his face. His gaze swept the room looking for her, and when he spotted her, a smile softened the hard planes of his face.

Annie's pulse missed a beat.

Jonah wasn't handsome in the classical sense. So why was he suddenly stirring this schoolgirl reaction in her?

She chastized herself. She was too busy making ends meet, fighting for her survival and reeling from her last devastating relationship to be in the market for a man. She had no business looking at Jonah as anything other than a regular customer at the diner. A mysterious man who'd rescued her from her attacker. The person who'd offered to show her techniques to protect herself and her family from further abuse.

"Haley, sugar, I have to go now. Be sweet for Rani and eat all of your dinner. Okay?" Annie watched Jonah cross the gym floor, his loose-limbed stride confident and relaxed. Her breath hung in her lungs.

Haley grumbled an unintelligible response as Jonah reached her.

"I'll be home soon, sugar. B'bye." She closed the phone and held it out to Jonah. "Thanks."

Taking the cell from her, he jerked his chin toward a nearby door. "Let's use the manager's office. It's quieter. More private."

More isolated. Her stomach flip-flopped as she fell in step behind Jonah.

"Hey, Frank," he called to the coach who was working with a boxer on a small punching bag. "Mind if we use your office for a while?"

The man eyed Annie, then sent Jonah a conspiratorial grin. "Be my guest."

After leading her into the windowless office with a sign that read Owner, Jonah closed the door behind him, muting the cacophony from the gym floor and spiking Annie's level of discomfort.

She was suddenly hyperaware that she was alone with a man she barely knew. The idea of being alone with Jonah both tantalized and frightened her. Drawing her purse against her chest, she glanced about the dim office. The decor was surprisingly upscale, with oil paintings and a leather couch. The large desk was covered with old photographs of a younger Frank posing with a pretty woman and a blond little girl.

"Why do I make you so nervous?" Jonah's question drew

her gaze back to him. He angled his head and studied her with a lazy sweep of his eyes.

She forced a smile. "You don't."

Sitting on the edge of the wooden desk, Jonah waved a finger toward her purse. "Your body language says otherwise."

Annie glanced down at her white-knuckle grip on her purse and the defensive position of her arms crossed over her chest. Knowing he could read her so easily didn't help ease her tension.

She sighed. "I'm just…out of my element here. I don't know you well, and this whole business with Hardin and the money I lost has—"

"Stop." He said the word softly, but with enough cool command to freeze the words on her tongue.

Her gaze snapped up to his.

Jonah folded his arms over his chest and drilled her with his dark green eyes. "Let's get one thing straight. You didn't lose that money. You don't owe Hardin a thing. You were mugged, and the money was stolen. Period."

Annie opened her mouth to reply, but no sound came.

"As for your other points…" Jonah shrugged one shoulder. "Maybe you don't know me real well, but if you'd let me take you to a quiet dinner somewhere, we could talk and remedy that."

Her heart pounding in her ears, Annie gaped at him. "Like…a date?"

He nodded. "And if I'm right about you, you're not as out of place at this gym as you'd have me believe."

Already reeling from his invitation to dinner, Annie needed a moment before his last comment registered. "What do you mean I'm not out of place? Do I look like someone who enjoys punching a bag for thrills?"

His face sobered, and he pitched his voice low. "No. But

I think you've been used as a punching bag by some bastard you once trusted."

Annie's head swam, and an odd buzzing rang in her ears. She staggered drunkenly to the nearest chair and dropped onto the seat.

Slowly, he moved toward her and crouched beside her. "Maybe a father. Maybe a husband or boyfriend. Am I right?"

Practiced denials sprang to her tongue but shattered under the weight of his piercing gaze. She struggled to draw a breath. "How… Why would you think—"

"Because I've been there."

Annie's breath backed up in her lungs. She shook her head, not sure she'd heard him right. Did he mean he'd been an abuser—or been abused?

Jonah nodded, his expression open and guileless. "I've seen what you've seen. I know the emotions you've known. I recognize the signs."

He reached for her left cheek and gently grazed her scar with his knuckle.

Mortified, she jerked away and scoffed. "That's from a car accident. I shattered my cheekbone and couldn't afford a fancy plastic surgeon after the emergency surgery."

The lie tumbled easily from her lips, while a hurricane of confused emotions twisted inside her. Guilt, relief, embarrassment, anger, frustration…

How did she begin to sort it all out?

"Part of that is probably true."

Clenching her teeth, she shot him a tight scowl. "Are you calling me a liar?"

He wrapped his hand around hers, and she flinched. Undaunted, he squeezed her hand. "I got good at lying about my injuries, too. To teachers, neighbors…even myself. It wasn't easy to tell anyone my dad had a nasty temper, and he'd beat us and our mom with little provocation."

Icy fingers clamped around her heart. Torn between empathy and wariness, she stared into his jade eyes, searching for some hint of insincerity. But his unflinching gaze shone with compassion and honesty.

Unsure what to do with his revelation, Annie gripped the edge of the chair and listened to the thundering of her pulse in her ears. "Why are you telling me this?"

"I wanted you to know I understood what you'd been through, and I know how—"

Annie stiffened, fury coursing through her blood. She shoved to her feet, balling her hands and glaring at Jonah. "Stop it! You can't begin to know what I've been through! And I don't know what your life was like growing up with a father who hurt you. Don't you dare try to tell me—"

"All right." He put a hand on each of her shoulders, and she tensed, realizing the mistake she'd made.

Her stomach knotted. Her mouth dried. Dear God, if she'd ever lost her temper and challenged Walt that way, she'd have paid dearly.

Inhaling sharply, she held her breath, bracing for Jonah's answering wrath.

Instead, he murmured softly, "I'm sorry. You're right. I only meant—"

When a tremble raced through her, he paused, his brow lowering in a concerned frown. Cupping her chin, he lifted her face toward his, his thumb stroking her jaw.

His tender gesture, so opposite the raw power she'd seen him display moments ago, caught her off guard. The warmth of his fingers, the crisp scent of soap that clung to him, the lulling calm in his voice had her senses reeling. Her head swam, and the heat of a blush prickled her skin.

"Relax, beautiful. You're safe with me. I swear it. I will *never* hurt you." A husky growl of conviction emphasized his vow, a stark contrast to the tenderness of his touch.

Annie couldn't speak, couldn't move. Confused emotions tangled inside her. Part of her wanted to trust Jonah and believe the warm promise in his eyes. Another part of her remembered too clearly the brute violence he'd employed defending her in the alley last night and the power behind his punches in the boxing ring only moments ago. Despite his kindness and gentle touches, she'd witnessed Jonah's fierce strength and skill. Her body's reaction to him was only the natural response to being near so much virile magnetism. Wasn't it?

When she didn't respond, Jonah lowered his hand and stepped back. He sighed and glanced away, his expression pensive. "Annie, I asked you here because I have a bad feeling about what happened last night."

Sinking back onto the chair, she rubbed her throbbing temple and shoved aside distracting thoughts of Jonah's allure. "That makes two of us. Hardin isn't likely to forget the money I lost any time soon. He's going to make my life miserable until I repay him."

Jonah popped his knuckles restlessly and frowned. "I wasn't referring to Hardin."

She glanced up. "What do you mean?"

"I don't think your attack was random. I think the guy who stole the money was waiting for you, that he was expecting someone to be making that delivery for Hardin."

A chill shimmied through her. "Waiting for me?"

"I can't go into detail, but…I have reason to believe the money you were delivering was profits from a gambling ring that Hardin had laundered through the diner's accounts."

Her stomach seesawed. Annie's emotions had spun in

every conceivable direction in the past few minutes, but Jonah's claim made her head reel. Hands shaking, she hugged herself and drew a ragged breath.

"The man who mugged you may have intended to kill you so that you couldn't make an ID. Or Hardin may have picked you to make the delivery because he thought you'd be least likely to talk, that he could keep you quiet through intimidation. Or…there are other scenarios possible, but they all boil down to this—you're involved now. You're in danger."

Chapter 5

This couldn't be happening. Not now. Not again!

Nausea flooded Annie's gut, and a bitter taste rose in her throat. She shook her head. "No. I can't... I didn't d-do anything. I don't know anything. I—I—"

Jonah dragged a hand over his mouth. "Like it or not, because of that delivery you made, because of the theft, you are involved now, and you're going to have to be careful. Watch your back. Take precautions."

Annie muffled a half gasp, half sob.

She'd just spent months escaping a possessive and vengeful husband, seen him brought up on charges of stalking and murder, feared for her life and her children's. She'd only recently started piecing her life back together, finding some sanity and calm.

As he wrapped a firm, warm hand around her wrist, Jonah's gaze drilled into her. "You need to be able to protect yourself. I want to show you a few basic techniques to deter an attacker."

She shook off his hand and narrowed her eyes, suspicion tickling her neck. "How do you know all this? What proof do you have that Hardin's doing anything illegal?"

"I don't have anything solid enough to take to the authorities yet, but—"

"You didn't want me to call the cops last night. Why?" Her mind clicked, reviewing from a new perspective her attack, Jonah's rescue and his defense of her with Hardin that morning. "Are you involved in whatever's going on at the diner?" She rose and stumbled away from Jonah. "How do I know there really is a gambling ring or money laundering or...or—"

Her chest seized, and her stomach pitched at the idea of unwittingly becoming ensnared in unlawful dealings at the diner. The turkey sandwich she'd eaten at lunch roiled in her belly and threatened to come back up.

Jonah sighed. "I know because...I've spent the past six months on this investigation."

"This *investigation?* You're a cop?"

"I was. In Little Rock. But I left the force about a year ago, right before I moved here."

Mentally she reviewed everything she'd heard the other waitresses say about Jonah. "You told Susan you worked at the paper mill. That was a lie, wasn't it?"

He blew a deep breath out through pursed lips. "Yeah. That's my cover."

Annie's heart tapped a staccato rhythm, and she studied Jonah with new eyes, doubt and distrust nipping at her. "Your cover? Who are you? *What* are you? Why should I trust you? What do you want from me?" The questions tumbled from her in increasing volume as her fear mounted.

He quieted her by touching a finger to her lips. "I don't

work for anyone. This investigation is personal for me. I've been looking into the gambling ring and money laundering because of a friend of mine. The men involved in the ring swindled Michael out of his entire retirement savings."

A sympathetic pang gripped her chest. Annie understood the gravity of such a loss. She lived paycheck to paycheck and couldn't imagine how she'd survive if her income disappeared.

Jonah stepped back and propped himself against the scarred desk again. "Last night, I asked you not to go to the cops because I was afraid police involvement in your mugging would scare some of the players into hiding. I'm getting close to nailing these bastards, and I didn't want any unnecessary outside law enforcement to rock the boat before I get the evidence I need."

Annie shook her head trying to wrap her mind around the scenario Jonah laid out. "Wh-what kind of evidence?"

"I need to see for myself exactly how the operation runs, who is involved up the chain. I'll need to videotape a transaction or record incriminating conversations. If I can get them, bank records, computer files, a log of wagers, any kind of paper trail to support my case." He wiped his palms on his jeans and shook his head. "But the deeper I get into their organization, the dicier it gets. These men have a lot of money at stake. If they get spooked, they'll protect themselves and their interests in the operation by any means possible. Even murder."

A numbing chill crept through Annie. She stared at Jonah, questions spinning through her brain, yet she couldn't make her tongue work. The weight of the situation settled on her lungs, squeezing the breath from her. By trying to save her job, had she embroiled herself in a scheme that could cost her her life?

The air in the tiny dark office vibrated with tension. Jonah held her gaze, his green eyes difficult to read in the dim light.

Swallowing the pressure in her throat, Annie voiced her doubts. "How do I know you're telling me the truth? Why should I trust you?"

"Your attack last night was real enough, wasn't it? Hardin's fury over the stolen money was no act. I've no doubt he's up a major creek right now with whoever that money was going to."

Joseph Nance. The name Hardin had given her flashed through her mind, but she kept silent, playing her cards close to her chest until she could figure out for herself who she should trust and where Jonah really fit in the dangerous scenario he described.

"I know I've dropped a bomb on you. I understand how scary this must be. But I need you to believe that I am the only person at that diner looking out for your interests. I want to protect you from any fallout, but you'll have to trust me."

Her trust had been shattered by the last man she gave it to and would be hard-earned for Jonah. Another biting chill nipped her skin. "What do you want me to do?"

"Nothing right now. But stay alert. Keep your eyes and ears open. And learn how to defend yourself." He pushed away from the desk and moved close enough for her to feel the body heat radiating from his skin. "That's where I come in."

Jonah reached for Annie, noting the wariness that shadowed her eyes. When he touched her arm, she stiffened and pulled away.

"What are you doing?" Alarm flashed in her mahogany eyes.

"Getting to the business at hand. Teaching you some defensive moves to protect yourself."

Her stance relaxed a fraction, but her expression remained cautious. He understood that caution better now. Her story about a car accident causing her facial scar aside, she hadn't denied his conjecture about her history of abuse. Her body language had told him all she didn't say. He had to proceed carefully. The last thing he wanted was to cause Annie any more pain.

But her protection was paramount, and he couldn't be with her twenty-four seven.

"Let's start with the basics." He squared his feet in front of her. "Your best strike points are your attacker's eyes, his groin and his throat. Concentrate your efforts there. Okay? Like this…"

Jonah lifted his arms to demonstrate the best hand position for a throat strike.

Annie rubbed a hand down her arm, her expression dubious. "I don't know. Fighting back will only make him mad, make him hurt me more."

Jonah lowered his hands and stepped back. He remembered how Annie had shut down last night, retreating into herself and giving her attacker no resistance. "Do you believe your life is worth fighting for?"

Her chin lifted, surprise flickering across her face. "Of course."

"Do you? Deep down, do you truly believe your life is worth defending at any cost? Because to save your life, you may have to do things that are difficult, or embarrassing, or impolite or disgusting. You have to believe you're worth it and be willing to do whatever it takes. Gouging eyeballs, biting until you draw blood…"

She winced and pulled her arms closer to her body.

Jonah scratched his jaw, reassessing his approach with Annie. His first task was helping her overcome her skittishness. Maybe showing her a few simple, less invasive moves would help build her confidence.

"Lower your arms to your sides," he said, doing so himself. When she complied, he gave her an encouraging smile. "Now I promise not to hurt you. I just want to show you a couple tricks you can use."

Her brow puckered skeptically.

"What would you do if someone grabbed your arm like this?" He wrapped his hand around her wrist with a secure grip.

She gasped and tried to jerk her arm back. He held tight.

"Instinct tells you to pull back, but unless you're stronger than your attacker, that won't work, will it?"

She raised a startled look from her wrist, meeting his gaze. "So…what do I do?"

Beneath his fingers, the flutter of her pulse beat harder, faster. He became acutely aware of the delicate softness of her skin, the poignant blend of hope and vulnerability in her expression and the answering thump of his own heart.

For weeks now, he'd been intrigued by Annie, attracted to her, and the protective instincts she brought out in him only deepened the connection he felt. Knowing how satiny smooth her skin felt stoked the fire that smoldered in his blood when he was around her and teased his imagination. *Steady, boy.*

"Step closer to me." When she hesitated, he added, "Come on. Keep your elbow down and close to your body."

Drawing a shaky breath, Annie edged nearer.

"Okay, look what that did to my grip, the angle of my wrist."

Her wary gaze still on him, she tipped her head like a curious puppy, then glanced down at the awkward cant of his hand.

"Now make a fist and twist it up toward my thumb and over my arm."

She followed his directions and broke free of his grasp. Instead of smiling at her success, Annie scowled. "I didn't do that. You let go on purpose."

He chuckled. "Yeah, because I didn't want a broken wrist. Here. Try it on me, and I'll show you."

Annie gripped the arm he extended at his wrist, and he worked through the steps he'd just shown her slowly, repeating, "Step in. Arm close to you. Fist. Twist toward their thumb and—"

"Ow!" Annie dropped his arm and shook her hand as he broke her hold. She blinked at him, her expression stunned.

He sent her a satisfied grin. "You okay?"

"Yeah, I—" She wet her lips and stood taller. A bit of the skepticism melted from her expression, replaced by intrigue. "It works."

"Of course it works." He chuckled. "I'm not gonna teach you stuff that doesn't work. What's the point in that?"

"Touché." The corner of her mouth twitched, and a pink flush stained her cheeks.

Even that sultry hint of a grin scrambled his concentration and filled his chest with a warmth that expanded until he couldn't catch his breath. But her delicate blush reminded him that despite her full lips and temptress hairstyle, Annie was off-limits. He had nothing to offer the young mother except heartache, and she'd seen enough pain in her life.

"Okay, next move." He stepped behind her, catching her shoulders when she tried to turn toward him. "No, this time let's suppose someone comes up from behind and grabs you like this…" He circled her with his arms, pinning her arms to her sides, and tugged her back against his chest. Again, she stiffened under his restrictive hold.

The light floral scent of her shampoo teased his senses. He gritted his teeth, steeling himself when her futile attempts to break from his hold caused her fanny to buck against his crotch.

After a moment of panicked wiggling, her breath coming in shallow gasps, she stilled. "Let go. Please. I—I don't want to do this."

"Struggling doesn't do anything but wear you out, Annie. You have to use your head. Stay calm."

She gave a small nod and drew a tremulous breath.

"You can break his grip by dropping to the ground. Just lift your feet. But shift all your weight onto his arms. Or if you throw your head back hard—although not now, 'cause I don't want a bloody nose—your skull is hard enough to bash your attacker's face."

She tipped her head back slowly until she lightly bumped his face. Her silky hair tickled his nose and stroked his cheek.

Another spike of arousal sucker punched him, and he wrestled down the urge to nuzzle her neck. He cleared his throat and stepped back, allowing her to face him. "That move, uh… will at least catch him off guard."

Mentally he regrouped, concentrating on the details Annie needed to know. He had only to think of the dangerous people who could be gunning for her after last night and the importance of her knowing how to protect herself to bring him back to the task at hand. "That's a key thing to remember. If you can pull a surprise move on him, it gives you back the upper hand for a few seconds. Use those seconds to strike a debilitating blow that will help you get away. Got it?"

"What debilitating blows? I'm not Bruce Lee."

"Remember those strike points I mentioned?"

She hesitated. "Eyes, throat and…groin."

"Good. We'll get to the Bruce Lee part later. But first you

have to break his hold. Once you're free, pull out your pepper spray and prepare to douse him."

Her forehead dented as she frowned. "I don't have pepper spray."

"Get some. Keep it with you." He waved her close again. "Let me show you something else."

When he stepped toward her, Annie visibly shivered, and Jonah's heart squeezed. He hated the fear that flickered in her watchful eyes. Some bastard had really done a number on her. The mugging last night hadn't helped.

He pressed his mouth in a taut line, realizing that, more than the physical scars on her cheek, Annie bore emotional scars on her heart thanks to the rough treatment she'd received from a man she'd loved. Just as his mom had.

But understanding the source of her ghosts made it all the more important to him that he not add to her pain. He had to be careful not to give her false expectations, not to follow through on the desire that pounded in his veins. He had to protect her from himself.

He paused and held his palms up. "You up for one more demonstration?"

She hugged herself and, closing her eyes, inhaled a deep breath. Blew it out slowly. "All right."

Pride washed through him. Given her history, he knew any reminders of violence and her vulnerability had to be frightening, yet she was here, giving his lessons a fair shake. She had the core strength and resilience that were essential to rebounding from the knocks life had given her.

From behind her, he held her waist with one hand and pressed his other forearm against her throat. "There are two things you can do if you're being choked like this. First, turn your head to the side, into the crook of his arm. That repositions your windpipe so that you can get air."

She moved her head accordingly.

"Good. Perfect."

As he splayed the hand at her waist wider, snuggling her closer to his body, he heard the whisper of her breath catching. A tiny gasp. A feathery near sigh.

The sound shot fire through his blood. He could all too easily imagine her making sexy sighing sounds during sex. Her wispy breath caressed the arm he held to her throat.

Gritting his teeth, he stifled a moan. Jonah shifted his arm from her throat to complete the circle around her waist. Perhaps his idea of private lessons had been ill-advised. The intimate contact required to teach the defensive moves correctly would test even a monk's willpower. Especially when working with a woman as attractive and intriguing as Annie.

He took a moment to gather his composure, blocking out the mental images of stroking her pale skin and exploring the soft curves that were currently nestled against him like a custom-fit glove.

"If he's holding you—" Jonah stopped, hearing the rumbling, husky quality that darkened his tone and left no secret of his arousal. The subtle tensing of her muscles told him she hadn't missed the shift in the atmosphere, the crackle of sexual tension. He cleared his throat.

Without warning, Annie went limp in his arms. The sudden weight on his arms, the shift in his center of balance sent him sprawling forward. Just as he'd told her it would.

Using lightning reflexes, employed a half second too late to avoid falling, Jonah twisted, landing beside her rather than crushing her with his weight. His shoulder caught the brunt of the tumble, and he rolled to his back, his breath jarred from his lungs.

Annie scrambled away, climbing to her feet and edging to

the far side of the room. With her head bowed to her hands, she stood with her back to him, shaking.

Jonah pinched the bridge of his nose. So much for protecting her from himself and reining in his attraction to her.

Private lessons were too intimate, too personal. Their proximity clearly intimidated her. But how was he supposed to help her learn defensive maneuvers without driving himself insane touching her, having her body close to his?

Perhaps more than self-defense lessons, Annie needed to exorcize personal demons. Fortunately, he knew where she could get help with both.

Chapter 6

Annie struggled for a breath and fought to calm the trembling that racked her muscles. She'd known she'd been wrong to come here tonight the minute she realized the kind of gym Jonah frequented. But her real mistake had been something she'd never expected.

She dragged in a cleansing breath and tried to ignore the weight of Jonah's stare. She knew he was waiting for an explanation of her sudden panic. But how did she explain what she didn't understand herself? Working one-on-one had been intimidating at first, but seeing how effective even simple moves could be had buoyed her confidence.

That self-assurance had shattered when he wrapped her in his restrictive hold. The binding hold of his arms had frightened and enticed her at the same time. How screwed up was that?

One minute his hold reminded her of being grabbed in the alley last night, spiking her anxiety. The next moment Jonah spoke his instructions in her ear and her tension dissolved, replaced by an odd thrum of desire.

Having his arms locked securely around her gave her a sense of safety she hadn't know in years. Feeling his body, a wall of strength and heat, pressed against hers made her head spin and her skin tingle. The scent of soap and man filled her nose and enticed her like forbidden fruit.

Then Jonah described an attack scenario for his demonstration that raised a cold sweat on her temple and stirred a fresh swell of panic in her chest.

She'd been fine, though, until she'd heard the change in his voice. His tone had dipped to a sexy rasp that told her she wasn't alone in her attraction. She'd sensed the jolt of awareness that rippled through him in the tensing of his muscles, the moist rasp of his breath on the back of her neck. And her body had responded with its own shudder of anticipation.

Squeezing her hands into fists, Annie tried to sort out the jumble of emotions churning her stomach and spinning her thoughts. Why did Jonah make her want to disregard all the painful lessons life had taught her about men?

"Annie, what's wrong?" The tender concern in Jonah's voice did little to calm the frenzy of activity inside her. The man confused her. Frightened her. Tempted her when she had no business ever giving another man a second glance.

Dear God, she'd just untangled her life and her children's from a controlling, abusive monster. The last thing she wanted was to become involved with another man. Especially one whose prowess in the boxing ring she'd witnessed herself. He could be lethal if he chose. So why did Jonah's gentle hands and warm eyes turn her insides to goo and scramble her sense of reason?

Turning, she forced a fleeting smile. "Nothing's wrong. I just…need to get home now. My kids…"

His steady probing gaze flustered her, and she snatched up her purse without finishing the excuse. Clearly, he knew she was lying.

"We've barely started. There's more you need to know. Important tactics—"

"No. I can't stay. I—"

"You need to protect yourself." He crossed the room, stopping her as she tried to sidle out the door. "Some other time, then? I'll be here again tomorrow. Same time."

She shook her head, avoiding the unnerving intensity of his dark eyes. "I have to work."

"Then you pick the day. I'll be here."

"I don't think so. I—I'll get some pepper spray and…I'll be fine." She edged closer to the door, raising her head only long enough to slant him a quick smile. "Thanks, though."

He placed his hand on her arm, and her pulse jumped. His touch scorched her skin and weakened her knees.

"Annie, you're in the middle of a bad situation at the diner. I don't know what's going to happen now that Hardin's money was stolen, but you need to take precautions. I don't mean to frighten you, but—"

"But you are." She sighed and forced the starch back into her bones as she lifted her gaze to his. "I am frightened. But not just because of everything you've said tonight. I'm scared of a lot of things. I'm afraid I won't have enough paycheck to feed my kids through the end of the week. I'm scared I'll tick Hardin off and lose my job. I'm scared that while I'm working sixty-hour weeks at the diner, I'll miss seeing my kids grow up. Haley lost a tooth today, her first, and I missed it!" Tears thickened her voice, but she plowed on. Once her vent started, she couldn't stop the tide of frustration and pain. "And most of all, I'm terrified that some ignorant parole board will let my ex-husband out of prison, that I'll have to go into hiding again so he can't kill me!"

Jonah straightened his spine and firmed his mouth as if satisfied to have his suspicions confirmed. But the hard edge in his expression softened and compassion warmed his eyes.

In a quieter, more ragged voice, she whispered, "So yeah, I'm frightened, and your talk of money laundering and goons coming after me to shut me up doesn't help. All I want is to raise my children in peace. I never wanted—"

She choked on a sob, and Jonah tugged her into his arms, holding her against his wide chest.

Annie dug her fingers into his T-shirt and rested her forehead under his chin. She hadn't meant to spill so much of her personal life at his feet. But the damage was done now. He knew more than anyone else from the diner. More than anyone other than her women's center counselor, Ginny.

"I've seen what you've seen."

"It wasn't easy to tell anyone my dad was a mean drunk..."

Could Jonah actually understand something of the horror she'd been through? The possibility caused a hard tug in her chest. The comfort and protection of his embrace tempted her to lose herself for a few precious minutes. To lower her guard and let him into her heart.

But relying on Jonah for her safety meant falling back into the traps that had imprisoned her in a violent marriage. Depending on any man for anything, whether security or shelter or her identity, would be a step backward. Wouldn't it?

Her kids were counting on her to be strong, to be self-reliant.

She swiped at her runny nose with the back of her hand and shoved out of his arms. "I have to go. I've already stayed too long."

"Annie, if you'd—"

Before he could finish, she jerked open the door and fled.

"Annie, wait!" Jonah's voice boomed through the cavernous gym, chasing her out to the street. Without looking, she knew he was behind her, that he'd follow her home as he had the night before.

Just as she knew the feel of his embrace and warm breath in her ear were sweet sensations she wouldn't soon forget.

Chapter 7

The next morning as Annie left for work, she paused at the edge of the parking lot and turned to wave at Haley, who watched from the apartment window. Her goodbye ritual, which Haley insisted on, took an ominous turn when she glimpsed a man for a split second before he darted behind a tree.

Her heart fluttering erratically, Annie smiled and lifted a wave to her daughter, while keeping an eye on the large live oak tree where the man had disappeared.

Jonah? Probably.

For some reason she couldn't fathom, he'd appointed himself her guardian. As she'd expected, he'd walked her home last night, having caught up to her several blocks from the boxing gym. She'd refused his offer to drive her, not wanting to be alone with him in the narrow confines of his front seat. Yet even outside, an arm's-length away, walking the city streets back toward her apartment, he'd crowded her.

His presence on her walk home had compounded the conflicting feelings her self-defense lesson had stirred. If Jonah was correct about the danger she was in, she appreciated his efforts to keep her safe. Yet the idea of needing a man's protection nettled her, especially now when she was supposed to be making an independent stand.

He had at least granted her wish for quiet, not bothering to make meaningless conversation. He'd only warned her to lock up when she got inside and bid her a good-night at the foot of the stairs to her apartment.

So why, if he'd walked *with* her last night, was he being so furtive this morning? Sighing her irritation, Annie spun back around and marched toward the bus stop. She didn't see him get on her bus when it arrived, yet the sense of being watched, being followed, stayed with her all the way to the diner. Annoying, cloying, unsettling.

By the time she reached work, she'd grown edgy and waspish, and she planned to give him a piece of her mind. What was he doing tailing her like some pervert when his warnings of danger already had her jumpy and looking over her shoulder? The nerve of him!

Annie stormed through the diner's front door and slammed her purse under the front counter with a huff.

"Whoa," a familiar male voice said. "I was going to say good morning, but obviously yours hasn't been so far, if your mood is any indication."

She snapped her gaze up to the smiling man sitting at the lunch counter.

Jonah. With a half-eaten plate of eggs and grits in front of him.

Her pulse scampered as her pique morphed to dismay. "You're here."

The corner of his mouth hiked higher. "Aren't I every day?"

"But if you're here, then who—" A chill slid through her.

One dark eyebrow dipped over Jonah's incisive stare. "Who what?"

Annie pressed a hand to her swirling stomach and shook her head. "I... Nothing."

Had the man behind the tree been her imagination? Had she really been tailed to the diner, or had she conjured the sensation because she'd expected Jonah to escort her?

She twitched her lips, the closest thing to a grin she could manage at the moment. "Forget it. I..."

She cleared her throat and tried to shake the jitters that danced down her spine.

Jonah's concerned gaze lingered, reminding her that just hours ago she'd been in his arms, held close to his masculine heat and strength. Yesterday, when his hands had been splayed intimately against her ribs, his warm breath fanning her nape, how could she not have entertained sexual images of him? And how did she keep those same images from taunting her this morning?

She fumbled to unfold a clean apron, and though she studiously avoided Jonah's gaze, she felt his eyes tracking her movements behind the counter.

Susan, one of the other waitresses, stood by the order window, her long blond braid trailing down her back as she rolled silverware into napkins. "Mornin', Annie. Am I ever glad you're here! It's been a zoo."

Annie returned a smile, glad for the distraction. "Good morning."

No sooner had the words left her mouth than the morning took a decided turn toward *bad*. Two regulars, the rude and intimidating men Jonah had been sitting with the night she was mugged, sauntered into the restaurant. The men slid into their usual booth, and the larger man snapped his fingers to call her to the table.

As if she were a dog he could summon to grovel at his feet. Annie's skin crawled, and she gritted her teeth.

Susan stepped over to top off Jonah's coffee. She gave the new arrivals a meaningful glance and rolled her eyes. "Want me to get their order for ya, hon?"

Jonah glanced over his shoulder toward the men in question. His shoulders tensed almost imperceptibly. If Annie hadn't been looking for his reaction, she'd have missed the subtle flinch. Why had Jonah been talking with the two men the other night? Were they involved in the gambling and money-laundering investigation he was conducting?

Hands shaking, she tied on her apron and shoved a fresh order pad in her pocket. She gave Susan a grateful smile and shook her head. "No. Let me go clock in, then I'll take care of them."

"Devereaux!" the shorter man called to Jonah.

Jonah sent Annie what she could only call a sharp, warning glance before he faced the men's table and nodded an acknowledgment.

The second man returned a nod, and Jonah carried his coffee over to sit at the men's booth.

Squelching the uneasy jangle inside her, Annie hurried into the kitchen to clock in.

"You're late!" Hardin shouted at her from his post beside the grill cook.

Without answering, Annie walked carefully on the slick floor and consulted the time clock as she punched her card. She was, in fact, ten minutes early.

He's trying to rattle you. As if she needed further rattling that morning.

Someone had followed her to the diner from her apartment. She was sure of it. If not Jonah, then who? And why?

And what was she supposed to make of that odd look Jonah had just sent her? Was he trying to tell her something? Serving the goons was unnerving enough without Jonah sending her unspoken signals.

Taking a deep breath for courage, Annie grabbed a coffeepot and headed to the goons' table.

Temporarily setting aside his concerns surrounding Annie's strange mood that morning, Jonah eased into the booth next to Pulliam and across from Farrout. "Morning, gentlemen."

Farrout arched one thick eyebrow. "You have something for me?"

So much for small talk.

Jonah fished in his back pocket, then slid a folded envelope across the Formica table. Farrout lifted the flap and verified the contents—a cashier's check for eight thousand dollars. The bookie sent him a dark look.

Jonah shrugged. "Like I said before, I'll have the rest at the end of the month, after I get paid."

Pulliam scoffed, and Farrout silenced him with a hooded gaze. "With interest."

His anger spiking, Jonah balled his hand, then sucked in a deep breath to cool his knee-jerk reaction. "You never mentioned interest the other night. We agreed that—"

"You want in or don't you?" Farrout interrupted, his tone flat.

Frustration gnawed at Jonah. He had to play by this scumbag's rules if he wanted firsthand knowledge of how the operation worked. He ground his teeth and finally gave a jerky nod. "How much interest?"

Farrout exchanged a look with his partner.

"Twenty-five percent," Pulliam said, angling his body to lean his back against the wall.

Jonah was ready to argue the point when Pulliam's gaze shifted.

The scents of fresh coffee and flowers alerted Jonah to Annie's arrival even before he turned. His libido snapped to attention. While she filled Farrout's and Pulliam's mugs with hot brew, Jonah inhaled deeply, and the floral aroma of her shampoo sparked memories of holding her body close at the gym. With effort, he shoved down his natural reaction to Annie.

For her sake, he couldn't give Farrout or Pulliam any indication there was any outside connection between him and Annie. He prayed she'd read his unspoken message warning her of the same before he'd joined the shysters at their table.

He hazarded a glance at her, but she kept her eyes on her pad as she took the other men's order. Before she left, her doelike eyes found his. "Anything else for you?"

Her gaze clung, asking more than just what food he wanted. Jonah schooled his face, wanting with every fiber of his being to reach up and stroke the worry lines creasing her brow.

He shook his head and tore his attention away before anything in his expression gave him away.

Once Annie left, Farrout got back to the business at hand. "Here's how it works. Your money goes into the pool with everyone else's. If your team wins, you split the pot with anyone else who had money on the winner. Minus our cut, of course."

Jonah frowned. "Your cut."

Farrout shrugged blithely. "Like your friendly office pool, but with higher stakes."

"And your rules."

"Exactly," Pulliam answered, a smug grin pulling his cheek. "We gotta make something for our services."

Jonah's gut churned. How could Michael have gotten mixed up with something so obviously crooked?

But Michael's perception had been altered. His gambling had become an addiction. Compulsive. An illness. The high stakes would have been as tempting to Jonah's mentor as a cold beer would be to an alcoholic.

"So how big is the pool? How many people have paid in?"

Farrout shook his head. "Proprietary information."

When Jonah scowled, Pulliam chortled. "What? You can trust us."

Trust them to fleece him like they'd fleeced Michael, perhaps.

Annie returned with the men's orders, and as she set Farrout's plate in front of him, he seized her wrist. "I didn't want toast. All I ordered was an omelette. Don't try to charge me for toast I didn't order, ya hear?"

Jonah bristled, remembering the thug's rough treatment of Annie a couple of nights earlier. He leaned forward, ready to rip the bastard's throat out.

But something in Annie's posture stopped him. Her mouth tightened, and color crept to her cheeks. Squaring her shoulders, she stared at Farrout's grip on her arm, then stepped closer to him. "The omelette comes with toast. There's no extra charge." She circled her wrist, twisting her hand toward his thumb. And freeing herself from his grip. *"Sir."*

She stepped back, her expression almost as stunned as Farrout's. Jonah bit the inside of his cheek to contain his proud grin and his chuckle of amusement at Farrout's expense. He wasn't in a position to gloat over Annie's victory while he had business of his own to conduct.

Farrout glared at Annie's back as she marched back to the kitchen. "She just lost her tip."

Jonah squelched his gnawing disgust for Farrout and focused on his goal. If his plan worked, he'd have the sweet satisfaction of ending Farrout's days of manhandling waitresses. Permanently.

He sat through the rest of his meeting with Farrout and Pulliam wishing he could scoop Annie into a bear hug and congratulate her for taking a stand, for her skilled use of the technique she'd only learned last night. He prayed that this demonstration of the technique's effectiveness would convince her to continue with the private lessons.

But did he want to teach Annie one-on-one for her sake— or for his? He couldn't deny his attraction to Annie. He wanted to spend more time with her, get to know her, explore the mysteries that surrounded her. But even without his nine years at the Little Rock Police Department, anyone could have figured out the intimate nature of the private lessons bothered Annie.

After Farrout and Pulliam left the diner, Jonah headed up to the lunch counter to pay for his breakfast. His encounter with the two bookies left him feeling contaminated, tainted by association. His gut told him these two lowlifes were responsible for conning Michael, sending him into the downward spiral that ultimately killed him.

Jonah itched to get into the ring and work off his frustration with the slow pace of his investigation. He needed to sweat off Farrout's invisible filth, which clung to his skin and infected his soul.

If you lie down with dogs...

Susan hustled over to the cash register to take his money, a wide grin at the ready. "Off to the mill, handsome?"

"You lied." Jonah mentally flinched remembering Annie's reaction to his cover of shift work at the paper mill.

"'Fraid so." He handed her his cash and managed a polite smile.

The blond waitress was attractive enough, and he usually enjoyed exchanging flirtatious banter with her. Today he only wanted to ruminate on where his investigation was going and how to crank it up to the next level without arousing suspicion.

"I think pot roast is on the menu for tonight." Susan handed him his change. "Tempt you to come back in for dinner?"

"Susan, you know it's not the food that brings me back every night." Jonah gave her a wink, then scanned the dining room.

He needed to speak to Annie in private before he left—and not just about her self-defense lessons. Something had spooked her this morning. When she'd arrived at the diner and seen him, the flush tinting her cheeks had waned to a ghostly pallor.

Jonah stalled, taking his time putting away his change and unwrapping a mint from the basket by the register. Finally, Annie bustled through the swinging door from the kitchen, casting a wary glance toward the table where he'd had his meeting with Farrout and Pulliam. Relief flashed over her face when she found the table empty.

Jonah moved behind the counter so he could speak to her without raising his voice. "Annie, do you have a minute?"

Spinning toward him with a startled gasp, Annie frowned. "You're not supposed to be back here."

He hitched his head toward the front door. "So follow me out, and we'll talk there."

She gave the dining room a meaningful glance. "I have customers."

"They'll wait. I just need a minute." He took her elbow and nudged her toward the front door.

With a sigh of exasperation, she accompanied him to the sidewalk in front of the diner.

The March sun warmed the air, and a spring breeze lifted her hair, revealing her scars. Annie quickly combed the tousled wisps back over her cheek with her fingers.

Tempted to thread his own fingers through the glossy strands, Jonah shoved his hands into his pockets. "They're not that noticeable, you know. I don't see why you cover them."

Annie shot a startled look toward him.

He angled his head. "Besides, sexy as that side part is, it hides your best feature. You have beautiful eyes, Annie."

She gaped at him for a moment as if she couldn't quite believe what she was hearing. "Is this what you brought me out here for? Patronizing flattery?"

He jerked his shoulders back. "Patronizing? I'm not trying to insult you."

She twisted her mouth into a dismissive frown. "What did you want to talk about? I have to get back to work."

"Why were you surprised to see me here when you got to work? What happened this morning on your way in?"

She crossed her arms over her chest and shrugged a shoulder. "Nothing."

But the nervous glint in her eyes betrayed her.

"The truth."

She cocked her chin up, but the protest on her lips died when he narrowed a hard gaze on her. With a resigned sigh, she turned to watch the traffic on the side street. "I thought you were following me. When I left my apartment this morning, I thought I saw…"

He waited for her to finish, but she only shook her head. "It was probably just my imagination." She slanted an irritated glance at him. "You've got me so paranoid about someone gunning for me because of that stolen money that I'm jumping at my own shadow."

An uneasy tremor rippled through him. Instinct told him that whatever she'd sensed, whatever she'd seen had been no trick of her imagination.

"Just the same, I think I should drive you home tonight, bring you to work when you—"

"No."

He reached for her arm, determined to make her understand the seriousness of the situation. "Annie, until I can be sure you're safe—"

"I said no." She wrenched free of his grip and took a big step back. "I'm not your responsibility, Jonah. I need to take care of myself."

"Then meet me tonight for another self-defense lesson."

Her shoulders drooped, and she shook her head. "I don't think so. I—"

"Annie, think about it—you've only had one lesson, and already you've put something you learned to use."

The corner of her mouth lifted, and she peeked up at him. "I surprised myself with that."

"Why are you surprised? You're a strong, capable woman. You can do anything you want if you apply yourself to it."

She rolled her eyes. "You sound like Ginny." Tipping her head, she met his eyes briefly. "She's my counselor at the women's center."

The simple statement told Jonah a great deal. The Lagniappe Women's Center counseled and aided women who'd been raped, abused or otherwise traumatized. This Ginny Annie referred to was likely responsible for helping Annie free herself from her abusive situation. A good ally to have in her corner. That Annie trusted him enough to confide having used the center's resources was progress.

Jonah grinned. "I like Ginny already."

Annie shifted her weight and sighed. "Look, I plan to buy a can of pepper spray on the way home tonight. I'll be fine."

"And what if someone really is following you? Pepper spray is a start, but to defend yourself from—"

"No!" She shuddered and raised both palms toward him. "Jonah, I appreciate your time yesterday and your concern for me, but… I just… I can't…"

When she hesitated, he asked, "Is it me? Is it working with me in private that bothers you?"

Her expression answered him even though she didn't. The awkward, apologetic look she gave him burrowed to his core. He'd suspected as much, should have known better.

"There's an alternative. The local police department offers ongoing self-defense classes for women at the training center on Wood Street. They meet four days a week at 5:00 p.m. The instructor is a woman. A police officer. The class is all women and teenaged girls."

She bit her bottom lip and furrowed her brow as if considering his suggestion.

"It's a good class. No charge. No commitment."

The knit over her eyebrows deepened. "And you know all this because…?"

Jonah balked. If he told her the truth, that he served as the training aggressor for the class, would his participation be a deterrent because of her discomfort around him? In the class, he wore a full-body, padded suit including a helmet with a face mask so the women could practice the defensive strikes without injuring him. Annie didn't have to ever learn he was involved in the class.

He opted for partial truth, hoping she'd forgive his sin

of omission if she ever discovered his deception. "The lead instructor is a friend of mine. She told me about the class."

Before Annie could answer, Susan appeared at the diner door. "Annie, we need you. Orders are backing up."

"I have to go," Annie murmured, brushing past him.

He caught her arm, felt her tremble at his touch. "Please think about it. Even if this business with the stolen money comes to nothing, you need to be able to protect yourself."

She set her shoulders and gave him a tight nod. "I'll think about it."

Thinking was a start, but not really enough. He had to convince her to take the class. Her life could depend on it.

Chapter 8

Annie's thoughts drifted to Jonah time and again throughout the day. She had to admit, even the little bit of information he'd given her last night about defending herself had been valuable. After weeks of being manhandled by Mr. Farrout, breaking his grip on her wrist this morning had been surprising. Exhilarating. Encouraging.

The idea of learning more from Jonah was tempting. But so was Jonah. Being around him at the diner, remembering how his defense demonstrations made her body hum and her knees weak, was difficult enough. She'd be crazy to purposely put herself in his proximity. In his arms. Alone. Even to learn self-defense, she couldn't justify torturing herself with something so...

Annie wiped her hands on her apron and chewed her bottom lip. What was the right word?

Forbidden? She certainly had no business taunting herself

with a physical relationship that could never be. She had no room in her life for a man, and she didn't do one-night stands.

Confusing? Jonah's fighting skills, his brute strength and size contradicted the compassionate concern he'd shown her and his gentleness when he'd touched her. So who was the real Jonah?

Intimidating? More than her ever-present fear of physical violence, Jonah's uncanny ability to read her, to guess her motivations, predict her responses and see through her excuses left Annie off balance.

"I wanted you to know I understood what you'd been through."

Even Ginny didn't claim to understand the turbulent emotions of Annie's abusive marriage, the terror, the self-doubt and self-recrimination. But Ginny had been raised in a healthy family, had a loving marriage to a wonderful man.

Jonah claimed he had experience with abuse, had grown up with a violent father. Was it possible he did understand her and the pain of her past?

"Yoo-hoo. Anybody home?" Susan asked, waving a hand in front of Annie and bringing her out of her deep reverie. "Table six is ready for his bill."

"Thanks." Annie pushed the distracting thoughts of Jonah aside as she flipped through her order pad and presented the businessman at table six with his check and an apologetic smile. "Sorry for the delay. Can I get you anything else?"

His gaze traveled slowly down her body and back up, lingering on her chest. "That's all today—" his focus shifted quickly to her name tag before he met her eyes "—Annie." He put peculiar emphasis on her name, and as he slid out of his booth, his grin could be better characterized as a smirk.

Annie returned to the counter, gritting her teeth. "Why do the smarmy guys always sit at my tables?"

"Luck of the draw. But you don't have a monopoly on scumbags." Susan took a couple of plates from the order window and sent Annie a commiserating look. "Just yesterday, I had a guy in here *with his wife,* and he grabbed my ass." She rolled her eyes and huffed in disgust as she carried the orders out to the dining room.

Annie did her best to shake off the heebie-jeebies the creepy businessman gave her and concentrate on her job the rest of the day. But thoughts of Jonah and his encouragement to take the self-defense class offered by the police department returned that afternoon when she left work.

On an impulse, Annie bypassed her bus stop and headed to the Lagniappe Women's Center. The staff at the center, in particular her counselor, Ginny Sinclair, had been instrumental in helping her leave Walt sixteen months ago. Ginny and her husband, Riley, had risked their lives to save her and her children and had become dear friends of Annie's. When Annie needed perspective, encouragement and straight answers, Ginny was always there for her.

Today, she needed a dose of Ginny's honesty and understanding.

Annie smiled to the receptionist as she made her way to Ginny's office door and knocked. Hearing Ginny call, "Come in," Annie cracked the door open and peeked in.

Her blond-haired counselor cradled her phone to her ear but smiled broadly when Annie stepped into the office. She waved Annie to a chair and rocked forward in her seat. "Gotta go, babe. Annie just arrived. I will. Love you, too."

Ginny sighed happily as she replaced the receiver, then lifted a glowing grin to Annie. "Riley says hi."

Annie returned a smile. Ginny's newlywed bliss was palpable, and Annie couldn't be happier for her friends, though she experienced a pinch of envy for the contentment that radiated from Ginny's eyes. Would she ever find that pure joy with a man or would Walt always cast a shadow over her?

Taking a chair opposite Ginny's desk, she took a deep breath. "I know I don't have an appointment, but I was hoping you had a couple minutes. Something's happened."

Ginny frowned. "What's wrong?"

Annie explained about the attack in the alley and the stolen money, the possibility that the diner was the hub of illegal gambling and money laundering. "Jonah thinks I could be in danger. He wants me to take a self-defense class, and he—"

"Whoa." Ginny held up her hand. "Back up a second. Jonah? Who is that?"

Annie glanced down at her lap where her hands fidgeted. "He's a customer at the diner. A regular. He...followed me the night I was supposed to make that delivery, and he... defended me from the mugger. Probably saved my life." She squeezed her eyes shut, picturing Jonah's rugged face, his warm green eyes. Her stomach twirled and pirouetted dizzily, but, surprisingly, the sensation was not an unpleasant one. Instead, thoughts of Jonah stirred her pulse with the exhilaration of a carnival ride.

Annie huffed and forcibly tamped down the tingling reaction. She had no business indulging in any frivolous schoolgirl distraction when her job, her life, her children's safety could well be in jeopardy. "Jonah...has made himself my guardian. He's taken it upon himself to teach me to protect myself or see that I take a self-defense class. He wants to drive me to and from work, and he..."

When she paused, Ginny said, "He sounds like a good guy to have on your side. So why do I get the impression you are less than thrilled?"

"I didn't ask for his help. Not that I don't appreciate his assistance the night I was mugged, but I...I don't want..."

Ginny leaned forward. "Spit it out. Don't edit your true feelings."

Annie took a deep breath. "I don't want to need him. I don't want to depend on him and get trapped in a relationship that's bad for me again."

Ginny picked up a pencil to doodle as she thought, a quirky habit Annie had grown familiar with in the past two years. "Is that where you think your association with him is headed? A romantic relationship?"

"I... No. I didn't mean... I just..." Annie sighed. "I don't know. I'm not looking for a relationship right now. Truly. But if I'm honest—"

Ginny raised a palm. "Honesty is the best policy...and all that jazz."

"I find myself thinking about him a lot. And I feel...safer somehow when he's around." Annie sighed, then hurried to add, "But that's the thing. I don't want to reach a point where I only feel safe with him around, where I depend on him for... well, for *anything*."

Ginny rubbed her chin, clearly weighing her response. "There's a difference between being emotionally secure and self-reliant, and isolating yourself out of fear. Don't be too quick to cut yourself off from people, Annie. We all need other people in our lives sometimes."

Ginny's gaze drifted to the wedding portrait on her desk, and the corner of her mouth lifted. "At its best, a loving relationship makes you a stronger, better person. The right man will complement you, not eclipse you. It's about give and take, sharing and supporting each other. Being a team where both partners contribute the best of themselves."

Annie stared at a knot in the hardwood floor of Ginny's office. Had her marriage to Walt ever been a partnership where they complemented each other? From the beginning,

Walt had taken the lead and made decisions about their future, their lifestyle, their finances. Annie had been left to follow…or be forced into compliance.

"I only just got my freedom back, my independence. Getting into another relationship now seems…" She fumbled for
the right word.

"So don't get into another relationship yet," Ginny said.
"That's not what I'm telling you. Just don't be afraid of building something special with a man because you're afraid of
losing yourself again. Because the right man will help you
discover all your best qualities, will support you and let you
shine. Just like you'll do for him." Ginny laced her fingers.
"Stronger together. A team."

Annie nodded, stashing the advice away to ruminate on
later. "And the other stuff I mentioned? The mugging, the
money laundering, the self-defense classes…what am I supposed to do with all that?"

Ginny stabbed her desk with her finger. "Take the class.
Knowing how to protect yourself is always a good thing. As
for the money laundering…I can call Libby Walters in the
D.A.'s office if you want an official investigation opened."

Annie shook her head. "No. Jonah doesn't want to involve
the local police yet. He's afraid one of the players will get wise
to his investigation and all his work will be lost."

"But if there is something illegal and dangerous going
on—"

Annie sat up straight, her mind made up. "Jonah is an ex-
cop. I believe he knows what he's doing."

Somehow saying the words reassured her. She felt no hesitation defending Jonah's handling of the investigation. What
did that say about her deepest, truest feelings?

Ginny arched an eyebrow. "You're sure? Because if you

ever change your mind about this, you can call me, and I'll have Libby look into—"

Annie gave a tight nod. "I'm sure."

"And the mugging. How are you handling that? Any nightmares? Trouble sleeping? Issues you want to talk out?"

"I've had…a few flashbacks of Walt's abuse." Annie fingered the hem of her uniform skirt. "Especially seeing Jonah using his fists so effectively." She paused and glanced up at Ginny. "Did I tell you Jonah spars as a hobby? He fights for fun. For exercise."

Ginny scowled. "Has he given you reason to think he'll turn that violence against you?"

"Not yet. In fact, like I mentioned, he's encouraged me to learn self-defense."

Relaxing in her chair again, Ginny absently scratched another doodle. "So…stay alert with him. Be watchful for signs he's dangerous, but…give him a chance to prove his worth, too." She glanced up, and her gaze invited a response. "What else has been happening?"

Gnawing her lip, Annie thought about the creepy sensation of being watched on her way to work. "Well, I get the feeling someone is following me when I come and go from the diner. But that could just be paranoia."

"Just the same, be extra careful. Take Jonah up on his offer of a ride. Better safe than sorry, huh?"

A knock on Ginny's door interrupted them, and the receptionist poked her head in. "Sally Hendridge is here when you're ready."

"Thanks, Helen." Ginny rose from her chair and circled her desk.

Annie took the cue that the meeting was over and stood, as well, only to find herself drawn into Ginny's friendly embrace.

"Take care of yourself, Annie. And give those sweet kid-dos of yours a hug from their aunt Ginny."

"I will." Annie backed out of the hug and picked up her purse. While Ginny made her feel more optimistic, in general, her friend had also given her a great deal to think about regarding Jonah.

Thinking in terms of a relationship with him was more than a little premature. Still, she reviewed everything Ginny had said as she left the women's center and headed to the bus stop.

Like that morning, the sensation of being watched dogged her on her trip home. She checked behind her numerous times, but never spotted any one person she considered a threat. But then her stalker, if there was one, wouldn't advertise his presence. Would he? Or was it, as she'd suggested to Ginny, merely her imagination and paranoia at work?

She tried to discount the odd feeling, but the next morning as she made her way through the predawn darkness to open the diner, the sensation returned in full force.

Finding the entrance to the diner unlit only heightened her jitters. Perhaps she should follow Ginny's advice and take Jonah up on his offer of a ride home. And she'd look into the Lagniappe P.D.'s class, if for no other reason than to calm the jangling nerves that made her commute to the diner and back home so tense.

Annie fumbled to key the front door lock but discovered it was already open. Odd.

Grumbling under her breath about Mr. Hardin's multiple oversights in closing the restaurant the night before, Annie started a pot of coffee and headed to the kitchen to clock in and collect the cleaning supplies she'd need to prepare the restaurant for opening.

Instead, she found Hardin sprawled on the office floor in a puddle of blood.

* * *

When Jonah arrived for breakfast at Pop's, a swarm of cops milled around the entrance and crime scene tape barred the gathering of reporters and curious onlookers from entering the diner. His heart rose to his throat as a black body bag was wheeled out by the coroner and loaded in a hearse.

Panic squeezed his chest, and he struggled to recall the waitresses' work schedule he'd conned Susan into showing him, knowing Annie wouldn't share her schedule willingly.

Friday. Annie was slated to open the diner.

Dear God.

Adrenaline pumped through him, jangling his nerves. A cold sweat beaded on his lip as he searched the crowd for Annie's face.

Years of experience with crime scenes that should have allowed him some professional distance vanished. When someone you cared about was involved, objectivity flew out the window.

He spotted Lydia and shoved through the horde of reporters and cameramen. Seizing Lydia's arm, he spun her around. "What happened? Where's Annie?"

The gray-haired woman scowled at him and fought his grip until recognition dawned on her face. "Oh, Mr. Devereaux, it's you. I thought you were another vulture reporter trying to exploit this tragedy for ratings."

She huffed indignantly and sent a scathing look down the sidewalk to the aforementioned scavengers.

Jonah fought down the rising fear that coiled inside him, forced his voice to remain calm. "What tragedy, Miss Lydia? What happened?"

"It's Hardin. Poor Annie found him shot dead in his office when she got here this morning to open the place."

Relief that the body bag hadn't been for Annie, and a gnawing concern for her trauma, tangled inside him.

Lydia shuddered and wrinkled her nose in dismay. "I can't even imagine how grisly and horrifying that had to have been for her," she said, mirroring Jonah's thoughts.

"Where's Annie now?" He cast another searching glance over the rubbernecking bystanders. "What happened to her? Is she all right?"

"Shook-up real bad, but not hurt." The older woman's face crumpled in sympathy. "Poor dear. Last I saw her, one of the cops had put her in the back of a cruiser to take her statement, get her out of the diner and away from the pushy reporters." She aimed a finger down the block. "Over there."

Jonah squeezed Lydia's hand. "Thanks."

He jogged down the street in the direction Lydia had pointed, searching each of the numerous police cars for Annie. When he spotted her, a curtain of dark hair shielding her bowed face, her thin shoulders hunched forward, her body rocking rhythmically back and forth on the rear seat of a cruiser, his gut twisted. Her body language reflected abject misery and terror.

A suffocating urgency to reach her, comfort her, protect her, grabbed him by the throat. He darted around the cluster of uniformed officers holding court on the sidewalk and knocked on the car window. "Annie!"

Her head jerked up, eyes wide. A gray pallor leeched her complexion. In seconds, the officers on the sidewalk assessed Jonah as a threat and seized his arms.

"Back off, sir," one cop ordered as he hauled Jonah back from the police car.

Annie scrambled to find the door handle, beating it with her fists when she found herself trapped in the cruiser's escape-proof backseat.

"That's my girlfriend," he lied. "I just want to talk to her! Can't you see she's upset?"

"She's a material witness. Until the detectives question her—"

"I know the drill!" Jonah released his frustration on the uniform. "I was on the job in Little Rock for nine years! I just want to hold her, calm her down." He shook free of the man's grip and shoved past another cop blocking his path.

"Sir, you can't—"

Jonah stuck his nose in the second cop's face. "Look, pal, you can stand right next to us and monitor our conversation if you want. We won't discuss the case. But I *am* going to let her out of that car." He met the officer's narrowed gaze with a dark glare of his own, then grated through clenched teeth, "Now get the hell outta my way."

With a determined stride around the cop, Jonah snatched open the cruiser door.

Annie lunged from the backseat and fell into his arms. "Jonah!" she gasped, her body trembling. "They killed Hardin! They shot him! Oh, God, Jonah."

He crushed her slim body to his chest, only to find his arms were shaking as much as she was. Just holding her, knowing she was safe, released the knot of tension that strangled him. He clung to her, stroking her back and sucking in deep restorative breaths.

"Oh, Jonah, it was horrible. There was blood everywhere, and his eyes—"

"Shh," he murmured into her ear. "Don't say anything now. We can't talk about the case until you've answered all the police's questions. Okay?"

She raised frightened eyes to his and nodded. A near-convulsive tremor shook her, and she dug her fingers into his arms.

"Is this my fault?" she rasped under her breath.

Jonah's gut clenched. "No!"

"But I—"

His grip tightened, and his gaze drilled into hers. "No! You can't think that way."

"We both know why this happened."

Jonah cut a furtive glance to the cop standing a few feet away, listening. He had to keep Annie from saying too much, incriminating herself or blowing his investigation.

She shivered, near hysterics. "A-and I'm the one who lost—"

He kissed her. Just a quick collision of mouths. Not the deep, intimate kiss she deserved and he hoped he could give her someday, but enough to shock her into silence.

Enough to tell him her lips were every bit as soft and sweet as they looked. Enough to fire both his libido and his primal protective instincts.

She blinked. Gaped. Lifted a trembling hand to her mouth.

Guilt kicked him. Perhaps now, when she was already vulnerable, shaken by Hardin's murder, wasn't the best time to complicate his tenuous relationship with Annie. Even if the kiss kept her from incriminating herself in front of the eavesdropping cop.

Blowing out a cleansing breath, he turned to the cop. "When will she be done here? I want to take her home."

The officer arched an eyebrow and flashed a suggestive I-just-bet-you-would grin. Jonah gritted his teeth, battling down the urge to wipe the smug look off the man's face. But getting arrested for assaulting an officer would do Annie and his investigation no good.

"We just have a few more questions to ask her. She was in shock earlier, and we were giving her time to calm down."

Jonah brushed the hair back from Annie's cheek and gently

massaged the tense muscles in her shoulders. "You feel up to some questions?"

Annie turned a wide-eyed glance to the policeman. "Can h-he stay with me?"

"Sorry. No." When her face turned a shade whiter, the man hitched his head toward the sidewalk. "He can wait right there, though. This will only take a minute."

Jonah took Annie's icy hands in his and squeezed. "I'll wait for you." He brushed a soft kiss on her knuckles and backed away. "You're strong, Annie. You can do this."

Her expression, as she cut a glance toward the cop, said she didn't agree.

Jonah leaned his back against the brick wall of the building next door to the diner and kept a close watch as Annie gave her statement and answered questions. He only caught snatches of the conversation. But having conducted more of these interviews than he liked to remember when he'd been on the force in Little Rock, he could fill in the blanks. Crossing his arms over his chest, he scanned the gathered crowd, scrutinizing faces, taking mental note of who'd come to rubberneck.

Could Hardin's killer still be lurking in the area? Somehow he doubted it. The killing could have been a robbery gone bad, but he doubted that, too.

Annie's instinct that the killing was related to the cash delivery stolen from her was much more on the mark. But in this day and age, where money could be transferred from one account to another with the click of a mouse and the blink of a cursor, why deal with cash and messengered deliveries? The whole scenario reeked. He was certain the thief had been waiting for Annie, the delivery a setup to squeeze Hardin.

Was the head of the operation getting greedy, trying to

eliminate the fringe players to keep more profit for himself?
Had Hardin become a liabilty?

Jonah clenched his teeth. He needed more hard evidence
soon so he could close his investigation, nail the bastards responsible. Before anyone else got hurt. Like Annie.

A cold ball of fear settled in his gut. Annie could easily
be the thief's next target if he thought she knew too much.

Time to change tactics with Annie. She still needed to
learn to protect herself, but Jonah wasn't about to leave her
safety up to a few lessons in self-defense moves. Whether she
liked it or not, he intended to stay at her side, watching her
back until he knew the men responsible for Michael's death
and Hardin's murder were behind bars—or dead.

Chapter 9

Cold permeated to her bones.

Annie rubbed her arms as she answered the cop's questions, but her hands did little to displace the chill that sank deep into her marrow. Hardin's lifeless stare haunted her whenever she closed her eyes. The metallic scent of blood overlaid by remnants of day-old grease lingered in her nose, churning her stomach with every inhaled breath.

"Do you own a gun, Ms. Compton?" the cop asked, jerking her attention back to the seemingly endless questions.

She blinked, stunned by the implication. Did they suspect *she* had killed her boss? That she had a motive to shoot Hardin?

And did it matter if she hadn't actually been the one to pull the trigger? Hardin was just as dead, and her careless loss of his money was why he'd been murdered. She knew that much with a horrifying clarity.

The icy numbness burrowed deeper. "N-no. I— I've never owned a gun."

"Do you have access to someone else's gun?"

She shook her head. "I didn't do this. I found him already...dead."

The cop was clearly unmoved by her denial of guilt. He fired a few more questions before finally flipping his notepad closed and eyeing her dispassionately. "All right. That's it. You can go for now, ma'am. But don't leave town. We may have more questions for you in the next couple days."

Annie nodded and wrapped her arms around her stomach, feeling she had to physically hold herself together or she'd shatter.

She glanced down the sidewalk to the spot where Jonah stood patiently waiting for her. Why turning to Jonah in this crisis felt right, she couldn't say, but when she'd seen him at the window of the police car, her relief had been immediate and immense. She'd held her breath as he fought to get past the officers blocking his path. She'd needed his calming comfort, his reassuring strength, and hadn't questioned why she'd instinctively known he'd come. As soon as the initial shock of finding Hardin dead had morphed into a bone-chilling fear for her own life, Jonah's had been the face she'd sought as the police gathered and morbidly curious crowds clogged the sidewalk.

Now he tucked her trembling body under his chin, his arms folded securely around her, and she let the tears she'd been holding at bay throughout the policeman's questioning wash down her cheeks.

His embrace was firm and reassuring without crushing her. The soothing strokes of his wide hand on her back eased the chaos and terror of the past hours. Nestled close to him again, she allowed her thoughts to drift back to the jolt that had shot through her when he'd surprised her with his kiss. More unexpected than the kiss itself was her body's electric reaction. If his intention had been to scramble her thoughts and distract her from the situation, he'd succeeded nobly for several breathless seconds. The tender caress of his lips had spun a soothing warmth through her terror-chilled blood.

"When you're ready, I'll take you home," he murmured, his warm breath stirring the hair at her neck.

Home. Her children.

A fresh wave of icy horror flashed through her. She stiffened and jerked back to stare at Jonah in dismay. "My kids! What if the people who did this go after my kids?"

Nausea swamped her gut. If anything happened to Haley or Ben...

Jonah's grip tightened slightly, and he took her chin between his fingers and thumb. "That's not going to happen."

Frowning, she pulled her chin from his grip. "You don't know that. They could be at my apartment now!" She glanced to the cluster of policemen half a block away and lowered her voice to a harsh whisper. "I'm the one who lost that money. If they did this to Hardin, then why wouldn't I be next on their list?"

"I'm not denying that you could be in danger. But I promise you, I won't let them hurt you or your kids on my watch." The rough edge to his voice, the penetrating heat of his dark eyes rippled through her with concentric waves. Another tiny piece of her trust surrendered to his firm persuasion.

Jonah had bulldozed his way into her life and appointed himself her counsel and guardian. She knew so little about him, and what she did know was conflicting and confusing. By all rights, she should be running in the other direction. She'd had enough of bossy, controlling men.

Yet Jonah's concern for her and her family seemed genuine. That alone was novel in her experience. Walt had been selfish, cared little for what his drinking and cruelty were doing to her and the children.

And Jonah had encouraged her to become self-reliant, empowered, confident. Walt had preyed upon her through fear and intimidation.

He nodded his head toward the parking lot. "My truck is over here."

She followed him to his pickup and climbed inside. As they drove to her apartment in silence, Annie's head pounded with questions, terrifying images of death and a numbing fear that she'd once more lost control of her life.

Jonah parked in a visitor's spot on the far side of the parking lot, and she climbed out of his truck. Relief poured through her when she spotted Rani and her children playing on the grassy quadrant between apartment buildings.

Jonah placed a proprietary hand at the small of Annie's back as they started across the crumbling asphalt.

Haley noticed her first, and her daughter's face brightened. "Mommy!"

She ran across the parking lot to intercept her mother, and Annie stooped, catching her little girl in a fierce, protective bear hug. Holding Haley, knowing her kids were safe, melted a layer of the chill in her bones.

"How come you're home, Mommy?"

"I...just got the day off." Clinging to her daughter, Annie inhaled the sweet scent of the baby shampoo Haley still used, and a rush of tender emotion washed through her. Her children were everything to her, and if she had to go into hiding again to protect them, so be it.

Haley pushed back from the hug. "Does that mean you can play with us? Can we play with my Barbies?"

Excitement and hope laced Haley's voice, and joy lit her eyes.

"In a little while. I need to…take care of a few things first." Annie stroked her daughter's hair and kissed her forehead. "But later, I promise to play Barbies with you."

Her daughter grinned her satisfaction, then turned a curious look to Jonah, who'd stayed back as she greeted her daughter.

"Who are you?" Haley asked, wrinkling her nose.

Annie sent Jonah an apologetic glance. "Haley, if you want to meet someone, you introduce yourself politely. Remember?"

"Oh, yeah." Haley scratched her nose and gave Jonah a measuring look.

Annie watched Haley's reaction to him closely. Jonah was the first new man she'd brought around the kids since the ordeal with Walt came to a head more than a year ago.

He stepped forward and held his hand out for Haley to shake. "I'm Jonah Devereaux, a friend of your mom's. Nice to meet you, Haley."

Jonah's hand swallowed her daughter's smaller one, and an uneasy tremor fluttered through Annie, a reminder of how vulnerable her children were.

Rani had reached them with Ben in her arms, and she gave Annie a worried look. "Ms. Annie, is everything all right?"

"Well, yes and no. The diner had to close today unexpectedly. I can watch the kids today."

Rani gave her a brief update on what the kids had eaten and when Ben had woken up that morning as she passed the toddler over to his mother.

"I'll call you when I know what's going to happen tomorrow. My plans are kinda up in the air right now," Annie said.

She sighed as Rani told the kids goodbye and headed toward her apartment.

If fearing for her life and her children's weren't enough, Annie hated the uncertainty this turn of events cast over her future. Would she have a job tomorrow? Would the diner close indefinitely? Would she have to leave Lagniappe to protect herself from the person who murdered Mr. Hardin?

As she herded Ben and Haley back toward their apartment, Haley stopped to play with the neighbors' cat. Eager to get the children inside, out of view of any eyes that could be watching her, stalking her, she opened her mouth to chastise Haley for dawdling.

But Jonah crouched beside Haley and joined her in stroking the cat's back. Annie paused, watching her daughter give the cat solid thumping pats.

"Gently," Jonah murmured. "See how he put his ears back? That means he's unhappy. You don't want to hurt him, right? Kitties like soft pats."

Haley gentled her touch and tipped her head. "Like this?"

"Yeah, good."

The lesson in kindness to animals caught Annie off guard. His concern that Haley not hurt the cat contributed to her confused feelings toward Jonah. She tried to reconcile Jonah's fighting skills with this protective and loving attitude toward animals.

A shiver raced over her skin remembering how safe she'd felt in his arms when he'd gotten her out of the police cruiser. How could someone who sparred as a hobby, who didn't hesitate to take on another man in a dark alley in hand-to-hand combat have such a gentle soul? The contradiction flew in the face of everything her personal experience taught her. She was risking a lot bringing Jonah home, exposing her children to him.

She prayed she didn't regret taking the chance later. But she needed answers from Jonah, and the diner wasn't safe for this particular discussion.

"Do you have a cat?" Haley asked. Her wide-eyed innocence twisted in Annie's chest.

Jonah blinked his surprise, then chuckled. "Well, no. Do you?"

"No, sir. Me and Mommy want one, but she says we can't. She says maybe we can someday."

Jonah arched an eyebrow and divided a smile between Haley and Annie. "And when is someday?"

"Haley, take Ben and go on inside. I'll fix you a snack when I get upstairs." Annie waited until Haley had led her toddling brother up the steps and closed the door before turning back to Jonah. "I don't know when someday will be. It can't get here soon enough for me." She gripped the railing to steady herself, recalling the darkest days of her life. "Someday is when I don't have to worry that my husband will hurt an innocent animal to scare or control me. I couldn't justify exposing a pet to Walt's volatile temper and cruelty."

Jonah's expression inexplicably tensed and softened at the same time, anger and empathy clearly battling for dominance.

"Someday," she continued, struggling to keep her voice steady, "is when I'm not on the run, living in hiding to escape the murderous intentions of my husband. I didn't know from day to day where we'd sleep at night, if Walt would find us and make good on his threat to kill me. A cat would have been impractical."

Jonah nodded, his dark eyes boring into her. Rather than rattle her as his intense gaze usually did, his focused attention encouraged confidence and soothed her frayed nerves.

She cleared the knot of emotion clogging her throat and added, "Someday is when I don't have to stretch my paycheck so thin you can see light through it. I can barely keep a roof over our heads and food in my kids' stomachs with what I earn."

The neighbors' cat wound through her legs, rubbing, and Annie bent to pick it up. Cuddling the feline close to her chest, Annie buried her face in the cat's soft fur. "I would love to let my baby have a pet, but cat food and vet bills aren't in the budget."

Jonah reached for her, but instead of patting the cat, he stroked Annie's cheek with his wide palm. "Someday may be closer than you think."

She scoffed and set the cat back on the ground when it squirmed. "How can you say that after this morning? Even if the diner reopens and I still have a job, Hardin was *murdered* because of that stolen money. How do I know I won't be next?"

Conviction and determination blazed in Jonah's eyes. "Because I won't let that happen. Hardin's isn't the first life lost because of these bastards, and if it is the last thing I do, I'm going to find the people responsible and see that they pay."

As Annie fixed her kids an early lunch, the bone-deep chill returned when Jonah's remark replayed in her head. Who else had been killed? How had Jonah become involved in investigating the gambling and money laundering?

Her children's restless squabbling drifted in from the living room where she'd left them watching TV with Jonah. She hurriedly finished draining the boiling water from the macaroni, eager to get back to the children and quiet their bickering. Jonah had to be uncomfortable around her fussy kids. Even the most stalwart soul could grow edgy around cranky children. Lord knew, the kids crying had been enough to set Walt off.

She shuddered remembering how often she'd had to run interference, bend over backward to keep the kids quiet when Walt was in one of his moods. And the backlash when her efforts hadn't been enough.

With those dark memories haunting her, Annie set the macaroni aside and rushed to the living room to break up her children's latest squabble.

"That's the way! Punch it again. Harder," Jonah said as she stepped around the corner from the hall. He held a sofa pillow in front of him, egging Ben to jab the cushion with his tiny fists.

Outraged, Annie snatched the pillow away, her temper spiking. "Stop it!"

Both Ben and Jonah lifted startled looks.

"Annie?"

"How dare you teach my son to fight! I risked my life getting away from my husband so that my kids wouldn't learn his abusive ways. I will *not* allow you or anyone to teach my son it is okay to hit!" Anger and hurt raised the level and pitch of her voice. Her body shook, and tears bloomed in her eyes as she glared at Jonah.

He raised a placating hand and rose from the floor to face her. "Your son already knows how to hit. I was trying to teach him to punch something *other than* his sister. I told him hitting a girl was never okay. I wanted him to redirect his frustration on an inanimate object."

Annie stared at Jonah, dragging in air and needing a moment for his explanation to pierce the skin of her anger. With her heart thundering, she recalled seeing Ben punch Haley in a fit of anger more than once. She'd asked Rani to do all she could to squelch the behavior when she saw it.

Her gaze darted to Haley, who blinked at her, wide-eyed and pale. Compunction plucked at Annie. She'd assessed the

situation at face value and unfairly jumped to a biased conclusion. Now she choked down the bitter fear and resentment
that strangled her and worked to calm her runaway pulse
before addressing her daughter. "Ben was punching you?"

Her daughter bobbed her head.

"Why?"

Haley poked out her bottom lip and looked away. "I took
his truck."

Annie inhaled a slow, deep breath. Counted to ten. "Go
to the time-out chair. You know not to grab your brother's
toys from him."

Her expression contrite, Haley sidled over to the chair in
the corner of the room. Feeling Jonah's gaze on her, Annie
steeled her nerves and schooled her face before facing him.
Rather than accusation, his expression was patient, forgiving. Her awkward guilt grew. "I'm sorry. When I saw you—"

"I understand."

She tipped her head, studying him. "Do you? Do you have
any idea how much it scares me to think of my son following his father's example? He was a baby when I left Walt, but
not a day passes that I don't worry that Walt's abusiveness
could be genetic."

A muscle in Jonah's cheek twitched. "Behavior is learned,
not inherited."

"I wish I could be sure," she murmured, shifting her gaze
to Ben, who'd toddled over to cling to her leg. He whined
and raised his arms to be picked up. Annie lifted Ben to her
chest and bear-hugged him. "Oh, Ben, what am I going to
do with you?"

Slanting her a lopsided smile, Jonah stepped closer and
stroked a hand down Ben's wavy baby hair. "You're gonna
be all right. Aren't you, little man?"

The loving gesture stole Annie's breath. Walt had claimed

to love their kids, but she'd never seen him show his affection with a tender touch, a softly spoken encouragement or a warm smile.

Ben lifted his head from her shoulder and, grinning impishly, wagged a finger at Jonah. "No hit."

Chuckling, Jonah caught Ben's finger in his hand and gently squeezed. "That's right, pal. No hitting Haley."

Annie's throat tightened, and she struggled to assimilate her new impressions of Jonah in the wake of the horror and gore she'd witnessed this morning at the diner. How did this caring, conscientious man fit in the landscape of violence and illegal activity she'd become embroiled in at Pop's? How did she reconcile this gentle side of Jonah with the violent skill she'd seen him employ firsthand?

Her mind spinning, Annie nodded toward Haley. "Once she's been in the chair two more minutes, will you bring her into the kitchen to eat?"

He tweaked Ben's chin. "Sure."

She backed out of the living room, knowing something fundamental had shifted in her relationship with Jonah, but too overwhelmed by the events of the morning to examine the change closely.

Their relationship? The word clanged in her head and made her stomach whirl. She didn't have a relationship with Jonah. He was a customer at the diner, nothing more.

But you don't kiss a man who is nothing more than a customer.

No, *he* kissed *her*. Annie's lips tingled from the mere memory of that brief kiss. Warm, sweet, breath-stealing.

And totally off-limits. She had enough upheaval in her life at the moment without complicating matters with a new relationship. When she was ready to become involved with a man again, assuming she ever was, she'd want someone stable, safe, considerate.

Not a man who'd elbowed his way into her life, for whom hand-to-hand combat was a sport, and who turned her emotions topsy-turvy with his soul-piercing eyes.

After settling Ben in his high chair, Annie finished mixing the cheese sauce into the pasta. She was just about to check on Haley when Jonah carried her into the kitchen on his hip.

Her daughter gazed at him with such implicit trust and admiration, Annie's heart hammered. She'd expected Haley to be much more circumspect around men following Walt's frightening behavior both before and after Annie had left the marriage.

Not that Haley hadn't been exposed to positive male role models, too. Riley Sinclair, her counselor Ginny's husband, for one.

Jonah situated Haley at the table and took a bowl from the counter. "Can I help serve?"

"I—" Before she could answer, Jonah had scooped a spoonful of mac and cheese in the dish and carried it over to Haley.

"It's too hot," her daughter complained without tasting her lunch.

"Can't have that." Jonah stepped up behind Haley and bent low over the table. "Help me blow out the fire."

Together they both blew on the bowl with their cheeks puffed, and Ben giggled.

"Me, too!" Ben's attempt to cool his food resembled a raspberry more than a puff of breath. Now both children giggled, and Annie's heart swelled. Her children's mirth sang through her blood, a lyrical, magical melody that she treasured more than gold.

When Jonah peeked up and winked at her, Annie's joy

over her children's laughter and Jonah's rapport with the kids morphed into a knee-weakening skip in her pulse. Her children had trusted and bonded with Jonah quickly and easily. Did they sense something about him that she'd overlooked, or was he preying on their innocence and naïveté to get to her?

Before he left today, she intended to find out.

Chapter 10

Jonah was examining Haley's baby picture on a side table in the living room when Annie finished settling the kids in for their naps. Her heart ached, knowing she'd not had a professional picture made of Ben as an infant. The early months of his life had been the tumultuous prelude to her leaving Walt, and the months since her divorce had been too financially tight, too busy with her hours at the diner to have her son's picture made.

But she needed to capture her son's early years on film soon, someday....

"Someday may be closer than you think."

Though she said nothing, Jonah turned as if he sensed her standing behind him. "Your children are precious. You've a right to be proud of them."

"Thank you." She managed a small smile of appreciation, then grew serious. Time for answers. "Tell me about your childhood."

Jonah raised his head, stood straighter, arched an eyebrow in surprise.

"You said you were abused. How bad was it? What did your mother do? How did it change who you were?"

Jonah inhaled deeply and dragged a hand along his jaw. His callused palm rasped against the shadow of beard on his chin as he released his breath slowly through pursed lips. "Wow. You know how to cut to the chase."

He jerked his head toward the sofa she'd gotten from the secondhand store. "Sit?" He settled on one end of the couch and patted the cushion next to him.

Instead, she took the rocking chair across the room from him and squeezed the knobby armrests. "I'm listening."

Jonah leaned forward, propping his forearms on his thighs and bridging his fingers. "I grew up in a white-collar neighborhood, went to a good school, had a circle of friends I hung out with. Most of the normal stuff."

He shrugged. "But every once in a while my dad would lose his temper and take out his frustrations on Mom. If I tried to defend her, I'd catch as bad as she got. He generally left my older sister alone, but even she took a backhand across the mouth for a sassy remark or an ear-ringing slap if she was in the wrong place at the wrong time. As I got older, when I sensed he was in one of his moods, I'd provoke him so that he'd come after me to start with instead of Mom.

"I lied to my teachers or whoever would ask about where my bruises came from. By the time I was thirteen, I'd started picking fights with kids in the neighborhood. Part of that was me venting my internal rage, and part of it was to cover the constant parade of injuries my dad gave me. I got the reputation of being a bully on purpose, so no one questioned the black eyes and split lips as much."

A bully. Annie shuddered.

"And your mother? How could she let this happen to you? I left Walt when I realized he could turn his violence against our kids next."

"She tried to protect me and got hurt for it. But she also lived in denial. Dad would apologize and beg her forgiveness, promise to change, tell her he'd get counseling and she'd stay. She loved the bastard for some reason, and I couldn't convince her to leave him. She died of cancer when I was fifteen. My sister was away at college by then, and I had no desire to live alone with my dad, so I left home."

Annie frowned. "And went where?"

"The streets for a while. Then I went to this gym one day, looking for work."

"As in a *boxing* gym like the one where we met the other day?" She couldn't hide the disdain in her tone.

He nodded. "Yeah, but in my hometown in Arkansas. For a while I did odd jobs, real menial stuff, in exchange for a cot in the locker room. Then I found out you could earn money working as a sparring partner with the guys who were training for competitions. I asked for that job and got it."

When she sent him a dubious look, he shrugged and flashed her a self-deprecating grin. "I had plenty of experience getting beat up, so why not get paid for taking a few hits?"

Annie stared down at her lap, her hands fidgeting restlessly. While her heart ached for the teenager Jonah had been, relying on the violence that was his father's legacy to survive, her new insights about his past only confirmed what she'd feared. Violence was a part of who he was. His casual attitude about hopping into a boxing ring to pound another man chafed against her memories of being Walt's punching bag.

"So you turned the abuse your father taught you into a profession?" She surged from her chair and paced across the living room, uneasy with the truths she was learning. How could she be attracted to another man with a tendency toward violence? What was wrong with her?

"A profession?" He snorted. "Hardly. I just made a few bucks exchanging jabs with guys in the evening. And sparring was nothing like the abuse I took from my old man. For one thing, I wore pads and headgear."

She spun to face him with a sigh. "My point is, when you got away from your father, rather than leave the abuse in the past, you continued fighting. It was a lifestyle for you. You *chose* to fight."

He met her gaze evenly. "I chose to heal. I chose to turn my life around and use what I knew to help other people in the same situation."

She blinked, gave him a humorless laugh. "Excuse me? How does sparring help other people?"

A muscle in his jaw twitched, and he took a slow, measured breath. "It doesn't necessarily. But being a policeman does, if you do your job right."

She sat straighter, remembering his telling her he'd once been a cop. She listened attentively as he explained.

"The thing is, the kid who went to that gym looking for work, the teenager who got into the ring to earn a few bucks isn't the same guy sitting here today. Back then I was full of rage, full of hatred for what my father did. I was confused, alone, just...mad at the world. But the owner of the gym saw something worthwhile in me and took me under his wing. He talked to me, listened to me when I was ready to spill my guts and helped me work through that anger I had pent up inside. He showed me how that fury was destroying me, how holding on to that anger hurt *me,* not my dad."

His words reverberated through Annie, and she hugged herself. She'd heard much of the same admonitions and advice

from Ginny. Ginny had been her rock when she'd felt overwhelmed by the turmoil and danger of leaving Walt. Annie
understood without his explaining further how important the
owner of that gym had been for Jonah.

Jonah rubbed his palms on his jeans and continued. "He
taught me to channel those bottled-up emotions and release
them through my boxing. I sweated out the grief and worked
off the tension and hatred. Took it out on a punching bag
so that I *didn't* blow a gasket one day and let it out on some
shmuck who ticked me off. I poured all the fear and frustration and rage I had for my father and what he'd done to us
into my workout and learned to fight a clean, fair fight in
the ring. No cheap shots. Keeping control and perspective.

"I'd been in a downward spiral, and he pulled me back
from the brink and set me on a better path."

"How so?" Annie leaned forward, enthralled by what she
was learning about Jonah's past.

He rolled a palm up. "I went back to school, joined the
police academy and was on the job for nine years before I
left the force."

Annie drew her eyebrows together and shook her head.
"Why did you quit?"

Jonah flopped back on the sofa and rubbed his hands over
his face. Grunted. "I guess I…answered one too many domestic disturbance calls and had had enough."

He clenched his teeth, and the distant look in his eyes told
her his thoughts were miles away from her living room, deep
in troublesome memories from his years as a cop. Annie's
heart thundered as color crept up his neck and flooded his
cheeks, his nostrils flared and his jaw tightened.

"Every time I'd leave a home where I knew abuse was happening, regardless of whether I'd been able to do anything to
help the people involved, I'd feel that frustration knotted up

inside me again, and I'd go to the gym to work through it, work it off." He inhaled deeply and expelled it in a whoosh. "But in all the years I was a cop," he said, meeting her eyes with a hard, level gaze, "I *never* lost my cool with an abuser— much as I wanted to knock the snot out of 'em. Never." He paused, letting that fact sink in.

A shiver chased up Annie's spine as all her conceptions about Jonah shattered and reassembled in new patterns. Her spinning thoughts made her restless, and she shoved to her feet, paced across the floor and back.

"So…boxing, sparring saved my life. The things I learned from Michael kept me on track, kept me sane."

Her pulse tripped, and she jerked her head up. "Michael. You've mentioned him before. He's the one you said lost his savings to the gambling ring that operates out of the diner."

Jonah nodded. "He was my mentor, my guardian angel when I needed him. He moved down here to Lagniappe a couple years ago to manage Frank's gym, the one we were at the other day." He paused and drew his eyebrows into a frown. "Michael was a good man at heart, but…he was no saint. Gambling became an addiction. When he lost his savings, he…lost hope. He was ashamed and thought he was out of options."

Annie heard the grief that vibrated in Jonah's tone. He sucked in a deep breath and pushed it out through pursed lips. "He…killed himself just over a year ago."

She gasped and pressed a hand to her mouth. "Oh, no. Jonah, I'm so sorry."

His jaw tightened. "I blame the thugs who stole his money for his death. That's how I got involved with this investigation. I wanted retribution for Michael. I wanted to shut down the bastards' operation and bring them to justice."

"Alone?"

He sighed and glanced away. "For the most part. Right now I'm just getting information, trying to figure out who's involved, how the operation is run. When I have all my facts laid out, enough proof to hang these guys, I'll take it to the authorities. But I don't want anyone, even someone on the fringes of this thing, to get away. I want solid information, hard evidence that no judge can toss out, no lawyer can explain away."

The passion in his voice fueled the fire inside Annie, the determination she had to free herself from the danger she'd unwittingly landed in. If she wanted to keep her kids safe, if she wanted to protect herself and still scrabble out a living, the criminals at the diner had to be stopped.

But she wouldn't sit back and leave it to Jonah to bring the men involved to justice. She would not be a victim again, would not passively let someone ruin her life again as Walt had done.

Screwing up her courage, Annie balled her fists and pulled her shoulders back. "I want to help. I can search Hardin's office for files or financial records, or—"

"No." Jonah shook his head.

Irritation tickled her gut. "But I have access to his office and can—"

"No! I can't let you get in this mess any deeper. It's too dangerous."

She crossed her arms over her chest. "It's not your decision whether I'm involved or not. And I'm already in danger. You said so yourself."

"Think of your kids, Annie. You can't put yourself in harm's—"

"I am thinking of my kids! The sooner we build a case against these creeps, the sooner I can get my life back."

"Not *we*. Let me handle this. The only reason I told you

what was going on is because you needed to be aware, be alert. So you could protect yourself. But now, with Hardin's murder, the stakes are higher. I have to be careful how I proceed. Changing anything now about the cover I've set up might tip someone off."

She pictured Hardin's bullet-riddled body and almost changed her mind. The idea of being so vulnerable, with an unknown enemy lurking, lying in wait, scared her senseless. She swallowed the bitter taste of fear in her throat and raised her chin. "All the more reason to let me search Hardin's office. You don't have the opportunity and the access I have. I can do this. I *have* to do this. I can't let fear or danger dictate my life again."

Jonah surged off the couch and strode over to her. "Look, I know how much you want this all to be over, and I respect your courage and willingness to help, but—"

"Courage?" She gave him a humorless laugh. "It's not courage, Jonah. It's desperation. Panic. I'm scared to death, but I have to do something before the whole situation explodes in my face. If there's even a chance I could be on their hit list because of that stolen money, I have to act. I won't sit by and risk my children getting hurt by this. It's necessity, not courage."

He cupped her cheek in his massive hand and stroked her jaw with his thumb. The comforting gesture sent ribbons of sweet sensation coursing through her, muddling her thoughts.

"Don't sell yourself short," he murmured, his low voice stroking her, adding to the pleasant hum vibrating from deep inside her. "Leaving your husband, starting over, standing up for what's right…you had to have a lot of courage to do all you've done. Being brave isn't the absence of fear—"

"It's doing what you must despite the fear. I know, I know." With a disgruntled sigh and a nod, she lifted her hand to his wrist and pulled away from his deliciously distracting touch. She needed to stay focused on the problem at hand. "Ginny practically tattooed that saying on my forehead. So, fine, call it what you want, but I need to help. Don't shut me out of this, Jonah."

He shook his head again. "If you want to do something to protect yourself, then go to the self-defense class at the police station we talked about. But stay out of this."

She raised her chin. "Fine. I'll go to the class. But I'm tired of sitting back while the world stomps all over me. I have to *do* something—with or without your help."

"Annie—" His dark brow lowered, and his eyes narrowed to slits. "If I agree to let you help, do you promise you'll follow my instructions? No going it alone or taking unnecessary risks. Understood?"

Her pulse fluttered with anticipation and dread. "I promise."

"Remember, these people have a lot of money at stake, and if they suspect you of meddling in the operation or feeding information to the police, they'll kill you without asking questions."

Her stomach pitched, but she steeled her nerves. She had no choice but to help Jonah. She couldn't live under this cloud of fear, couldn't bear the idea of her children living under a threat of danger. Wishing she weren't in this predicament didn't make it so.

"You promise you'll go to the class?" he asked, his eyes drilling hers.

She raised a hand. "Promise."

Sighing his resignation, Jonah drew her to the sofa and pulled her down onto the cushions beside him. "All right. Let's make some plans. I don't want to leave anything to chance. We have too much at stake."

* * *

Jonah angled the seat in his truck to a more comfortable position, settling in for the long night ahead. Annie would balk at the idea of him camping out on the street to watch her apartment, but the stakes in this case kept getting higher. He remembered her saying she'd thought someone followed her to work the day before. Coupled with Hardin's murder, he wasn't about to leave her home unguarded.

Acid flooded his gut when he thought of Annie becoming involved in his investigation. He should never have agreed to let her help him, but what choice did he have? He'd seen the determination and passion that fired her eyes. She'd have acted on her own if he hadn't let her help him. At least this way, he could keep closer tabs on her involvement.

He scanned the parking lot and the oak-tree-lined yard. Everything was quiet, dark, still. A stark contrast to the turmoil writhing inside him.

Telling her about his abuse, his history with Michael and his mentor's suicide had been wrenching. Painful. He never relived those memories if he could help it. But Annie had asked him point-blank, and she wouldn't have been satisfied with evasion or half-truths. He needed her to trust him.

The question he was left with, however, was where did they go from here? He couldn't deny his attraction to her. His feelings went deeper than the protective instincts she aroused in him. But given her history, knowing the hardships she'd already survived, he was the last person she needed in her life.

Even after he'd explained to her how he'd gotten involved with sparring, explained how the physical outlet for his emotions kept him sane, he'd seen the doubts and disapproval in her body language. She wanted nothing to do with any form of violence, even the controlled, therapeutic version he practiced at the gym.

Not to mention the fact that any future with Annie had to include being a father figure to her kids. And his only example of fatherhood was the horrid one his father had set. What kind of father would he be?

The notion of having a family, sharing his life with a wife and being a role model for children left him in a cold sweat. He wanted those things, deeply, but only if he was sure he could give his family what his father hadn't. Love. Security. Happiness.

He didn't have a clue where to begin creating a healthy family life. It wasn't that he feared he'd physically hurt Annie or her kids—he'd cut his hand off before he'd raise it against them—but there were so many other ways to fail a family. He'd be damned if he'd repeat his father's mistakes, but he didn't have any other point of reference. On the job, he'd faced down armed gangbangers without a second thought. But being a husband or father, being in a position to screw up the lives of those you love, scared the hell out of him.

Which left him with only one option. Never marry. Never have children. Never recreate the hellish existence that had passed for his childhood home.

Jonah dragged in a lungful of oxygen, his chest knotting with regret. As much as he wanted his own family, as much as he wanted Annie, he was destined to be alone.

Chapter 11

Two days later, the police released the murder scene, and the diner reopened. Annie arrived early for the breakfast shift, hoping to look around in Hardin's office before the diner filled with the morning rush.

She pressed a hand to her stomach, trying to calm the battalion of butterflies swooping in her gut as she stepped through the swinging door into the kitchen. The images and smells of the last time she'd walked through this door were all too fresh in her mind.

Enough dawdling. She had limited time before the rest of the kitchen help and waitstaff arrived. And the interim manager. Who would take Hardin's place and was he connected to the money laundering the way Hardin was?

She had no doubt whoever was in charge of the illegal operation would handpick Hardin's replacement.

Sucking in a calming breath, Annie pushed through the door and surveyed the kitchen as she crept cautiously back to the manager's office. Would the police have removed the financial records and computer drive for their investigation of Hardin's murder? What were the odds that, had there been any proof of money laundering before Hardin's death, the men responsible for his murder would have left any evidence behind to incriminate themselves?

Annie reached the door of the office and, knees shaking, turned the corner into the cramped office. No trace of blood or death remained, other than the faint chemical smell of the cleaner used to erase the evidence a man had been shot and bled to death on this floor.

An uneasy jitter crawled through Annie, but she shoved down her discomfort and set to work. She started with the file cabinet in the corner. The disarray of the papers and the haphazard order of the contents told her that someone had already rifled through the papers. But had it been the police... or Hardin's murderer?

Order forms and delivery slips from various grocery vendors were jumbled together with personnel applications and insurance documents. Records of health inspector visits had been jammed to the back of the top drawer, but she saw nothing resembling a financial ledger or a computer spreadsheet of expenses and profits.

Of course not.

Did she really think it would be that easy? That she'd flip through a few files until she found a neat and organized record of all past criminal activity along with a typed and signed confession of those involved?

She scoffed. Anything she found would be far more subtle. Just a piece of a bigger picture.

She moved on from the file cabinet to Hardin's desk. She rummaged through the center drawer but found nothing beyond basic office supplies and an opened pack of cigarettes.

Next she searched the deep side drawer where it appeared the most recent paperwork was kept. As she fingered through the files, she realized the kind of evidence she was interested in wouldn't be kept in the obvious places. Evidence of wrongdoing would be hidden. Protected.

Was there a safe? A bank lockbox?

She pulled the drawer all the way out and felt behind the hanging files. Nothing. Same with the next drawer she searched. Then, on an impulse, she pulled the center drawer all the way out, off its tracks, and emptied the contents onto the desk. As she flipped the drawer, her heart sank when she found nothing stuck to the underside other than a wad of very old gum.

"Looking for something?" a deep voice growled behind her.

Gasping, she whirled around, her heart hammering at the dark glower she met.

Martin Farrout.

A chill washed through Annie as she faced Farrout's intimidating glare. "Uh, sir, the kitchen is for employees only."

His black eyebrows beaded. "I'm well aware of that. And from now on this office is off-limits to anyone but the new manager." He paused a moment, his head cocked at a haughty angle.

A staggering heartbeat later, understanding dawned through the muddle of her spinning thoughts. "You're—"

"The new boss. Yes. So what are you doing snooping in my office?"

Annie's breath backed up in her lungs. "I—I was looking for—" She glanced at the mess she'd dumped from the center drawer. Grabbing the first item she saw, she held the opened pack of cigarettes out. "These. I…needed a smoke. Hardin let me have his when—"

"So you got 'em. Now beat it."

She jerked a nod, praying she'd returned the other drawers to enough order that he couldn't tell the full extent of her searching.

Scrunching the cigarette pack in her hand, she hustled out past the large man. He refused to step aside, so she was forced to turn sideways and sidle out of the office. Heart thundering, she rushed out to the dining room, where Lydia was chatting with the first breakfast customers. The older woman glanced at the cigarettes Annie squeezed and propped a hand on her hip. "I didn't know you smoked."

Annie pressed her free hand to her chest, struggling to calm her ragged breathing. "I don't."

Lydia gave a meaningful nod toward Annie's fist. "What are those for, then?"

Annie glanced down at her hand and sighed. "Nothing. I... was just—" She stopped herself, realizing something hard and distinctly uncigarette-like poked her hand through the paper packaging.

"The first step to quitting is admitting you have a problem," Lydia said with a teasing grin and a bump from her hip as she headed out to the tables.

Annie turned her back to the customers sitting at the counter and upended the crushed pack. Several bent cigarettes slid out—along with a small silver key that pinged as it clattered onto the counter. Why did Hardin have a key in his cigarettes? What did the key go to? She studied it, turning it over in her hand, her pulse picking up. Folding the key into her palm, she peeked into the packaging to be sure she hadn't missed anything else. Empty.

She brushed the cigarettes and empty package into the trash and jammed the key into her apron pocket.

Would Farrout be looking for that key? Would he suspect

her when he found it missing? Did the key unlock something here at the diner or was it part of Hardin's personal property?

She wondered if Jonah would stop by the diner today and what he'd make of the key she'd found. The key she'd *stolen*.

Her heartbeat thundered in her ears.

Stolen. If Farrout or the other men involved in this money-laundering scheme found out—

"You have any grape jelly? I'm allergic to strawberries," a woman at the counter asked, jarring Annie from her disturbing thoughts.

"Oh, uh, sure." She wiped her sweaty palms on her apron and took a moment to redirect her thoughts. As she turned to the tray where they kept the condiments, another man at the counter caught her eye, and her stomach dipped. The businessman who'd ogled her earlier in the week was back, his weighty gaze following her every move.

Her skin crawling from his discomfiting scrutiny, Annie found the grape jelly and handed it to the woman with the strawberry allergy.

She cast a surreptitious glance to the businessman as she moved the pot of decaf coffee that had finished brewing to a warming burner. He caught her eye and lifted his eyebrow and his mug. "I'll take some of that, doll."

Squelching the uneasy jitter that he elicited, Annie crossed to him with the coffee just as a handsome, familiar face arrived at the counter. Relief and pleasure spun through her as Jonah took his seat at the counter.

When had she decided his face, with his broken nose bump, the scar over his black eyebrow and his perpetual five-o'clock shadow, was handsome rather than rough-hewn? Comforting instead of daunting?

She'd have been the first to deny she'd formed any attachments to Jonah, yet the leap in her pulse and the lift in her spirits when she spotted him were undeniable. He held a central role in her thoughts lately, too, whether she was at home or at work, thoughts that had her lying awake at night with a restlessness stirring inside her.

He shook his head slightly, a subtle reminder of the warning he'd given her last night not to greet him with more than normal, businesslike attention. He wanted to keep their association as low-key as possible when at the diner.

"Morning," she greeted him casually. "Can I get you coffee?"

She wanted desperately to tell him about the key she'd found but knew now was not the time or place.

"Sure. And I'll have the sunrise platter." He lifted a corner of his mouth in a polite grin, but as she filled his mug, his attention shifted and his countenance clouded. She turned, curious to see what had darkened his mood.

Martin Farrout stood just outside the kitchen door, casting an imperious glance over the dining room like a ruler surveying his land. Her new boss's gaze lingered on Jonah, then skipped briefly to the businessman beside him before moving on.

"Our new manager," she told Jonah under her breath.

She could almost see the wheels in Jonah's head clicking, figuring how Farrout's appointment as manager fit into the money-laundering scheme and Hardin's murder.

Lydia returned from the tables, brushing past Farrout, and clipped new orders up for the cooks. "I could use some help out there if you can, Annie. Notoriety over Hardin's murder has brought out the morbidly curious this morning, and tables are filling up fast."

"Of course." Annie surrendered to the frenzy of the breakfast rush but kept tabs on Jonah's progress through his meal. She needed an opportunity to talk to him before he left.

He'd cleaned his plate and had nodded to her for his bill before inspiration struck. In tiny printing at the bottom of his order ticket she wrote *Meet me at restroom.* Jonah gave no visible sign he'd noticed her message as he checked his total and handed her his cash. She held her breath as he left his seat, glanced at the morning paper on the rack beside the cash register and took a toothpick from the dispenser on the counter. She tried to hand him his change, but he waved it away.

After pocketing his tip, she picked up a rag to wipe the counter and watched him make his way to the back hall that led to the bathrooms.

Relief unfurled in her chest, and she wiped her hands on her apron as she made her way toward the back hall, using the employee entrance from the kitchen.

Jonah stood by the pay phone at the end of the hall thumbing through a well-worn phone book. Glancing about to be sure they were alone, she hurried over to him and pulled the key from her pocket. "I found this in a cigarette pack in Hardin's desk." She kept her voice low, kept an eye on the door to the dining room. "Guess it's Farrout's desk now."

Wrinkling his brow, Jonah took the key from her palm and examined it. "Any idea what it goes to?"

"None. I didn't find it until after I left the office. Farrout caught me in the office earlier and asked what I was looking for. I had to make up a quick excuse and get out of there. I told him I was there for the cigarette pack, so I grabbed it and left. But I could try to get back in there later when he's not around and see—"

"No! If Farrout is already suspicious, it's all the more dangerous for you." Jonah bounced the key in his hand. "Besides, this looks more like a locker key. Like the ones at my gym or the kind at the bus depot."

She nodded her agreement. "So how do we find the locker it goes to?"

He shrugged. "I'll look into that today." He held the key toward the light and narrowed his gaze, studying it closer. "There's a number on it—223. That should help narrow the search."

"I want to go with you when you open the locker."

As soon as Jonah started shaking his head, Annie snatched the key from his hand and shoved it down the front of her waitressing dress and inside her bra. "You promised not to shut me out. I found the key. I want to go with you when you open the locker or whatever the key goes to."

Agitation shaping his expression, Jonah clenched his teeth and sighed.

She saw the businessman from the counter before Jonah did and cut off his protest, saying, "Yeah, that phone book is way out of date. You'd do better to just call information. Sorry."

Jonah's gaze flicked to the man in the pressed suit who strolled past them into the men's room. "Okay, thanks anyway."

As soon as the men's restroom door swished closed, Jonah whispered, "Annie, give me the key. I never promised you could be involved in every aspect of my investigation."

She backed toward the kitchen, whispering back, "I can get off at two, if Susan will cover my last hour. You can meet me at the bus stop on Third Street, and we'll go together from there to start looking for the locker this goes to."

"Annie." His tone dipped in warning. "Give me the key."

"I will." She backed to the kitchen door, mouthing, "At two."

At five minutes until two, Jonah sat in his car waiting for Annie at the Third Street bus stop stewing over her stubbornness and the cheap tactic she'd used to keep the key from him. If it had been anyone besides Annie, he'd probably have gone after the key without blinking. But he figured Annie was the last person who needed to be manhandled and groped—even if she'd all but dared him to with her ploy. He chuckled despite himself. Her moxie had caught him off guard, but he wouldn't be so easily outmaneuvered again.

The show of gumption also encouraged him. Beneath the layers of shame and intimidation her ex had heaped on her with his abuse lurked a strong, vibrant woman waiting to be freed. She just needed a safe environment, the right timing and the encouragement of people she trusted to revive the side of herself she'd forced into hibernation.

A few minutes later, Annie opened his passenger-side door and slid onto the seat. "So where do you want to start?"

He cranked the engine. "Not the gym. I checked, and those lockers are numbered one to one hundred. We'll try the bus depot first."

When they reached the bus station, Jonah took a gym bag inside with him. He placed a proprietary hand at the small of her back as he ushered her into the dingy brick building. They located locker 223 easily, and she handed him the key.

"Bingo," he said when the metal door opened.

Annie huddled in close as he examined the locker's contents. The light, feminine scent that clung to her was distracting. With effort, he focused his attention on the locker and not the thrum of his blood and the pounding desire to pull Annie into his arms.

Gritting his teeth and shoving down the hum of desire, Jonah pulled out computer CDs that lay on a top shelf and shoved them into his gym bag. Next he rifled through printed files stacked below. He handed Annie one of the files stuffed with pages of data. "Read through some of this and see what it is."

Jonah pulled out a file for himself and began flipping pages. His folder held financial records, long lists of deposits with names and—*hold the phone*—sports results listed by each entry.

His pulse roared in his ears as he scanned the list for a particular name. Michael's. The deposits were listed chronologically, and he skimmed quickly through the past several months until he found the sheet for the last month Michael was alive.

Beside him, Annie gasped. "Jonah, look at this."

She pointed to a page where a name and phone number had been scribbled at the top of the sheet.

"Joseph Nance?" he said, reading the name. "You know him?"

"Not exactly. But I know the name. That's who I was supposed to deliver the package of money to the night I was attacked. Hardin was very adamant that I only give the money to him."

Jonah's heart thundered in his chest. A name. He had a name.

He closed his file folder and pulled out his cell phone. "Read me that number."

As she did, he dialed. His breath hung in his throat as the phone rang once, twice.

"Lagniappe P.D. Detective Nance speaking," a gruff voice answered.

Jonah pulled his eyebrows together, stunned speechless. Nance was a cop?

"I'm sorry. I have the wrong number." As he thumbed the disconnect button, Jonah lifted a confused gaze to Annie.

She frowned, gripped his wrist. "What? Who answered?"

"Apparently Nance is a detective with the Lagniappe police."

"The police? So…Hardin was working with the cops to bust the gambling ring?"

"Or we have a crooked cop on the force taking payoffs." Jonah stroked the stubble on his cheek and mulled the turn of events.

"Or someone ratted Hardin out, and he was being set up for arrest," Annie countered.

"Anything's possible, I suppose." He nodded toward the file in her hand. "What else you got in there?"

"It's an accounting of receipts and expenses for the diner, but…I don't see how it can possibly be right. According to this, the diner consistently brought in more than five thousand dollars a day. Maybe a large restaurant can do that kind of business, but Pop's Diner doesn't do that kind of volume." She lifted a knowing gaze. "Methinks these are the cooked books you were looking for."

He grinned at her antiquated language. "Methinks so, too."

Annie's smile morphed to a frown, and she scowled as she turned her gaze to the locker. "I don't know, Jonah. This all seems…too easy. You've been working this case for months, making only baby steps of progress—"

"Well, that was intentional. Hard as it was to sit back while the investigation inched along, I didn't want to send up any red flags, either. I took baby steps in order to gain Farrout's trust. I wanted to fit in at the diner before I approached him. Impatience can blow an investigation."

Jonah studied the way the harsh fluorescent lights of the bus depot danced over the soft curves of Annie's face. He needed the same kind of patience with her. He had to take baby steps until he'd earned her trust. Annie was worth waiting for.

On the heels of that thought, a chill unrelated to the hyper-cold air-conditioning skimmed up his back. What business did he have harboring any ideas of a future with Annie? And if he didn't intend to hang around and be part of her ready-made family, he had no right to give her any misleading cues, either. The absolute last thing he wanted to do was hurt Annie.

Annie propped a hand on her hip and shook her head. "What I mean by too easy is, it's as if Hardin had packaged all this information together, building a case against the people involved. It's all here, laid out with everything except the bow on top."

Jonah refocused his thoughts, considering Annie's point. "True. So maybe he was about to turn it all over to the cops. Maybe that's why he was killed."

"Or maybe this is all a setup. Maybe none of this information is real, and if we take this to the authorities, we expose ourselves to the higher-ups in the operation without having anything that will actually stick."

Jonah clenched his teeth and made two decisions. "Regardless of what all this means, I know two things. First and most important, you're out. I don't want you connected to any of this if it should blow up in my face."

"But—"

He held up a hand, cutting her off. "Second, we won't decide anything here and now. I need time to study these files and put all the pieces together."

She closed the file in her hands and handed it back. "I can still be of help to you. Let me go over these records with you."

Jonah started shoving the contents of the locker into the gym bag and shook his head. "I've already involved you more than I should have."

She put a hand on his, and his heart fisted when he met her pleading gaze.

"I need to do this, Jonah. I need to feel I'm doing something to make my life better, safer. For too long, I've drifted along letting life happen to me and suffering because I gave others too much control over my life. Please don't ask me to sit on my hands now. I am involved whether I like it or not."

He drew a slow breath, his respect for Annie blossoming inside him. He grazed his fingers along her chin. "I appreciate what you're saying. I understand and applaud you for wanting to change your life. But if I allowed you to get mired deeper in this muck…"

"I'd still be in danger, through no fault of yours." Turmoil swirled in the depths of her dark eyes, landing a sucker punch to his gut.

Before he could counter her argument, she glanced at her watch and bit her bottom lip. "Which reminds me…I want to go to that self-defense class at the police station that you mentioned. It starts in thirty minutes. Can you drop me off?"

Jonah nodded, relieved to hear she was taking her personal safety seriously. "Of course."

Studying the rest of the locker's contents would keep until that evening. Making sure Annie stayed safe was his top priority, and the class was, for the time being, the best means to that end.

Besides, he was headed to that class himself—though he decided it was best that Annie not know of his role.

Chapter 12

Jonah let Annie out at the door to the gymnasium housed at the back of the Lagniappe Police Department. A hollow ache filled her as she waved goodbye to him and watched him drive down the block and out of sight. She'd see him again soon enough. At the diner tomorrow, if nothing else. So why did parting from him cause this bittersweet emptiness inside her?

She wasn't falling for him. She couldn't be growing attached to a man at this delicate crossroad in her life. She'd only been free of Walt a little more than a year. Too soon to give her heart again. But since when did love follow any prescribed schedule?

She barked a harsh laugh as she turned from the street. Love? Now she was really rushing things. Jonah was a friend. Nothing more.

With a cleansing breath, she faced the large brick building that housed the city police department. The name they'd found on Hardin's file flashed in her mind. Joseph Nance. *Detective* Nance.

If she marched inside the station now and found Detective Nance, told him everything she knew, could this whole frightening scenario finally be over?

Or would she create an even bigger nightmare for Jonah?

"Impatience can blow an investigation."

She owed it to Jonah to do things his way. She trusted him to figure out the whos and whats of the criminal activity at the diner in his own time.

Warmth flooded her veins as she turned that truth over in her head again. She trusted Jonah. No small feat.

The class had already gathered around a set of floor mats in the center of the gym. She hesitated, remembering how intimidating the private lessons with Jonah had been. Even knowing he wouldn't truly hurt her, his strength and sheer masculinity had resurrected so many vivid memories of Walt's power over her.

Annie was having second thoughts about joining the class when the instructor spotted her lurking by the door and waved her in. "Hi! You're not late. We're waiting for our practice aggressor to arrive. Please have a seat."

Taking a deep breath for courage, Annie walked toward the mats.

"I'm Jan, the instructor, and you are...?"

"Annie."

"Welcome, Annie." Jan flashed a warm smile. "Feel free to join in or just watch today. Whatever you feel comfortable with."

Annie sat cross-legged on the floor next to the other women and pressed a hand to her jittery stomach. As much as she wanted to leave, wanted to crawl into a safe cave somewhere and pretend Hardin hadn't been murdered, she hadn't been mugged and she hadn't divorced or ever been married to Walt in the first place, wishing didn't make those things true. *"Do it for your kids."*

She only had to think of the years she'd let Walt intimidate and hurt her, think of any man doing the same to Haley, to know she had to do something now to turn her life around. She wanted to pass on strength and courage to her daughter, not a legacy of fear and doubt. Putting Haley's innocent face front and center in her mind's eye, Annie raised her gaze to the instructor and squared her shoulders.

"Remember, you *can* protect yourself, and you have a right to protect yourself. Your job is to convey those ideas to your attacker. Frankly, most aggressors are looking for an easy target. If you send him the message that you won't go down easily, that you know how to defend yourself and are willing to hurt him to protect yourself, there's a good chance he'll back off and look for an easier target." The instructor paused when the locker-room door creaked open. "Ah, here's Joe now." To Annie, Jan said, "That's what we call the volunteer in the suit. Generic Joe. Mr. Any Man."

A man, decked from head to foot in a heavily padded suit, lumbered into gymnasium. With a slow, stiff gait, impeded by the bulky pads, he approached the mats where the class had gathered.

None of the other women seemed daunted by his hulking appearance, but Annie couldn't help shifting uneasily. The man's face was completely hidden, the bulky suit and shielded helmet conjuring images of masked horror movie monsters. She had the prickly sense that the man's attention was focused on her as he took his place in the center of the mats. Digging deep in her floundering willpower, she fought the urge to flee from the room.

The woman beside Annie offered to be the first to practice the defensive moves the instructor demonstrated. Annie watched in fascination as the petite woman shouted at the padded man, commanding him with a forceful tone, "Stop! Get back!"

The demonstration continued with the diminutive woman striking the pretend attacker's face mask with an upward arc of her palm, then following with a knee to the groin and a sharp kick to his kneecap. The women applauded as the man lifted a hand and hobbled back. The class continued in this way for the remainder of the hour.

As the instructor gave final instructions and dismissed them, Annie glanced around the circle again, her outlook buoyed by the positive mood of the other women. The support and encouragement they gave each other fed the constructive energy of the class.

Other than Ginny, Annie hadn't had a network of friends or support for a long time. The idea of these women becoming a base of encouragement and help appealed to her. Maybe they could understand the struggle she faced, the seemingly insurmountable odds. Jan touched Annie on the arm as the group scattered and "Joe" clomped back toward the locker room. "Thanks for coming, Annie. I hope you learned something and that you'll come back."

She nodded. Though the class had seemed intimidating at first, she'd gained a new perspective as she watched the other women.

Annie grabbed her purse and headed outside. What a day!

Her thoughts drifted to the cooked financial records they'd found in Hardin's locker, and her heart pattered with a combination of hope and trepidation. Having that proof of illegal activity put her and Jonah in an even more dangerous position. But Jonah's investigation took a huge step forward. The sooner he resolved the case and the people responsible for

Hardin's murder were caught, the sooner she'd be safe and could move on with her life.

Finding that evidence, taking the self-defense class... Annie inhaled deeply and let a warm tingle of satisfaction and accomplishment flow through her. They were baby steps perhaps, but any forward progress was better than wallowing in the mire her life had become. Taking back control in her life rather than drifting along at the mercy of the pervading winds felt good.

Hadn't there been a time in her life when she'd met daily challenges with a zest for life, when she'd felt confident and capable and ready to leave her mark in the world?

Yes—before her world had narrowed to the handsome Special Forces soldier who'd married her as he left for overseas duty—and returned a different man.

The hiss of hydraulics and squeak of brakes called her attention to the bus arriving at the stop across the street. Her bus. Shaking off memories of Walt, she clutched her purse to her chest and jogged to the corner. With a quick glance left and right, she checked for oncoming traffic and stepped out into the street.

Suddenly, tires squealed.

A man shouted, "Annie!"

From the edge of her vision, a blur of steel and dark glass streaked toward her.

A wall of muscle plowed into her from behind.

Asphalt bit her hands, her knees.

A crushing weight landed on her, knocking the breath from her lungs.

The same weight wrapped around her, rolling her aside as a car raced past her head, missing her by inches.

Adrenaline spiked through her blood, and a violent tremor

shook her. Trapped by the dearth of oxygen in her lungs, a scream lodged in her throat.

"Annie! Are you all right?" Large hands roamed over her face and arms.

She blinked, struggled to draw in air. Jonah?

Her heartbeat staggered as his rough-hewn features swam into focus above her.

"Honey, answer me! Are you hurt?"

Her joints ached. Her palms and knees stung. Her head buzzed numbly.

"No," she rasped.

Jonah examined her bloodied hands and swore under his breath.

"Wh-what are y-you doing here?"

He steadied her with a hand under her arm as he helped her to her feet. "I intended to give you a ride home from the class. I had a hunch they might try something like this." He sighed and glanced around at the people who gawked at them from the sidewalk. "Although I didn't think they'd make their move in such a public place."

She stumbled numbly beside him out of the path of traffic. Slowly the buzz of terror that filled her ears faded, allowing his words to sink in. She jerked her head toward him and drilled him with a dubious stare. "You think that was deliberate? That that car was trying to run me over?"

His mouth pressed in a taut line, his jaw stiff. "They pulled out from the curb the second you stepped into the street, gunned the engine and drove straight at you. Seems pretty conclusive."

A chill washed through Annie as she felt the tingle of blood draining from her face. She looked down the street, not certain what she was searching for. "Well, maybe they just didn't see me…or maybe…"

"Annie, they didn't stop." He put one hand on each of her shoulders and met her eyes evenly.

A fierce quaking started deep inside her, working outward in concentric waves of terror. She knew what he would say before he said it, but hearing the words, acknowledging the truth, made the event all the more frightening.

"Honey, this was no accident. They tried to kill you."

Chapter 13

Jonah kept a close eye on Annie as he drove her back to her apartment. For someone who'd almost been killed, she seemed too calm. He worried that her reserve meant she was in shock, though when asked direct questions, she gave coherent answers.

Her hand trembled when she raised it to brush her hair from her eyes, and her pale complexion told him she wasn't totally unaffected by the near-miss with the speeding car.

But when he thought about her past, all the tragedy and trauma she'd survived, a new concern presented itself to him. After Hardin had been murdered, she'd shown surprising composure and detachment also. Maybe Annie was suppressing her reaction, bottling up her emotions as she'd learned to do in her marriage. If so, she was a ticking bomb. How much trauma could she handle before she broke?

She gave her children a brave smile when they rushed to greet her in her kitchen. Haley held a fat cat in her arms, though Annie seemed to barely notice. She hugged both of the kids at the same time and held on to them even when they wiggled for release.

Finally Haley and the cat fought free of Annie's embrace. "Mommy, can Fuzzy sleep with me tonight?"

Annie blinked at her daughter and stared at the cat as if just seeing it for the first time. "What's that cat doing in here?"

"I let him come in to play. I named him Fuzzy. Can he stay in my room tonight?"

Annie drew a slow careful breath. She seemed so tired and disoriented, Jonah stepped closer, in case she toppled.

Smoothing a hand over her forehead and into her hair, Annie shook her head. "Baby, that's the Smiths' cat. You can't keep him. The Smiths would miss him too much."

"But, Mo-om—"

Jonah intervened when the whining started. He took the cat from Annie's daughter and carried it to the door. "Maybe you can play with Fuzzy again tomorrow. Right now he has to go home for dinner. Okay?"

The cat scooted out the opened door and trotted away.

Haley glared at him, her lower lip poked out in full pout mode. "When can I have a cat, Mommy?"

The tortured, world-weary look in Annie's eyes when she glanced at her daughter shredded Jonah's heart. She rubbed her temple with her fingertips. "Someday, sweetie."

Rani strolled in from the next room, her arms full of toys. "Sorry about the cat. I didn't think it would hurt for her to play with him inside for a little while. Then she started talking about keeping him and—" The babysitter winced. "My bad."

Annie shook her head. "It's okay." She hesitated, still looking dazed. "Have the kids eaten dinner?"

"Yes, ma'am. And Ben's had his bath. I was just putting the toys away when you arrived."

Thanking the babysitter, Annie showed her out before sending Haley off to get ready for bed. Her worried eyes met his then, and she tipped her head. "Will the couch be all right for you?"

Jonah lifted an eyebrow. "Pardon?"

"You were going to sleep in your truck and watch my apartment again like the other night, weren't you?"

"You saw me?"

She nodded. "Rather than try to dissuade you from your guard duty, I figured I'd offer you a more comfortable post. I'm not sure I want to be alone tonight."

A tender ache swelled in Jonah's chest. Annie looked so fragile, so near breaking, and the powerful urge to pull her into his arms, kiss away any fear or doubt that weighed her down nearly suffocated him. "The sofa is fine."

She gave a quiet, stoic nod. "I'll get you a pillow and blanket."

She disappeared down the hall, and Jonah sighed his frustration. He hated the resignation that shadowed her gaze. She needed to tap the fiery, fighting spirit he'd seen before, the determination that blazed in her eyes when she talked of protecting her children. Annie needed to approach her own safety and happiness with the same moxie. Through the screened helmet of his "generic Joe" suit, he'd noted her withdrawn and dubious body language at the self-defense class.

Not that he expected her to overcome years of intimidation from her marriage in one session, but so much of her healing and her progress in the class would depend on her attitude. The attempt on her life had clearly rattled her, shaken what confidence she had. She was teetering on the edge of giving up. He couldn't let her retreat into that cave of defeat. His gut told him Annie had a vibrant, core strength. He needed to find a way to revive her hope, fan the fire inside her and give her the courage to fight back.

The desire that Michael had lost. The hope that had been snuffed out in him by the bastards who swindled him.

The hot burn of acid bit his stomach, and he gritted his teeth. He wouldn't let Farrout and his men, or whoever the hell was involved with the attempt on Annie's life, rob Annie of her will to rebuild her life.

Focus, Annie scolded herself for the umpteenth time that day as she let her thoughts drift to the dark car that had hurtled toward her yesterday. She'd already mixed up three special orders thanks to her drifting attention. But every time a car horn blasted on the street outside, or the distant whine of a siren sounded over the murmur of the lunch crowd, her mind jumped back to the instant terror, the jolting realization that someone had tried to run her over.

And the heady rush of warmth and security when Jonah had scooped her into his protective arms.

Stop it. She gave her head a brisk shake to clear the images of Jonah's long legs and broad shoulders curled uncomfortably on her sofa this morning.

"I need two cheeseburgers, well done, hold the onions please." She slapped the order slip under a clip on the order wheel and started scooping ice into glasses for tea. Had they said sweet or unsweet tea?

Damn it. She had to get her mind back on work. She couldn't give Farrout any reason to fire her now. She filled the glasses with sweet tea, going with the odds. Most Southerners took their iced tea sweet. As she carried the drinks out to the customers, she glanced to the front door, waiting to see Jonah arrive.

He'd left her apartment before sunrise, making himself

scarce before her kids got up, then waited in his truck to drive her to work. He'd dropped her off just before the breakfast rush, and after promising he'd stop by for lunch, he'd kissed her scarred cheek.

The memory made her pulse stumble. What would it be like to kiss him? Not a chaste, sweet kiss like he'd startled her with after Hardin's murder, but the kind of long, deep, soul-shaking kisses lovers shared. What would it have been like to lie down beside him on her narrow couch, nestle herself in the crook of his body and let him hold her in his arms?

She huffed, irritated by the track of her thoughts. She had no business considering such intimacies with Jonah. Wasn't it bad enough that she'd grown so dependent on him that she didn't feel safe in her apartment without him sleeping on her couch? She couldn't add a physical relationship to the mix, couldn't complicate a relationship that already confused her.

Annie wiped her damp palms on her apron and sent another glance to the front door as a new customer strolled in.

Not Jonah. She squashed the pluck of disappointment and took the bill slip and cash the man at the next table handed her as she walked past.

"Keep the change."

"Thank you, sir." She mustered a smile for her customer and headed back to the counter to ring up the sale. The mundane task was not enough to keep her head from straying back to the question: What was happening between her and Jonah?

The shared attraction was obvious. The common goal of rooting out and stopping the people threatening her life and running the money laundering at the diner was a given. But what about after that threat had been eliminated? Assuming they could find the people involved and stop them before—

"How was your class yesterday?" Susan asked, hustling in from the dining room with a tray full of dirty dishes.

Annie took a moment to focus her train of thought. "My class?"

"Yeah. When you asked me to cover your afternoon hours, you said you had some kind of class."

"Oh, right. It was…fine."

Susan tipped her head and grinned. "Fine? That's all you can say? You sound like my kid. How was school? *Fine.* How'd you do on your math test? *Fine.*"

Annie dropped the change from the man's ticket into the community tip jar. "Okay, it was…intimidating at first since it was my first time going. But I guess I learned a little bit."

Susan grunted. "Better. So…what the heck kind of class are you taking down at the police station anyway?"

Annie shrugged, hoping to minimize the truth. "Self-defense. So, was the dinner hour busy last night?"

She prayed her change of topic would steer Susan away from questions about why Annie felt the need to defend herself or other queries of a personal nature. The less her co-workers knew about her private life, the better, as far as she was concerned. Especially when it came to her relationship with Jonah. If someone connected the two of them—

"Howdy, ladies."

Annie's head snapped up at the sound of the familiar baritone voice. As if her thoughts had conjured him, Jonah took a seat at the counter, dividing a smile between her and Susan. A thrill of pleasure spun through Annie, though she worked to hide her reaction. Curling her fingers into her apron, Annie bunched the material in her hand and gave Jonah a quick nod of acknowledgment.

"Order up!"

Annie rushed to the kitchen window and took down the plates waiting for her. Balancing the plates, two in her hands and two on her arms, she cast a furtive glance toward Jonah as she headed out to the dining room.

The heat and intimacy in the hooded glance he returned almost made her trip.

Oh, Lord, she was in trouble. How did she fight the powerful magnetic pull she felt toward him?

Jonah hadn't had an opportunity to speak privately with Annie before he left the diner after lunch. He'd spent the better part of the morning going over the files they'd retrieved from Hardin's locker at the bus depot. Based on the organization of the files, the specificity of the incriminating information in the documents and the detective's name at the top of one of the most recent printouts, Jonah was convinced Hardin was working with Detective Nance to expose the money laundering. Whether as part of a plea arrangement, as revenge against the other parties in the criminal operation or out of some civic-minded sense of duty, Jonah had yet to determine. Hardin could have had any number of motivations for helping the Lagniappe police detective gather evidence, and dead men couldn't explain themselves.

Which gave a new light to Hardin's murder. Perhaps the manager's death was less about the stolen package and missing money than it was about silencing an informant.

Had the higher-ups in the gambling and money-laundering ring suspected Hardin's betrayal?

Jonah rubbed his temple, pondering all the new angles, as he parked behind the police station and headed in the back entrance to the gymnasium. In the men's locker room, he began dressing in the bulky gear he wore for the self-defense class and wondered if Annie would show up.

Given twenty-four hours to assess her situation, had the

attempt on her life yesterday fired her resolve to take back control of her life or had it scared her into retreat?

She'd all but ignored him at the diner today. Probably a smart idea. They were already risking a lot spending as much time together away from the diner as they did. Anyone could see them together on the street or outside her apartment.

Jonah bit the inside of his cheek as he mulled that point. While he didn't want Annie and her kids alone in her apartment until he'd neutralized the threat against her, he couldn't risk jeopardizing the investigation, either.

He'd have to devise a way to be more discreet about his arrival and departure from Annie's home. Just in case her apartment was being watched.

After donning his protective gear, Jonah lumbered out to the padded mats where the women waited. He was relieved to see Annie sitting with the other ladies. Soon he needed to tell her the role he played in the class. Somehow keeping his identity secret felt like lying to her. But he hadn't wanted to scare her away from the classes.

Jan acknowledged him and turned to the women. "Who wants to go first?"

Jonah glanced at Annie. She stared at the floor, but her body was stiff, her hands balled. Suddenly, she surged to her feet.

"I will." Her voice was strong, yet Jonah heard the warble of nerves.

Pride swelled in his chest for her courage, her willingness to defeat the doubts and move forward.

Annie stepped forward, squared her shoulders and lifted her chin, but Jonah saw the shadows of trepidation darkening her eyes.

Come on, honey. You can do this.

"All right, Annie. Joe is going to be a kidnapper in a parking lot. It's night, and he approaches you as you are walking to your car. What do you do first?"

Annie took a deep breath. "Warn him away."

Jan nodded. "Right. Do that."

Jonah moved toward Annie, taking an aggressive stance.

He saw the panic flare in her eyes. "No. Stop. Get back," she said in a raised voice but without any real command.

Jonah kept coming.

"Louder, Annie. Say it like you mean it," Jan coached.

Raising her hand, Annie stumbled back. "Stop!"

Nervous energy quivered in her voice.

Jan glanced at Jonah and waved him away. "Let's try it again. Annie, put more force behind your words. Your tone has to tell him you will *not* be his victim. Stop!" Jan barked the word and several ladies, including Annie, flinched, startled by her shout. "Get back!" Jan tipped her head. "See the difference?"

Annie nodded, and Jan waved Jonah forward again.

He moved faster this time, growling as he lunged forward. Annie gasped and threw her hand up. "Stop! Get back!"

Jan smiled and clapped. "Much better!"

Jonah lumbered back, keeping an eye on Annie's reaction.

She opened and closed her hands, then wiped her palms on her uniform skirt.

"Okay, now suppose he doesn't stop. I want you to fight him off with anything and everything you've learned here. Don't hold back." Jan gave a nod to him, and Jonah sucked in a deep breath before closing in on Annie again. Bracing. Hoping.

Come on, Annie. Let me have it.

Raising wide, apprehensive eyes, Annie backpedaled. When he grabbed her arm, hauling her into a restrictive hold, she gasped, tensed.

"Fight back, Annie. Joe won't hurt you, but a real attacker would. You can't be afraid to inflict some damage yourself."

Annie struggled some, tried a puny jab or two with her elbows. Jonah tightened his grip and stumbled back a step with her, simulating a kidnapping. "Get in the car," he grated in a low voice.

Annie's breathing grew ragged, fast. She was hyperventilating.

Without waiting for Jan's directive, Jonah released Annie.

After giving Jonah a quizzical look, Jan noticed Annie's irregular breathing.

"Annie, are you okay? Calm down. You're safe here. This is just practice, remember. Do you want to sit down and rest a minute while someone else tries?"

Clutching a hand to her chest, Annie shook her head and fought to slow her breathing. "No. I—I have to try again."

A mix of concern and admiration swirled in Jonah's gut. He understood her motivation, knew the need that drove her. But the fear that brightened her eyes made her seem fragile, ready to break.

"You're sure?" Jan asked.

Lifting her chin and inhaling deeply, she nodded. "Just… give me a second. I…" She shook out her hands and closed her eyes, clearly drawing on her inner strength.

A few members of the class clapped and shouted encouragement. "You can do it."

"Go get 'em, girl."

"Hang in there."

When she opened her eyes and faced him, Jonah saw the same doubts and hesitation. The fear.

And he knew he had to do something. He had to make her dig deep into the well of her buried emotions, had to remind her of what was at stake, had to help her past the hurdle of intimidation her husband had heaped on her.

His heart hurt, even as he did what he knew would galvanize her.

"What's the matter, bitch? Didn't your old man ever teach you your place?" he growled from behind the protective mask.

Annie's head snapped up, alarm blanching her face.

"Your kids are gonna grow up without a mommy, 'cause I'm gonna kill you," he taunted in a dark growl, hating the pain he knew his barbs caused while praying his tactic worked.

From the periphery of his vision, he caught the stunned, querying glance Jan sent him. He was out of line, breaking protocol.

But he didn't care. Only Annie mattered. She needed to get past her anxiety, and anger was the best way he knew to trump fear. He tapped into her protective rage. The fury of the injustice done to her. The hostility toward her husband that she'd suppressed for years.

The women watching murmured to one another with expressions of dismay and disgust. Annie gaped at him, quivering, her cheeks flushing, her eyes full of confusion, hurt and horror.

Pain squeezed his chest as he stepped closer and stuck his helmeted face close to hers, grating, "Are you going to let your husband win? Are you going to let fear win? As long as you listen to the doubts he put in your head, you give him power. If you want a better life for yourself and your kids, then prove it."

Tears sparkled in her dark eyes. But he'd reached her. He saw the instant his message penetrated her fear. Like a light switch flipping on the power to her private reserve of energy and guts, Annie's gaze lit with passion and determination.

Her posture shifted. Her muscles tensed. Her expression filled with raw emotion and fire.

"Now hit me, Annie. Fight for your life, damn it. You deserve to live, and you deserve a good life. Now show me you care. Show me you want to be free of your past."

Jonah grabbed her around the waist, and she reacted instantly, landing a swift knee to his groin. The blow had power behind it, strength and anger.

Thank God for the protective pads.

"That's it, Annie. Fight back. Don't give him an inch," Jan coached.

Jonah made another move to subdue Annie, and she swung her hand up toward the face mask, demonstrating a nose strike. Jonah's head snapped back from the unexpected force of the blow. The class cheered.

"Great job," Jan said. "Who wants to be next?"

He shook off the hit and turned toward Annie. Despite Jan's dismissal, Annie clearly wasn't finished with him. She had a lethal glare narrowed on him, and she charged. Again she lashed out with a nose strike, then a strike to his throat.

"Annie?" Jan called to her, concern lacing her tone.

Annie didn't seem to hear. Jonah recognized the intent, the emotion blazing in her eyes. She'd tapped a wellspring of poisonous memories, and the flow of bitter emotion had rushed to the surface.

He held a hand up, stopping Jan when she tried to approach Annie and calm her. Self-defense techniques dissolved into a flurry of unbridled frustration and hurt and anger. Tears streamed down her cheeks as she swung at him, pounding him with tightly clenched fists. Annie's grunts of exertion and emotion as she pummeled his protective suit ripped through Jonah's gut. This catharsis was good for her, he told himself, even as his heart broke seeing her unleash her temper, her suppressed bitterness and sense of helplessness.

After several minutes, when Annie's rage hadn't cooled, the first whispers of doubt crept in. What had worked for him when Michael had goaded him to release his bottled-up anger in the gym might not have been the best approach for Annie. Who was he to tell her how to heal?

His heart thundered, and worry wrenched his chest as her meltdown continued. She seemed to have blocked out all but the target of her flailing fists and feet. Teeth gritted, Annie sobbed and snarled and lashed at his chest. Even through the protective suit the force of her blows reverberated through him.

"Jonah, stop her. She's going to hurt herself," Jan called to him over the buzz of the stunned women who watched.

"Annie, that's enough." He tried to catch her swinging hands, but the protective suit made him awkward.

"You animal! How could you do this to me?" she screamed, her eyes unfocused. He hated to think what horrible beating, what demeaning taunts she was reliving. Seeing her anguish clogged Jonah's throat with regret and sympathy. Shared pain.

His hand came away with a smear of red on his palm. Blood. Annie's blood.

She'd opened wounds on her knuckles from the force and frequency of her strikes to the padded suit, but she seemed oblivious to the condition of her hands.

Guilt swelled in Jonah. He'd provoked her, he'd goaded her into this rage. He had to do something to stop her, had to talk her down somehow and be there for the aftershock.

Chapter 14

"Annie, stop! It's over!" Jonah yanked the face mask off, so he could see more clearly. So she could see his face and know who was with her. So he could claim responsibility for his part in her breakdown.

He wouldn't hide from his part in this.

Her lashes kept coming, though she seemed to be running out of steam.

Around them, he was aware that Jan had dismissed the class and ushered the other ladies out of the gym.

Following her violent outburst, her uncontrolled sobs, Annie gasped for breath. Her final swings were devoid of energy.

"Annie! Annie, listen to me. I'm here. You're safe. It's over." He gently swiped a tear from her cheek. "It's over, honey."

Stiffening, she jerked her gaze up, blinked at him. Confusion muddied her expression.

He peeled open the top Velcro fastenings of the padded armor and shucked his arms out so that the pads hung from his waist. Sweat plastered his T-shirt to his chest, but, free of the suit, he could at least breathe easier, move without so much bulk.

"Annie? Are you with me? Are you okay?"

Her breathing was still ragged, and her eyes flashed with turbulent emotions.

Jan crossed from the gym door where she'd seen the class out. She brought an ice pack and a clean rag with her, both of which she handed to Jonah. "Want me to stay, to talk to her?"

He shook his head. "No. I'll take her home when she's ready. Go on."

"You're gonna be okay, friend." Jan squeezed Annie's shoulder, and Annie flinched.

Jonah extended a hand, unsure how he'd be received. "Come 'ere, honey. You're safe now. Take a deep breath."

Slowly Annie's surroundings sharpened into focus through her tears.

The gymnasium at the police station. The self-defense class. But everyone else was gone. She was alone with "Generic Joe."

She gave her head a clearing shake. The memories had seemed so fresh, so real.

But Walt wasn't there.

Jonah was.

She narrowed her gaze on him, wondering if he was another illusion.

Jonah was Joe? He'd been the one taunting her, egging her on to vent her rage?

She rubbed her arms. The air-conditioning blowing on her perspiration-damp body left a chill on her skin. Or maybe the iciness came from the remnants of her flashback, the wake of her tantrum.

She'd really lost it. Snapped. The anger, once she'd allowed it to sneak to the surface, had almost consumed her.

Annie shivered, stunned by the power of the fury and loathing that had washed through her. Fresh tears puddled in her eyes. Would she ever feel normal again? Would Walt always taint her life, even from behind bars? Could she ever heal the deep emotional scars he'd gouged in her soul?

"Annie?"

She raised her gaze to Jonah, who studied her with a dark veil of concern shading his expression. A prick of embarrassment jabbed her. What must he think of her after witnessing her meltdown?

She sniffed and wiped the wet tracks from her face. "Sorry, I—"

"Don't you dare apologize." His voice trembled, and she'd have sworn he had tears in his eyes. He stretched his hand toward hers, then gently wrapped his hand around her aching fingers. "Gimme…"

He placed an ice pack on her knuckles, and she winced when she saw the raw scrapes. She felt equally chafed and bleeding inside. Shaken.

Her legs buckled, and she no longer had the strength to stay on her feet. With a weary sigh, she crumpled to her knees. Her shoulders sagged, and she stared at the reddened knuckles in disbelief. The hot well of tears, nudged by shame and frustration, tainted with the bitterness of her marriage to Walt, flowed down her cheeks as she quietly sobbed. She'd gotten good in days past at crying without making any noise. So her children didn't hear her. So Walt wouldn't know, wouldn't make an issue of it.

Jonah sank down on the mats beside her. When he tugged her closer, she didn't have the energy, the willpower to refuse.

Besides, collapsing against the solid strength of his chest, resting in the embrace of his arms held great appeal. He scooted awkwardly closer, the protective Joe suit impeding him somewhat.

Laying her head against his chest, she listened to the drumming of his heart, steady and soothing. Her fingers curled into his damp T-shirt, while his hands rubbed her back the way she calmed Haley after a bad dream.

Annie closed her eyes, inhaling the musky, masculine scent of his overheated skin, tinged with sandalwood and spice. His fingers combed through her hair and stroked her cheek. Every gentle touch and comforting caress lulled her deeper into a time and place where only the two of them existed.

Her tears slowed as she slowly gained her composure. But as the adrenaline and tension that had fueled her tantrum waned, she found a different source for the rapid beating of her heart, the heady swirl of desire that hummed inside her.

After losing herself to her emotions, scaring herself with how easily she'd lost control, Jonah's embrace was a safe haven. Had she really found this gentle man intimidating before?

His fingers worked their magic, massaging the tension and tightness from her neck muscles, and she relaxed against him. Wrapping her arms around his chest, she clung to his solid strength like a life raft in a turbulent sea.

The last thing she wanted was to fall back into a position of need, dependency and defeatism that had trapped her in her unhappy marriage. Yet in Jonah's arms, though she leaned on him now for physical and emotional support, she didn't feel needy or weak. Jonah gave her peace of mind, encouragement, the affection of friendship.

Or was it more than friendship with Jonah?

She pushed aside the ugly dregs of her flashbacks of Walt's abuse, of Hardin's murder, of the attempt on her life, and she concentrated on more pleasant memories. The soft kiss Jonah had surprised her with the day Hardin had been killed. The warmth in his eyes when he'd met her children. The sweet quiver of expectation that rippled through her when he'd lock his penetrating green eyes on her. His gaze said he could see straight through her, knew her darkest secrets and blackest fears...but accepted all her flaws without reservation.

"Better?" he murmured.

She nodded. *Much. Thanks to you.*

He shifted slightly, and she realized how long she'd subjected him to a rather awkward position, huddled on the dusty floor mats.

Though her anguish had faded, she wasn't ready to leave the comfort and sweet refuge of Jonah's arms, his warm touch.

Unwise though it might be to get involved with another man when her life was in such disarray, she wanted to cherish these few moments alone with him. She wanted to block out the reality of cars trying to mow her down. She needed to forget for a moment the vortex sucking her into the shadow of illegal activity at the diner, and the specter of finding her boss murdered.

"Annie," Jonah said, breaking the still silence. "Forgive me. I shouldn't have pushed so hard, sweetheart. I'm sorry."

His voice cracked, and she tipped her chin back to meet his gaze. The sorrow and compassion she found staring back at her arrowed deep, warming her from the inside out.

"The things you said—"

"Were awful," he interrupted, regret darkening his eyes.

"Hurtful. I'm so sorry. I was just trying to get you mad enough to get past your fear and hesitation."

She lifted a corner of her mouth in a melancholy grin. "It worked."

"Too well. I shouldn't have—"

"I'm glad you did. Maybe this was what I needed. You said boxing, working out on the punching bags was cathartic for you."

"But we're all different. Maybe you just needed to leave the baggage in the past and move on. Maybe I did more harm than good. Annie, I never want to hurt you or cause you more pain."

How could the words *hurt* and *pain* ever be associated with Jonah? She'd never met a man so kind and gentle, so understanding and generous. But his comment made her think, made her dig deep for her own understanding of what it would take for her to feel safe again. When would she feel her life was her own again?

Haley and Ben sprang immediately to mind. Everything she did was for her children, their happiness, their future.

"When I know my children are safe, when I can know they're provided for and will grow up healthy and happy—" She peered up at Jonah. "That's all I want."

A deep crease puckered his forehead. "And what about you? What about your happiness?"

She lifted a shoulder in a tired shrug. "Maybe someday…"

Jonah gripped her chin, and his fierce gaze drilled into hers. "Annie, listen to me. You deserve to be happy every bit as much as your children do. You deserve to seize happiness with both hands and hold on to it. It is your right."

The passion in his tone and intensity of his magnetic gaze burrowed deep inside her, shook her to her core. "I—I know."

"Do you?"

The air in her lungs stilled. Could she really find the joy for life she'd had when she was younger? She wanted desperately to reclaim the hope and promise, the simple pleasure life offered.

"Promise me you will go after whatever it is you truly want, whatever it is that will make you happy again, Annie." Jonah stroked his fingers through her hair until his palm cradled the back of her head. "Promise me you will fight for your happiness."

Staring into his fathomless eyes, how could she refuse? A fist of bittersweet emotion squeezed her throat. "I promise."

Jonah dipped his head and touched his lips to hers. The warm caress of his lips spun a sweet pleasure through her blood, and she savored a taste of what that happiness might be. She leaned into the kiss, enticed by the tender persuasion of his mouth.

Jonah angled his head and captured her lips more fully, yet his kiss remained infinitely patient, his touch light and careful.

Annie raised a hand to his shoulder to steady herself and curled her fingers into his damp shirt. The tip of his tongue teased the seam of her mouth, and she opened to him. She was shocked to realize the breathy sigh that whispered through the quiet gym was hers. After a moment, she grew impatient with his caution, his restraint.

Hadn't he just made her promise to go after whatever made her happy? For a few precious moments, she wanted to lose herself in Jonah's kiss, in the mind-numbing sensations he stirred and the gentle comfort of his caress. Drawing on the boldness he'd encouraged in her and the assurance that she was safe with this caring man, Annie slid her hand to Jonah's nape and pulled him closer, drawing hard, more deeply on his lips.

A satisfied moan rumbled from his chest, filling Annie with a heady sense of empowerment. She'd taken the initiative, and she had elicited that husky growl of pleasure from him.

Though Jonah matched her intensity, he never pushed her past the limits she set. The quiver of restraint in his muscles told her he'd surrendered the pace to her. That evidence of his control gave her the confidence to sink against him and explore the hard ridges of his muscled back with her fingers while her tongue darted into his mouth, testing, seeking more.

Finally, Jonah laid her back on the floor, covering her with his wide body and pressing her into the mats with his weight, his heat. Annie's heart thrashed against her chest like a trapped animal, her blood rushing past her ears with a deafening whoosh.

He paused long enough to gauge her reaction, his eyes dark with desire, his breath lashing her cheeks with hot, ragged puffs. She answered his unspoken query by raising her mouth to his again and tunneling her fingers into his short, cropped hair.

Jonah raked his palm along her thigh, under the skirt of her waitress uniform. His touch skimmed tantalizingly close to the spot where her body wept for his touch, but his fingers skittered away, raising a delicious shiver on her skin. He moved his hand up along her hip to the dent of her waist, then cupped her breast through the ugly fabric of her uniform. Even with the barrier between them, her nerve endings fired, and her nipple beaded, aching for his touch.

She mewled her approval without breaking their kiss. Jonah had offered her a glimpse of the kind of passion and freedom she'd never had before, and she didn't want to squander any part of it. The press of his body and the heat of his mouth on hers thrilled her, terrified her, tempted her.

Somehow through the dizzying bliss, a tiny voice whispered to her.

What was she doing? How could she give herself to Jonah and not lose her heart, not set herself up for heartache?

Her head spun, and the thrum of pleasure shouted down the voice of caution and doubt in the back of her brain. Here with Jonah, no one was trying to kill her. She didn't have to face her mountain of unpaid bills, and she could escape the memories of the man who'd started her life on this downward spiral.

When Jonah moved his kiss to the fluttering pulse at her throat, Annie drew a shuddering breath.

"Annie," he murmured against her skin. His voice rasped with unspent desire. Jonah raised his head and gulped oxygen. "We have to stop. This is…the wrong time. Wrong place."

His words slashed through the lusty fog she'd lost herself in, and she blinked her surroundings into focus. A ripple of shock shot through her.

Dear God, had she been ready to make love to Jonah in the middle of the police station gymnasium?

Mortified by the total loss of her senses, she bolted upright. The sweet hum of passion fled, doused by the cold wash of reality.

"Annie?" Jonah placed a soothing hand on her arm as she dragged in the stale air of the gym.

Her pulse pounded at her temples. "Yeah…wrong."

With his fingers, he angled her chin toward him. "No, I said wrong time and place." He brushed his thumb along her bottom lip, still swollen from his crushing kiss. "Everything else about kissing you was…nirvana."

The sound of a door closing down the hall echoed through the empty gym. Glancing in the direction of the noise, Jonah shoved to his feet and extended a hand to help her up. "Let me take you home."

She inhaled, searching for the shreds of her composure, then clasped his hand.

Once he'd hauled her to her feet, she hugged herself and rubbed her arms self-consciously.

"Will you be all right for a couple minutes while I put this thing away?" He indicated the padded suit that hung from his waist.

She nodded, and Jonah lumbered off toward the locker room, already ripping open the Velcro enclosures on the protective pants.

While she waited for Jonah, Annie's thoughts traveled a windy, troubled path. Jonah was Joe. That's how he knew of the class. Why he'd recommended it.

And why he'd been close by yesterday when she'd gotten out of class. When the car had tried to run her down. When he'd saved her life.

Are you going to let your husband win? Are you going to let fear win?

She experienced the same bone-chilling dread that had kick-started her breakdown in class. Sometimes fear could be a stronger motivation to act than anger. For her, the idea that Walt could still be controlling her from his prison cell because of his legacy of intimidation frightened her more than anything else. She would do whatever it took to be free of Walt's lingering effect.

"What the heck kind of class do you take at the police station anyway?"

The kind that helped you climb out of the morass of anxiety and self-doubt your ex-husband left you in.

Annie purposefully moved her musings around that mental quicksand. Dwelling on Walt now would only depress her, and she wanted to hold on to the last wisps of cloud nine where she'd drifted briefly with Jonah.

Nirvana, he'd called it. She closed her eyes and tried to recapture the sweetness of those moments, but her mind snagged on another memory instead.

"What the heck kind of class do you take at the police station anyway?"

She frowned as Susan's question replayed in her head.

"Ready to go?" Jonah's voice jarred her from her introspection. "Hey, what's wrong? Why so serious?"

"I never told Susan where my class was. So how did she know?"

Chapter 15

"Are you sure you didn't mention the police station when you asked her to cover your shift?" Jonah asked later in his truck as they drove toward her apartment.

Annie leaned her head back on the seat and closed her eyes. "I don't think so. But maybe. I— No. No, I'm sure I didn't."

Annie's revelation didn't worry him much. Susan struck him as an astute listener, a curious sort of busybody, but not a killer. Still, he wasn't comfortable leaving the loose end unexplained. "Did you tell anyone else where you'd be? Someone else could have told her."

She cut a sharp glance toward him. "Only you."

He arched his dark eyebrow. "I didn't say anything, if that's what you're thinking."

"You asked who I'd told." Sighing her fatigue, Annie raked her fingers through her hair. Jonah's gut tightened remembering the silky feel of her hair twined around his fingers. The soft crush of her lips against his had packed a more powerful punch than he'd have imagined. One small taste of Annie wasn't nearly enough. Her eager response at the gym had rocked him to his core.

Wrong time, wrong place. But someday…

His body thrummed with the expectation, anticipation. He wanted to make slow, sweet love to Annie as much as he'd ever wanted anything in his life.

But she had to make the first move. No way would he push her, pressure her. He'd wait until she was ready if it killed him. Which, judging by the pressure in his jeans, the pounding at his temples and the fine sheen of sweat on his back, might be sooner than later.

Jonah cleared his throat, bringing his attention back to the discussion at hand. "We'll keep an eye on Susan. If you see or hear anything suspicious, let me know. Meantime, be on your toes around her. Okay?"

She nodded, wet her lips. "Will you stay for dinner?"

"If you want me to." He parked on the street a couple of blocks from her apartment, in case her parking lot was being watched. When she didn't answer, he angled his body toward her on the seat, waiting.

Finally she peered up at him through a fringe of dark eyelashes. "I do."

Her gaze clung to his for a breathless moment before her focus shifted to his mouth. Drawing her own lip between her teeth, she inhaled a choppy breath.

"I can't promise much more than cold-cut sandwiches and canned peaches. I need to get groceries, but I have to wait for payday."

When he stroked her chin with a bent finger, he felt the tremble that chased through her, heard the catch in her breath. He knew better than to offer to buy her groceries. A woman searching so fiercely for her independence would see the offer as charity and flatly decline. "A sandwich sounds fine. But if you'd rather, I could take you and the kids out for a burger somewhere. Or I know an Italian place where the kids could get spaghetti and the manicotti is out of this world."

The expression in her eyes softened. "You sure you want to start dating a mother with two kids? I thought the idea of kids gave most single men cold sweats."

He grinned. "I like your kids."

She climbed out of his truck, and he escorted her through the maze of other buildings in her complex and across the yard behind her apartment.

Getting involved with Annie's family did unnerve him a little, but not for the reasons she might assume. Family was just a concept that carried too much history for him, not enough useful experience to feel confident in that realm.

"If calling it a date bothers you—" He shrugged. "Call it 'I know you're tired, and I thought I'd offer an easy out from cooking.'"

She cocked her head as they made their way to the back entrance to her building.

"Making a sandwich is hardly cooking. And if Ben throws one of his two-year-old tantrums at the restaurant, I doubt you'll still be calling it an easy out."

She had him on that point. He hadn't the faintest idea how to deal with any aspect of parenting young kids. His father was the last model of discipline he'd ever use, and his mother had been withdrawn and all but absent in his life.

Turning up a palm, he said, "Your choice."

She squeezed his hand. "Thank you, but not today. I'm beat, and the kids need to be in bed in an hour or so."

"Another time?"

She poked her door key into the lock and flashed a half grin. "Yeah. Maybe. Someday."

Someday. She'd said the same about when she'd get the cat she wanted. A pluck of disappointment tugged at him. She deserved more than to keep her dreams, her desires on ice while she dealt with life's hard knocks. He hated to think of Annie putting her life on hold, suspending all her happiness until *someday.*

While Annie paid the babysitter and started the sandwiches, Jonah listened as Haley jabbered excitedly about the DVD Rani had checked out of the library for them to watch. The best he could figure, the movie started as animation, then switched to live action, and involved a prince and a talking chipmunk. Beyond that, he lost track of the girl's convoluted explanation.

"Come on," she begged, tugging his hand. "We can watch it now!"

"Dinner first, Haley," Annie said without missing a beat as she set four places at the table. "Wash your hands. Time to eat."

Haley whined her protest, and Annie visibly tensed. The past few hours, to say nothing of her shift at the diner, had taken their toll on her. A fussy child was the last thing she needed.

He had no notion how a parent normally dealt with cranky complaints, but his instincts told him distraction was a promising option. "Haley, have I shown you my magic trick?"

Forget that he had no real trick. Haley was hooked. Eyes wide, she gaped at him as if he'd hung the moon. "You know magic?"

Annie tipped her head, giving him a curious look.

Jonah scrambled for a plan, making things up as he went. "Sure, but…you need clean hands for this trick. Let's wash up, okay?"

Hands clean, Haley sat down at the table with him, watching expectantly.

Um...

"I can...make this sandwich disappear!" Jonah picked up his sandwich and waved a hand over it.

"Do it! Make it disappear!" Haley squealed, and Ben clapped his hands.

Annie's cheek twitched in amusement.

Jonah ate the sandwich in three large bites.

"Ta-da!" he mumbled around his mouthful of food. He waited for the inevitable look of disgruntled disappointment from Annie's daughter. Instead, she giggled and rolled her eyes.

"That's not magic!"

He chewed some more so he could speak. "It's not?"

"No!" The girl laughed, but she picked up her sandwich and eyed it. "I can make my sandwich disappear, too!"

And she did.

"Thank you," Annie mouthed from across the table.

After dinner, he helped clear the table, then followed Haley to the living room with Ben while Annie finished cleaning the kitchen.

The Disney movie held Haley's rapt attention as Jonah took a seat on the couch. Ben glanced at the television occasionally but was more absorbed in stacking his wooden blocks and knocking the towers down.

After watching the process for a while, Jonah moved to the floor with Ben. Rolling a wooden block in his fingers, Jonah replayed the afternoon's events in his mind.

He prayed Annie's meltdown today had been her needed catharsis. But now she needed a healthy outlet for the future, a safe environment where she could continue the healing process. Ginny would provide some of that counseling and support.

But would that be enough?

Annie was strong, but even the bravest woman needed a soft place to land when the world crashed around her. A soul-deep yearning tugged inside Jonah, twisting, aching. He wanted to be Annie's safe harbor, her confidant, her life partner so much his teeth hurt. But that damn niggling voice that had been whispering to him for weeks now wouldn't be quieted. The uneasy feeling that committing himself to her and her family would be a disaster.

Ben's tiny hand grabbed the block Jonah held, and the brush of those tiny fingers reverberated to his marrow. How could he ask Annie or her children to tie themselves to him when even he had doubts about his ability to be part of their family?

A movement at the edge of his vision told him Annie had come to the living-room door. He glanced up at her and curled up one corner of his mouth. She returned a twitch of a grin, her gaze flicking from one child to the next. A mother hen assuring herself that her chicks were safe.

Haley crawled forward and punched the volume up on the Disney DVD. The cartoon princess who'd landed in real-life New York City had just arrived at a costume ball.

"Bok."

Jonah glanced down at Ben, who held a block out to him. "Yeah. Block. That's good, buddy." He took the offering from the boy's chubby hand and slanted a look toward Annie.

Her attention, like Haley's, was riveted on the television screen as the princess and the handsome New Yorker who'd befriended her swirled around the dance floor. A melancholy ballad played and glittery confetti surrounded the starry-eyed, star-crossed couple.

Jonah sat back, leaning against the sofa and watched Annie stare at the fairy-tale movie. Tears sparkled in her eyes and wistful longing transformed her expression. His heart slowed, stuttered at the sadness on her face and his new insight.

The woman who'd raged and pummeled her imaginary attacker today until her knuckles bled was a died-in-the-wool romantic at heart. An optimist who'd had her dreams of happily ever after brutally ripped from her.

The desire to put a smile on Annie's face, whatever the cost, slammed into Jonah with a force that stole his breath. If anyone in the world deserved a happily ever after, Annie did. She'd survived so much, been so brave and strong for her children.

He shoved to his feet, his muscles protesting, and pulled the coffee table out of the way. Stepping over to her, he held out his hand. "May I have this dance, pretty lady?"

Annie blinked at him, stunned, then shook her head, swiping jerkily at her damp eyes. "No…Jonah, I can't—"

"Sure you can." He took her hand and tugged her close, despite her startled gasp.

"What are you doing?" She stiffened and gaped at him with wide, dubious eyes.

"Trying to dance, but you're not following my lead." He tugged harder, until she stumbled into his arms. He was a clumsy dancer at best, but he shuffled his feet in a sidestep, and Annie staggered along with him, still staring at him like he'd lost his mind.

He anchored her slim body closer, so she wouldn't fall as he swept her around in small circles, careful not to trip on Ben's blocks. He wiggled his eyebrows at her. "And I've never darkened the door at an Arthur Murray Dance Studio."

A small awkward laugh snuck from her, and she turned up the corner of her mouth. "I can tell."

He sent her an expression of mock affront. "Hey! I'm not that bad!"

The movie music swelled, and he swooped her around in grander twirls. Annie clung to him to keep her balance, her eyes brightening.

Haley noticed them dancing and jumped up from the floor. She giggled and clapped her hands. "Me, too. I want to dance!"

As her daughter twirled and pirouetted around the floor, Annie's smile grew, and her cheeks flushed. A genuine smile blossomed on her lips, and her face glowed—all the encouragement Jonah needed to continue swirling around the confines of her living room, colliding with Haley. When the little girl tumbled onto her bottom, he broke his hold on Annie long enough to scoop the girl onto his hip.

Haley squealed her delight as the three of them continued to dance and spin. Annie's laughter joined her daughter's giggles, and Jonah's chest filled with a bittersweet pleasure and satisfaction. Annie's smile and lyrical laugh were intoxicating. He'd give anything to know he could make Annie this happy for longer than a few moments of silliness. As he'd suspected, her smile transformed her face from attractive and intriguing to knockout beautiful.

Haley wiggled to be put down again, and he let her slide to the floor without breaking his hold around Annie's waist. Once Haley scampered down the hall, calling something about her princess crown, Annie lifted a grateful smile and a teary gaze to his.

Jonah's heart clenched, and he tucked Annie under his chin as they made another circuit around her small apartment. Like that afternoon, the crush of her petite body against his made his nerve endings crackle and spark. Holding Annie, the sweet scent of her shampoo filling his senses, taunted his libido. He craved her kiss, the touch of her skin against his.

But as they danced, her smile warming him to his core, the hum of his body took a dangerous turn. His heart was involved. Her laughter bubbled inside him like a disinfectant cleansing the poison and pain from his soul.

The music from the DVD slowed, and Annie lifted a heart-breaking gaze that punched Jonah in the gut.

He was in trouble. The mix of emotion filling Annie's damp eyes was much like that of the Disney princess as the dance with her true love ended. Longing and reluctance, gratitude and regret, and—probably the hardest for Jonah to bear—hope.

The last thing he'd wanted to do was build false hopes for Annie. He was no one's prince. He couldn't give her a story-book ending. Dancing with her had been a mistake. Encouraging her romantic notions only set her up for more heartache when he couldn't fulfill her happily ever after.

But, damn it, seeing her smile, knowing he'd made her laugh, giving her even a few moments of happiness after the gut-wrenching day she'd had had been worth it. Hadn't it? Or was it just his own selfish need to feel he'd slayed a dragon for her, given her a few minutes of lighthearted joy when the rest of her world seemed so difficult?

Even after the ballad stopped, Annie stood close to him, her eyes searching his as if they held all the answers to her problems.

His pulse hammered. Big trouble.

When he brushed a hand along her cheek, she trembled and raised her lips. Need slammed him, knocking the breath from him. As much as he wanted to kiss her, he couldn't, *wouldn't* mislead her about his ability to give her a fairy-tale ending. Instead, he pressed a kiss to her forehead and stepped back.

A shadow of disappointment, colored with embarrassment, dimmed the spark in her eyes as she stepped out of his arms. Guilt kicked him in the shin.

"Look, Jonah!" Haley pranced back into the living room wearing a plastic tiara. "I have a crown like Giselle's."

Her daughter's arrival provided a welcome distraction, and an excuse to tear himself from the temptation Annie served. He cleared the thickness from his throat. "Hey, princess. Don't you look pretty?"

"Can you dance with me again?" Haley lifted her arms to him.

Annie hugged herself, clearly still fighting an onslaught of emotions. "Haley, I…I think it's your bedtime."

Jonah gritted his teeth, struggling to sort out for himself the shift in his feeling toward Annie. So much had changed today. He'd be wise to leave, to get some distance to clear his head.

Haley pouted, and her shoulders slumped. "But, Mommy—"

"No whining, please."

Jonah tweaked the girl's chin. "Hey, another time. I promise."

Annie avoided his eyes as she stooped to collect Ben's blocks and pile them in a basket. "You, too, Ben. Go get your jammies for me. Haley, brush your teeth."

The kids, with mixed degrees of protest, toddled toward their bedrooms, leaving him alone with Annie. He crouched beside her and helped collect blocks.

"You have a beautiful smile. You should use it more often."

His comment stopped her. Her hand hovered over a block, shaking. Finally, she looked up, and confusion and pain clouded the dark eyes that moments ago had held such joy and hope. "What do you want from me?"

He rocked back on his heels. "Only for you to be happy. And safe."

"Do you see yourself as part of that happiness? Is that why you're here?"

His gut pitched. Why was he here? What was he doing inserting himself in her family dynamic if he had no intention of staying?

"I'm here because you had a rough day, and I wanted to be sure you were all right. I thought you could use a hand with the kids tonight."

And because he knew Farrout and his cohorts still saw her as a threat to be dealt with. She was still in danger.

His answer clearly didn't satisfy her. She frowned as she moved the basket of blocks to a corner of the room, then dropped onto the sofa. "Why do you feel that's your job? I'm not your responsibility. You don't owe me anything. It's not your fault my life is in the pitiful shape it's in."

"Maybe not, but I want to help." He took the seat beside her on the couch and resisted the urge to brush her cheek again. The wary distance that had returned in her eyes told him his touch would be unwelcome.

She picked at a loose thread on the sofa cushion for a moment, then raised a level gaze. "I'm not looking for someone to rescue me. I refuse to depend on anyone ever again." Steely determination colored her tone.

"Especially not a man."

She squared her shoulders and scowled. "I didn't say that."

"You didn't have to." He raised a hand to interrupt when she opened her mouth to protest. "I don't blame you. The men in your life so far gave you reason to be cautious. But I'm not your husband. I'm not Hardin. If you don't want me in your life, I'll leave. But I'm worried about what's going on at the diner and how it could all play out. I want you to be safe, and I want you to know you can trust me."

She stared at him for several long, tense seconds, gnawing her bottom lip. Every one of her conflicting emotions played across her doelike eyes as if he were watching her thoughts on a monitor.

"I'm so scared, Jonah. Not just because of the mess at the diner. I'm scared of the future. When I think about raising those two babies by myself, supporting them with my pathetic paycheck, trying to teach them right from wrong...I feel overwhelmed. Alone. But..." She shivered and rubbed a hand along her arm. "But when I think about getting involved with someone again... Oh, God, that scares me the most. I don't want to spend my life alone, but how can I risk...?" She closed her eyes and swallowed hard. "What if they turn out to be like Walt?"

Her honesty grabbed him by the throat, simultaneously spreading warmth through him and chilling him to the bone. While he was flattered that she trusted him enough to reveal her fears, her worries echoed the doubts that had dogged him, haunted him with increasing frequency as his feelings for Annie deepened.

While he'd cut off his own hand before he'd ever raise it against a woman or a child, his memories of family life, the legacy of his own painful youth warned him away whenever he considered marriage. Family. Children.

Despite the drumbeat of caution pounding in his brain, Jonah dragged a hand down his jaw and looked for a way to reassure Annie. He wouldn't lie to her. But he wanted so badly to give her even a morsel of the hope she deserved.

"When the right man comes along, you will have the wisdom and discernment that your experience gives you to know, in your heart, whether he's like Walt or not." The notion of

Annie with another man scraped him raw. But if he couldn't give her what she needed, didn't she deserve to be happy with someone else?

Of course. But that didn't make it any easier for him to think of another man touching her, holding her, making love to her.

His gut knotted, and his mouth dried, but he forced the words she needed to hear from his tongue. "When the time is right, you'll know you're ready to commit yourself to a relationship."

Her expression softened. "I want to believe that."

"Then do. I believe it. One hundred percent."

The tender longing that lit her eyes made it difficult to stay on his side of the couch. As much as he wanted his next breath, he wanted to press her back in the cushions and convince her with his kiss that he was the one who could make her happy, that he was the one she was looking for.

But Haley ran into the room, providing the diversion he needed to regain his focus and control.

"Done brushing. See?" She flashed her teeth.

Annie seemed equally relieved for the distraction. She lifted a corner of her mouth in a grin of approval. "Very good. Now scoot to bed. I'll be back in a second to read you a book."

"Can Jonah read to me tonight?" her daughter asked, trotting over to flop against Jonah's legs.

Annie shook her head, clearly ready to protest.

Though his gut tightened at the notion of helping with something as domestic and familial as tucking Haley into bed, Annie was exhausted, and if reading Haley a book would help her, he'd read a whole library.

"If it's okay with your mom." Jonah sent Annie an inquisitive glance. "I don't mind. Really. You tend to Ben."

Her stunned look told him what words didn't. He ex-husband had never volunteered to help put the children to bed. When it came to raising her kids, she'd been as alone in her marriage as she was now.

Haley tugged his hand, and Jonah rose to follow the girl to her bedroom. She scampered under the covers and grabbed a book from the foot of the bed. "This one. It's my favorite."

Jonah glanced down at the title. *Skippyjon Jones.*

"And you have to do the Spanish accent like Mommy does," Haley added as she scrunched down under her sheet.

"A Spanish accent, huh?" Jonah scratched his chin, already having second thoughts about the task he'd volunteered for. He cracked the book open and began reading the humorous tale of a Siamese cat who thought he was a Chihuahua. Hearing a noise in the hallway, he glanced up and saw Annie's shadow on the wall outside Haley's door. Annie hovered by the door, out of sight, no doubt listening—whether protectively monitoring his interaction with her daughter or simply curious to hear his attempted Spanish accent, he couldn't say. It didn't matter. In her place, he'd do the same.

He turned the page and continued reading.

"Jonah?" Haley interrupted.

"Yeah?"

Haley angled her head on her pillow to peer up at him with brown eyes, much like her mother's. "Do you think my mommy's pretty?"

He grinned and nodded. "I do. I think she's beautiful."

"She has a scar on her face." Haley wrinkled her brow as if deep in thought.

"I know. So do I. See?" He pointed to the scar over his eyebrow. "I've had that since I was just a kid."

She winced. "Does it hurt?"

"Not anymore."

"My daddy broke Mommy's cheek. She had to have surg'ry. That's why she's got a scar."

He heard a soft gasp from the hall, and his chest tightened imagining Annie's concern for her daughter.

Please, God, give me the right words for this little girl.

"You know your daddy can't hurt you or your mom anymore. You're safe."

She nodded matter-of-factly. "Daddy's in jail."

"Right." He looked down at the book again, half expecting Haley to ask another question, but the girl stared silently at the stuffed cat clutched in her hands. He could let the subject drop, finish reading the book and escape the topic relatively unscathed. But avoidance never solved anything. More important, he needed Haley—and Annie—to know his true feelings. "You know what? I think your mom's scar is part of what makes her so beautiful to me."

Haley glanced up, giving him a funny, wrinkle-nosed grin. "Really?"

"Really. To me, it's like a badge of courage. A sign of her love for you and of her incredible inner strength. Even though your daddy's in jail, she's made a new life for you and Ben. Sometimes it's hard to be a mommy, but she's one of the best mommies I've ever met."

Haley smiled and bobbed her head.

"Her scar tells me she's willing to do whatever it takes to protect the people she loves." Jonah tapped the girl's nose with his finger. "That's pretty brave, huh? Pretty awesome."

"Yeah." Haley hugged her stuffed cat tighter. "And that's why you think she's pretty?"

Jonah shrugged. "That and her beautiful eyes, and her smile—"

"And her hair?" Haley volunteered, grinning.

"Yep."

"And her mouth?" She giggled.

She'd digressed to silliness now, and Jonah groaned internally. He scrambled mentally for the best way to nip the laundry list in the bud. "Head to toe. I think all of your mom is beautiful. Okay?"

"Like a princess?"

"Sure. Like a princess."

"Are you her prince?"

"I, uh—" His mouth opened like that of a fish out of water. He should have seen that one coming. Conscious of Annie still listening at the door, he chose his response carefully. "Aren't princes supposed to be handsome and charming?"

"You're handsome and charming," Haley said guilelessly.

Jonah chuckled and scratched his jaw. "Well…thanks, sweetie. But I think your mom gets the deciding vote on that."

"Mr. Jonah?"

Fearing another side trip into territory he didn't want to cover, Jonah waggled the book in front of her. "Shouldn't we finish the story now?"

Haley ignored his question and sat up in her bed. Leaning in to hug him, she whispered, "I hope Mommy votes for you."

His heart lurched, and a tangled mix of emotions squeezed his chest. For someone who didn't want to be part of a family again, he'd sure gotten himself in deep with Annie's. So how did he get out without hurting her or her kids?

And why did the idea of future bedtime stories stir such a bittersweet longing in his soul?

Chapter 16

Annie dabbed at the tears tickling her cheeks as Jonah stepped out of Haley's room and pulled the door shut. Her heart gave a heavy throb, so full of affection and gratitude, she thought it might burst.

Clearing his throat quietly, he studied her face. With the pad of his thumb, he dried one of her tears and twitched the corner of his mouth into an awkward smile. "I see you heard my attempt at a Spanish accent. Maybe if we're lucky, the child won't have nightmares of monsters who roll their *R*s."

She grinned through her tears. "Joke all you want. But what you did for her...for me...just now..."

A knot choked her throat, but she forced it down, determined to tell Jonah what was in her heart. "Just so you know—" She rose on her toes and wrapped her arms around his neck, leaning into his large, taut body. "I think you are both handsome and charming." She kissed his cheek. "Gentle and kind." She brushed her lips over his. "A fierce protector and an honorable man."

He heaved a weary sigh and stepped back, his gaze troubled. "Annie, I'm no prince."

She studied the deep lines of worry and fatigue in his craggy face. "I…I'm not looking for a prince."

A muscle in his jaw twitched, and he met her gaze evenly. "Aren't you?"

Annie squared her shoulders, shoving down the knot of disappointment that rose in her chest. "I know better than to believe in fairy tales."

He shook his head. "You can't lie to me. I saw the look in your eyes tonight, the longing and hope."

She scowled, disturbed by the notion he saw through her so easily. "What do you mean? When? What look?"

Jonah edged close again. He tucked her hair behind her ear, leaving the jagged scar on her face exposed, much as her soul felt bared when he drilled her with his dark eyes. "You deserve more than I have in me to give. I will do everything in my power to make sure you and your kids are safe, to stop the people responsible for scamming Michael. But I don't know how to be what you need after that."

A bitter pain slashed through Annie, and she jerked away from his gentle caress. Her spine stiff, she glared at him through hot tears. "I don't need anything from you. I've been alone for most of my life and survived just fine! I'm not your charity case, Jonah. If that's what you think, then you can just…go. Leave now."

"Annie, I didn't mean—"

"No, it's better this way. I don't want my kids growing attached to you if you plan to leave us when this is over. They've been hurt enough."

"I would never intentionally harm you or your kids, Annie.

Never. If you want me to leave, then I will." His stubbled jaw firmed, and he set his mouth in a taut line, though his gaze stayed soft and warm.

Jonah's eyes really did reflect his soul. Her heart did a tap dance inside her. Her emotions played a vicious tug-of-war. She felt safer with Jonah nearby, but how did she justify depending on him, allowing him to become any more deeply rooted in her children's affection. Or hers.

She answered with a jerky nod, and he sighed his resignation. Pain clawed her chest, knowing she'd put that defeated expression on his face.

He patted his hip where his phone was clipped. "I have my cell with me if you need anything. I'll be watching your place from my truck and can be back up here in seconds."

"Jonah…" An invitation to sleep on her couch again was on the tip of her tongue, but she swallowed it. She'd given him an opening to deny his intention to walk away at the close of his investigation at the diner, but he'd kept silent. Better that she begin untangling him from her life now.

Nothing had changed, despite the tantalizing glimpses of a better, happier life she might have with Jonah. Depending on a man for her safety, her happiness, her strength, only led to heartache and disaster. Experience had taught her that in the harshest way. She'd be a fool to forget that lesson.

Jonah was still in his truck, parked just down the street from her apartment, when Annie left for work the next morning. When she spotted him, her pulse leaped like a schoolgirl's. She'd missed sharing a cup of coffee with Jonah this morning, his hair sleep-tousled, his cheek bearing the impression of her couch upholstery like a tattoo. Being around his easygoing companionship in the early morning hours had started recent days with an optimism she'd not had in years.

Knowing how cramped and uncomfortable his truck had to have been overnight stabbed her with a sharp edge of regret. She acknowledged him with a raised hand but ignored his signal when he waved her over. Turning, Annie hurried to the bus stop on the corner, hearing him call to her, then crank his engine.

Accepting a ride from him to the diner as she had done in recent mornings would be the easy way out. With his investigation winding down, she had to return to doing things for herself, looking out for her own interests, breaking the fragile bonds they'd formed.

"Annie, come on. What are you doing?" he called from his truck as he double-parked on the side street.

Thankfully, her bus chugged toward the stop just as Jonah climbed from his front seat. She couldn't bear a confrontation.

"I don't know how to be what you need…."

His rejection last night had gnawed at her all night, kept her tossing and turning through the dark, lonely hours. A heavy ache pinched her chest as she hustled onto the city bus without a backward glance.

What did Jonah think she needed? What demand had she made of him that he thought he lacked? She'd tried so hard not to ask anything of him, not to assume anything about their relationship. And despite her best intentions, she *had* developed a relationship with Jonah, though she was at a loss as to how to define it.

Her skin prickled at the memory of the sweet pressure of his lips on hers, the pleasure of his kiss. He'd wanted her as much as she'd wanted him, hadn't he? Had she misjudged what happened at the police gymnasium? After all, she had just suffered an emotional meltdown. Maybe he'd just been offering pity sex. Had she thrown herself at him in some desperate moment of weakness like a cheap tramp?

Her face heated with mortification. Jonah, being a gentleman, had not taken advantage of her and had stopped her from making the next great mistake of her life.

Her heart squeezed, and she blinked back the moisture that puddled in her eyes. If making love to Jonah would have been such a mistake, why did she still long with every fiber of her body and soul to sink into his arms and lose herself in his kiss, his touch? Deep inside her, she knew Jonah would be infinitely gentle, generous and attentive as a lover. That was the nature of the man she'd gotten to know these past weeks, the man she'd learned to trust, the man who'd stolen her heart when she wasn't looking.

But Jonah had made it clear last night the affection was one-sided.

"I don't know how to be what you need...."

Stifling the self-pity that nipped at her, Annie dug deep inside her for the shreds of determination and hope that she'd clung to like a tattered blanket since she walked out on Walt almost two years ago.

She'd survived just fine before she'd let Jonah into her life, and she had to do the same again. Though she couldn't stop him from playing guardian, she didn't have to indulge the fantasy that he would ever be more than a transient part of her life. As she always had, she'd focus her energy and her life on giving her kids the best childhood she could as a single, working mother.

The bus slowed with a hiss of its brakes, and Annie made her way to the door, giving the driver a polite smile as she stepped down to the sidewalk. Before she'd even walked a block, Jonah's truck was beside her on the street.

"Annie, I know you're mad. You have every right to be. But your safety has to come before your pride. Please, get in the truck."

She waved a hand down the street. "It's only another block."

The car behind Jonah honked, but he ignored it. "We need to talk. About us."

She lifted her chin but kept her gaze forward as she strode toward the diner. "There is no us, Jonah. You made that perfectly clear last night."

"Annie—"

She flicked a hand to cut him off. "No, it's fine. You're right. I guess I just let the emotions of the day get to me. It's better this way."

"It's not that I don't want to be with you, Annie. But I don't—" He bit out a curse word. "I can't have this conversation through the window of a moving truck. Annie, please get in."

"I'll be late for work." Sighing, she stopped walking and faced his truck. "We can talk tonight, if you want. But you don't need to make any apologies or excuses. There is no us. I get that. I'm okay with that. I just forgot that in a moment of weak—" To her dismay, her voice cracked, and scalding tears clouded her eyes. She pressed her lips in a tight line and swung back toward the diner, her steps brisk and clipped.

"Damn it, Annie. You're not weak. Just give me five minutes to—"

The rest of his plea was silenced as she breezed through the diner's front door and it closed behind her.

Jonah appeared at his usual seat at the counter within minutes, but Annie left it to Susan to wait on him. By mutual agreement, their interaction at the diner was to remain casual and all-business. The true nature of their relationship might not be a secret if someone was, in fact, following her, watching her apartment, but she decided discretion was still in order.

Annie did her best to pretend the weight of Jonah's gaze didn't follow her as she served breakfast to the other customers, but the prickle of awareness told her without looking that he was monitoring her every move. Her hands shook as she poured coffee for her customers, and her stomach stayed in knots. Ignoring Jonah was tantamount to pretending there wasn't a bull loose in the china shop. She felt his commanding presence in every cell of her body.

"Annie." His voice thrummed through her as she searched behind the counter for more sugar packets. Cautiously raising her gaze, she met the dark intensity of his eyes and a shudder rippled through her.

"May I...have some more coffee?"

She glanced at his full mug and sent him a skeptical look. "Aren't you going to be late for your shift at the mill, Mr. Devereaux?"

He returned a chagrined smile, but the unspoken plea in his eyes raked her heart with razor-sharp talons. He hesitated, then his shoulders sagged. "Touché. Then just my bill."

What had put that hint of pain in his gaze? Was it guilt? Regret? Or something deeper and more personal?

Her throat tightened, and she had to swallow twice before she could speak. "I'll get your waitress."

After Jonah paid for his breakfast and left the diner, Annie tried to bury herself in waiting tables, refilling saltshakers and making idle chatter with customers. But her head and her heart were filled with questions about Jonah and the poignant look he'd given her as he walked out the front door.

At lunchtime, Annie glanced toward the door as new customers came in. Ginny and her husband gave Annie a smile and a wave as they chose a table and sat down. Her spirits lifted, seeing her friends, and she hurried over to their table.

"Wow, y'all are a sight for sore eyes." She gave them a weary smile as she handed them each a menu.

Ginny cocked a blond eyebrow. "Oh? Something wrong?"

Annie gave Riley a side glance and shrugged. "Just, um…"

Ginny's husband cleared his throat and slid back to the end of the booth seat. "If you'll excuse me, ladies. I think I'll… grab a newspaper from the machine by the door."

Annie sent the handsome fireman an appreciative grin. "Thanks, Riley."

He gave her cheek a friendly kiss as he left her alone to talk to Ginny.

Ginny's gaze followed her husband to the front door, her happiness glowing in her cheeks. "For a guy, he's pretty perceptive."

Turning her attention to Annie, Ginny captured Annie's hands and pulled her onto the seat beside her. "So, what's up? Would your glum mood have anything to do with the guy you mentioned last time we talked?" She knitted her forehead and waved a finger as she thought. "Jonah? Was that his name?"

Annie tugged up a corner of her mouth in a wry grin. "Riley's not the only perceptive one."

"Well, don't forget, I was in a quandary over what to do about Riley not that long ago. I recognize the look."

Annie toyed with the string of her apron. "What look?"

"The one that says you are crazy about this guy, but you're scared to death to take a shot at being happy with him."

Annie leaned back against the booth seat and frowned. "Who says I would be happy with him? What if what I really need is to forget about having any man in my life and concentrate on raising my kids?"

"Is that really something you want to do alone?"

"No. But Walt didn't leave me much choice in that matter."

"Sure he did. He divorced you. You can give the kids a

new father. Question is, is that what will make you happy? Is Jonah who will make you happy?"

Annie idly traced a crack in the tabletop. "Ginny, we're getting way ahead of ourselves here. Jonah hasn't even said he wants to be more than my guardian until this mess with—" She caught herself and glanced toward the counter where Susan was ringing up a customer. She lowered her voice. "This other mess I told you about. I still have that hanging over my head."

Ginny leaned closer, matching Annie's quiet tone. "Maybe it's time you went to the police with your suspicions and the information you've found."

Annie shook her head. "Not yet. Jonah has a plan and I trust him. When he's got everything he needs for the police to make their arrests, then he'll turn it over to the authorities. But he's afraid if we involve the cops too soon, the people involved higher up will close shop and go into hiding. Or cut their losses some other way to protect themselves. Jonah already suspects that is why Hardin was murdered."

A frown dented the bridge of Ginny's nose. "Annie, I don't like you being involved in this. Get out. I'll help you get another job. You don't have to stay here if—"

"I can't quit now. We're too close to catching the people behind this thing." She cast another surreptitious glance toward Susan. "Besides, leaving the diner won't end the threat to me. I have reason to believe these people know I have information about their operation. That threat doesn't go away just because I quit. You know the saying, keep your friends close—"

"And your enemies closer," Ginny finished for her. "Oh, Annie. Please be careful."

She nodded. "I will."

Ginny's worried gaze clung to hers for a few more seconds before she shifted in her seat. "And what about Jonah?"

"What about him?"

"Do you love him?"

Annie sputtered, and her face grew hot. "I—I—"

Ginny grinned. "You're blushing. I think I have my answer."

Annie averted her face. "Ginny, I don't know how to feel about him. And after last night, it may all be a moot point anyway."

Ginny tipped her head. "Why? What happened?"

A rock lodged in Annie's gut. "He all but told me he's not interested in a future with me."

Ginny squeezed Annie's hand. "What exactly did he say?"

"That he can't be what I need him to be."

Ginny arched an eyebrow. "Ah. He's afraid."

"Afraid?" Annie jerked her eyebrows into a frown. Fear was the last thing she'd ever associate with Jonah. And yet...

She thought of the haunted look in his eyes this morning, the uncertainty in his voice when he begged for a chance to talk.

"Afraid of what?"

Ginny leaned back and shook her head. "Could be almost anything. You know him better than I do. Maybe he's afraid of hurting you. Didn't you say his size and his fighting skills scared you? Do you think he's worried about—"

"Oh, no." Annie vehemently shook her head. "He would never hurt me or the kids."

As soon as the words left her mouth, Annie heard them echoing through her head, heard the certainty in her voice and waited for the niggling of doubt that never came. When had she come to this conclusion? When had Jonah convinced her of his trustworthiness and honor? How did she know in her heart of hearts that she was truly safe with Jonah in every way?

She didn't know how or when she'd known. But she was sure of it.

Ginny's bright blue eyes lasered into her. "Maybe it's not physical pain he's afraid of causing you. Maybe he's afraid of commitment or failure or letting you down. He could be worried about breaking your heart—or you breaking his."

Annie inhaled sharply. Had she let Jonah's brawn and rough-around-the-edges appearance blind her to his Achilles' heel? Jonah had told her about his history with his father, his grim childhood, the pain of losing his mentor last year. Could her tough-on-the-outside protector be hiding a vulnerable heart?

When Annie didn't respond, Ginny said, "Either way, my question to you remains the same. Do you love him?"

Ginny's query flustered Annie, made her feel trapped and panicky. "I think...I could. I'm happier when I'm with him. He makes me feel braver, stronger, more hopeful."

Turning up a palm as if to say the answer was obvious, Ginny flashed her a satisfied grin. "Then fight for him. You stood up to Walt, saved yourself and your kids from his abuse and started a new life. After everything you've struggled to achieve, don't give up on the one person who can give you the love you deserve. These past few weeks, you've learned you're safe with him. Now show him he can be safe with you, that you won't let him be hurt, either. Show him he doesn't have to be afraid of a future with you. Just don't let him go without a fight."

Annie's heartbeat thundered in her ears. After years of withdrawing to protect herself, of shutting down and pulling in to avoid conflict, could she throw herself into the fray, to put her heart in the line of fire for the chance at a future with Jonah?

As she weighed the risks of such a bold leap of faith, Annie noticed Susan staring at her from behind the front counter. The other waitress gave her a stern glare and then a meaningful hitch of her head to the rest of the dining room. Customers were waiting.

Annie shoved to her feet. "I…need to get back to work. I have tables waiting."

As she turned away, Ginny grabbed her hand and sent her a penetrating look. "Trust your heart, Annie. Allow yourself to be happy. You deserve a man who will cherish you and fill your life with joy. Don't let what happened with Walt skew your vision with Jonah. I almost made that mistake with Riley and would have blown the best thing that ever happened to me."

Annie pulled in a deep breath. "Okay."

"And…can we get two cheeseburgers with sweet iced tea? I'm famished." Ginny gave her a wide, cheerful grin.

"Of course." She hustled to the order window, scribbling Ginny's request on her pad. If she'd thought talking with Ginny would help calm her whirling thoughts and confusion, she'd sadly miscalculated.

Trust her heart? Fight for Jonah? She didn't know where to begin. The realization that she felt truly safe with Jonah eliminated what Annie had believed was her main reason for not getting involved with him. Yesterday she'd almost made love to Jonah at the police station gymnasium. Clearly, physical chemistry wasn't her problem.

His instincts and interactions with her kids warmed her heart, so she couldn't blame parental protectiveness for her reluctance. Having experienced his gentleness, his compassion, his loyalty, his honor, how could she question what kind of husband he'd be?

But Ginny had challenged her to do more than admit her feelings for Jonah. Ginny wanted her to act on those feelings, drop her defenses and muster a courage she wasn't sure she had inside her. What would happen if she let herself love Jonah, gave him her body, heart and soul, and he still walked away when his case here at the diner was solved? That was the issue that scared her spitless. She'd already lost so much.

But wasn't Jonah worth the risk?

A niggling unrest stirred in her gut, a desperation that lit a fire in her soul. The same inner voice had roused her from the nightmare of her dysfunctional marriage and given her the courage to save herself and her children from Walt.

She'd faced down her demons before when her life was on the line. Tonight, she would put her love on the line for a chance to be happy, a chance to share the kind of love she'd always dreamed of. She'd risk her heart—for Jonah.

Jonah spent a frustrating day going over the files from Hardin's bus-station locker but found himself distracted by thoughts of Annie's sweet kiss. That afternoon, he rhythmically lashed the speed bag at the boxing gym. He'd hoped that exhausting himself with an intense workout would expel the thrum of desire that wound him tight.

Hammering the punching bag should have given his mind something else to focus on besides the wistful longing in Annie's eyes last night, the musical sound of her laughter as they danced and the poignant ache in his heart as he'd put Haley to bed. Instead, giving his body over to the repetitive motion of his workout gave his brain free rein to review the same images over and over again.

He'd done the one thing that scared him most, the one thing

he'd sworn not to do with Annie. He'd become involved with her family, grown attached to her kids, developed deep, complicated feelings for her. How did he extricate himself from the relationship without hurting her and her family? Without losing a piece of his own heart and soul?

Bad enough Haley had begun thinking in terms of him marrying Annie, but if Annie interpreted his recent actions as a promise of a future, an expression of feelings deeper than friendship, he was bound to let her down. Considering the cold shoulder she'd given him this morning, he guessed his withdrawal last night had already hurt her.

He gave the bag an especially forceful punch. Damn it! Hurting Annie was the last thing he'd wanted.

But had that stopped him from kissing her senseless at the Lagniappe P.D. gym? Had he considered the repercussions when he'd engaged her daughter in a cozy, fatherly chat at bedtime? Watching her home from his truck would have been safer for his own sanity and not created the intimate connection he now felt for Annie and her kids.

But had he weighed the risks when he'd slept on her couch?

Apparently not. Because in unguarded moments, even he conjured fanciful ideas of what it would be like to help Annie raise her children, or wake in the morning beside Annie rather than on her lumpy sofa.

Heat coursed through his veins as he imagined himself wrapped around Annie's naked body, making love to her night after night. Perhaps creating a child of their own. His heart fisted. He couldn't deny how much he wanted Annie, how sweet the promise of joining her family was.

But too many unknowns cast a specter over that homey ideal. How did he build a loving family with Annie when his own family had been so screwed up? Sure, he could try to make Annie happy, try to give her kids the kind of fatherly role model they needed, but trying wasn't good enough. A wife and family wasn't something he could attempt and risk failure. Annie had already had one husband fail her. She deserved more than his bumbling attempt to fill a role he knew nothing about.

He refused to add to her pain. He simply couldn't commit to Annie without assurances that he could make family life a success. But with a lack of experience to draw from and with innumerable cases of marital hell etched in his memory thanks to domestic disturbance calls while on the job in Little Rock, he knew far more about what not to do than how to get family relationships right.

Gritting his teeth, he pounded the speed bag until sweat blinded him and his arms ached.

"Hell, man! What's gotten into you?"

Catching the swinging bag with one hand, Jonah turned to Frank and swiped stinging perspiration from his eyes with his forearm. "I'm sorry. What'd you say?"

"I asked what got into you. You were beating that poor bag like a man possessed. What gives?"

After shucking his gloves, Jonah picked up his towel and wiped his face and arms. "Just have a lot on my mind. I needed to let off a little stress, clear my head."

Frank chuckled. "Did it work?"

Jonah scowled. "Not as much as I'd hoped. I'm still not sure what I'm going to do."

"A woman or money?"

"Excuse me?"

"Well, a man's problems usually boil down to either his lady or his finances. So which one's got you all in a twist?"

Jonah hesitated. Did he really want relationship advice from the stodgy owner of the gym? He scoffed as he tossed his towel back on his gym bag. The advice and guidance

Michael had given him had saved his life, and Michael had run the gym in Little Rock. He glanced up at Frank. "A woman."

"Marry her."

Jonah arched an eyebrow and cocked his head. "What?"

"Between my wife and daughter, I've lived with women for more than thirty years. I know how they think. If your woman's got you this tied up in knots, she's gotta mean more to you than a casual roll in the sack. I say, man up. Marry her and quit waffling."

"But I'm not—"

"On the other hand, if you're already married, and she's giving you this much grief—"

Jonah folded his arms over his chest, curious where the older man's generalities about female relationships would go.

"—chances are she's probably at least partly right about whatever she's steamed over, so suck it up, buy her some flowers and tell her you're sorry. You may have to eat some crow, but at least it will get you off the couch and back in the bedroom."

Frank hadn't missed the mark by much. Jonah had to admit thoughts of moving off Annie's couch and holding her in her bed had been part of what wound him so tight. He could have made love to Annie last night, if his conscience hadn't been gnawing at him. Her kiss outside Haley's bedroom had been full of unspoken promises. The air around them had crackled with desire and expectation.

A sultry fantasy of Annie peering up at him through her sexy curtain of hair while she reclined on starched white sheets taunted him. Jonah's libido kicked him where it counted, and he muffled a groan.

Frank shrugged. "I'm just telling you what I've learned—

both in marriage and as a business owner. Sometimes you have to sacrifice to get what ya really want."

The gym owner gave a satisfied nod as if he'd just solved world hunger and the energy crisis. "Right now, what I really want is a cold beer and a wide-screen TV to watch the basketball championship. Wanna join me?"

Jonah perked up. He'd almost forgotten the final round of the college tournament he'd bet on with Farrout. He should watch the game, so he'd be able to talk about it with some authority when he met up with Farrout later.

Frank stared at him, waiting for an answer.

If he could get the television away from Haley, perhaps he could watch the game at Annie's. He didn't want her unprotected tonight, and she'd promised to listen tonight to his explanation of why he'd balked last night. Anticipating *that* conversation raised a sweat on Jonah's forehead unrelated to his workout.

He shook his head. "Thanks, Frank, but I'll watch it at home."

"With your lady friend? Ha. Good luck with that." Frank waved a dismissive hand, then jerked his chin. "Who ya pulling for?"

"UNC."

Frank scoffed. "They don't have a chance."

Shrugging, Jonah tossed his towel on his gym bag. "My gut tells me they'll pull it out, no matter what the oddsmakers are saying."

With a tip of his head, Frank gave him a measuring glance. "You sound pretty sure of your team. Wanna put a little money on that?"

Jonah sighed and scooped up the straps of his gym bag. "Already did."

Frank's eyes widened, and he folded his arms over his

chest. "Ya know…if you're interested in making some serious coin on the game, I might know someone who could hook you up."

A chill skimmed down Jonah's back. Was Frank the one who'd sent Michael to Farrout? Could Frank have information about the gambling ring Jonah needed?

The gym owner smoothed a hand over his silver hair and lifted a shoulder. "Think about it and let me know. Stanley Cup is coming up, the Masters Tournament, NBA finals. Plenty of opportunities to make a little on the side if you're interested."

Frank strolled into his office, waving good-night to another boxer.

As Jonah headed into the locker room to shower, he made a mental note to quiz Frank further on his connections to sports betting. For now, he had more immediate concerns—like ten thousand dollars riding on a college basketball game and a single mother of two who made him want things that were out of his reach.

Chapter 17

When Jonah rapped on her door that evening, Annie's heart gave an answering knock. She smoothed her hands down the slim skirt she'd changed into after work, denying to herself that she'd dressed to impress Jonah. But in truth, she felt frumpy in her waitress uniform. If she wanted to convince him to take a chance on a relationship with her, she needed every scrap of confidence and all the positive vibes she could scrounge.

"Hi," she said, standing back to let him in. Her voice sounded breathy and seductive even to her own ears. But just the sight of him, his hair damp from a recent shower, the evening sun casting shadows across his face that highlighted the masculine cut of his jaw and cheekbones, sucked all the oxygen from her lungs.

The lopsided grin he gave her coiled around her heart and filled her with a longing so powerful she ached.

"Trust your heart," Ginny had said.

Right now her heart was telling her to grab hold of Jonah with both hands and never let go. This man, with his dark gaze that could see through to her soul and a tender touch that never failed to turn her bones to mush, had snuck past her defenses and stolen her heart.

His gaze slid over her, drinking in the narrow blue jean skirt that emphasized her hips and the white cotton T-shirt that made the most of her unimpressive cleavage. His pupils rounded as his perusal lingered at her lips before drifting to her scarred cheek.

On an impulse, she had pinned her hair back from her face with a cloisonne clip, leaving the harsh jagged marks exposed. Her scars were a part of who she was now, and tonight she wanted no secrets or barriers between her and Jonah.

She held her breath, anxiously waiting for his reaction to the prominence of her scars, until his mouth curled in a warm grin. "Hi yourself. You look…beautiful."

Her pulse pattered, and her cheeks heated with pleasure. The way he looked at her, like a cat ready to pounce, made her feel pretty for the first time in years.

She cleared the nervous tightening from her throat. "Have you eaten?"

"I—"

"Jonah!" Haley squealed as she bounded in from the living room wearing her plastic tiara. Ben toddled in behind his sister, and a drooly grin lit his face when he saw their guest. Her daughter hugged Jonah's legs, and he stooped to lift her into a bear hug.

"Hi, princess. How are things at the castle?" he said, tweaking her nose, then tousling Ben's curls. "Hey, slick. How's the block business?"

Haley giggled, and Annie's heart somersaulted. Jonah had a natural rapport with her kids and showed none of the stiff reluctance she'd seen when other men got around children. His ease with her kids went a long way toward assuring her she'd made the right decision, allowing him into their lives.

For dinner, they shared a delivered pizza, Jonah's treat and an indulgence the kids reveled in. With their stomachs full of pepperoni pizza, Haley and Ben were in a better mood when time came for their baths and bedtime. Jonah read *Skippyjon Jones* to Haley again, then disappeared to the living room to watch a basketball game while Annie settled Ben into his crib for the night.

Once both children were soundly sleeping, Annie sat next to Jonah on the couch and tucked her feet under her. "Who's playing?"

"UNC and Kansas." He sent her a side glance, then turned back to the television. "This is the final round of the NCAA championship."

"Mmm." An uneasy prickle nipped her spine. Walt had been especially grouchy and sensitive to interruption when he'd been watching sports. She'd quickly learned to make herself scarce on nights when her ex watched a game.

Disappointment knotted her stomach. She'd hoped to have time tonight to talk openly with Jonah about her feelings. The game on TV didn't bode well for a discussion or any intimacies.

When a commercial came on, Jonah turned to face her and swiped a hand down his face. "So…kids asleep?"

She nodded. "Will this be on much longer? I'd hoped we could talk."

His eyes softened, and he stroked her chin. "I'd like that, too." He hitched his head toward the TV screen. "This is the tournament I bet on with Farrout. I need to see how it shakes out, but I want to talk once it's over. There's only about ten minutes left in the game."

His explanation both lifted her spirits and twisted new strands of dread inside her. Even if she settled things with Jonah, nothing was settled with the gambling and money-laundering operation.

Working to tamp the apprehension the problems at the diner knotted inside her, she covered his hand with hers and nodded. "I can wait ten minutes."

He winced. "It could go into overtime."

His boyishly apologetic expression was so far from the irritated glower Walt used to give her, she had to smile. "Okay, but no shouting at the TV. You'll wake the kids." Pulling her lips in a flirtatious grin, she snuggled closer to him and threaded her fingers through his hair. "And I'd really like them to stay asleep."

The lift of his eyebrow and darkening of his gaze spoke of his intrigue with her intimation. "I'll keep that in mind." Jonah slid an arm around her waist and pulled her closer. "Help me pull for my team. I've got ten grand riding on this game."

Annie jerked away from him. "Ten grand? Where did you get that kind of money?" Immediately, she shook her head and held up a hand. "I'm sorry. That's not my business. It's just...that much money is—"

Jonah laced his fingers with hers and kissed her palm. The soft brush of his lips on her sensitive skin sent a delicious thrill spiraling through her.

"You have a right to know. The money is from an insurance settlement. My dad was killed in a car accident a couple years ago."

She caught her breath, sympathy plucking at her. She knew the mixed feelings he had toward his father and the confused emotions he'd have experienced because of the loss.

"A guy ran a red light and T-boned him," he continued.

"The other guy's insurance company offered a healthy settlement if my sister and I signed papers saying we wouldn't sue. Dad also had a good bit of life insurance listing my sister and me as beneficiaries." He gave a cursory glance to the television, where the game had resumed. "I hadn't wanted anything to do with my dad when he was alive, and I sure as hell didn't want to profit from his death. I took the money and put it in the bank. Left it there. Didn't want anything to do with it, until—"

When he paused, ducking his head, Annie slid a hand along his cheek, then lifted his chin to meet his gaze. "Until?"

"When Michael died and I decided to investigate who was behind the gambling operation, I resigned from my position on the police force in Little Rock and moved down here. I've been living off the money from my dad's death for the past year. Michael was more of a father figure to me than my dad ever was. It seems like poetic justice somehow that the money I inherited be used to catch the people behind Michael's death."

"Poetic justice, indeed."

After a drawn-out moment where the world seemed to still around them, his gaze dipped to her mouth.

Her lips gravitated to his, and a low moan rumbled from his chest. The vibration reverberated through Annie, licking her veins and encouraging her to be bolder, to take what she craved without fear or regret. She sealed her mouth over his and teased the seam of his lips with her tongue.

Jonah's arm tightened around her, and he tugged her onto his lap. His fingers burrowed into her hair, and he met her questing tongue with his own. Every velvet stroke spun her senses reeling faster. She clung to Jonah for support and could feel the rapid-fire beat of his heart against her chest. A bulge at his fly ground intimately against her hip. Knowing that she'd roused his body to that state emboldened her, filled her with a sense of power she hadn't know in years. In Jonah's arms, she felt feminine. Respected. Cherished.

Her restless hands skimmed over his wide shoulders, along the muscle and sinew of his arms, then settled on his hard chest. Her fingers curled into his shirt, and she raised her eyes to his, breathless from his kiss. The heat and hunger blazing in his gaze sent shock waves rippling through her, firing every nerve. Her whole body quaked with need and strained closer to him. "Jonah, I want…"

Her breath hung in her lungs. She should stop now, retreat. Protect herself from inevitable pain. She might not fear physical abuse from Jonah, but the risk to her heart was too great. If she gave her body to Jonah, she'd lose a piece of her soul to him, too.

Trepidation dried her throat, and she nervously wet her lips. His gaze tracked the quick swipe of her tongue. His grip tightened, and smoky desire darkened his eyes.

"What do you want, Annie?" His husky growl stroked her like a physical caress. "Name it, honey. Anything."

His warm hands framed her face, and he brushed butterfly kisses to her nose, her cheeks, her closed eyes. His tenderness touched a raw, aching place deep inside her, soothing, calming. His warmth thawed the chill of fear that had frozen her, paralyzed her for too long.

"Trust your heart."

Even if it cost her a piece of her soul, she wanted the respite his arms offered from the turmoil of her life. She ached for the sweet joy and heady bliss of his kiss.

After years of running, bone-deep pain and endless nights of loneliness, she desperately wanted a few stolen moments of happiness, of escape, of…*Jonah.*

"This," she whispered, her voice catching. "I want this. I…want you."

A heartbreaking expression molded his face. Moisture clung to his eyelashes, and a shocking vulnerability shaded the bright yearning in his eyes. "Are you sure?"

The tremor of wistful longing in his tone shook Annie to the core.

He could be worried about breaking your heart—or you breaking his.

Her chest clenched, realizing that Jonah's need and doubts echoed her own. Her pulse tripped over the idea her warrior protector bore scars from his own past. Was it possible Jonah needed her as much as she needed him? Did her kiss offer him the same balm to old hurts as his did to her? Could two broken spirits, two wounded birds find solace and hope with each other?

"It's about give and take, sharing and supporting each other."

Ginny was right. More than anything, Annie wanted to give Jonah the hope and happiness, the healing that his patience and gentleness had given her.

Annie dragged in a shaky breath and stroked her fingers down his cheek to cup his jaw. She touched her lips to his, felt his shudder. "Make love to me, Jonah."

After checking on her children, Annie joined Jonah in her bedroom, her heart tapping an anxious tattoo. She walked in just as he pulled a small foil packet from his wallet and tossed it on the bedside stand.

Her heart turned over. *Always the protector.*

Hearing her enter, he glanced up, and a muscle in his jaw bunched. "Just so you know, you're safe with me."

Annie bit her lip, a flutter of anticipation dancing in her belly. "I know."

His mouth pressed in a hard line, and his gaze narrowed on her. "What I mean is…I don't sleep around. I don't take sex light—"

She pressed a finger to his lips to stop him. "I trust you."

His throat convulsed as he swallowed, and his pupils rounded. He tugged her close and sighed into her mouth. "Annie, sweet Annie…"

She sank into his kiss, ribbons of pleasure unfurling inside her. When he skimmed his lips over her chin and down to the pulse point at her throat, shimmering sparks danced over her skin. His hands worked under her T-shirt and massaged her back, strumming the bumps of her spine and lulling her with tender strokes.

Weeks of tension and anxiety melted by degrees at his touch, and she gave herself over to the magic of his hands.

Bracing her hips securely against his, he leaned her back and ducked his head to nuzzle the valley between her breasts. The arch of her body pushed her hips more intimately against the ridge of his arousal, and with a sway of her body, she rocked against him. A low moan rasped from his throat. The effect she had on him thrilled her, heightened her own pleasure, made her bolder.

Grasping his shoulders, Annie straightened and stepped back. Holding his hot gaze with hers, she whisked her shirt off and let it drop on the floor. Her bra followed, and Jonah released a stuttering breath as he palmed her bared breasts. He molded and shaped her gently before shifting his hands so he could roll her nipples under his thumbs.

Staggering sensation pulsed through Annie's blood, a hot rush that melted her bones and made her legs buckle. She curled her fingers into his shirt, gasping for a steadying breath. Jonah pivoted with her in his embrace and lowered her carefully to the bed.

He stood beside the bed only long enough to yank his own shirt off and shove his jeans down his legs. He kicked free of the pants, then braced himself on his arms above her.

Annie drank in the sight of his toned muscles and broad chest dusted with black hair. Rather than frighten her, his brawn and powerful potential made her feel safe, protected. She brushed her hand across the taut skin, savoring the warmth and texture, lightly scraping his nipples with her fingernails and smiling when she felt his answering shudder. Her gaze followed the path she blazed with her fingers, until a wide jagged patch of pale skin stopped her cold.

A long scar stretched across his lower abdomen. She sucked in a sharp breath. "Jonah, what…?"

He glanced at her with heavy-lidded, passion-drunk eyes and shrugged. "A punk with a knife resisted arrest."

She pulled back to appraise him with fresh eyes and re-newed concern, and she noticed a small puckered circle on his shoulder. She touched it. "And this?"

He groaned. "Do we really need to catalog all my scars *now?* We could be here a while."

A poignant ache squeezed her chest, and she tipped her head, her gaze scanning him. "Oh, Jonah."

How many more scars did he have? More important, how did she help him heal the internal wounds that stitches and bandages couldn't help?

Jonah had been surrounded by violence all his life, been its victim, learned to use it as his tool for catharsis. A hot stab of pain lanced her heart, understanding all too well the kind of pain he'd endured.

But Jonah, despite his inauspicious start in life, despite the odds against him, had turned his life around, joined the police force, become a defender, a protector rather than succumbing to the violence that had marred his life. With Jonah on her side, how could she not overcome the obstacles her own life had thrown at her. A burning determination fired in her gut, a conviction that a better life was within her grasp if she had the courage to seize it, to fight for it. And Jonah was a huge part of the life she wanted for herself and her children.

Tears clogged her throat as she gazed up at him. She captured his lips with hers and poured everything that was in her heart into her kiss. Drawing her closer, he pressed her into the mattress with his weight, and she wrapped her legs around him. Jonah explored her body with tender roaming caresses and sultry kisses until she quaked with longing and burned with need. She reveled in the freedom to enjoy his taut muscles and masculine angles with equal leisure and passion. When he settled between her legs, she arched toward him, her body aching to feel the heat and weight of him inside her.

In short order, Jonah sheathed himself with a condom and rolled her on top of him. "You're in control, Annie. You set the pace."

A blissful contentment and trust, a sense of rightness and fulfillment swelled inside her until she couldn't breathe. She held Jonah's gaze, savoring the moment as he entered her. Somehow she sensed her whole life had been leading to this moment, this man. Everything she'd suffered, all she'd sacrificed and lost only made this moment that much sweeter. She belonged with Jonah. They bore the same scars, yet together they were stronger, better. Whole.

Tears of joy stung her eyes as her body stroked his, and the heat and need pounding through her blood coiled tighter, burned brighter— until she shattered in his arms.

She clung to him as he sighed her name and shuddered

with his release. Then, in the still darkness of her bedroom, they held each other. Silent. Still. Complete.

Safe in Jonah's embrace, Annie drifted into the first truly peaceful sleep she'd had in years.

Jonah folded an arm behind his head and stared into the inky blackness of Annie's bedroom. With his free hand, he stroked Annie's silky hair and listened to her deep, even breathing as she slept.

He'd been unprepared for the way making love to Annie would rock him to his marrow. Beyond powerfully satisfying sex, joining his body with hers had felt so fundamentally right, like a homecoming, that something had shifted in his soul and grabbed him by the heart. He'd known sleeping with her was a mistake, that it would make giving her up harder and would hurt her more deeply when he had to leave. But when she'd looked at him with her heart in her eyes and asked him to make love to her, denying her request, when every fiber of his body ached for her, had been impossible. He'd thought he could give her the pleasure and comfort she deserved and keep his heart out of the mix, keep the emotional distance that would allow him to walk away when it was over.

He'd been wrong. So wrong.

He blinked hard when the sting of tears burned his eyes and brutally shoved down the bout of self-pity. He had to think of Annie, not his own bleeding heart.

Because if he'd learned nothing else tonight, he'd seen the truth of his feelings for her. He'd fallen in love.

His chest throbbed as bitter regret and frustration raked his chest with sharp talons. No matter how it hurt him, he had to do the right thing for Annie. He couldn't give her the family, the future, the happiness she deserved, and he had to stand aside so that another man could.

Jonah gritted his teeth until his jaw throbbed. Thinking of Annie in another man's arms, building a life with her, burned in his gut like acid.

But she needed better than the patchwork attempt at a real family that was all he had to offer. For him, failure was unthinkable, inexcusable. Annie had survived one bitter marriage, one damaged attempt at family without burdening her with his tarnished history. He couldn't risk her happiness should he bomb as a husband and father.

But in the short hours until morning, he could soak up as many precious memories as possible. Then, when daylight came, he had to do what was best for Annie.

He had to let her go.

Chapter 18

Jonah was gone.

Annie blinked and groped sleepily on the bed beside her when her alarm clock beeped the next morning. His pillow still bore the dent from his head, and his scent clung to the sheets, but he'd already risen and disappeared from her room.

Disappointment stabbed her. She'd wanted his face to be the first thing she saw that morning, had hoped for a few stolen kisses before she stumbled to the shower.

But perhaps his discretion was for the best. Maybe it was better that Haley and Ben didn't find a man in their mother's bed when they tiptoed in for their morning snuggles.

Even though she didn't have to be at work until that afternoon for the late shift, Annie dragged herself out of bed and into the kitchen to start a pot of coffee. She checked the living-room couch for Jonah, then glanced out her window toward his truck. Not only was Jonah in neither place, but his truck was gone, as well.

The first niggling doubts squirmed restlessly inside her as she returned to pour a cup of the fresh coffee. Where could he have gone? And why hadn't he told her he was leaving?

A tousle-headed Haley staggered into the kitchen and dropped into a chair with her stuffed cat tucked under her arm.

"Morning, sunshine." Annie pushed aside her nagging questions and disappointment over Jonah's absence to concentrate on her daughter. Mornings like this, when they could share breakfast together and have time to play before she left for work, were rare, and she didn't want to waste a minute.

Haley yawned and scratched her ear. "Can we make pancakes, Mommy?"

Annie took out a frying pan and smiled at her daughter. "Absolutely."

Tar Heels Win Nailbiter, the front page of the sports section read. Jonah sat in his truck and sipped the convenience-store coffee he'd bought when he got the newspaper and scanned the game summary. While he'd been making love to Annie, his team had pulled out a narrow victory. He should be happy. Instead, he felt rotten. After the most amazing night of his life, he'd woken to the reality that Annie could never be his and the day had gone downhill from there.

Well…except that his team had won. Unable to muster the appropriate satisfaction for his winning bet, he tossed the newspaper aside and took another throat-scorching gulp of his coffee. Pulling out his cell phone, he dialed Farrout's number. When the bookie answered, Jonah forced a note of satisfaction to his tone and gloated, "UNC by three. I believe you owe me some winnings, Farrout."

A moment of silence followed during which Jonah pictured Farrout's narrow-eyed glare and glowering countenance. Then, "Tonight at Pop's. At eleven. I don't like a crowd around for transactions."

Jonah inhaled deeply. Annie worked the late shift.

He really didn't want Annie anywhere around when he did his business with Farrout, but he didn't feel he had the luxury of contradicting the bookie. "I'll be there."

Farrout disconnected without comment, and Jonah returned his phone to the clip on his belt.

Things were beginning to fall into place. He had Hardin's files, and if he wore a wire tonight, maybe a camera in a lapel pin, he could get proof of the gambling transactions Farrout ran. Perhaps it was time to bring his investigation to a head. He wanted the business finished, wanted the people involved behind bars so Annie would be safe, so Michael could rest in peace and so he could move on with his own life.

His gut roiled.

A life without Annie.

He imagined her disappointment upon waking alone, and he clenched his teeth. When he'd dressed in the predawn hours, she'd looked so peaceful, he hadn't had the heart to tell her he was leaving. Acid bubbled and seared inside him, and he groaned. In truth, he hadn't had the guts to look into her wide, vulnerable eyes and break her heart.

He needed to go by her apartment before she left for work, explain himself. Or maybe he could drive her to the diner that afternoon, and he could use the time alone to tell her the decisions he'd made. Jonah sighed miserably and pinched the bridge of his nose where a headache was starting. How did he look the woman he loved in the eye and…rip her heart to shreds?

His cell phone trilled, and he checked the caller ID. It was the call he'd been waiting for. "Devereaux."

"I got your message," his caller said.

Jonah cranked the engine of his truck. "We need to meet."

Annie waited all day for Jonah to show up at her apartment. Or call. Something. Anything. But she heard nothing.

The dinner hour came and went at the diner without any sign of him, as well, and Annie's dread, the certainty that something had gone horribly wrong last night that she hadn't realized, continued to grow. Was Jonah gone for good? Had he been conning her all along, looking for a vulnerable woman to get in the sack? Had she fallen for pretty lies and smooth talk, and now that he'd slept with her, he'd moved on?

She swallowed hard, forcing down the knot of hurt and disappointment that choked her. Around ten o'clock, she cleared a table for an elderly couple who'd come in for a late-night dessert.

"Two apple pies, one à la mode, one plain," the old man said.

"I'm lactose intolerant," his wife volunteered as the elderly gentleman patted her wrinkled hand.

The loving gesture brought a fresh sting of tears to Annie's eyes. Was it so wrong to want the kind of love this couple shared? A lover, a partner, a companion for her retirement years? The kind of happiness that Riley and Ginny had? She'd thought Jonah might be the one she could spend her life with, grow old with. But the later it got without word from Jonah, the dimmer that hope looked. As badly as Walt had hurt her physically, the pain of losing Jonah when she'd just begun believing she could be happy with him stung far worse.

Clearing her throat and forcing a smile for the elderly couple, Annie said, "One plain, one à la mode pie coming up."

As she shuffled behind the counter to begin serving the

pie, Susan moved up beside Annie. "Aren't they sweet? Look at him holding her hand." Susan sighed. "So romantic."

"Mmm-hmm," she hummed, and gave a jerky nod, not trusting her voice.

"Hey, are you all right?" Susan asked. "You look…upset."

Annie shook her head. "I'll be fine. I just—" The rest of her sentence hung in her throat as Jonah strolled in the front door and took a seat at a booth instead of his usual place at the counter.

His eyes met hers and held for a moment before he glanced away. Annie's heart thrashed in her chest and rocks settled in her gut.

"Oh. I see." Susan's voice pulled Annie's attention back from Jonah. The other waitress gave her a smug grin and hitched her head toward Jonah's booth. "Man trouble. Am I right?"

Annie released a shuddering breath. "No. I… Don't be silly. Jonah's just…a friend."

"Riiight." Susan sauntered away, tossing a knowing grin over her shoulder.

Annie finished scooping up two slices of apple pie for the elderly couple and carried their desserts out to them before approaching Jonah. She squared her shoulders and pasted a smile on her face, determined not to let him see how his disappearing act and silence had hurt her. "Hi, you. I missed you today."

He flattened his hands on the table and gave her a brief grin. "Sorry about ducking out this morning without saying anything. You were sleeping so peacefully, I hated to wake you."

She shrugged. "I wouldn't have minded."

He looked away guiltily. "And I had some things to take care of today. I got busy—"

"Jonah, it's okay. You don't…owe me any explanations." Hating the wobble in her voice, she squeezed the pen in her hand until her fingers blanched.

"No, it's not okay." Jonah grabbed her hand and pulled her down on the seat beside him. "I should have called or stopped by or something. I'm sorry, Annie. Truly. You deserve so much better than to be treated like a one-night stand." His tone rang with passion, conviction…and regret.

Her spirits lifted a little, dared to hope.

"The thing is," he said, his voice more hollow-sounding now, "I messed up last night, Annie. I shouldn't have slept with you, shouldn't have misled you, and I'm sorry."

Her heart plummeted to her toes. "Misled me? What do you mean?"

He sighed heavily and scraped a hand over the bristles of his unshaven jaw. "I never wanted to hurt you, honey. Please believe that."

"Jonah?" Her throat closed, and the dread she'd been feeling all day settled on her chest like a lead weight. "What are you saying?"

He stared down at the table, wouldn't meet her eyes, and his evasion told her what he couldn't.

"You're dumping me."

"Annie…"

"No, *dumping* isn't the right word. That implies we had something to start with, something you were ending." Anger and hurt sharpened her tone as she struggled to keep her tears at bay. She would not cry over him, would not show him her pain. "But I guess we never really had any kind of relationship for you to dump me from…other than the pity sex, of course." She shoved out of the booth, and he seized her arm.

"Annie, wait! You've got it all wrong. I care about you. I…I love you, but…"

Her pulse jumped. Freezing, she gaped at him as he fumbled, clearly as shocked by his confession as she was.

After a moment to catch her breath, she shook her head. "You can't say 'but' after 'I love you.' Love has to be unconditional, or it's not really love."

He raised his eyes to hers, and the anguish and pleading in his green gaze wrenched her heart. "I'm sorry, Annie. I want to be with you, to give you everything you deserve. But I don't know how."

She sank slowly down on the booth seat again, feeling numb, confused, cold. "I don't understand. If you really love me, then…" She caught her bottom lip with her teeth, her chest tightening until she couldn't breathe.

A muscle worked in his jaw, and he chafed her frozen fingers with his thumb. "I tried to warn you the other night not to fall for me, not to put your hope and faith in me. I could tell your deepest desire and dream was to have someone who could promise you a happily ever after. But that someone isn't me."

She glanced toward the table where the elderly couple fed each other apple pie, and she couldn't deny Jonah's assertion. She did want happily ever after. But didn't everyone? Was that wrong?

"Why do you think we wouldn't be happy?"

"Maybe we would be…for a while. But I don't know how to be a husband, how to be a father, how to be a family. When I think about my dad, the awkward, painful way our family operated, the lies and deceit, the distance, the anger, the isolation…" His voice cracked, and he swiped a hand down his face. "I don't ever want to go through that again. I don't want you to have to deal with my ghosts, and I can't promise you a future when I can't be sure if I'll get it right. I want you to be happy—for always—but I don't know if I can be what you need."

"So you won't even try?"

"You deserve better than just an attempt—"

She jerked her hand away from his and lurched to her feet. "Why don't you let me decide what I deserve?" She drew a shaky breath and blinked back the burn of tears. "I have work to do." She took two steps toward the kitchen before turning back. "Do you want to order anything?"

He met her glare with a sad, apologetic gaze that burrowed deep into her breaking heart. "Your forgiveness?"

His image blurred, and she swiped angrily at the moisture clouding her eyes. "I'm sorry, sir, but we're fresh out of forgiveness tonight."

With that, she hurried to the ladies' room for the privacy to fall apart.

As the hour grew later, the diner emptied of customers, and as Jonah watched Annie studiously avoid him, he felt increasingly empty inside, as well. He couldn't leave things so raw and unsettled between them. He needed to talk with her again, make her understand his decision.

"I'm sorry, sir, but we're fresh out of forgiveness tonight."

Annie's parting shot replayed in his head, and as always, her words kicked him in the gut. She had reason to be angry, to hate him. Despite his best intentions, he'd hurt her. Deeply. He wasn't sure he could forgive himself for that.

A few minutes before eleven o'clock, Farrout and Pulliam came in the front door of the diner, and Jonah braced himself. Farrout said a few words to Susan and swept an encompassing gaze around the empty diner before joining Jonah at his booth.

Annie stopped what she was doing and watched the men

with wide, frightened eyes. Jonah longed to wrap her in his arms, keep her safe.

When Pulliam flipped the lock on the front door and headed into the kitchen, a chill of suspicion washed down Jonah's neck. He met Farrout's narrowed gaze with one of his own. "You have my payout?"

Farrout lifted a shoulder. "We'll get to that. First, you have something I want."

Jonah didn't show the other man any reaction, but a cold spike of apprehension drilled his chest. If something was about to happen, if Farrout had caught on to his investigation, Jonah wanted Annie safe, wanted her out of the diner.

He took a moment to appraise Farrout, then answered coolly, "I don't know what you mean."

"I thought you'd say that." Farrout leaned forward and pitched his voice to a low growl. "I want Hardin's files. I want whatever you took out of the locker at the bus depot, and I want whatever your girlfriend stole from my office."

Inside, Jonah's nerves were jumping, but he kept his gaze steady, his body still. "For starters, I don't have anything of Hardin's. All I got at the bus depot was a bag of my gym clothes I'd stashed there before a trip."

Jonah leaned across the table now, matching Farrout's aggressive cant. "But clearly you've been following me, which I resent and which begs the question, *why?* What do you have to hide?" He paused, but Farrout only glared. "And I don't have a girlfriend, so I have no idea what is missing from your office. Maybe you should be asking your lackeys these questions, 'cause I sure as hell have no answers for you."

Farrout sent a dark glance and a nod toward the counter where Pulliam propped, chewing a toothpick. In a heartbeat, Pulliam circled the counter and grabbed Annie's arm. Snak-

ing an arm around her waist, he hauled her close, and Jonah
tensed, alarm streaking through him.

"Perhaps we should ask your girlfriend the same questions.
What do you suppose she'd have to say?" Farrout asked, his
tone gloating.

Jonah squeezed his fingers into a fist and growled, "Leave
her out of this."

"Oh, but she is a part of it, isn't she? She was Hardin's
courier the night a small fortune went missing, and she was
with you at the bus depot and later at the police department.
I caught her snooping in my office the other day, too. Start
talking, Devereaux. What's your game? What are you after?"

"I just want the money I won on the basketball tourney. I
put ten grand on UNC."

Farrout frowned and tipped his head. "I don't recall any
wager like that on UNC. Pulliam, you remember Devereaux
placing any bets?"

"Nope."

Jonah struggled to cool the fury rising in him. He glanced
over to Pulliam, who had pulled Annie's arms behind her
back. A chill washed through Jonah.

Dear God, don't let them hurt Annie.

Jonah weighed his options and made his decision. "You
let Annie walk out of here, and we'll talk." He leaned forward, nailing Farrout with his glare. "We'll talk about how
you killed Michael Hamrick."

"Word I heard was Hamrick offed himself." Farrout's negligent shrug, as if Michael's death meant nothing, fanned
Jonah's rage. "Anyway, I had nothing to do with his death."

"You had everything to do with it. You cheated him out
of his retirement savings just like you're trying to cheat me
now. You destroyed his life."

"I didn't make him place his bets. He was an addict. He

lost his money all on his own. I'm just a businessman, all too happy to make a profit wherever I can."

Jonah forcibly swallowed the bitter reply on his tongue, fought the urge trembling in his arms to smash Farrout's face. He couldn't, wouldn't give Farrout the power to make him lose control. He wasn't his father, and he would never let his life go down the violent path his father took.

He glanced again to Annie, whose dark eyes were wide with fear. "Tell your goon to take his grubby hands off Annie," he grated. "Now."

"Give me Hardin's files and whatever else your girlfriend stole from my office," Farrout countered. The man's eyes were flinty, emotionless.

Jonah didn't like the imbalance in this standoff. Farrout held all the cards, and Jonah had everything at stake. Because Pulliam had Annie. The woman he loved.

And that gave his enemy the upper hand.

Annie's heart knocked wildly in her chest. She was a liability to Jonah.

Every time Jonah glanced her way, she became more certain. As long as he was distracted by what Pulliam might do to her, Jonah was working from a disadvantage. She had to do something to even the odds. Stall for time.

When Pulliam grabbed her, she'd watched from the corner of her eye as Susan sidled into the kitchen. Surely Susan or the fry cook, Daniel, had called the police by now.

Annie clung to the hope that the cavalry was on the way. Her breath hung in her throat, knowing instinctively that her life was at a pivotal point, a defining moment. What direction fate took her depended largely on her response to the crisis, the choices she would make. She refused to wait helplessly for rescue, refused to be the victim of another man's abuse. In order to help Jonah, she had to help herself.

Mentally, she reviewed what she'd learned at the self-defense class, the things Jonah had coached her on. While a plan of attack coalesced in her mind, she followed the tense confrontation between Farrout and Jonah.

"What makes you think I have anything of Hardin's?" Jonah said. His body language said he'd gladly leap over the table and rip Farrout's larynx out at the slightest provocation. That he hadn't throttled Farrout at his first chance spoke volumes to Annie about Jonah's control over his emotions, his restraint with the sparring skills he knew so well. Admiration swelled in her chest.

"Because I don't believe in coincidence. You showed up in the Fourth Street alley just after Hardin's delivery got nabbed. Your girlfriend was Hardin's courier, and she was snooping in my office the day the diner reopened." Farrout's glare narrowed on Jonah. "And my man saw you take a gym bag into the bus depot to a locker we saw Hardin use a week earlier. Given all that, what would you think?"

Annie swallowed hard. Farrout had them cornered. She'd seen enough nature shows to know what even the weakest animals did when cornered. They fought.

Annie took a deep breath, sent up a silent prayer…and fought back.

With all the force she could muster, she slammed her head into Pulliam's nose.

The thin man wailed in pain and released her wrist to cradle his face.

Hand freed, Annie grabbed a metal water pitcher from the counter. Twisted. Swung it in a powerful arc toward Pulliam's head.

"Damn bitch! You broke my—"

The pitcher smashed into the man's head with a resounding thunk. He wobbled, eyes rolling back, then crumpled onto the floor.

The scuffle of feet behind her yanked her attention to Farrout. The rotund man lurched to his feet. With his black gaze locked on her, he reached inside his jacket.

Jonah sprang a millisecond behind Farrout, tackling the giant man as he drew his weapon. He kicked Farrout's feet out from under him with a sweep of his leg and pinned him to the floor.

Farrout's gun fired, the blast deafening.

Annie gasped and stumbled back.

In a seamless move, Jonah reached for his ankle and came up with a small gun of his own. He jammed the gun against Farrout's head and grated, "Drop your weapon!"

Farrout struggled, cursing and bucking. Jonah jerked Farrout's arm into a painful-looking, unnatural angle. "Drop it, or I'll break your arm."

Growling an obscenity, Farrout let his gun clatter to the floor. Quickly, Jonah stuck his own gun into the waist of his jeans and palmed Farrout's larger gun.

Annie froze, stunned at what she'd just witnessed. But Jonah had served for many years with the police. Of course he knew how to subdue a man twice his size.

Jonah dug plastic bindings from his pocket and secured Farrout's hands behind his back. Bound his feet. Then shackled him to the leg of the nearest table with handcuffs.

Farrout continued to spout filth, and Jonah grabbed his throat in a hard pinch at his carotid artery. In a moment, Farrout passed out.

Jonah looked up at her. "Don't worry, he's not dead. He'll revive in a few minutes."

Annie released the breath she hadn't realized she was holding. Could it really be over? Relief swept through her, welling tears in her eyes and making her knees tremble.

Swiping perspiration from his forehead, Jonah asked, "Are you okay?"

She nodded, a smile blossoming on her lips. But Jonah's gaze shifted to something behind her and hardened.

Spinning around, Annie found Susan behind her. The waitress's mouth was pressed in a grim line. Her glare was icy.

And she aimed a gun at Annie's heart. "Not so fast, sweet cakes. We have unsettled business, and the boss is on his way."

Chapter 19

When he saw the revolver pointed at Annie, Jonah's gut roiled. He shoved away from Farrout's inert form and, rising to his knees, he swung Farrout's 9 mm toward Susan.

Annie had mentioned her concern that Susan had known things Annie hadn't told her. He'd downplayed the significance, discounted the importance of Susan's comments.

He'd screwed up. Failed Annie.

Acid guilt gnawed inside him, rebuking him.

"Lower your gun, Susan," he commanded, his tone firm but calm. "No one else has to get hurt. Just put it on the floor and step back."

Susan's answering laugh had a bitter edge. She stepped closer to Annie. "You wish."

Jonah's hands sweated, but he kept a firm grip on the 9 mm he had aimed at Susan.

Annie backed away from Susan until her back came up against the wall. "Daniel!" she yelled. "Call 911!"

Susan lurched forward, grabbed Annie's arm. "Sorry, honey. Daniel left twenty minutes ago. Pulliam sent him home when he and Farrout arrived."

While Susan's attention was shifted to Annie, Jonah pushed smoothly to his feet.

Susan jerked her head back toward Jonah and poked her revolver behind Annie's ear. She tightened her grip on Annie's arm, and Annie winced. "Stop right there, Jonah. I don't want to hurt her, but I will."

Annie grew still, her eyes pleading with him. *Now what do I do?* her gaze asked.

Jonah dug deep for the professional detachment he needed. He had to treat this situation like any other he'd encountered on the force. Let training take over. Keep his emotions out of it.

But he'd never been in a standoff with the woman he loved caught in the crosshairs. How could he live with himself if anything happened to Annie? What would he do without her in his life?

A ball of cold realization settled in his gut. By ending their relationship and walking away, he'd already cut her out of his life. Because he feared the unknown. Because he couldn't bear to revive memories of his childhood. Because he was a coward.

Yet Annie had found enough courage to face her past, her demons, her fears. Enough to leave her abusive husband. Enough to give a future with him a chance. Enough to help him stop Farrout and his men.

Because she loved her children. Because she loved him.

Jonah's heart constricted. Annie had trumped fear...with love.

If he loved Annie, how could he do any less?

He ground his teeth together, battled down the doubts and

questions jabbing him. He had to focus on freeing Annie. If he could keep Susan occupied, distracted, he had a chance. If his plan was falling in place as arranged, backup was coming. He just had to buy a little time.

"What are you doing, Susan? Why are you involved in this?" Jonah asked.

Annie chewed her bottom lip, tried not to think about the muzzle jabbing her skull. Her children needed her. She couldn't die here. Wouldn't leave her babies without a mother. She might not know how to get out of this macabre turn of events, but she had faith in Jonah. She trusted him with her life. And if she found an opportunity to help the situation, she'd act.

Susan snorted in answer to Jonah's query. "I'm not stupid. I know easy money when I see it. Why wouldn't I want my cut? Besides, you could say it's my family legacy."

Jonah furrowed his brow. "What do you mean?"

Susan shrugged, and the gun poked Annie harder. "My father runs the operation. He let me in on the action. Working at his diner is just my cover, so I can keep an eye on the people who work for him."

"Your father is the Pop of Pop's Diner?" Jonah's tone was calm, conversational. But Annie saw the cunning and purpose that blazed in his eyes.

"That's right. Pop himself. I'm the one who found out what Hardin was up to." Susan gave a smug-sounding chuckle. "I knew Hardin had been in trouble with the cops recently for some drug violation. When those charges went away a little too easily, I got curious. And Hardin started acting funny."

"Define funny," Jonah said, his weapon never wavering.

Annie watched him, amazed by his cool confidence, waiting for some clue from him as to what he needed her to do.

Susan grunted. "Hardin started acting nervous and looking crappier every day. Like he wasn't sleeping. Like the stress was eating his lunch.

"I warned Pop something could be up, and Pop had someone follow him. Pop's guys saw Hardin take a bunch of files from the diner to the bus depot. Then a little eavesdropping gave me enough information to help arrange someone to intercept the transfer of cash and gambling records to his police contact. We had all the proof we needed to justify eliminating Hardin. He'd become a liability."

Annie tensed. "Y-you killed Hardin?"

Susan scoffed. "Hell, no. Not me. Pop has men on his payroll to do that."

"Farrout and Pulliam." Jonah nodded to the men unconscious on the floor.

"Maybe. Or the guy who jumped Annie in the alley. Maybe someone else. I don't know who. Don't care."

Annie felt Susan shift her weight, draw her body up and press the gun harder against her head. She blew out a frustrated huff.

"Damn it, enough talking. I didn't mean to say that much. Now…put your gun down, Jonah, or I'll…I'll hurt Annie."

Jonah's eyes narrowed almost imperceptibly when Susan hesitated. Annie could swear she saw the wheels in Jonah's brain turning.

Rather than lower his gun, Jonah curled his finger around the trigger. "You don't want to hurt Annie, Susan. She's your friend. She's a mother. She's not involved in my investigation." He paused, narrowing his eyes again. "On the other hand, I have no qualms about shooting a woman."

His penetrating gaze met Annie's eyes then and held. Drilled her with their bright intensity. A chill crawled down Annie's spine, certain he was trying to tell her something.

Still holding her gaze, Jonah said calmly, "If you hurt Annie, I won't hesitate to *drop* you in the *blink* of an eye."

His gaze clung to hers another heartbeat, before he shifted his lethal stare back to Susan. His unflinching green eyes blazed with intent.

Then he blinked.

Annie dropped like a rag doll.

A single blast shook the room, and Susan screamed.

From the floor, Annie glanced back to see Susan clutch her shoulder, drop her gun and slide down the counter to the floor.

"You bastard!" a male voice growled. "What have you done to my daughter?"

A familiar-looking, silver-haired man stood in the door to the kitchen.

Pop had arrived.

Jonah re-aimed the gun toward the new arrival.

And his pulse kicked when recognition dawned. "Frank?"

The gym owner snatched up the gun Susan had dropped and swung it toward Jonah. "I can't tell you how disappointed I am to see you here, Devereaux. You're one of my best sparring partners. I hate having to kill you. You're gonna be missed at the gym."

"*You* own the diner? *You're* behind the gambling and money laundering?" Jonah heard the disbelief in his voice and shook off the lingering shock to focus on the problem at hand. Namely, the gun in Frank's grip.

Jonah cut a quick glance to Annie. She'd grabbed a clean towel and pressed it to the wound on Susan's shoulder. Ever the caregiver. Even though her patient had just held a gun to her head.

Frank strolled closer to Jonah. "Folks were all the time wagering on sports at my gym. I saw a way to make a profit and took it. I'd bought the diner years back, and it proved the simplest way to clean the money, filter it into special accounts. But as an operation like mine grows, problems come up. People you thought you could trust turn on you to save their own skin."

"Hardin?"

Frank jerked a nod. "Good riddance. The man had proved unreliable at best. He got greedy. Got careless. I should have taken him out years ago."

Jonah drew a slow breath for composure. "And Michael Hamrick? You fleeced him. Before he died, he told me the operation he'd gotten tangled up with had welched on paying him what he was owed on winning bets. That you duped him into investing his life savings on high-stakes games."

"No one held a gun to his head, if that's what you mean." Frank smirked. "He took care of that himself."

White-hot rage exploded in Jonah. Ducking his head, he charged at Frank. "You son of a bitch!"

"Jonah, no!" Annie launched from the floor, threw herself at Frank.

Grabbed for Frank's gun.

A flash. An earsplitting blast. A gut-wrenching cry.

With a gasp, Annie collapsed against Jonah, the front of her apron marred by a bright red stain.

"Annie!" Jonah sank with her to the floor, horror ripping through his chest.

Frank reangled his weapon.

Glass shattered. Men in uniform breached the front door. Guns at the ready, Lagniappe's finest swarmed the diner.

"Freeze! Police! Lower your weapon and lie facedown with your hands out!"

As the police filed in, Frank sighed defeat, set his gun on the floor and lay down spread-eagle as ordered.

Jonah shot an angry look at the man leading the charge. *Joseph Nance.* "About damn time! Annie's been shot! Get an ambulance *now!*"

Chapter 20

"Mommy?" The sweet tiny voice cut through Annie's drug-induced haze. A small hand touched her cheek, and she blinked Haley into focus. On some level she knew she was in the hospital. The beeping monitors and medicinal smells told her that much. But her daughter held her attention, made her heart swell.

"Hey, darlin'. How's my girl?" she rasped, her throat raw and aching.

"I'm okay." Her daughter snuggled closer, bumping her ribs. Annie gasped as a sharp pain ripped through her chest.

"Say, princess, why don't you sit here with me? Remember I told you your mommy didn't feel good?"

Annie angled her head, searching for the man who'd spoken.

Jonah sat in a chair beside the hospital bed. Unshaven, clothes wrinkled, hair mussed, he'd never looked better to

Annie. His eyes met hers, and she read the questions there.
The doubts.

"I don't know if I can be what you need."

Fresh pain, unrelated to the bullet that had ripped through
her, slashed her heart. Despite the dramatic events at the diner,
nothing had been resolved between her and Jonah.

Haley climbed onto Jonah's lap, and he gave her daughter's head a loving stroke and cuddled her close. "Don't be
scared," he murmured to Haley. "Remember I told you how
strong your mom is? She's going to be fine."

Haley nodded and glanced back at her mother. "Mr. Jonah
says you're a hero, Mommy. You saved his life and helped
catch a bad guy."

"He said that?" Annie raised her eyebrows and shot Jonah
a querying look.

"Don't worry. I gave her the Saturday-morning cartoon
version. I figured a well-filtered version of the truth was better than a lie." He looked unsure of himself, and Annie tugged
up a corner of her mouth.

"You were right. Thank you for your discretion."

Jonah sighed, relief replacing a fraction of the tension lin-
ing his face.

"Where's Ben?" Annie croaked.

Jonah whispered something to Haley, and her daughter
slid from his lap to hand Annie a cup of ice chips.

"Thanks, sweetie."

"Ben is with your friend Ginny. She offered to keep Haley,
too, but nothing would do for Haley until she saw her mommy
at the hospital."

A scuffle of feet drew Annie's attention to her door. Ginny's
husband came in with two large cups of coffee. When Riley
noticed Annie was awake, he paused and grinned. "Hey, wel-

come back, Sleeping Beauty. I don't know what kind of drugs they gave you, but they sure knocked you out."

Annie wrinkled her brow. "How long was I asleep?"

Jonah checked his watch. "About thirteen and a half hours." He grinned sheepishly and added, "Thirteen hours and thirty-six minutes to be exact. Longest thirteen hours and thirty-six minutes of my life."

Riley handed one of the coffees to Jonah and tousled Haley's hair. "So now that you've seen for yourself your mom's okay, what say we let her rest and go give Ms. Ginny a hand with your brother?"

Haley gave her mother a dubious frown, but with a few more reassurances, she allowed Riley to lead her from the room.

Then Annie turned to Jonah, nailing him with an expression that was all-business. "You stayed with my children overnight?"

He nodded. "I wanted to here with you, more than anything. But I knew your priority would be your kids, so I stayed with them. Burned up the phone line calling the hospital every five minutes to check on you, but…"

Annie grinned. "My hero."

He pulled his eyebrows into a skeptical V. "I don't know how you can say that. I let you down. You wouldn't be here if—"

"I'm here because I was dumb enough to try to get Frank's gun away from him."

"No, you were brave enough to act when my life was at risk. I owe you one."

She shrugged carefully, but even the small movement caused her ribs to burn. "You've saved me more than once. Call us even."

Jonah's cheek twitched in a weak grin, and he lowered his gaze to his hands.

Annie broke the awkward silence. "What did my doctors say? Last thing I really remember is the EMT giving me something for pain. Then I passed out."

"The bullet's angle was shallow, but it hit and broke a rib. You'll be in some pain for a few weeks, and they want you to take it easy to allow yourself to heal."

Annie gave a soft laugh. "Did you tell them there's no such thing as rest for the mother of two young kids?"

Jonah shot her a warning look. "Annie...do as your doctor says. Ginny, Rani and I will help with Haley and Ben."

A seed of hope lodged deep inside her. "You?"

He met her eyes warily, a heartbreaking sadness dimming his eyes. "If you'll let me. I know I hurt you, Annie. Everything I said the other night... I..." His eyes closed, and he dragged a hand over his face, the picture of misery.

"Jonah, before you tell me you don't know how to be a husband and father, think about what we've already done together."

His gaze found hers again, and he cocked his head. "Go on."

"Every time I thought the worst had passed the other night, that the nightmare was over, something else would happen. Susan showed up with a gun. Then her father did. I didn't know what to do, how to get us out of the pickle we were in, but I had faith. Between us, we got through it. We survived by working together, and the bad guys were caught." She paused, frowning. "They were all caught, right? The whole mess at the diner is over. We don't have to worry about anyone else popping out of the shadows?"

Jonah nodded. "The four at the diner were arrested and taken in for questioning. Farrout and Pulliam, hoping to buy lighter sentences, started singing like birds. Names, addresses, the works. As we speak, the rest of Frank's cronies are being rounded up." He nodded. "It's really over."

Relief washed through her, and she closed her eyes, replaying the moment the police had swarmed the diner. One face in particular stood out. "The smarmy businessman," she mumbled. She jerked her gaze back to Jonah. "Joseph Nance? He'd been in the diner before. I recognized him, because he'd watched me so close every time he came in, it gave me the creeps."

"Hardin had contacted him but had been really vague about what he wanted with the police. So Nance got suspicious when Hardin was murdered. He'd started his own investigation by the time I called him."

She arched an eyebrow. "So that's how the cops knew what was happening last night? Somehow I didn't think that was coincidence."

"Naw. After going through Hardin's files, I decided it was time to bring in the authorities. I called Joseph Nance, showed him what we had, and we made a plan. I was wearing a mic last night. They heard everything and knew when to step in." He paused. "Detective Nance has offered me a job with the Lagniappe P.D."

Annie caught her breath. "Will you take it?"

He nodded. "I plan to."

Annie sank back in her pillows, digesting it all. "I guess all this means I'm out of a job, though." She chewed her lip, wondering how she'd make ends meet now.

"Think of this as opportunity knocking. You can do whatever you want with your life, Annie."

She curled her fingers into the sheet, letting her deepest desires filter to the light. "Ginny told me once the women's center offers scholarships for women who want to finish their education. Maybe I'll go back to college. The local university has a student worker program and family housing I can look into."

Jonah smiled. "I like that plan."

One problem had been resolved, but the greater threat to her happiness remained.

"Jonah," she started again carefully, her heart rising to her throat. She had to convince him their love was worth taking a risk. "Considering all we've been through already, how can you doubt our ability to make a marriage work? And I say *our* ability for a reason. Because you won't be alone anymore. We'll be a team."

Jonah caught his breath, and she saw warmth flash in his eyes, chasing away some of the shadows darkening his expression. The seed of hope in her chest planted roots.

He rose from the chair and sat on the edge of her bed. He stroked her face gently and held her gaze. "We do make a good team."

She covered his hand with hers. "I know the idea of family brings back painful memories, but I want to be there to help you face down those ghosts from your past…if you'll let me."

He answered her by kissing her palm.

Encouraged, she forged on, "I know that our life together will have bumps and potholes along the way, problems to overcome. Every marriage does. But last night—for the past several weeks, in fact—we've met every challenge we faced *together* and seen it through. We can do the same as a family, no matter what life throws at us."

He leaned close and pressed a kiss to her forehead. "Last night when Susan had that gun on you, I was terrified she'd hurt you and I'd lose you. Then I realized I'd already lost you, because I'd let fear rule my heart instead of my love for you, and I was ashamed of myself." He placed a soft kiss on her lips. "You deserve so much more."

She tensed. "Jonah, don't let fear keep you from being part of our family. I've seen how you are with my children. You're kind and gentle and protective, but you're also appropriately firm and instructive when you need to be. You have good instincts with them. You know what they need to hear to ease their fears without misleading them. The fact that you knew they needed you last night more than I did speaks volumes to me. You put them first. Trust those instincts, and you'll be a wonderful father."

He dragged a crooked finger along her jaw. "I know you're probably right, I…just have to sort some things out."

Annie stroked his face. "Jonah, what…what more do you need to know?"

He squeezed her hand, and the vulnerability that flickered in his gaze stole her breath.

"Only that you trust me."

She knitted her brow, concerned where Jonah was leading. "You know I do."

"Good. Then rest now." He kissed her lightly and backed away from the bed. "And know that I love you."

A few weeks later, Annie was putting the final touches on her hair, clipping the strands away from her face the way Jonah liked it, when she heard the doorbell.

"It's Jonah!" Haley squealed as she sped past the bathroom door.

Down the hall, Annie heard Jonah greet her daughter and son, and her heart gave a little kick. Quickly she snapped her hair clip in place and smoothed her hands down her slacks before hurrying to join her kids and Jonah.

When she rounded the corner to her living room, Jonah

swept an appreciative gaze over her and smiled brightly. "Hello, gorgeous."

"You're early," she said with a teasing scowl.

"I couldn't wait any longer to see you again. And I had a surprise for you that wouldn't keep."

"A surprise?" She noticed for the first time that he held one hand behind his back. Visions of boxed chocolate or cut flowers tickled her imagination. She lifted the corner of her mouth. "Do tell."

"I hope you like it." Jonah drew a deep breath and produced from behind him…a kitten.

Haley cheered. Ben giggled. "Kitty!"

Annie gaped, and Jonah flashed her a devilish grin. "Way I see it, every *new family* should have a pet."

Ignoring the children's outstretched and eager hands, he stepped closer to Annie and settled the tiny black-and-white tabby in her arms. Pinlike claws dug into her blouse, and a sweet fuzzy face peered up at her. Annie's heart melted. "She's precious, but—"

"No buts. You said you wanted a cat *someday*. When you were safe from Walt, and your life calmed down, and your future looked bright." He brushed his fingers along her cheek and lowered his voice. "I know you were hoping for a ring, but…for now, will April do?"

"April?"

"That's what I've been calling the cat…to mark the month we started our new life with our new family." Jonah's eyes glowed with warmth and love. "A token of my promise to be the best husband and father I can."

She wrapped an arm around Jonah's neck and kissed him soundly on the lips. When Haley reached for the kitten, Annie surrendered the fuzz ball to her daughter's hands. "Gently, Hal. She's just a baby."

"I'm gonna call her Pookie," Haley cooed as she rocked the kitten in her arms.

"Pookie?" Jonah pulled a face.

Annie laughed as tears of joy sprang to her eyes. "Pookie, April, whatever... I love my surprise. And I love you, Jonah. You helped me find myself when I was lost."

Jonah drew her into the circle of his arms, smiling warmly. "And you gave me the courage to claim a new family when I was drifting and alone."

"So are we partners? Can we tackle the future as a team?"

"You've got a deal." Joy lit Jonah's eyes, and he rested his forehead on Annie's. "Welcome to someday."

* * * * *

COMING NEXT MONTH from Harlequin®
Romantic Suspense
AVAILABLE AUGUST 21, 2012

#1719 THE COP'S MISSING CHILD
Karen Whiddon
Cop Mac Riordan thinks he's found the woman who might have stolen his baby. But will she also steal his heart?

#1720 COLTON DESTINY
The Coltons of Eden Falls
Justine Davis
When kidnappings of innocent young women bring FBI agent Emma Colton home, she never intends to end up longing for Caleb Troyer and his peaceful Amish life.

#1721 SURGEON SHEIK'S RESCUE
Sahara Kings
Loreth Anne White
A dark, scarred sheik hiding in a haunted monastery is brought to life by a feisty young reporter come to expose him.

#1722 HIDING HIS WITNESS
C.J. Miller
On the run from a dangerous criminal, Carey Smith witnesses an attempted murder. But she can't run from the handsome detective determined to keep her safe.

You can find more information on upcoming Harlequin® titles, free excerpts and more at www.Harlequin.com.

HRSCNM0812

REQUEST YOUR FREE BOOKS!
2 FREE NOVELS PLUS 2 FREE GIFTS!

ROMANTIC
SUSPENSE
Sparked by Danger, Fueled by Passion.

YES! Please send me 2 FREE Harlequin® Romantic Suspense novels and my 2 FREE gifts (gifts are worth about $10). After receiving them, if I don't wish to receive any more books, I can return the shipping statement marked "cancel." If I don't cancel, I will receive 4 brand-new novels every month and be billed just $4.49 per book in the U.S. or $5.24 per book in Canada. That's a saving of at least 14% off the cover price! It's quite a bargain! Shipping and handling is just 50¢ per book in the U.S. and 75¢ per book in Canada.* I understand that accepting the 2 free books and gifts places me under no obligation to buy anything. I can always return a shipment and cancel at any time. Even if I never buy another book, the two free books and gifts are mine to keep forever.

240/340 HDN FEFR

Name _____ (PLEASE PRINT) _____

Address _____ Apt. # _____

City _____ State/Prov. _____ Zip/Postal Code _____

Signature (if under 18, a parent or guardian must sign)

Mail to the **Reader Service:**
IN U.S.A.: P.O. Box 1867, Buffalo, NY 14240-1867
IN CANADA: P.O. Box 609, Fort Erie, Ontario L2A 5X3

Not valid for current subscribers to Harlequin Romantic Suspense books.

Want to try two free books from another line?
Call 1-800-873-8635 or visit www.ReaderService.com.

* Terms and prices subject to change without notice. Prices do not include applicable taxes. Sales tax applicable in N.Y. Canadian residents will be charged applicable taxes. Offer not valid in Quebec. This offer is limited to one order per household. All orders subject to credit approval. Credit or debit balances in a customer's account(s) may be offset by any other outstanding balance owed by or to the customer. Please allow 4 to 6 weeks for delivery. Offer available while quantities last.

Your Privacy—The Reader Service is committed to protecting your privacy. Our Privacy Policy is available online at www.ReaderService.com or upon request from the Reader Service.

We make a portion of our mailing list available to reputable third parties that offer products we believe may interest you. If you prefer that we not exchange your name with third parties, or if you wish to clarify or modify your communication preferences, please visit us at www.ReaderService.com/consumerschoice or write to us at Reader Service Preference Service, P.O. Box 9062, Buffalo, NY 14269. Include your complete name and address.

HRS11B

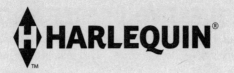

*In the newest continuity series from Harlequin®
Romantic Suspense, the worlds of the Coltons and their
Amish neighbors collide—with dramatic results.*

*Take a sneak peek at the first book, COLTON DESTINY
by Justine Davis, available September 2012.*

"**I**'m here to try and find your sister."

"I know this. But don't assume this will automatically ensure trust from all of us."

He was antagonizing her. Purposely.

Caleb realized it with a little jolt. While it was difficult for anyone in the community to turn to outsiders for help, they had all reluctantly agreed this was beyond their scope and that they would cooperate.

Including—in fact, especially—him.

"Then I will find these girls without your help," she said, sounding fierce.

Caleb appreciated her determination. He *wanted* that kind of determination in the search for Hannah. He attempted a fresh start.

"It is difficult for us—"

"What's difficult for me is to understand why anyone wouldn't pull out all the stops to save a child whose life could be in danger."

Caleb wasn't used to being interrupted. Annie would never have dreamed of it. But this woman was clearly nothing like his sweet, retiring Annie. She was sharp, forceful and very intense.

"I grew up just a couple of miles from here," she said. "And I always had the idea the Amish loved their kids just as we did."

"Of course we do."

"And yet you'll throw roadblocks in the way of the people best equipped to find your missing children?"

Caleb studied her for a long, silent moment. "You are very angry," he said.

"Of course I am."

"Anger is an…unproductive emotion."

She stared at him in turn then. "Oh, it can be very productive. Perhaps you could use a little."

"It is not our way."

"Is it your way to stand here and argue with me when your sister is among the missing?"

Caleb gave himself an internal shake. Despite her abrasiveness—well, when compared to Annie, anyway—he could not argue with her last point. And he wasn't at all sure why he'd found himself sparring with this woman. She was an Englishwoman, and what they said or did mattered nothing to him.

Except it had to matter now. For Hannah's sake.

*Don't miss any of the books in this exciting
new miniseries from Harlequin® Romantic Suspense,
starting in September 2012 and running
through December 2012.*